Old Soldiers

Robert M Penner

BeWrite Books

Published internationally by BeWrite Books, UK.
32 Bryn Road South, Wigan, Lancashire, WN4 8QR.

A CIP catalogue record for this book is available from the British Library

ISBN-10: 1-905202-38-5
ISBN-13: 978-1-905202-38-6

Also available in eBook format.

Produced by BeWrite Books

Cover image Adam Freeman © 2006

For Monica

Robert Penner's life has been a slow westward migration across Canada, from his early years in Manitoba, to his education in Alberta and his new career in British Columbia. Trained as a physician, his first novel, *Old Soldiers*, combines an intimate knowledge of his professional field with his keen interest in history. He works as a gastroenterologist in Kelowna, where he lives with his wife Monica and their son Daniel.

Old Soldiers

Chapter 1

Dr Darren Johnston was full of nervous energy. He combed the same hairs he had straightened just moments before, picked at invisible lint on his shirt and then re-formed his troops for another attack with the comb. Far from unruly, his hair lay unperturbed in the same straight part he had worn for over five years. Still unsatisfied, he tried a last time to improve it. Several strained minutes passed in front of the mirror. He even put on his white lab coat to adjust his nametag before knotting his tie and putting on the gold tie clip his brother had given him as a graduation present. Finally feeling better about his appearance, he removed the coat and folded it carefully into his bag.

Glancing across the room, he noticed the lab coat he had worn at work for the last four years. The coat of a medical student, it was shorter than his new one, and having accompanied him into the trenches, it now bore permanent stains that no amount of cleaning would ever remove. The one he would wear today, on the other hand, had been carefully ironed last night as Courtney looked on and suppressed laughter. He did not care if his change in attitude towards his lab coat amused her, because the one that now lay crumpled in the corner had suddenly become a part of his past. It was the coat he sensed patients viewed with disappointment when a kid who was not even a doctor yet arrived to get their story at three o'clock in the morning. Nurses had looked at him in that coat and told him to get orders co-signed by the resident. Today he would walk into a new hospital with a new coat on, and he would sign the orders for himself.

Before turning to face Courtney he thought maybe he should burn the old coat. He had considered keeping it as a souvenir of his long years of training, but as he looked at the stains of who-knows-what on its sleeves, he realized maybe he would be better off destroying it.

"Are you going to hang around here all morning or do you have actual work to do?" Courtney was leaning up on her elbow and smiling at Darren from their bed.

He reached for a pillow from the chair next to his dresser and tossed it at her. She made a show of blocking it, and then stuck out her tongue.

She knew he was excited about starting his residency. If the careful preparation of his clothes and the painful hour at the ironing board had not revealed his anxiety, then his restlessness while trying but failing to fall asleep certainly had. She teased him, excited on his behalf, and sensed his tension lessen with gentle prodding.

Now, despite ample opportunity to sleep late, she was fully awake. On this important day in Darren's life, she had few plans. Darren was briefly distracted from his preparations and savoured the way she moved as she rolled across the bed and reached into the nightstand drawer. She threw back her long straight hair that, like his, could be described as dark brown, but that Darren would be horrified to hear qualified with such pedestrian prose.

Courtney grabbed a pile of prints and sorted through the many pictures from the Mexican vacation they had taken to celebrate her graduation from law school. They had returned Saturday, leaving just enough time for Darren to make feverish preparations for today, but Courtney had already bought an album and would no doubt begin sorting photographs today.

"Look what a nice tan I had while we were there," she said.

Darren smiled a smile he reserved only for her. Somehow he was not surprised she might believe it had started to fade after only two days. Nevertheless, as intended, her comment drew his eyes towards the smooth, darkened skin of her back and away from her eyes that mischievously stalked him from the nightstand mirror.

"Why are you so quiet?" She dropped her pictures and rolled to face the door as he headed for the kitchen. Darren paused and faced her, so she took advantage of his attention. "Don't look so terrified. Just remember, you're fine as long as you don't kill anyone."

Darren's bland expression turned quizzical at her unexpected advice. He recalled an occasion, on the last day of his clinical rotations as a medical student, when a patient became suddenly short of breath. The man's skin turned blue as he gasped for air and desperately clutched at the bedrails. A nurse standing nearby seemed unsure whether she should look to Darren for a medical decision or demand that he move quickly to find someone more senior. It was a horrifying experience marked by deepest uncertainty. Darren never dreamed of trying to manage the situation by himself at that time, and had called the resident before initiating even the most basic efforts to help the man. Afterwards he had wondered whether administering oxygen should have come before rushing to the telephone, but no one had faulted him for getting help when he may have been in over his head.

Today, with only a single day more experience, he was the resident and could be called upon to help a desperate student.

"Nothing to fear but fear itself." Darren's clichéd response was monotone, and he fidgeted with the keys in his pocket. Courtney pushed further.

"That, and big scary spiders. You can be afraid of those, too, if you want to." She rolled off the bed in an attempt to dodge his sudden lunge. His anxiety was replaced with laughter as he threw blankets over her head and wrestled her to the ground.

"Don't crush the pictures!" She interrupted their antics and told Darren to get moving or he would be late.

He was still laughing when he finally arrived in the kitchen, and when he reached into the cupboard for a box of cereal, he found his stomach unready to accept an offering so early in the morning. Darren and Courtney had partied late and slept in until noon while they were in Mexico, so six o'clock in the morning suddenly felt like the middle of the night. Darren poured milk into his bowl anyway, knowing he would be uncomfortably hungry later if he did not force himself to have some breakfast.

Munching purposefully with his full bowl in one hand, he made his way out of the kitchen and opened the front door of the apartment. While reaching for the morning newspaper, he manoeuvred to avoid spilling his breakfast. He scanned the pictures and titles on the front page on his way back to the kitchen table. As a medical student, he had always rushed out the door without a morning second to spare, but now he was going to work instead of school, necessitating a maturation of his morning routine. He diligently tried to read an article on national trade deficits before finally conceding and flipping to the comics. After finishing his favourites, he absentmindedly stared at the page while making his mental list of what he would need to make it through the day.

He had packed his stethoscope and his reflex hammer. He had a tiny binder he used to write out equations and normal laboratory values. He had put most of his small library of reference books in his bag, and now the only question was how many of them he could fit into his lab coat pockets. He had packed a lunch the night before and put a granola bar in his pocket in case he got hungry during rounds.

Now Courtney was watching him from the hall that separated the kitchen and living room from their bedroom. As he looked up, she assumed a seductive pose in her tattered housecoat. Wiping milk from his chin, he smiled but resumed his mental inventory.

"Maybe I can get a couple of pictures framed today so we can hang them up. This hallway is so gloomy and empty. I think we should go with the blue paint in the bedroom." Courtney strolled around the apartment. Her voice waxed and waned in volume as she moved from room to room within Darren's audible range.

"Yeah, things still look pretty bleak," Darren agreed. Courtney disappeared into the living room and reappeared with an armful of books. She continued circling, ready to swoop down on any shelf with a combination of karmic factors making it suitable to display her precious tomes.

They had not been in the new apartment for long. In fact, unopened boxes still sat in the living room awaiting attention. As if to confirm Darren's thoughts, she began reciting her schedule out loud.

"I guess I should go and get some more groceries this morning, and then I should see where I can find the best picture frames. That way I can have this hallway looking good when you get home." Her arms still full of books, she could not prevent her housecoat from slipping revealingly.

"That would be great," Darren mumbled through a mouthful of cereal, too preoccupied to notice. He imagined how long it would take to get to work and decided he had better catch the 6:50 bus rather than the 7:05. He hurried the rest of his breakfast.

"After that, I guess I can get back to work on these boxes." Courtney set her books on the kitchen counter and continued her slow lap of their living space, finding jobs for herself.

"I can help you with those when I get home." Darren was not keen on the job, but noticed when Courtney arranged their storage space he often found his things buried under a layer of hers. He had once joked to a friend that future archaeologists would think he had been from a much more primitive civilization than hers, because his computer games would be found in a lower layer of soil than her shoes.

"Don't you worry about that, Dr Johnston. I'll just take care of these little things while you go out and heal the sick." After returning to their bedroom, she retrieved their photo album. With a pen in hand, she held up the album as though it were his schedule, and did an impression of a diligent secretary.

Darren laughed. He realized he had been in a world of his own all morning, and Courtney had finally broken it open. He walked over and kissed her hungrily, pulling her close to him. She dropped the album to the floor. When he let go, she slapped his chest, feigning indignation.

"Dr Johnston! What would your mistress say if she knew that you were making advances on your secretary?"

He laughed and kissed her again, quickly on the cheek. She picked up the album and a mess of scattered pictures as he got his knapsack organized.

"This reminds me." Courtney became serious again as she flipped through their pictures. "Sheila and Kevin will be getting married next week. Maybe we should send them a card."

They had met Sheila and Kevin on their trip to Mexico. Sheila and Kevin had complained that they had to go on their Mexican honeymoon before their wedding, because Sheila's family insisted on taking them to Switzerland afterwards.

"Sure, if you want." Darren had found them generally pleasant, but often tedious. It was hard to rouse even feigned sympathy for the couple whose parents had more money than he could make in ten lifetimes, particularly when their every comment seemed to creep insidiously towards the subject of cash. Empathizing with the fabulously wealthy was not any easier after he and Courtney had used up the last of their credit lines on their trip to Mexico. He cringed, thinking of how much debt they had accumulated while in school. It had always been tempting to spend a little more than they could afford. The banks were enthusiastic to lend money to students in professional faculties, so now he had thirty thousand dollars of debt in his personal line of credit in addition to student loans, and she had twelve thousand more. Now they would be paying the interest on their loans from his resident salary and from her part-time job. While Darren knew their financial future together seemed very bright, neither of them came from families with money to spare, so debt was an uncomfortable companion while lucrative salaries remained in a hypothetical future.

Courtney finished law school while he did medicine, and although she would otherwise have planned to start articling now, the uncertainty about what city would select him for a residency program gave her cause to hesitate until they knew where they would be living. For the short term she had found herself a part time job in a bookstore that started in two weeks, so they would have two meagre incomes instead of one.

Courtney never complained that her career was briefly taking a back seat to his, and Darren appreciated that. He did notice the subject of marriage entered into conversation more frequently now that they had officially moved in together, even only as a strategic reference to Sheila and Kevin. They both occasionally joked that Courtney was the breadwinner of the home when the job she landed paid eight dollars and fifty cents an hour. They heard that a resident's salary only worked out to six dollars an hour and Darren wondered at the hours he would be working.

Sure that he had himself ready to go to work, Darren closed his knapsack and got his coat from the hall closet. Courtney hugged him after he got his coat on, and locked her eyes with his.

"You're going to do great today. I'm really proud of you."

Once again she had successfully pulled him out of the self-centred little world he had built. Suddenly he felt more confident. He knew Courtney loved him, and somehow she always knew the appropriate counsel to make him feel best, and at what moment to use it. She also saw right through him. While he was preening in front of the mirror and trying to look sharp in his new lab coat and nametag, she sensed just how worried he was. Worried about knowing enough, worried about patients counting on him, worried about how he would look in front of the more senior physicians, and worried about proving to himself that he really could be a good doctor.

"Thanks," he said. "I love you a lot, you know."

They kissed again as he was on his way out the door and she surprised him with a slap on the backside when he turned to go.

He turned to blow her a kiss on his way down the street but she was looking at her forearm, realizing she was not wearing a watch.

Walking towards the bus stop that could get him to the University Hospital, he imagined that later in the year he would desperately want a car, but today was only the first of July and the summer sun was a nice companion. In fact the first part of his trip to work made for a very refreshing walk through his new neighbourhood.

His was the only low-rise apartment for several blocks. Mostly small houses were on this street, and many were rental properties for university students. As he drew nearer the campus, some of the houses displayed Greek letters representing the fraternities they housed. In September those houses would shake with constant parties. University students would tend kegs on the porches, and studying would be put aside for dancing and carousing. With their trees draped in toilet paper and lawns drenched in vomit, these houses were proud symbols of undergraduate study and Darren missed it already. His fraternity had been a small affair, and with his thoughts of getting into medical school his studying had been intense. Nevertheless, a pit formed in his stomach as he imagined the responsibility that he was about to assume. Suddenly the stresses he had felt before a big exam felt insignificant indeed.

As Darren walked past the fraternity houses and into more of a family oriented neighbourhood, his thoughts returned to what he had in store. When he saw his first patient today he could finally introduce himself as, "Dr Johnston", a title in which there would be a certain comfort. It would be much easier than deciding whether to introduce himself as "Student Intern Johnston", or just as Darren.

Now having imagined his introduction to the patients, he imagined all the illnesses they might have. His head swam with all the diseases he had learned about in textbooks but had never encountered. He imagined all the treatments that needed to be instituted on an emergent basis that he did not know how to administer. Suddenly the pit in his stomach grew larger and threatened to rise into his throat. As he arrived at the bus stop on the edge of campus, he felt that he must be visibly anxious to those around him. He sat down and took several slow deep breaths. Calmer, he now wondered: *If I'm this worried just because it's my first day of work, what kind of a nervous wreck will I be when a patient crashes in front of me?*

He only waited a few minutes before the bus appeared down the street. Approaching, its silhouette grew slowly after he picked up his bag and stood to wait. Walking up the steps into the bus, he showed the driver his pass and took a brief look at the other passengers. Most looked tired and not particularly enthusiastic about starting another day. A couple read novels and one leafed through a day-timer, planning her schedule for the day. Darren concluded that they must all be on their way to very ordinary, tiresome jobs. None, he thought, had quite the excitement in store that he did.

As he found himself a seat near the back, he imagined one of the passengers beginning to have a seizure or chest pain, and thought that the other passengers would all be frightened and unsure what to do, but that he could stand up and say: "Don't worry, I'm a doctor."

For a moment he felt so proud of himself that he almost wanted to stand up now and say it anyway. "Good morning everyone, I'm Dr Johnston." He laughed quietly at himself for the ridiculous image of surprising these morning commuters with his egocentric but bland introduction. His angst returned as he began wondering what he would do if someone on the bus really seized or had chest pain and realized that he did not know.

Darren was jarred back into awareness of the present as his bus reached the last stop before the hospital. As the bus drove on, the people in the street surrounding him all seemed to have a destination in common. Some wore hospital scrubs or nurse uniforms; others were dressed in suits or skirts. As they drew nearer the large complex that made up the university hospital and its supporting buildings, they were drawn towards it like grains of sand sliding through an hourglass. The hospital was a huge monster of glass and steel, and, as it began to dominate the horizon, Darren thought back to the last time he had been there.

A few months beforehand, he had come to town to interview

for the residency position that he was starting today. He had wandered the halls of the hospital in the hopes of gaining some familiarity with its innards. At one point he had arrived in an isolated white hallway with a tall ceiling. Incomprehensible modern art in huge frames dotted the walls between sharp, angular signs that pointed to myriad complex destinations. One tiny window above eye level was leaking sunlight into the otherwise sterile enclosure. Feeling very small and intimidated, he had found it necessary to reassure himself that he would do well in his interview. He had begun rehearsing a brief litany.

"I belong here. The interview will go great, because I was made to work here. I am going to be a great doctor and I am going to do it here." The walls had towered over him and the ceiling had vanishing into an artificial sky miles above. The feeling of intimidation had not receded when he had entered the interview room.

"What kind of research experience do you have?" The question came from the elderly gentleman in white who might have invented Aspirin for all Darren knew.

"What do you feel that you can contribute to our institution?" The lady's stethoscope cascaded over her shoulder like another strand of her long hair. It had the appearance of an extra limb she could control with greater certainty than ordinary mortals could use their hands and feet.

The interview had been a terrifying experience, but he had survived and even won one of the residency positions at the hospital he was now approaching. Darren pulled the cord signalling that his was the next stop.

The wind hit his face as he stepped out of the bus, and not too far above him a helicopter flew home to its eyrie atop the university's Emergency Department. The feeling of the walls towering over him was acute once again, but this time there was the added knowledge that someday soon the unfortunate passenger of that air ambulance might be on her way to see him.

Chapter 2

The intensity and quality of any experience can be coloured by one's expectations. By eleven o'clock, Darren was to find himself completely lost in the basement level of the hospital asking the cleaning staff for directions. Having expected no less than being called upon to save lives the instant he entered the door, Darren found his day was all the more frustrating and mundane.

It began when he stepped off the bus and moved with a crush of people into the hospital's main entrance. His new career was then launched with a brief orientation and a stack of paperwork required for claiming his paycheck. The man who conducted his orientation was a tall and imposing figure who made Darren imagine an old-school drill instructor. He introduced himself as Kevin Briggs and took Darren, along with seven other new doctors, around the hospital in a whirlwind tour. Walking at a rapid pace that kept his long white coat constantly flapping in the air, he pointed out landmarks in staccato fashion and made rapid turns through the corridors. Darren often needed to jog to keep up. As they passed the CT scanning area, one of the others volunteered a question. "Dr. Briggs?"

"Oh, I'm not a doctor." Kevin Briggs responded before stabbing his finger out to right and left, pointing out nuclear medicine, the fluoroscopy suite and the vascular interventions laboratory.

The resident whose question had been ignored leaned close to Darren. "What's up with the white coat if he isn't a doctor?" he whispered. "And who is he anyway? And what the hell is a 'vascular interventions laboratory'?"

Darren only shrugged, not knowing the answer to any of the questions. He quietly laughed to himself but rapidly silenced when Mr Briggs angrily swung his head in the direction of the sound. Darren resumed his silent pursuit and turned his eyes in the direction of the resident who had asked the questions.

"I'm Eddy. Radiology resident. First year." Eddy introduced himself quietly, casting a glance in Kevin Briggs' direction. He did not want to be caught talking.

"I'm Darren. I'm starting internal medicine." Darren spoke quietly as well. They missed several of the important landmarks on the tour in their few seconds of discussion, but Darren was pretty sure that he would never be able to find his way back anyway. When the tour finally came to a close, Mr Briggs handed out schedules. Darren took a look and noticed that he and Eddy had been assigned to a clinical teaching unit together. Kevin Briggs informed them that they should go to the hospital unit where their patients were located and contact the senior resident on their team.

Darren and Eddy went together in search of Unit 43. Their schedule indicated that their senior resident would be Layton Leigh. It took almost half an hour for Eddy and Darren to figure out where they were going, but in that time they talked, and got to know each other a little better.

"I can't believe they're making me do two months of internal medicine," Eddy complained. "At least I'll get it out of the way early, but the other radiology residents call it 'eternal medicine', so I'm guessing it's going to be a long two months."

Darren knew that internal medicine was not every doctor's cup of tea. As students they had all done clinical rotations in medicine, surgery, pediatrics and obstetrics. Darren was glad to be finished with the specialties that held no interest for him. Now in the intern year, most residents were required to complete a broad rotation through a number of specialties. This was where Eddy found himself now.

"If I wanted to spend my time looking after one-hundred-year-old people, I would have gone into internal medicine like you. Man, I wish they'd just let me check out their X-rays instead of dealing with their body fluids and stuff." Eddy made a disgusted look at this last aspect of patient care, but Darren just laughed. Getting your hands dirty was part of the territory.

Years ago medicine was divided into two groups of specialists. The first group was the surgeons. They had not always been doctors, resulting in the tradition in many Commonwealth countries that practitioners of that specialty are referred to as "Mister" or "Miss" rather than "Doctor". Drawing their professional ancestry from the ranks of barbers or butchers, the surgeons remain the specialists in cutting. The other group of specialists was the physicians, or internists, who could be thought of as the specialists in drugs and other non-surgical interventions. The surgeon-apothecary, who practiced a bit of each, could be thought of as the precursor to the general practitioner, or family doctor.

While Eddy had signed on for further training in radiology, a much newer specialty, Darren had thrown in his lot with the internists, deciding during medical school he would train in internal medicine, but knowing there remained many more choices for him to make. After three years of general internal medicine, he would need to make a decision again. For each organ system in the human body, there is a subspecialty of medicine and one of surgery. For the brain there are neurologists and neurosurgeons; for the heart there are cardiologists and cardiac surgeons, and so on. Like many of his colleagues in first year (the intern year), Darren was not sure whether he might complete his training in general internal medicine or try to learn a subspecialty. Either way, he had years ahead of him to decide. For now, he was mostly interested in surviving his first year.

Eddy and Darren's journey through the hospital continued in circuitous fashion until they encountered an information desk. Eddy wisely obtained a map of the building, but became disoriented and traveled in the wrong direction. He proudly pointed when he was fairly sure that they were where they were supposed to be.

"Right through there," he gestured at a set of double doors, "should be the medicine wards."

Darren erupted into laughter when they walked through the doors into an outdoor courtyard. Eddy looked frustrated and turned the map over in his hands, wondering which way was up. Darren sat down on a bench and wiped tears from his eyes, his frustration lessened by the only entertaining event in an otherwise terrifying first day. Now Darren and Eddy were alone in the courtyard except for a lone figure lying down on another bench. Noticing a white lab coat thrown over the stranger's seat, Darren concluded he must also be a resident.

"Excuse me." He approached the man as Eddy studied his map.

"What can I do for you?" The other resident opened one eye and then raised his eyebrows. He remained supine, apparently reluctant to interrupt his relaxation.

"We're new residents here and we're lost. Can you tell us where the medicine units are?"

"What program are you in?" The young doctor retained his relaxed posture.

"I'm in internal medicine, and Eddy there is …"

"Medicine? That's fabulous. My name's Chris; I'm in medicine as well." Now Chris reached up his hand to shake Darren's and struggled into a seated position.

"Are you just starting today too?" Darren asked. He shook Chris's hand while wondering whether he and Eddy had been the only new recruits to get lost in the hospital complex.

"No. I'm in second year," answered Chris, "I'm starting my Intensive Care Unit rotation."

"Wow." It was all Darren could think to say. He did not think he had ever even been in an Intensive Care Unit, but it sounded very intimidating. Chris apparently read the uncertainty on his face.

"It's not so bad." He paused and stifled a yawn while Darren and Eddy waited in anticipation. "You just don't know what to expect yet. I can take it easy 'cause I've already seen what's coming." He paused again, this time searching for the poetic phrase that would describe everything the internship year had to offer. "It sucks."

Darren was not sure whether Chris's relaxed attitude was making him feel better or worse, but the directions Chris gave him sorted out where he and Eddy were going. As they re-entered the hospital, Darren turned back to ask Chris the question that had been on his mind.

"If you're starting in the Intensive Care Unit today, then how come you're having a nap on a park bench?"

"Because I have fifteen minutes to spare," answered Chris, "and I never pass up the opportunity for a nap." He laid his head down again but looked up to speak before the door swung shut behind Darren and Eddy. "I suggest that be a policy that you take up as well. You're going to need to sleep every chance you get this year."

Eddy and Darren continued their quest through the hospital, this time with a more purposeful sense of direction, and even managed to find the internal medicine wards.

"Here they are," said Eddy as they approached the first ward, "Unit 45. We should just have to cut through here to get to 43." He gestured down the hall in front of them, but they had only gone a few steps when they were startled by claxons sounding overhead and a voice over the loudspeaker:

"Code Blue. Unit 45. Code Blue. Unit 45."

"A cardiac arrest? On Unit 45? That's where we are!" Eddy stood stunned, looking at the ceiling from where the loudspeaker had sounded, as though the action must be happening above them.

"Come on!" said Darren, pulling Eddy in the direction of one of the patient's rooms. A nurse in the doorway pointed their way to the arrest and the two of them moved quickly, finding a scene of confusion. A patient lay on a bed in the center of the room looking inhumanly pale and motionless. Nurses appeared to race in circles.

One was fidgeting with the patient's intravenous while another retrieved a bag mask from a cabinet in the wall. Both seemed ready for someone to take charge, and Darren winced as he realized that it should be him. He stood, still stunned in the doorway, and tried hard to think of what he should do first. Eddy tried to melt into the wall next to him as Darren thought back to his life support training.

Okay, what comes first? he thought. *First I need to figure out if the patient has a pulse.* He was glad to have finally thought of something useful, and he meekly asked the nurse who was standing by the patient's intravenous pole: "Does he have a pulse?" but was interrupted by a violent shove to the back of his shoulder.

"Excuse me," barked one of the critical care nurses who came crashing through the door with a cart full of monitoring equipment. Darren found himself face down on the floor but looked up as more people poured into the room and leaped into pre-assigned tasks. Before Darren had even gotten to his feet the critical care nurses had placed two new IVs into the patient's arms, someone had initiated chest compressions and a tall woman had stormed into the room announcing, "I'm the coronary care resident. Who's taking airway? Do we have a pulse? What's on the monitor? Excellent! Continue chest compressions. Who has the patient's chart? What's the clinical history? Did you say pericardial effusion? All right, get me a 60cc syringe and a 14-gauge angiocatheter." The words streamed out of her mouth in a continuous flow. Darren could not even hear the answers to her questions, but she seemed to be proceeding based on a flow of information from the room around her. As she barked out commands, people listened and things happened. Darren's vision blurred as he saw that she was about to plunge a needle into the patient's chest. He felt he should sit down, but realized that he was still on all fours on the floor.

Moments later the coronary care resident stepped away from the patient with a syringe full of yellowish fluid and said,

"Excellent! We have a pulse. Would you take over? I have to get back to the CCU. Great." She stepped away from the patient and another resident stepped in to take her place. She set down her syringe on a tray and stripped off a pair of gloves that Darren had not even seen her put on. As she walked back towards the door, she saw Darren and Eddy cowering in the corner and asked them: "First day, guys?" They both nodded, being too stunned to manage conversation. "My name's Rochelle. I'm one of the third-year residents in internal medicine. I guess I'll see you around." Before leaving she added: "That was pretty exciting, wasn't it? I'll bet you didn't expect to see a pericardiocentesis on your first day."

Darren stood silent for another moment. He could not believe that he might soon be called on to do whatever the hell it was that Rochelle had just done. When he arrived at the scene he had not even mustered the courage to walk all the way into the room. As his feeling of dread intensified, he wondered if he should just walk out of the hospital right now and never come back or if he should go look up the word P-E-R-I-C-A-R-D-I-O-C-E-N-T-E-S-I-S in a dictionary. Eddy tugged at his arm.

"Do you want to go get a coffee? I think I need to sit down for a few minutes."

"I don't think we have time," answered Darren. "We have to go find Layton."

"You're right," answered Eddy. "By the way, thanks for pulling me into the room. I think we did a lot of good here."

"Shut up," said Darren, shaking his head.

When they finally found Unit 43, Darren and Eddy met Layton at the nursing desk where he was getting sheets of paper from the computer printer. Even while Layton was seated, Darren could see that he was over six feet tall. He had slightly dishevelled blond hair and looked overweight. As Layton saw Darren and Eddy approach, he inferred by their white coats and baffled appearances that they were his new juniors, and addressed them immediately.

"I'm glad you guys are here," he said. He explained he was the third-year resident who would be their senior, but fumbled and dropped his papers as he reached to shake their hands. The smile on his face and his sincere greeting made his young colleagues feel welcome even if he was messily pulling scattered papers into a heap on the ground.

"Dr Smith wants to round at three o'clock, so you have a few hours to sort out who your patients are. Here are some lists of the patients. I assigned ten to each of you, and I jotted down some chores that have to get done for each of them. I'll take care of the rest for now."

When Layton stood from behind the computer, Darren and Eddy noticed that he was wearing hospital scrubs under his white coat.

"Expecting to get messy?" Eddy pointed to Layton's garb, already worried at the prospect of being exposed to something distasteful.

Layton looked down at what he was wearing and then smiled. "No, I changed into these last night. I was on call."

Darren winced. He thought of just how long Layton must have been in the hospital. If he had started work the previous morning, he had already been working for over twenty-five hours straight. He looked pretty good for someone who had been awake that long.

"That reminds me," added Layton, "here are the call schedules. Everybody's favourite." He handed Eddy and Darren each a sheet of paper. "Darren, you're on call on Wednesday. Sorry Eddy, you've got to be on call tonight." Darren glanced down at the sheet Layton had handed him. The calendar printed on it showed a name for each day. Darren's name was beside about every third. That meant that besides the 'regular' workdays that he would put in every Monday to Friday, he would be required to stay in the hospital working every third night as well. His heart sank a little when he saw how many weekends his name was beside. When on call on Saturday, he would be working twenty-nine hours from seven a.m. Saturday until some time around noon on Sunday. That hardly left him a weekend, and he noticed that he would be working Saturday or Friday and Sunday together on about every second weekend. Since working all weekend did not mean that he would be getting a weekday off, that left him only four days off a month. The only bright side was that he did not have to be on call tonight, like Eddy.

Being on call did not mean going home with his pager on. For the most junior doctors around, being on call meant staying up and working in the hospital all night. He took some consolation in the fact he would be able to find his way around the hospital for two days before he would be left on his own overnight.

Eddy was equally dismayed at the sight of his call schedule, and seemed terrified at the prospect of being on call this first night. He made a face as he examined the schedule and addressed Layton as he looked up. "I guess you get used to working hours like this?"

"Are you kidding?" Layton answered. "For the last three years of my life I have been constantly tired. I don't think a minute goes by that I would not gladly lie down and sleep for twelve hours if I only had the time. I haven't had time to study a single page in months. Now I haven't slept for thirty hours and I have a research proposal to work on tonight." He stared into the distance and his eyes glazed slightly as he added: "I feel like I'm dying."

Darren laughed nervously, assuming that Layton must be joking. Surely the senior residents enjoyed having a laugh at the expense of their frightened juniors. Layton turned his gaze back towards Eddy and Darren and smiled in return. He left Darren with the feeling that he might have been exaggerating, but only slightly. Darren was suddenly not sure that he was going to enjoy working with Layton. His meeting with Chris had left him slightly baffled, but Layton gave him a tangible feeling of dread.

Layton left them then to get some of the chores done on his own patients, and Darren started on the first patient on his list. The name of the patient, "Edna Wilson," and her age, "72," were beside her diagnosis, "acute pancreatitis," and the chore that Layton had laid out for him was to "check ultrasound results."

So, by eleven a.m., Darren was still on a wild goose chase around the hospital looking for the ultrasound department. He had spent about twenty minutes meeting Mrs Wilson, hearing about the abdominal pain that led to her admission and learning that it was now much improved. Following that, he had tried to sort out the workings of the computer at the nursing desk. He had been given a computer password at his morning orientation, but did not find that it got him very far, and had fumbled with a list of unintuitive commands that the charge nurse assigned him: "For the patient's radiology reports, you just type XWN. For the lab reports, you press 'Function G' and for their pending medications you type their identification number and birth year followed by the '℘' symbol." He learned that ultrasound results dictated by a radiologist would not be available for a day or two. To find out what the test showed, he would have to go to the ultrasound department and ask someone. The cleaning staff was very helpful, and pointed him in the right direction. Unfortunately, with so many obstacles in the way of Layton's errands, by three o'clock he had only figured out six of his patients, and had only finished the errands on four of them. His stomach was growling because he had skipped lunch in an attempt to get his work done. He returned to Unit 43 and met Layton for their afternoon rounds with Dr Smith. He told Layton how little of his work he had finished, but Layton just answered, "Well, that's not bad for your first day. Rounds are going to go slowly today anyway."

Eddy arrived a few minutes later looking shaken and breathing quickly, as though he had been running. "I'm not even nearly finished the stuff you laid out for me."

"That's OK, Eddy," Layton answered.

"It took me forty-five minutes to find the CT scan reporting area and then I couldn't find my way out. I was just trapped in there until a patient in a wheelchair showed me the way."

"It's all right. Dr Smith will know that you guys are new and he won't have very high expectations of your work today."

They spent the next few minutes gathering the charts of all the patients on their list. Dr Smith arrived just as they were finishing. "Have you got everything organized for me, Dr Leigh?" he asked

Layton. Dr Smith was tall, elderly, and very well dressed. His clean white coat shone with crisp creases, paralleling his immaculately parted white hair, and his name was embroidered above his breast pocket, which held a gold fountain pen. He was a stark contrast to Eddy, who was only a little over five feet tall. Eddy's white coat was rumpled and every pocket was filled with internal medicine reference books. His stethoscope hung precariously around his neck looking like it would drop on the floor at any moment. Eddy frequently reached up to adjust it. He wore cotton pants that draped a little too low over his tennis shoes, and a blue dress shirt with the top button undone.

"I hope so, Dr Smith," Layton answered. "These are your new interns, Eddy Bofors and Darren Johnston." As they shook hands with Dr Smith, Darren noticed that the number of books in their pockets seemed, inversely, to indicate the seniority of the doctors. Dr Smith's pockets were empty, except the gold pen at his breast and a stethoscope in his hip pocket. Layton had a small reference book in one pocket and a tiny black binder in the other. In contrast, Darren and Eddy held small libraries of books packed into every available inch of pocket space.

"Let's get started, shall we?" Dr Smith moved towards the collection of charts his residents had accumulated on a small cart. Darren noticed a hint of an accent to his voice. It sounded sort of English, but not quite. He calculated that it was a mixture of Sean Connery's accent from an early James Bond movie, and Margaret Thatcher. He found himself imagining former British Prime Minister Thatcher ordering a martini when Dr. Smith's voice surprised him, "Why don't we begin with Mrs Wilson? Who can tell me about her?"

Darren took her chart in hand and the time-honoured format of teaching rounds began. Dr Smith, as the specialist in internal medicine, had been in his clinic most of the day. In that time his residents looked after the day-to-day aspects of his hospitalized patients' care. He would come to see the patients once a day to guide their long-term management. In theory, he would reward the residents for their hard work by spending time teaching them the art of medicine. The rounds began as Darren provided a summary of Mrs Wilson's condition.

"Mrs Wilson is a 72-year-old woman admitted three days ago with acute pancreatitis. Today she states that her abdominal pain is improving and …"

"Why did Mrs Wilson have the misfortune of acquiring pancreatitis, Dr. Johnston?" Dr Smith asked.

"I think because she had gallstones. Her ultrasound showed gallstones." Darren was glad that he had completed that errand.

"Dr. Johnston, could you tell us about the other possible causes of her pancreatitis?"

Darren thought about cases he had seen as a medical student, and recalled some common causes. "I guess that alcohol is a pretty common cause. Trauma too. You could get pancreatitis if you were in a car accident or something. But she doesn't drink and she didn't have any trauma." Dr Smith continued staring at Darren as though not believing he was finished. The uncomfortable silence lasted several seconds, and Darren could feel himself starting to sweat. Dr Smith remained immobile. Layton was also impassive, standing directly behind him. The only person moving was Eddy, whose hands continually fidgeted with his stethoscope, and whose eyes darted back and forth from Darren to Dr Smith.

"Can you help out Dr Johnston, Dr Leigh?" Dr Smith addressed Layton without turning his gaze from Darren.

"Drug-induced causes include steroids and diuretics. Hypertriglyceridemia is also a cause. Pancreatitis can be a complication of ERCP." Layton rattled off the list as though it had been written in front of him.

"You forgot scorpion stings." Dr Smith completed the list, apparently unimpressed by Layton's rapid response.

"Scorpion stings?" Darren thought. "Who the hell ever heard of someone getting stung by a scorpion in Canada?"

"Now, Dr Johnston," Dr Smith went on. Darren wished he were on a first name basis. The title of "Dr" seemed more like a taunt than a mark of respect when he was being asked basic questions he could not answer.

"What is the probability that Mrs Wilson will die of her illness?"

"I guess not very high," said Darren. "She seems to be getting better."

"Are you familiar with Ranson's criteria?" Dr Smith continued as though he had not heard Darren's attempt at a response.

"I've heard of them." He thought that if he tried hard he might even remember one or two of the factors that predicted mortality in pancreatitis, but he did not care to try for this audience. He could sense that he would get grilled if he were incorrect.

"That is not quite good enough," answered Dr Smith. "I will ask you again about pancreatitis tomorrow morning. You have something to study tonight."

Darren visibly sagged. He hoped at least that this session of questioning was complete. Unfortunately, Dr Smith continued. "What is her serum lipase level today?"

Darren started leafing through the chart looking for the laboratory value. Before he could find it, Layton answered. "Nine hundred and fifty four."

"Good. And what is her alkaline phosphatase?" Darren continued leafing, but Layton beat him to it again.

"Ninety six."

Darren was not sure how Layton managed to keep these numbers on the tip of his tongue. It seemed particularly amazing since Layton had spent the day dealing with the thirteen other patients on the list that he and Eddy had not been assigned. Although Layton had seemed clumsy, inarticulate and dismayed at their first meeting, Darren was suddenly impressed with his ready knowledge. On rounds he was a medical machine.

"Very good. Let's go in and see her, shall we?" The group of them walked into Mrs Wilson's room and asked her a few questions before Dr. Smith examined her. Eddy was looking at Darren with terror in his eyes. He clearly did not want to go through this kind of interrogation about the patients he had seen.

Rounds continued in the same format until six thirty in the evening. Eddy had been breathing hard with anxiety every time they saw his patients, but somehow Dr Smith always reserved his difficult questions for Darren. More remarkably, Layton always seemed to have the answers. As Dr Smith left, Darren was acutely aware that he was not entirely sure of the plan for some of his patients. He attacked their charts again, trying to sort out what the therapeutic plan was for each of them, and trying to remember their laboratory data.

"Well, that went pretty well for a first day," Layton concluded. "Why don't you head home, Darren. I'll get Eddy ready for his night on call. I just got paged that there's an admission in emergency for you to see, Eddy, but I'll show you where your call room is first." As Layton left the ward with Eddy, Darren stood in disbelief. He was amazed that Layton thought things had gone pretty well, considering that he felt like he had been made a fool every time he opened his mouth. He reviewed the patients' charts for another half-hour, before beginning to worry about all the subjects he had to study before the next day's morning rounds. He got his things and headed out of the hospital.

Courtney was completing dinner preparations when he arrived home.

"How was your day?" she asked.

"Okay," he replied, already heading for his desk to hunt through textbooks.

"For a guy who finished his exams a month ago, you sure are keen to hit the books." She was laying out his meal on the table. "Why don't you save that for after dinner?"

Darren complied, but ate quickly and returned to his studies. Courtney cleaned up while he read. Later, she hovered over his shoulder and turned on his desk lamp. The sun had set while he was reading, but he had not noticed darkness creeping into the room.

"Either today was so exciting that you can't stop thinking about the wonders of medicine, or it was so tedious that you need to search your textbooks to renew your interest." Courtney sat on the desk beside the textbook he was trying to read. "Was it pretty exciting?" Darren finally paused from his intent reading and pondered her speculation.

"No, it wasn't," he answered. "It was kind of a let-down, actually. There was a cardiac arrest and I just got pushed out of the way. All I did was try to find my way around the hospital all day, and then try to figure out what was going on with a bunch of patients who had been in hospital for a while. Most of them were just slowly getting better. There wasn't much of anything to do for them."

She slipped off the desk and into his lap, putting her arms around his neck, and raised her eyebrows, prompting him to supply the details that she knew were missing.

"Dr Smith seems to know everything about everything, and he wants me to know it all too. I don't even care to think what tomorrow will be like if I haven't read everything that I said I would." He shifted in his seat so that she slid off his lap. She patted him on the shoulder as she walked away towards their bedroom.

"Don't stay up too late," she said as he buried his head in the books.

The next morning, Darren arrived half an hour earlier for work. He understood that they would usually round with Dr Smith in the morning. Their afternoon rounds the previous day had only been to accommodate newcomers to the team.

As a medical student, Darren had taught himself several tricks for memorizing vast amounts of information. He had been in the classroom for a gruelling forty hours a week, and often had major exams twice a week. Unfortunately, despite his techniques for cramming his head full at the last minute, he knew that all too often he would have forgotten most of it within days. Last night he had treated this morning like a big exam. He had memorized Ranson's criteria. He knew all the major causes and complications of acute pancreatitis. Dr Smith had promised to grill him on these and a dozen other subjects and he was ready. Now he spent the early hours of the morning cramming every piece of his patients' laboratory data into his head in anticipation that Dr Smith would question him on that too.

Rounds were due to start in about twenty minutes when he looked up from the patients' charts to see Eddy entering the ward. Although Eddy looked slightly dishevelled at the best of times, this morning he looked defeated and demoralized. From top to bottom it was clear he had been up all night. His hair was unwashed and uncombed and his eyes were bloodshot. He was no longer wearing his clothes from the previous day but was wearing scrubs that were bloodstained down one leg. He held a large Styrofoam cup of coffee. As he fell into the chair next to Darren he tremulously set his cup on the nursing desk.

"What happened to you?" Darren asked.

"Internal medicine, that's what. I can't believe you want to do this for a career."

"What's with the blood on your pants?"

"Ah, Jeez. You already know my feelings on body fluids. I changed my scrubs after the first time somebody puked blood on me. The second time I just changed my shirt. I guess I didn't notice that other stain."

"How many patients did you admit last night?" Darren was starting to worry about his impending nights on call.

"Eleven. Can you believe it? Each one took me over an hour. And that's between the times I spent looking after crashing patients on the ward. One of them had to go to the Intensive Care Unit. My pager went off so often it seems weird now that it's quiet. I was writing orders all over the hospital, and I don't even know any of this internal medicine crap. I just hope I haven't killed anyone."

Layton strolled onto the ward, looking sharper today in a shirt and tie. He smiled when he saw Eddy. "Rough night?"

"You know it," Eddy answered.

"Don't worry. The Call Gods like to give everyone a tough first night."

The three of them reviewed the patients on the ward before Dr. Smith arrived. They began their rounds by seeing all the patients that Eddy had admitted overnight. It was almost lunch by the time they got to the patients Darren knew. Now he felt confident that he would shine. He had put a lot of time into memorizing lab data and reading about the subjects on which Dr Smith had promised to quiz him.

He was certainly surprised when they reviewed Mrs Wilson in a few brief minutes and Dr Smith did not ask him a thing. Darren thought of pleading: "You promised to quiz me on Ranson's criteria!" but held his tongue. Instead, when they saw the next patient, one that Layton had reviewed, Dr Smith chose that moment to begin.

"Dr Johnston, perhaps you can list for us the most common bacteria involved in ventilator-associated pneumonia."

Darren was furious. He had spent hours reading about pancreatitis, and he was not going to get a chance to showcase his knowledge. Not only that but now he was going to look like a fool again.

Meanwhile, he couldn't help noticing that Eddy was acting like a zombie. Darren was not sure what the point was of having him on rounds after he had worked for over twenty-four hours, and the coffee Eddy had so eagerly consumed had not helped. He did not focus his eyes on people who spoke to him, and did not seem to be concentrating on the conversation. Darren wondered how Layton, who had complained yesterday that he was always tired, managed to look so fresh, given that he could not have gotten more than about eight hours of sleep last night and that after missing a whole night. Thinking of his own sleep schedule, Darren felt sure that he would need to have slept for a full twenty-four hours to look as good as Layton did this morning.

Suddenly Eddy's comment about hoping he had not killed anyone hit home. Darren began to seriously worry that gaps in his knowledge would put people in danger when he was on call the following night. Perhaps knowing Ranson's criteria or the common bacteria involved in pneumonia would play an important role. After rounds with Dr Smith were done, Darren reviewed his patients even later into the evening than he had on Monday. Afterwards, when he went home, he headed single-mindedly for his desk. Again, Courtney had made dinner for the two of them, but this time he ate at his desk. He tried to read up not only on what Dr. Smith said he would be questioned, but also about subjects pertinent to the other patients on the ward.

It was midnight when Darren finished reading. He winced as he realized that he was going to sleep tonight but might not be able to go back to bed for thirty or forty hours. He wished that he had not stayed up so late.

As he got ready for bed, he wondered where Courtney was. He went into the living room of their small apartment and found her quietly reading a novel on the couch.

"Sorry I've ignored you all evening," he apologized. "I'm kind of worried about what call will be like tomorrow. Poor Eddy looked like hell today. He didn't get to go home until three in the afternoon, so he had worked for about thirty-two hours straight."

Courtney quietly looked up from her book as he spoke. She paused for a moment before responding. "It's OK. I'm sure that you won't be this preoccupied forever. It's just really new for you." She smiled mischievously as she continued: "I'll give you two weeks. After that I'll expect you to ask me about my day."

Darren knew Courtney was joking, but he also knew that he had no idea how she had spent her last two days.

"I'm sorry. Why don't you tell me about what's been going on with you?" He tried to salvage the situation.

"That's okay," she answered, "I know you're tired. Why don't you go to bed and we'll catch up later. I'm going to read my book a little longer."

Darren agreed that he would put aside more time for them later, but paused before going to bed. "Nuremberg? Why is that name familiar?"

"Legal history," Courtney paused, and then gently scowled at Darren's lack of recognition. "I'm reading about the famous trials for Nazi war crimes after World War Two."

"Why?" Darren yawned.

"I need to keep up with the law this year, but if I try to read text books I won't remember a thing. I need books with legal issues and interesting stories behind them." She placed her bookmark, and closed the book into her lap. "You need to go to sleep, you're nodding off on your feet."

Darren agreed. As he drifted off he felt guilty that he would not be able to continue their conversation for a while, since he would not be home for two days.

The next morning Darren felt better prepared when Dr Smith arrived for rounds. The first patient they saw had asthma. When Dr Smith questioned him about treatment of asthma he was able to offer fairly complete answers. After he had answered two questions in a row correctly, though, the rules of the game seemed to change. Now Dr Smith's questions strayed from the realm of clinical relevance and into the vast stores of knowledge hidden in textbooks that no one would ever read.

"Which prostaglandins are most important in the exacerbation of asthma attacks?"

Darren had no idea. Prostaglandins were a series of hundreds of molecules named mostly only with numbers or letters like "prostaglandin 11b." He could not even imagine why anyone would care to remember which ones did what. But just as he felt sure he had been asked a question that no one would know the answer to, Layton gave it. Much of their rounds continued in the same fashion.

"This patient we treated with a sulfa drug has a rash," Dr Smith began. "What type of drug eruption might he have developed?"

"A Stevens-Johnson rash," Darren answered. He was suitably

impressed with himself for knowing an answer, but again Dr Smith took the game to a new level.

"Who was Johnson?"

Now Darren was lost again. Who cared who Johnson was? There were thousands of medical eponyms, and there was no point in knowing historical data about all of them. Dr Smith turned to Layton.

"Dr Robert Johnson was a nineteenth century Welsh physician," Layton coolly responded.

"Very good, Dr Leigh. I'll see you on rounds tomorrow, gentlemen." Dr Smith walked off the ward, leaving Darren staring in disbelief at his senior colleague.

"How do you know all that crazy stuff? You said yesterday that you never have time to read! You'd have to read the whole bloody Library of Congress to find some of that stuff you were spouting today!"

"This falls into the category of survival skills on rounds. Let's go get Eddy, and then I'll give you some tips before you start your night on call." Layton put his hand on Darren's shoulder and led him off the ward.

They began walking down to the Emergency Department. Eddy had been dismissed from rounds in order to admit an elderly lady in the Emergency Department. He had been gone for almost two hours, but as Darren and Layton entered the ER, Eddy's voice echoed from behind a curtain. They heard some of the questions he was loudly asking of a partially deaf lady.

"Please, Ma'am. Why have you come to hospital?" As the sound of his question reached Darren and Layton, Layton smirked slightly, recognizing a very basic error. Followed by Darren, Layton pulled aside the curtain and stepped into the area. Inside, they found an exasperated looking Eddy yelling questions at a very elderly lady dressed in a knitted shawl and hat. Beside her was a large suitcase. She was intent on providing a detailed answer to his question.

"It all started when I drove my car to the store. I met a very pleasant gentleman who was wearing a nice hat, because that was the style at the time. I think that I was with my niece. Her name is Amy, do you know her?"

Eddy looked towards Layton, desperation in his eyes. Layton took Eddy's shoulder and they walked outside the curtain.

Layton asked, "You've been talking to this lady for two hours?" He seemed to be having trouble controlling the laughter building inside him.

"She just keeps getting off topic," Eddy pleaded. "I can't even figure out what her symptoms are."

Layton smiled and they walked back into the curtained area. He said: "I was going to give Darren a few tips about surviving rounds, but clearly I need to teach you each a few things about the basics. Let me help you finish this history." He looked towards the confused woman and asked several questions in rapid fire.

"Where are you?"

"I'm at home," she answered confidently.

"What year is it?"

"1954."

"You see I'm wearing this white coat and stethoscope. Do you know who I am and why I'm here to see you?"

"You're my son."

"Thank you very much, Ma'am." Layton took Darren and Eddy out of the curtained area to the physicians' work area. As the three of them sat down, he asked Eddy: "Do you really think that you're going to get any information out of that lady?"

"She should at least be able to tell me what her symptoms are," Eddy defended himself.

"She doesn't have any symptoms," Layton said. "Did you see that suitcase?" Darren and Eddy nodded. "Her family is either not coping with her at home, or they're going out of town, so they just dropped Grandma off at the hospital. Have you ever heard of a sick person packing a suitcase to go to the hospital?" He reached across the desk and picked up her chart. "Here is some personal information that the nurses got about her. Try phoning the contacts and see if you can get a hold of her family. If you don't have any luck, we'll have to admit her until a social worker can see her."

Eddy reached for a telephone, but Layton stopped him. "Wait. I promised Darren I'd teach him some good stuff, so you should listen too. I should tell you guys about surviving rounds."

"I don't see how a few tips will cut it," Darren interjected. "It's a matter of knowing the answers to all sorts of crazy questions. I'd have to sit down and read for months to figure out some of the stuff you talked about today."

"It's simpler than that," Layton said. "Remember when Dr Smith asked me about those stupid prostaglandins? I don't know a thing about any prostaglandins, except a few things that are on a research poster outside Dr Smith's door. I guessed that the question he would ask would relate to the molecules that he has been researching. That's a trick the old guys like to use. If they can't think of anything relevant, they just ask you about their own research. At least they know that inside and out."

"That's all fine, but how the hell did you know who Johnson was?" Darren jumped in again. Layton laughed before explaining.

"That's another trick. You see, in the nineteenth century, people were just starting to figure stuff out about medicine, so they had a lot of things that needed new names. In those days you could do anything and get your name on it. So I guessed that Johnson was a nineteenth century physician. Next, I figured out that Dr Smith is Welsh. No matter where Johnson is from, Dr Smith is likely to think that he's Welsh. I didn't have to study anything to figure that out, I just had to watch sports on television. If you ever see the Welsh rugby team, some years so many players are named Smith or Davies that they have to refer to all the players by their first names. Besides, Dr Smith has that same accent."

"Is Johnson even a Welsh name?" Eddy cut into the conversation. "And what if you had been wrong?"

"The answer to your first question is: it doesn't matter. Like I said, no matter where the guy was from, Smith probably thinks he was Welsh. Your second question doesn't matter either. Smith doesn't even know who he is. If we hadn't known the answer, he would have smiled knowingly and said: 'there's something for you to look up tonight'. He just ran out of questions to ask, so he was grasping at straws. I made up the name Robert Johnson, and Smith didn't call me on it. That confirms my hypothesis." Eddy and Darren looked on, dumbstruck. "That's enough of the basics for today, guys. You'll figure out a lot of this stuff for yourselves this year. For now I'd better get Darren ready for tonight."

Layton took Darren to show him his call room, and they left Eddy to finish up in the Emergency Department. The call room had a bed, telephone and washroom. Layton informed him that the bed would be uncomfortable, but he also said that Darren would be lucky to lie down tonight. If he was unlucky, he would be running around the hospital all night and would be an exhausted zombie, like Eddy had been yesterday, by the time morning rounds came around.

As Darren put away his things in the call room, he thought about the number of tricks he had learned today. Unfortunately, he realized that few of them would be of any use tonight. Unlike the day, when Layton and Dr Smith were around to answer his questions, Darren would be on his own, and he did not think that knowing the names of Welsh rugby players would be helpful. He checked his watch and began dreading the arrival of five o'clock.

Chapter 3

Darren almost expected the excitement to begin the instant his watch struck five. Suddenly he was the doctor on call for General Internal Medicine for the entire hospital. If any patients ran into trouble that needed immediate attention, he would be the one who got called. But no one called. Not at five o'clock, anyway. Not at 5:03, either. Darren looked at his watch again. So far, so good. At 5:05 his pager rang as he was about to check his watch again. He was still sitting at the nursing station on his clinical teaching unit, after just finishing the chores Layton had laid out for him. A phone was directly in front of him and he was able to answer the page immediately.

"Hello, Unit 58."

"Dr Johnston, medicine."

"Hello, Dr Johnston, are you looking after Mrs Keilor?"

"Whose patient is she?" There were several units full of inpatients in internal medicine, and Darren was responsible for all of them. Other doctors looked after most of them during the day. Other clinical teaching units like Dr Smith's looked after some.

"Dr Weber." He was another internist, and Darren was responsible for his patients while on call.

"Yes, I'm responsible for her. I'm not familiar with her case, though."

"She's a sixty-four year old woman with pneumonia. She has a headache. Can we give her a Tylenol?"

"Sure. Up to two tablets every six hours as needed."

"Thanks. What was your name?"

"Johnston."

"Thanks."

That had not been too bad. Darren felt in control of the situation so long as all he was doing was ordering Tylenol for headaches. He checked his watch again. Layton would be back in the hospital at 7:30 a.m. He had already made it through seven minutes, and now he had only fourteen hours and twenty-three minutes to go before he would be back at the security of morning rounds, where more senior doctors would know the answer to his every question.

Soon his pager went off again. This time it was for a patient with an abnormal serum potassium level. He ordered an intravenous potassium infusion and continued feeling that everything was within his grasp. He walked to the elevator and went to the basement where there was a small lounge for residents on call. There he lay on the couch, turned on the television and tried to relax. It was 5:19 when his pager went off a third time. This time it was the Emergency Room physician, calling him to see a patient.

"Hi. Dr Lang here. I've got a seventy-four year old lady with a urinary tract infection that needs to be admitted to medicine."

Here was something that might be interesting. After completing a brief exchange, Darren hung up the phone and headed for the Emergency Room. He was already thinking about what would be the best type of antibiotics for her, and what kind of complications she might have developed. On his way up the stairs to the ground floor, he realized that in his excitement he had not asked the patient's name.

In order to obtain that last and most important piece of information, he was able to find Dr Lang amidst the sea of patients waiting on stretchers, in chairs and even on hospital beds lining the hallways. Almost six hours later, at 11:00, he felt like he had personally waded into that sea of agonized people. He had admitted five of them and answered eleven calls from the wards, but he had not once left the Emergency Department.

He felt tired, but still optimistic as he completed the admission orders for his latest patient. Now he had only one more patient left. It was a man with pneumonia. He picked up the man's chart and glanced past several curtained areas at the one where the man was waiting. The man did not seem to be in any significant respiratory distress, so Darren began taking his time to review the information that was already on the chart. He was interrupted when his pager rang. He quickly answered the call.

"Dr Johnston, medicine."

"Hi, Dr Johnston. This is Nurse Reynolds on Unit 71. Mr Stevens here is feeling very short of breath."

"All right. How long has this been going on for?"

"I'm not sure."

"Okay, what is he admitted with?"

"I'm not sure of that either. I'm not his nurse. She's on her coffee break."

"I'll be right up."

Darren replaced the chart he was reading in the rack at the doctor's workstation. As he turned to leave the Emergency Department, a more senior resident in neurology who had been seated next to him commented, "That must have been Unit 71. I noticed they didn't know a bloody thing when you asked. So, what's the matter? Did somebody sneeze?" She laughed at her own joke, but Darren remained serious.

"No. Someone is short of breath." Shortness of breath was a serious symptom, one never to be ignored. It was both uncomfortable for the patient and often representative of serious disease.

"Sure they are. Enjoy your trip." The neurology resident looked back to the chart she was reviewing, again laughing to herself. Darren shook his head and continued towards the wards.

Conscious that he was getting behind on his work, Darren hoped to finish quickly with the patient upstairs. On his way up the elevator, he began running through the list of common conditions that could make someone short of breath. He realized that this could take longer than he had hoped, since all the conditions he thought of were serious and required rapid medical intervention. As he walked onto Unit 71, a nurse at the desk confronted him. She directed him to the appropriate room. There, he found a middle-aged man comfortably reading a newspaper.

"Hi, I'm Dr Johnston. The nurses tell me you are short of breath." The man seemed surprised to see him, and paused before answering.

"Yes. I guess I am."

"How long have you been short of breath for?"

"About a week. I came into hospital for it. The doctors told me I had a blood clot in my lungs." He paused again before finishing and gestured towards his intravenous line. "It's getting better since they put me on the IV."

Darren frowned. Had he really come all the way up here, at midnight, with a patient waiting in the Emergency Room, to be told about a symptom that had been appropriately treated for a week? He returned to the nursing desk and wrote a brief progress note. In the meantime his pager rang twice more, once for a patient to see on the ward, and once for another admission in the ER. More importantly, he was having trouble recognizing which calls were important and which could wait. He thought back to the neurology resident who had immediately known that his call from Unit 71 would not be about anything important. Now Darren found himself wondering if he was leaving critically ill patients waiting while he dealt with trivial calls.

On his way to his next call, the hospital seemed extremely large and empty. The stark white corridors that normally seemed to close in around nervous visitors, now stretched off into infinity. The halls were essentially empty, with only the echoing sound of Darren's footsteps to fill them. Occasionally Darren would walk past a room with an IV pump beeping for attention, and sometimes past a room with a patient moaning in pain. The further he walked, the more alone he felt, and the more he thought of Courtney who would be asleep now in their bed. He felt at that moment like he had left his old life behind and had stepped into a vast world within the white walls surrounding him.

It was one o'clock in the morning by the time he got back to the Emergency Department. The ER was filled with sights and sounds. Some people were yelling, some were quietly reassuring loved ones. Machines made whining, hissing and ringing sounds and an overhead speaker was constantly calling for this or that doctor. The charge nurse immediately confronted him.

"What are you doing with bed number twelve?"

"You mean the guy with chest pain?"

"No, you're thinking of bed fourteen. Bed twelve, the one around the corner."

As the nurse corrected him, Darren wondered why the nurses insisted on describing patients by their bed number. How on earth was he supposed to remember which bed was which?

"Oh, the fever." It occurred to him that maybe he and the nurse could communicate more effectively by using the patients' names, but rifling through the notes he kept on scraps of paper in his pocket, he realized that he had not written down "the fever's" name. He did, however, recall what he had done for the actual fever, the diagnosis rather than the person attached to it. "I wrote orders for antibiotics and for admission to medicine."

"You might want to put those orders in the order rack so people can find them, *Doctor*." This was not the first time that Darren had heard his professional title spoken sarcastically. It was not the same way as Dr Smith said it. When Dr Smith said the word it carried haughty connotations that left Darren feeling unworthy. He quietly apologized and returned to the man's chart he had first seen over an hour before.

He spoke with the man, and realized that he was only mildly ill. He had been having a cough and fevers for almost two weeks, but had managed to walk to the hospital from five kilometres away. He had an obvious pneumonia on his chest X-ray, so Darren felt confident giving him antibiotics to take at home. Remembering from medical school that patients were always most satisfied when given an explanation of their condition, he explained his diagnosis to the man, and gave him a prescription. He asked the patient if he had any questions.

"No," replied the slightly dishevelled man in his sixties as he turned towards the exit without his prescription. Darren was not sure why the man would leave without treatment, but decided the man must have concerns that had not been addressed.

"Is something wrong, Sir?"

"I thought you were going to make me better."

Darren presumed that he hadn't adequately explained his treatment plan, so he tried again. "I prescribed you some antibiotics, Sir." He realized that perhaps the situation was more complicated. "Will you have trouble affording the prescription?"

"No. I took antibiotics already and I'm not any better. Some doctor prescribed me some pills a week ago. He thought I had nothing serious. He was probably racist."

Now the situation started to make sense to Darren. "How long did you take the pills for, Sir?"

"Two days."

Everything made sense. The man felt that the previous doctor had blown off his concerns, so he had only taken part of his prescription and then given up. Perhaps the patient was justified in his attitude that the previous doctor had not him seriously because of his race. Now his pneumonia had gotten worse. Darren smiled, sure that the situation could be remedied by some improved communication.

"The pills take a few days to work. You have to take the entire course for your pneumonia to resolve." He began to hand the man the prescription again, but the man only turned again to leave.

"I thought you were going to make me better. Maybe you're just another racist."

Darren just stood in disbelief with the man's chart in one hand and the unfilled prescription in the other. A nurse arrived and began speaking to him.

"What are you doing with bed eight?"

"Pardon me?" Darren started to respond as his pager beeped. The sudden sound distracted him. He looked down at his belt to see the pager display.

"Bed eight. What's your plan?" she repeated.

"You mean the pneumonia?" As he answered, his pager rang again. He was having trouble concentrating on so many things at once.

"Yes. Mr ..." she paused to look at the name on the chart he was holding. Having turned off the ringing of his pager, he looked at the chart as well.

"Mr Cardinal!" They both spoke in unison.

"He left without treatment," Darren finished.

"You have to get them to sign a 'Refusal of treatment' form if they leave without treatment, *Doctor*!" There was that sneering pronunciation again.

Darren began to explain the situation when his pager rang a third time. Looking down at the pager, he noted his own white coat and nametag. Instead of feeling proud of them, he wished he could tear them off to get people to leave him alone. When he looked back up, the nurse was gone. He walked to the nearest phone and began to answer his pages.

"Dr Johnston. Medicine."

"Hi, Dr Johnston. Mrs Jenkins on Unit 63 can't sleep and wants a sleeping pill. Can we give her a lorazepam?"

"What is she admitted with?" Darren did not want to prescribe something harmful, and knew that sleeping pills can cause problems if people are having trouble breathing.

"I don't know."

"Does she have any allergies?"

"I don't know. You see, I'm not her usual nurse."

"All right. I'll stop by and look at the chart."

"Thanks."

Darren hung up and answered his second page. "Dr Johnston. Medicine."

"Hi, Dr Johnston, this is nurse Whelan on Unit 12. I have here a sixty-three year old woman, named Edna Spence, admitted with tuberculosis."

"Okay." Darren had a pen and paper in hand and began jotting down the details.

"Her complications include a left pleural effusion, and her lab work shows …" Darren was ecstatic. Finally he was being given enough information to make a decision about the patient's urgency. The diligent nurse continued. "Anyway, she has a headache. Can we give her a Tylenol?" Darren's head dropped into his hands, and the pen and paper fell to the floor.

"Sure, go for it."

"One to two tablets every four to six hours?"

"Yup."

Darren's frustration was building as he hung up the phone and answered the third page. It was about two thirty in the morning and he was starting to feel his fatigue acutely. This time the call from the ward was about a significant problem with a patient with liver failure. He went to see the sick patient, leaving the sleeping pill fiasco for later.

It was four o'clock when he finally finished his work and headed for his call room. He had been on his feet for most of the twenty-one hours he had been in the hospital, and his legs ached and he longed to get into bed. He was glad that Layton would be back in the hospital soon, because the liver failure patient had been quite complicated, and he had questions he needed to ask. He figured he had dealt with the most pressing issues and the rest could wait until morning. Now he was just glad that if all went well he would still get three hours' sleep. Despite his severe fatigue, he had trouble falling asleep for about half an hour as he continued to think over the problems with the liver failure patient. Finally sleep overcame him. It seemed like the instant he drifted off he was in a complex dream where the chaotic sounds of the hospital took on physical form and chased him in endless circles. He awoke to the beeping of his pager. He rubbed his eyes and reached to turn on a light. The clock read 5:13, so he had slept for less than forty-five minutes. Without sitting up, he reached for the telephone. The call was from an emergency physician with another patient for him to admit. That would take about an hour, and effectively put an end to thoughts of getting any significant amount of sleep. He pushed himself up in bed and his entire body revolted. His eyes felt sore when he moved them, and all his muscles were stiff. He could not believe that he would spend every third night this way.

Chapter 4

When Darren arrived in the Emergency Department, the casualty officer who had consulted him smiled. "Nice nap?" He chuckled, and Darren reached up to realize that his hair was standing on end. Darren grumbled and flattened his hair with his hand, thinking that he had been sleeping for less than an hour. Despite ongoing fatigue, he looked to the rest of the world as if he had been asleep all night.

He made his way to the washroom and splashed water on his face before searching for his new patient's chart. This one was a man named Kurt Doering, who had apparently come in with confusion. Darren was feeling fairly confused himself at five a.m. He glanced past several of the stretchers before finding the one that held his patient. Sure enough, stretcher number eighteen was occupied by a man who looked distinctly disoriented. He was a big man, over six feet tall and broad in the shoulders with a thick mane of grey and white hair. Now robed in a flimsy hospital gown, he was lying on his stretcher and staring up at the ceiling. His eyes darted back and forth, seeing things no one else could. Periodically he would stab out at some invisible object with one of his large hands. His face bore a look of complete concentration as though solving some timeless paradox, but his eyes were somehow vacant, revealing that the paradox was within. One of his bare feet extended out from under his blankets but he made no effort to cover it.

Beside the bed stood his wife. She was a tall woman with white hair tied in a bun who wore a long dress that in no way betrayed having been hastily thrown on at five in the morning. Simply the way she stood with one hand on the bed rail and the other draped at her side held a certain grace. Darren thought that she must have been very beautiful when she was young, and even now, well over sixty, she had features of an attractive precision.

"Good morning, Ma'am. I'm Dr Johnston." He reached out his hand to shake hers. She began to reach towards him, but paused to ask a question.

"What is your first name?" She smiled. Her face radiated warmth and she made Darren think of a schoolteacher expressing satisfaction with a question well answered.

Darren's pause before answering must have been imperceptible to an observer, but concealed a multitude of swirling thoughts. This was one of the first days of his life in which he could introduce himself as "Dr Johnston." Now this lady casually wanted to know his first name. Although her demeanour was nothing but warm and friendly, he found himself feeling threatened. If he let his guard down for just a moment he could find himself looking at a woman who could be his grandmother. She was a woman with a lifetime of experiences behind her and all the wisdom that came with them. A woman who might call him from his games in the front yard onto the porch where she would give him freshly baked cookies and lemonade on a beautiful summer day. Then this man on the stretcher could be his grandfather, sitting comfortably inside the house and working on a model of a sailing ship. This crazy man in the hospital, wallowing in the captivity of delirium, could emerge from the house and tell Darren stories with a twinkle in his eye. They would be stories that told volumes about the joy of seeing children grow up when you have already grown old.

"My name is Darren." But this man on the stretcher was not his grandfather. He was a crazy old guy who was in the hospital at five in the morning, and Darren was going to have to figure out what was wrong. The information he would need to help him was at the fingertips of this graceful old lady who smiled back at him as she said: "It's nice to meet you Darren. I'm Mary Doering. I suppose that you would like to hear the story of why my husband is here."

"Yes, please."

"I suppose that it all began about a week ago. Kurt began talking to me about the war. That's the Second World War of course. First, he started telling me about the days just before the war started. His family's fortunes had not been good but things were improving when Hitler took power. I am sure that having grown up in Canada, you think of Hitler as an evil tyrant. That he was, but what you have to understand is, the Germans were very poor in the 1930s. They initially saw him as a man who was moving the country in a positive direction. He also stood up to what they saw as oppression from the countries that had won the Great War."

Now Darren was wondering if Kurt Doering was the only one who was confused. Mrs Doering's diction had the precision of an English teacher. He could almost imagine that she was teaching him a lesson. But what in God's name could all this nonsense about prewar Germany have to do with her husband becoming confused? Nevertheless, Darren continued listening. He had learned in medical school that there were dangers inherent in interrupting a patient early in an interview. If he came to ask this lady about her husband's confusion and focused the conversation to the exclusion of all else, then she might not remember to tell him that her husband had a fever yesterday or even that he had surgery. Darren needed to give the patient (or, in this case, his family) time to get the story out. He could do so with open questions like: "How have you been feeling lately?" That way a patient could tell him what was on his or her mind. When Darren had the general idea, he could ask closed questions such as: "Has the headache gotten worse?" That kind of question would give him the information he needed, but no more, and might leave the patient waiting to give Darren a last crucial piece of information, but without a question to bring it out. Keeping all this in mind, Darren let the story continue. Mary Doering had been talking, but he had not been concentrating. He did notice that she seemed to have reached an important crossroads in the tale.

"So it was after he had worked in construction for several years that he joined the army. It was then that life was just getting back on track for him and his first wife."

Fatigue hit Darren like a hammer to his head. Listening to this story was using up precious time, time that might have been used to grab a quick nap before morning rounds, but now here he was waiting, without gaining any useful information about the patient.

"Ma'am, when did your husband first become confused?"

"Like I've been saying, I first noticed that something was wrong about a week ago, when he began talking about the war. He had never talked to me about the war until last week. Never in almost fifty years of marriage. It was a time of his life that he put entirely behind him. He rarely even mentioned his first wife. I think that she died while he was away fighting. I suspect that was part of the reason that he emigrated to Canada. He had nothing to stay in Germany for. It was ironic because it was Canadian soldiers who had taken him prisoner."

Darren finally felt like he had gotten to the point of the story. Unfortunately, if it took him this long to get every answer from her, he would be here all day. He decided he had better ask some closed questions.

"So he started acting strangely about a week ago. Did he just gradually get more confused from there?"

"Yes. He just said strange things and seemed forgetful for a few days, and then last night he began pacing and talking to himself after I put the lights out. Finally I got him to lie down, but by then he was muttering to himself and staring into space so I brought him here."

"Does he have any medical problems?"

"No. He has always been healthy as a horse."

"Does he take any medication?"

"None."

"Any allergies?"

"No."

"Does he smoke?"

"Oh, yes. He smoked ever since the war. Apparently his doctor told him to start in order to calm his nerves. Doctors would never say that today!" Why did she always want to talk about World War II? Darren continued with his rapid-fire questions to get things moving.

"Did he have any other symptoms over the last week?"

"He seemed thirsty all the time and his cough got worse. He always coughs a bit in the morning, but the last few weeks there was some blood on the tissue he coughed into."

"Thank you, Ma'am. This has been very helpful. I'm going to examine him, and then I will have a look at the lab work that the emergency physician has drawn. I may have a few more questions for you afterwards."

"Oh, thank you. I'm sure you will be able to help him, Darren." There was his first name again, but Darren felt good. Mrs Doering was quite a charming lady when she got to the point, and he really wanted to help her husband. She smiled at Darren as she stepped aside to let him examine Kurt, and again Darren had the feeling of being watched by a proud schoolteacher. He worked through his physical exam, but did not find any clues to help him sort out Kurt's confusion. Kurt remained disoriented through the whole process, unaware of who or where he was.

After the physical examination, Darren looked at Kurt's lab work. His serum sodium was very low. That could certainly cause his confusion, and together with the story that he was thirsty all the time, suggested that his body was abnormally retaining water. Just why that should happen was still not clear. After looking at the laboratory values, Darren walked across the Emergency Department to look at Kurt's chest X-Ray. Across two nursing desks and through a mess of health care workers, Mrs Doering still smiled at him as he put the X-Ray up to the lighted view box. Suddenly the answer was clear. In Kurt Doering's left lung was a large tumour. As a heavy smoker, he must have developed lung cancer. Lung cancers sometimes cause a condition that leads to water retention. All the extra water lowered his blood salt concentrations. That was what made him confused.

There was no satisfaction for Darren in solving this human puzzle. The most potentially rewarding thing he had done all night, the most interesting use of a sea of information, only meant that he was about to become part of a horrible tragedy. Mrs Doering was still watching him hopefully from across the department, and now he realized he would have to give her worse news than she had ever received. But he could not break the news cleanly to her. He could still not be one hundred percent sure that this was cancer until he had a sample of the tumour. He would have to tell her that her husband "probably" had cancer. Darren was not sure if leaving her the hope that he was wrong would be helpful, or if it would only impede her inevitable grieving.

He felt a pit in his stomach as he walked back across the department. She watched him walk towards her and the smile slowly left her face. She could already tell that the news was not going to be good. Darren wanted to tell her that he was not yet sure what was wrong. He wanted to wait for a biopsy to be done, and then maybe Dr. Smith would give her the news. It hurt him just to keep walking towards her, but as he stopped in front of her he knew that he had to tell her. He had to tell her that her husband of many years was going to die. Kurt Doering had been healthy as a horse a week ago, and had not even realized that his smoking had already killed him.

"How are the results?" Mrs Doering's face betrayed caution. She seemed to know what he was going to say, but could not make herself believe that the news could really be that bad. Darren thought briefly about the easiest way to say what he had to say. There was no easy way.

"It looks like he has lung cancer." Darren's face was impassive as he forced out the words. Her face also remained emotionless, but somehow the strength of her grief hit Darren like a slap across the face. He could almost feel the air sucked from his lungs. But had he only imagined her grief, thinking of how he would feel in her place? Perhaps the very fact that her expression remained neutral in the face of his awful words had somehow communicated to his subconscious that she was in terrible pain. Although no tear ever ran down Mrs Doering's face, Darren was sure he had seen the hint of one forming. Her single tear, carefully blinked away, had produced the subtlest glistening in the corner of her eye at a moment before the word "cancer" had completely left his lips. Before the news had even registered in her brain, something in her nervous system knew that her entire life was about to change. She was about to lose her husband.

"I see." Mrs Doering paused for a moment and fidgeted with her purse. "How sure are you?"

"The only way we can be sure is to obtain a sample of the tissue in his lungs. It will likely be a few days before we can be certain."

"Are you going to be able to help him?"

During his childhood, Darren had learned that the best way of getting along with other people was to make compromises. There was always give and take. Now the back of his mind screamed at him that it was time to give. She had woken in the middle of the night. She had waited for hours in a frightening and unfamiliar Emergency Room to get some answers. Darren had just given her the worst possible news she could imagine. Now he owed her something. He had to be able to help.

"I don't know. I'm sorry." Darren felt helpless, helpless and useless. He looked down at the floor and could hardly bring himself to raise his gaze towards her. His eyes briefly focused on three drops of blood on the ground, and he wondered where they had come from, but forced himself to focus on the task at hand, and tried his best to give Mrs Doering a better answer. "I think the confusion is from water retention. People with lung cancer sometimes get the syndrome of inappropriate antidiuretic hormone …" His pager rang as he spoke, and he realized that he had begun speaking very quickly. "So his, um, sodium level is very low." He stopped. He had clearly lost her, and felt foolish for starting to blubber on in medical jargon. Her wonderful eyes that had seemed so full of warmth just a few minutes ago were no longer focused in his direction. He took her arm and led her back to the chair beside her husband's bed. She sat down, but her eyes remained focused at a great distance. Darren felt he had to keep trying to be helpful.

"It will take some time for us to arrange the tests we need. Why don't you go home and come back after you've had some sleep. You're probably very tired."

"I'll just stay with him if you don't mind," she said. "I can't imagine going home. After more than forty years, I can't remember what it is like to sleep without him." Darren reached to get her a box of tissues because she looked like she might start to cry. She thanked him, and he walked away to his work area to write admission orders for Mr Doering. On his way to the desk, he answered the page that had interrupted him earlier. It was one of the wards calling, letting him know that someone's potassium level was low. After the most emotionally draining night of his life, he could not believe he was still responsible for such mundane nuisances. He felt he must have done enough tonight, and he must be able to go home to Courtney now. No such luck, as he got down to the business of writing orders.

When he was through in the Emergency Department, he headed back for his call room. Now it was six o'clock in the morning, and he hoped that he would be able to get just a touch of sleep before starting morning rounds. On his way, thoughts were spinning around in his head about what had just happened. The Doerings had been married for longer than he had even been alive. He wondered what it was like to lose someone that you had been close to for such a long time. He thought back to Mrs Doering's comment that she could not remember sleeping without her husband, and he was sad to know she would have to learn to now, when she needed the support of her husband the most.

Darren fell to the mattress still wearing his hospital scrubs. He felt sleep approaching quickly, but stopped to kick off his shoes and check the clock on his pager. The time was 6:05, and he set his alarm for 6:45. That would give him a brief nap before getting started, and would give him time to get ready for rounds.

Despite the intensity of emotions that had been around him, he managed to fall asleep instantly, but when his pager awoke him, he blinked back tears. He was not sure if emotion had caught up with him or if he was just so tired that his body could no longer take it. Reaching his arm out to turn off the pager was physically painful. As he checked the number he had been paged to, he noticed that the clock read 6:11. For the second time, he wondered how he would survive call every third night.

Chapter 5

Later, Darren glanced at his watch again; it read 7:30a.m. His first night on call was officially finished. He lumbered back towards his call room from the wards where he had just taken care of several problems that effectively ended any chance of further sleep. His body felt both heavy and light at the same time as though marionette strings were pulling at his limbs. As people walked past him in the hallway he laughed to himself that they must feel they are up early. Meanwhile, for him, it was very, very late. His mouth felt dry so he opened and closed it several times to get rid of the feeling, and he realized he had worked the last twelve or fourteen hours without anything to eat or drink. With that in mind, he thought perhaps he should grab breakfast, but a wave of nausea broke against his throat, robbing him of the desire to respond to his metabolism. On his return to his call room he took several things from his overnight bag and decided he should have a shower. His whole body felt sticky, which was not surprising, given that he had been working in the same clothes for eighteen hours. On his way to the shower room down the hall, he began to dread that morning rounds were going to start soon. By the time he was finished showering, the team would be ready to start, and he had not reviewed his patients at all.

In the residents' shower room he found himself a towel, then made his way to one of the shower stalls. He lingered in the shower, enjoying the warm water cascading over him and easing his sore muscles. Part of him wanted to hurry and be ready for rounds, but another part just wanted to leave and go home to bed.

The two inclinations compromised on a slightly extended shower. As he dried himself off, the cold air woke him up a bit. He simply could not get the feeling he was one hundred percent awake. As he got dressed in a fresh set of hospital scrubs, he noticed Chris had just entered the shower area. Although Chris had not even showered yet, he looked much better than Darren. Chris must have been on call for the Intensive Care Unit last night, so Darren ventured a question.

"Did you get some sleep last night?" To look so enthusiastic to start his day, surely Chris must have slept.

"Nope. Not even a minute's worth."

"How on earth do you look so good? I feel like I had too much to drink last night, but without the benefit of having a good time!"

"Oh yeah. It must have been your first night on call last night. How did it go?" Chris smiled. Something about his demeanour suggested he knew not only how it had gone but had a good idea how Darren had felt all night.

"It was without a doubt the worst night of my life. I can't believe I have to keep working until rounds are done at lunchtime. And after that it doesn't seem reasonable I only get to go home for eighteen hours before I'm back again. And then it seems even less reasonable that I'm on call again, so I'm here for another thirty straight hours. Last night almost killed me. How am I going to do it again?"

"What was so bad about it?"

Darren was taken aback by Chris's response. He could not imagine why Chris, knowing what kind of night it was, would ask this needless question. Nevertheless, something about the way he asked it suggested there was a lesson to be learned from the answer.

"I'll tell you what was so bad about it. The nurses treated me like I didn't know anything, and sometimes they were right. Half the patients didn't seem to want my help. My pager went off every few minutes whether something important was happening or not, and it wasn't always easy to tell the difference. I had to tell a

woman that her husband had lung cancer. That alone was enough
to make me want to go straight home, but I was the only one here
and my pager just kept ringing. I wasn't always sure what to do
when it rang, and I think there was some pretty important stuff
happening. That's why it was so bad."

"Did you kill anyone?" Chris's permanent smile remained
painted on. Darren's eyes clouded, as though Chris's face might,
by a simple trick of ocular accommodation, deconstruct into
Monet's tiny brushstrokes.

"No. I didn't kill anyone." Foolish question.

"Then I guess nothing went irreversibly wrong, did it?" As
Chris finished speaking, part of Darren wanted to wipe that stupid
smile off his face, but the rest of him burst out laughing.

"No. I guess it didn't." Darren felt a little better with the events
of the previous night put in that light, but there was something that
left him unsatisfied. "So you still haven't answered my question.
Why are you looking so good if you were up working all night?"

"I'll tell you what your problem was. You probably got about
an hour of sleep last night, broken up into three or four parts. Am I
right?" Darren nodded. "If you keep going to bed, you're just
teasing your body and letting it think it's bedtime. That's why you
have that gross shaky feeling all over. It's okay if you can grab a
few hours, but once it's obvious that you're going to be up all
night, you have to just roll with the punches and stay up."

His advice sounded reasonable enough, but surely Chris must
have had a rough night to keep him up so long. "So what were you
up to all night?"

Chris's smile widened at the question. "Oh, I had a cool time. I
put in three central lines and two arterial lines. I intubated a guy
who was in respiratory distress and got him all fixed up on the
ventilator. It was fun."

Darren grimaced. *Fun indeed.* As a medical student, Darren
had put in two central lines, the long intravenous catheters
threaded into large veins, like the jugular in the neck, used for
intravenous access, or to pass devices like pacemakers into the

heart. The memory was not a pleasant one, and it reminded him of an anxious and challenging hour spent under the withering gaze of a chief surgical resident. As for arterial lines, going into arteries instead of veins, Darren hadn't yet had to place one, but Chris was clearly excited about having the chance to put them in and demonstrate the considerable skill required. "So I guess the Intensive Care Unit was pretty crazy last night." Darren was realizing that despite the stress his patients had caused him, Chris had dealt with much sicker patients all night.

"You could say that. The one guy died while I was putting in his arterial line. He had requested a 'Do not resuscitate' status earlier so we didn't start CPR."

"What did you do?" The discomforting thought of having someone die in front of him, while powerless to help, dawned on Darren.

"I finished his art-line."

Darren was taken aback again. "Why on earth would you finish the procedure if he was already dead? What the hell good is the art-line going to do?"

"I don't know, but I was almost finished. Besides, the art-line tracing gives you a super confident diagnosis of death. You can really be one hundred percent sure that they have no pulse."

Chris's smile had still not faded. He did look up and to the right a bit as he talked about "diagnosing" death. It was as though he had just thought of something very useful he was storing away to recall on important occasions. Until then, Darren had never seen Chris take his eyes off the person he was speaking to. He was very intense in a relaxed sort of way.

Darren paused for a moment, realizing Chris certainly had a different perspective on death than he did.

"How many of your patients died last night?"

"Um, three, I guess. Well, have a good rest tonight." Chris turned to leave, but Darren called him with one more question.

"Does it get any easier?"

Chris continued walking and did not look back at Darren as he spoke. "No. But you do get used to it. Try to have some fun!" He raised his arm in a casual wave as he left the change room. Did something in his tone of voice suggest perhaps his permanent smile, no longer within Darren's view, had finally faded during this most cheerful of suggestions?

Had he tried, Darren would have failed to rally a cheerful reply. The taste of the horrible news he had given Kurt Doering's wife still lingered on his tongue like a sour appetizer that preceded a course of Chris's casual attitude towards death and illness.

Chapter 6

The date was August 5, 1944, but Unterfeldwebel Kurt Doering of the Luftwaffe had long since lost count of the days. He and his men had been in a fighting withdrawal for weeks, and now every day seemed to blend into the next. He looked down towards the ground as his heavy boots crunched against the gravel that made up this narrow road, adjusted his heavy pack and shifted its weight on his shoulders, then returned his eyes to his route. Hedges more than eight feet tall lined the road on either side. This made it a narrow corridor just wide enough for a single horse-drawn wagon to pass. One was approaching now, so Kurt's column of men eased up against the hedge on their right. The sky seemed to darken as they moved over, because most of their light came from the glow of the setting sun on their right side. Now, they were in the shadow of the hedge.

The sound of gravel churning under the wheels of the wagon was loud against the profound silence that enveloped the countryside. The men were quiet, as was often the case during a long march. Kurt imagined perhaps four years ago the men of the Wehrmacht had joked and sung boisterously as they marched towards victory in France. He had never known such a march. For these last weeks they had marched always away from the coast from which British soldiers were fast advancing.

Now the quiet of dusk was broken by the sound of hurried footsteps approaching from behind Kurt. Oberjäger Hans Schultz lit a cigarette as he neared. He offered one to Kurt, but as always Kurt declined with a quick shake of his head. Hans knew very well that Kurt had never smoked; in fact, Kurt often gave Hans his cigarette ration. Nevertheless, Hans always offered. When almost everyone smoked, it would seem both incongruous and impolite not to make that gesture.

"We did some good work today, Herr Unterfeldwebel. Tommy will find a lot of surprises for him." Hans smiled as he reminded his sergeant of the day's exploits. Kurt shared Hans's enthusiasm, but as always, the Unterfeldwebel's face remained impassive in the presence of his men. He could feel himself smile inwardly, not so much out of approval of the work the men had done as out of amusement at Hans's overly formal greeting. The two had become fast friends during their time together in the Fifth Fallschirm-Jäger Regiment, Third Division, and despite extensive unit reorganizations, they had always found themselves in the same platoon of about thirty men, almost always in the same section. While no one in their platoon would doubt that Kurt and Hans were friends, Hans was always a corporal quick to obey orders and beyond reproach in his formality.

"Yes, I think that Tommy will have a difficult time today." Kurt once again shifted the weight of his pack as he used the common nickname for British soldiers. While Britain was a formidable empire and its soldiers were ordinary young men like those of the German army, "Tommy" was a faceless enemy, easy to despise. Long ago Thomas Atkins had been a compatriot of the Duke of Wellington; today, to the Germans, Tommy was a dehumanized foe that could be shot and killed without guilt.

One of Kurt's men called forward.

"Do you remember the wine bottle, Herr Unterfeldwebel? That was class!" The wine bottle had been an interesting exercise. In the cellar of an abandoned farmhouse, one of the men had discovered a well-aged bottle of Bordeaux. After finishing the bottle, they decided that the British would likely be equally impressed. They refilled the bottle with wine of a lesser vintage – urine – and reinserted the cork. The wine bottle was gingerly placed on a windowsill where Tommy would be likely to find it as he passed.

What the unsuspecting British soldier would not likely notice was the tripwire to an anti-personnel mine concealed in the wall from the inside.

The corners of Kurt's mouth rose just slightly as the men laughed and congratulated each other for their cunning. He did not mind the men finding satisfaction in the unusual work they had been doing lately. After all, most had become more quiet and withdrawn since they began booby-trapping their dead.

As the laughter died, the men quickly returned to their silent march. They were tired from long marches, and it did not help that they had been doing so much of their marching at night. Two soldiers of the German army passed by in the opposite direction, but hardly turned to look at Kurt's section. There was a civility between the branches of the armed forces these days, occasionally tested by individual hostilities. It was no secret they marched at night because the enemy air forces had free reign of the skies during the day. The parachute divisions of the Luftwaffe, like Kurt's, were not expected to play any part in keeping the sky safe, but still, Kurt's men sometimes felt the hostility that was directed by the army at Hermann Goering, who had been so optimistic with his promises of victory in the air.

The tensions between the Heer and the Luftwaffe, however, were nothing to rival those between the Wehrmacht and the SS. Although an organization with many branches, the SS was known by most for its frightening and sadistic troops who seemed to have materialized outside the armed forces' normal chain of command in the years before the war. Initially the elite among the street thugs who had won elections for Hitler with their fists and clubs, the SS had made a place for themselves by exterminating the leaders of the country's other prewar paramilitaries. Now they were a small army of their own. Fiercely loyal and disciplined, they were feared by all, but never respected as fellow soldiers by Germany's Wehrmacht.

Kurt and Hans marched on with the other men of their section. Up ahead the road narrowed from its already minimal width.

There, another group of men from Kurt's division was laying barbed wire and a sign that read: "Achtung, Minen!"

"Who would have imagined that the fearless soldiers of the parachute divisions would be reduced to laying down fences?" Hans asked of no one in particular. Kurt quietly nodded. They had indeed been doing work that was not in their usual line of duty. While they had not yet been directly involved in the combat that had been ongoing since D-Day, the men of Kurt's section had always been near enough to hear the guns in the distance. They had always been close enough to feel the wrath of the enemy bombers as well. Far from counterattacking, their role had become the laying of traps to slow the British advance while German forces bought time to form a defensive line. Their handiwork often took the form of mines or explosives with clever tripwires, but in this case, the men used a sign to leave only the impression of a minefield when they had run out of explosives. That could slow an advancing army too. Besides the traps they lay, other means of confusing the enemy included steps as simple as reversing road signs.

As Kurt and Hans continued marching, Hans took brief looks through the gaps in the hedges on either side of the road. Lush fields covered the landscape, often with picturesque farmhouses surveying them. As they passed the narrow point in the road where the sign indicating an imaginary minefield was placed, Kurt noticed that a machine gun crew was setting up behind the hedge. Even in the midst of the retreat the Germans left small groups of soldiers to hit the enemy quickly, then join the retreat themselves. This crew clearly had the intention of shooting up whatever group of sappers the British sent forward to clear the imaginary minefield.

The work the paratroopers were doing was unusual not because it was unheard of among the soldiers' duties, but because of who was doing it. Often engineers were assigned tasks like the one that the paratroopers were doing here, but in the confusion that reigned around the Allied landings, many people were doing work for which they had not been trained. Not only was Kurt's training more suited to leading paratroopers into combat, his position in the command structure was generally as part of a platoon. Now he found himself commanding a section of eleven men, with the hopes that they would soon be able to rendezvous with the remainder of their unit.

Kurt took a quick look around him and made sure that the men of his section were staying together. As always, they marched quickly and efficiently, and, despite carrying out unfamiliar tasks, they performed admirably. Although six of them had only recently been transferred to this section, drawn from entirely different paratrooper regiments, they had all seen combat in some form. These men were all volunteers and had all been extensively trained. Kurt's jaw tightened at the thought of the poorly trained conscripts that were finding their way into battle more and more often, but he laughed to himself as he recalled some of the training that seemed useless now.

"How many practice jumps did we do together, Hans?"

"I don't think I can count that far. I think that Schuler has probably done the least. Schuler?"

"Yes, Herr Oberjager Schultz?" Schuler jogged a few steps to catch up with his corporal.

"How many practice jumps have you done?

"Only one real drop. Many practice drops from the tower."

Hans paused for a moment, and then questioned his sergeant: "Herr Unterfeldwebel, do you think we'll ever jump into combat now?"

"I don't know." Kurt could not imagine that they would have the opportunity to drop behind enemy lines the way the war was going. He could not even imagine that the Luftwaffe could keep enough planes safely in the air in order to get them there. His face remained expressionless, as it always did when what he was thinking might hurt the morale of his men.

"Hard to believe when they have such important work for us on the ground!" Schuler exclaimed, getting a few laughs from his comrades. Hans scowled at him and barked, "That's enough, Schuler!" But his face softened into a lopsided grin as he said it.

The sky again seemed to darken as the road turned slightly west and the sun approached the horizon. As he slapped a mosquito from his neck, Kurt thought further about the training they had done. The regiment had seen heavy combat in Africa, and Kurt and Hans were two of a very small number of veterans who had remained with it following reorganizations. After their African battles, most of the regiment had been taken off the line. While many of its remaining troops were sent to Russia, a small administrative support group was left from which to build a new regiment in western France. There, Kurt and Hans had watched the formation of the new regiment, and participated in its training for a planned invasion of Malta. The invasion was to be led by paratroopers, but with France now under attack by the Allies, Malta seemed as far away as Japan.

"What do you think, Schultz? Are these mosquitoes worse, or the flies back in Africa?"

"There can't be anything could be worse than these damned mosquitoes!" interjected Schuler as he took several swipes at pests on his arms. The bugs were intensifying their attack as the sun set. "Whenever I'm on watch, it seems that there's one circling my head over and over, deciding where to land. Now I can't even remember what it's like to be without this itch."

"As usual, ignorance has no shame," remarked Schultz, scowling at Schuler for his interruption. "These mosquitoes are nothing compared to the flies in Africa."

"How could flies be worse?" called a private from further back in line. "They don't even bite! I wouldn't have all these welts if we were surrounded by flies."

"Is it time we teach these tenderfoots a little about the bad old days, Herr Unterfeldwebel?" Hans smiled at Kurt and turned to walk backwards, giving a lesson to the less experienced men behind. Kurt simply nodded and continued marching.

"In Africa, the flies were like a blanket that constantly covered you. They didn't come out at dusk like these little nuisances." He slapped another mosquito from his arm. "They were on you twenty-four hours a day. When you tried to eat, they were on your food. When you took a deep breath, they were in your mouth. When you woke up in the morning, they were in your ears. They were everywhere. Do you remember the simple solution that came from headquarters, Herr Unterfeldwebel Doering?" He smiled towards Kurt again. Perhaps a slight facial response crossed Kurt's lips, but only Hans could see it as he continued. "They told us how to put out fly traps. They even suggested we burn the dead ones."

"So what was wrong with that?" asked Schuler.

"What was wrong with that? I'll tell you what was wrong with that, young Schuler." Hans assumed the posture of a schoolteacher giving a lesson as he continued. "Dead flies attract flies!" The men broke out into laughter, as much from Hans's pantomime as from his story, and howled even louder as he tripped and fell on his backside from trying to walk in reverse. Now even Kurt laughed along with them.

"I think that's enough instruction for tonight, Hans. You're going to hurt yourself." Again Kurt realized how much he appreciated his men. As their sergeant, he did not think it appropriate to be laughing along with them too much, but he enjoyed the mirth all the same. Some of his professional distance no doubt arose from his more advanced age. At almost thirty, he often felt like an old man among children. He had only joined the Luftwaffe three years earlier, but had moved through the ranks and gained immeasurable experience in a very short time, with his age and maturity likely a crucial factor in his rapid promotion. Nevertheless, it was reassuring to know that he was commanding combat veterans and not incompetent rookies. The days three years earlier, when he himself had been inexperienced, seemed impossibly far away. The learning by humiliation was woven invisibly into the tapestry of his experience, and the stream of unanswerable questions that had so humbled him had surely been directed at someone else.

As the men's laughter subsided, Kurt suddenly became aware of the sound of distant gunfire. The sounds of battle from afar were always present, and often went unnoticed. Through the background noise, good soldiers could quickly pick out signs of danger, as Kurt's men did now. From the distant north came the scream of Allied dive-bombers. While an untrained observer might not be able to pick the sound out from the other din of battle, Kurt's men obviously knew it well. Although they continued to march at ease, they crowded slightly closer to the side of the roadway, readying themselves to dive for the cover of the hedge. Fortunately, the sound of the dive-bombers remained distant and the aircraft did not approach. The soldiers' vigilance had increased, but they had not become unsettled, not even when their bodies recognized the sound of the bombers as the sound of approaching death. One did not have to be attacked by the dive-bombers many times to make that association. When the scream became louder the bullets would rain down, and this fifty calibre steel rain was designed to rip the wood of staunch buildings or the metal of armoured vehicles to shreds. A near miss still passed through the air with enough shockwave to throw a shoulder out of joint and could kill a man by breaking pieces of concrete off a paved road and hurling them as deadly shrapnel. It was a rain that had been falling all too often lately since the enemy won control of the skies. It was one that was more hated by the men than the impersonal crash of artillery shells, because when the bullets rained from Allied aircraft, you knew that Tommy was looking right at you and choosing the moment you would die.

Heartbeats slowed a little as it became obvious the aircrafts were not approaching, and Hans moved closer to Kurt. He spoke softly enough that the men behind would not hear. His voice was much more serious than it had been when joking with the men.

"Do you think it is true that we are surrounded?" No doubt the sound of aircraft nearby reminded him of the gravity of their situation.

"I don't know." Kurt was truthful about his uncertainty, but he had his suspicions. Men of the Wehrmacht had been marching in both directions on every road they took. More and more combat troops seemed to be doing the jobs of engineers, and more headquarters troops were being prepared for close combat. Organization was definitely suffering, since it was no longer clear whether counterattacks would be aimed north or west or south, and Hans suspected his men had been lucky to be spared close combat so far, but that the decisive battle was fast approaching. Now they neared a junction in the road and he noticed a road sign. A ladder was mounted at its base, and a soldier was climbing to rearrange the signs to confuse advancing armies. Before the signs were changed Kurt noticed that they were on the road to Falaise. He wondered whether that might be the future name of a great German victory or defeat.

Looking further forward down the road, he noticed a column of soldiers approaching. Unlike Kurt's men, these men lacked primal recognition of aircraft in the distance, and far from easing to the side of the road, they continued in almost parade-ground formation. Their uniforms were tidy and they looked impossibly young. Having just been thinking about the imminence of the battle that could decide the future of the Reich, Kurt thought of the slogan on every Wehrmacht soldier's belt buckle:

"GOTT MIT UNS"

As he faced the inexperienced conscripts, he hoped it was true.

Chapter 7

Kurt was in a pleasant marching rhythm. As the green soldiers passed his section on the left, he chose not to notice them. But there were so many. He felt as though he had walked for days with this column of men passing in the opposite direction when the sound of voices from behind forced him to pay greater attention.

"Look at all the heroes off to fight the British!" Kurt recognized Schuler's voice as the source of the taunt. He turned to look and saw that Schuler was laughing and pointing at the clean uniforms of the new recruits. Now that his attention was focused on the young infantrymen marching past, Kurt briefly recalled his own life at their age. Many of them looked only seventeen or eighteen years old. At eighteen he had been an aspiring architect hard at his studies, and his only thoughts of war had been stories of the war of 1914 told by his uncle, but his uncle was notoriously quiet on the subject. Once again Kurt felt like an old man among children, even though he was only in his late twenties. Now, for a fleeting moment, he wondered what his life would have been like had it been touched so early by war. His eyes caught those of one of the infantry, and he saw them filled with fear. The young soldiers seemed awed by the veteran paratroopers walking away from the front. Their eyes were searching, questioning. They seemed to ask, "What is the future going to bring?" The young fools had no idea what to expect and now they looked at the sweat, dirt and blood on the uniforms of the paratroopers to give them the answer. Kurt was caught by the irony that in fact he and his men were not returning from combat. They were just continuing the stepwise job of creating nuisances for the enemy during a less than organized retreat. Kurt turned to continue marching but Schuler's taunts continued.

"Are those medals on your uniform? I did not realize that the Iron Cross was being given for keeping your room tidy."

Kurt turned an angry glance to Oberjager Schultz, who stepped out of line and moved purposefully towards Schuler. Schuler had all but stopped marching, and two infantry soldiers were standing near him receiving his taunts, so stunned that they did not even defend themselves. As Schultz forcefully pushed them out of his way and grabbed Schuler by the collar, Schuler's look of self-satisfaction dissolved. Kurt could taste the irony that the least experienced of the paratroopers was the first to brag to these recruits. Of course Schuler had taken quick advantage of the fact that the paratroopers were filthy and seemed to be returning from a battle, because the awe that fact inspired in the green infantry made them easy targets for his taunts. For just a moment Kurt sympathized with them, but the moment was fleeting. As Schultz manhandled Schuler towards him, Kurt remembered that the inexperience of conscript soldiers could mean death to those who fought alongside them.

"Perhaps you think that marching with your section is not a high enough priority?" Hans Schultz yelled as he hauled Schuler up before Kurt. Schuler was silent and pale. He had clearly hoped to win approval from the more experienced paratroopers by bullying the young recruits. Now that his efforts were only winning him discipline, his boisterous exterior shrunk quickly back to size. Kurt meted out his sentence.

"Herr Oberjager Schultz, I think that Jäger Hans Schuler would like to inspect the route for five kilometres up ahead. He should do so double-time and then return with a report on the condition of the road." Having received his orders, Schultz had only to glance in Schuler's direction to send him running ahead. Schuler's heavy pack bounced on his back and he braced himself for a workout. He had shown himself to be a loudmouth when placed in the presence of his juniors, but Kurt retained some sympathy, since Schuler had never been an unreliable soldier.

Kurt pointed down the road and gestured in Schultz's direction. Schultz assembled the section, most of which had slowed to a halt when the disruption began, then the corporal shouted instructions and they resumed their march. Kurt had noticed that his men were considerably outnumbered here by soldiers of the army. With animosity boiling under the surface between the Heer and the Luftwaffe, he felt compelled to do all he could to ensure that Schuler's immaturity did not result in an eruption of hostilities. He walked towards the lieutenant who was in charge of the infantry.

"I apologize for my soldier's outburst, Herr Oberleutnant. It will not happen again."

"Fine, Unterfeldwebel." The lieutenant was a younger man than Kurt. He looked sharp and professional, but as they exchanged salutes Kurt saw something in his eyes. It was the same combination of fear and awe worn by the troops the young Lieutenant commanded.

As Kurt turned and returned to his section, he chided himself for the bit of sympathy he had felt for the young infantry. Now he felt glad only that they were marching in the opposite direction. If they were nearby, their inexperience could kill him as surely as it was about to kill all of them.

He hated them.

He silently thanked Wehrmacht protocol that he could address the lieutenant only by his rank. He did not want to know that man's name. That young, ignorant lieutenant was only a piece of meat that was about to be ripped to pieces by the wrath of British bombers and tanks. Looking at Kurt, the eyes of those infantrymen had been probing his face, his clothes, and his rifle. They had been searching for any clues as to what to expect in battle, what to expect from a vastly superior enemy, what to expect from themselves. Most of them would never learn the answers.

Again Kurt felt glad to be back with his section, even with Schuler, who would shortly be jogging back from his disciplinary run. Deitrich Schuler had seen combat. Some weeks ago, before this section had been detached from its parent platoon, Schuler had been attached to a different unit within the division. At that time Schuler had been involved in a firefight with some enemy soldiers. In Kurt's mind, that proved two things about him. The first was that Deitrich Schuler had had a brief taste of true combat during which he could learn some of the lessons that could only be learned through experience. Second was that he had proved himself not to be among that fraction of men who could never survive as soldiers. When an army was fighting in advantageous circumstances, that fraction was not always killed in their first taste of battle. They were always marked, though. When the fighting got tough, those men would always have their numbers drawn sooner or later.

Kurt thought for a moment about the other group of young men whose paths he had occasionally crossed recently. The 12th SS Hitler Youth division was positioned nearby. Kurt tensed while contemplating the prospect of dealing with them. Unlike teenage conscripts that would occasionally be sent into battle, the young soldiers of the Hitler Youth were not clueless blunderers. Even Hitler Youth units that had not yet endured combat were frightening to those around them. There was something about troops inspired with fanaticism and devoid of the fear of death that was unsettling. They were dangerous. Unfortunately, they could be as dangerous to the troops they fought alongside as to the enemy.

Kurt reflected on their delicate situation, and began talking with Hans Schultz about their experiences fighting alongside some raw recruits while in Tunisia.

"Hans, I was thinking again of Africa." He moved into step alongside Schultz.

"The flies again? I still say these mosquitoes are no match." Hans smiled and swatted at his arm.

"No, I was thinking of some of the men we fought with. Those young recruits we just passed reminded me of some of them."

"I know. Me too. Do you remember the young man that lost his pictures?" Hans had smiled warmly after joking about the bugs, but his face hardened as he mentioned the soldier from their shared past.

"I do," answered Kurt. "When the American artillery started raining down, we all took cover. Not him. He just stood out in front of the foxhole looking left, then right. The shells were crashing down, but he just stood in the middle of them. It was a wonder he wasn't hit." Kurt recounted the story that he and Hans both remembered so well. Some of the men now marching with them stopped their conversations to listen. Soon most of the section was listening in rapt attention. As though on cue, Hans picked up the story where Kurt had finished.

"So many shells. There were pieces of shrapnel ripping past him. One tore the leg of his pants and I think that another grazed his helmet. He just kept standing there. When we finally grabbed him and dragged him into the foxhole, he just looked stunned. After we stared at him for a few moments, all he had to say was, 'I lost my pictures.'" Hans paused and closed his eyes tight for a moment before finishing. "I guess he lost his pictures of his girl back home. It's bizarre that it suddenly occurred to him to try and find them in the middle of that firestorm."

"So what happened to him?" One of the paratroopers named Betzner asked from behind Kurt and Hans.

"Killed the next day," Kurt responded.

"I think that he got himself together and that night he started writing a letter home to get another picture," Hans added. "The next day he took a bullet in the head. He had survived that artillery barrage while standing out in the open, but I think he actually got hit while he was sensibly taking cover. One of the men sent the letter he had written, but the picture never arrived with our unit. I suppose either the letter got lost or his girlfriend found out he was dead and didn't answer." Hans's voice trailed off as he finished. "Do you remember his name, Herr Unterfeldwebel?"

"No."

As the men walked on, most were quiet for a while. Many had

similar stories about soldiers who were new to combat. Many were thinking of those stories now. Few of them could, or chose to, recall names of the dead who had never been around long enough to get to know their comrades. Kurt thought more of the story, and recalled the detail Hans had forgotten or chosen to omit when telling it to the men. He and Hans had grabbed the man by the ankles to pull him under cover. Kurt could still remember the smell and feel of the man's urine that had run down his leg.

"Africa sounds awful." Betzner called out from behind again. "How did they keep you in the Luftwaffe after you had to survive the heat and all those flies? If they were worse than the bugs here, I would have surrendered with the Italians just to get out of there!" That got a laugh from the men, who had become rather sombre.

"There were some fun times," Hans answered. He smiled now and looked to Kurt, as though Kurt should remember the story he was thinking of. Kurt made a show of shrugging and left Hans to do the talking. The sound of artillery in the distance remained a constant background, but few of the men noticed any more. The sun drifted below the horizon as Hans talked, and the men were engulfed by darkness. The road was bumpy and irregular, but several recent nighttime marches had trained them to find their footing. Hans stumbled slightly as he spoke.

"The Unterfeldwebel and I were sent on some ridiculous errand. At the time, I was a lowly Jäger like all of you." Boos and hisses echoed from the men, but Hans smiled and continued. "We had to go get some papers from headquarters or something."

"Ration cards. We were picking up boxes of ration cards," Kurt interrupted.

"Of course. We were picking up ration cards. Anyhow, there are not always great landmarks in the desert. The bugs certainly don't give out directions. So Unterfeldwebel Doering and I realized after a while that we were driving this car in circles for hours with these boxes of cards in the back. He had a map out while I was driving, but there was nothing to tell us what direction we were going. Our compass was broken." The men crowded closer to hear his story. Kurt shook his head as Hans continued talking, thinking of how much he seemed to enjoy the men's attention. A dog barked in the background. It was likely from the farmhouse they were passing on the right, but the French countryside was obscured by darkness.

"Finally, we could see a group of tents by a junction in the road. They didn't look familiar but we thought that maybe the soldiers there could give us some directions. I drove the car up right in between two of the tents and some men came out to greet us. They were Americans! Somehow we had driven directly past the front line and into an American camp." A few gasps and some scattered laughter came from the men. Hans paused, apparently for dramatic effect.

"I got ready to drive as fast as I could back the way we came, but the Americans already had their weapons drawn and they would have killed us both. Kurt just put his hand on my shoulder and whispered to slow the car down. He even started waving at the Americans with a big smile on his face!" As Hans kept the men interested with his tale, Kurt had noticed something odd. Except in private, Hans rarely used Kurt's first name. Now he had used it in his story, but Kurt was not sure of the significance of the indiscretion. Hans continued.

"The Americans walked up to the car with their guns drawn, and our Unterfeldwebel began talking to them in the few words of English he knew."

"What did you say?" came some voices from the section.

"I told them 'Good Evening.'" Kurt was almost smiling but still deadpan.

"Of course he did," interjected Hans. "Our unterfeldwebel is always polite. Even to Americans." He smiled momentarily, hoping for some laughs from his audience, and then scowled when he got none. The men were too caught up in the suspense to enjoy his humour, but their patience was rewarded when he resumed. "So there we were, completely surrounded. The Americans who had come out of their tents called to some others who came out as well. They were all armed, and we had only two rifles between us. Mine was buried under the boxes in the back of the car! We had no chance. But there was Unterfeldwebel Doering, waving and talking to the Americans. I had no idea what he was saying, but the Americans started looking almost as confused as I was. Before I could make sense of anything, he pointed at a spot on the ground and they all started putting their guns down. I thought I was seeing things when about fifteen of them finished laying down their arms, and then came up to the car. Unterfeldwebel Doering reached into the back and started handing them ration cards. I had no idea what was going on, but I handed them cards as well, until each of them had one. Finally Unterfeldwebel Doering yelled some more cheery remarks at them, and then told me to drive away. He told me to drive quickly, but not so quickly as to look nervous."

By now the men were stumped. Hans paused for dramatic effect again, but his brief silence was immediately interrupted by the cries of the men.

"What did you tell them, Herr Unterfeldwebel?" one of the men asked.

"What the devil were they supposed to do with German ration cards?" called out another.

All eyes focused on Kurt. He shrugged, as though nothing of great significance had occurred, and then completed the story. "I told them 'Good news! We will not need to fight today.' I furthermore told them that their commander's surrender had been accepted, and the Wehrmacht troops who had encircled them would be sending military police to collect them shortly. I told them to hold onto their red cards, which indicated that their surrender had been accepted and they had been promised safe passage. I then told them to lay down their weapons, collect their cards and await further orders."

As Kurt spoke, Hans began laughing so hard that tears filled his eyes. The rest of the men stared in silent disbelief. Hans wiped away tears and asked, "Didn't you even salute them with a 'Heil Hitler' as we drove away?"

"I don't remember, but I don't think so. I was too busy telling you to change the pants you had just shit in." Now the men erupted into laughter. Even Hans resumed his mirth, and had to hold his stomach from the pain of laughing so hard. Betzner asked the question that was on everyone's mind.

"So what happened when you got back? You must have won a medal."

Hans tried to answer, but his words came between gasps of laughter. "We got disciplined for weeks because we had lost some of the ration cards. We even had to empty the fly traps!" Some of the men joined Hans in laughing, but some were still in a state of such disbelief that they remained silent.

It was several minutes before the section was marching in orderly fashion again. Soon Schuler's silhouette was evident on the road ahead as he returned from his disciplinary reconnaissance. He was breathing hard as he reported to Kurt.

"Herr Unterfeldwebel, the road remains in similar condition for several kilometres ahead. Of interest, there is a farmhouse about two kilometres up which looks like it could provide excellent lodging for the remainder of the night."

"Thank you, Schuler. Return to your position in line."

Schuler's face had seemed hopeful as he made his report. The men were all tired from a long march, but Schuler exceptionally so. The other men were hopeful as well, now there was a possibility the march would soon be over and they could get some rest.

Kurt and Hans spoke briefly and decided it was an appropriate time to end the march. If a comfortable farmhouse was available to rest in, then that was even better. As they approached the property on which the house stood, Kurt had the men stop at the gate. The house was two storeys and seemed an ample size. About one hundred metres of lush grass separated the house from the gate, and the tall ever-present French hedges rimmed the property. Behind the farmhouse were large gardens, but in the darkness it was impossible to see details. As always, when bombers frequent the skies, the house's windows were blackened. Kurt hoped that this might be the property of a family that had fled when combat approached, but even if it remained occupied, that did not mean that an arrangement could not be made for eleven weary soldiers.

Hans spoke: "Shall I take three men forward to have a closer look?"

"Yes, carry on." Although the men frequently complained to each other about marches, their footwear or any number of other nuisances, Kurt, as the man in charge, remained necessarily quiet. That did not mean, of course, his feet were not equally sore. He was happy to let Hans take three men forward to check out the farmhouse, and as Hans left, the remaining men immediately fell to the ground. Many lit cigarettes, some removed their boots, but all enjoyed the few minutes of relaxation. Kurt went a few steps to a large stone, which made a comfortable bench, and rested his legs there.

Clouds parted in the sky, and suddenly the moonlight was bright enough to read by. Kurt became aware of a weight in his breast pocket, and no sooner had the light improved than he removed it. It consisted of a small paper package, containing letters he had received from his wife earlier that day. Although written at different times, three letters had arrived all at once. He had read the first letter immediately, but saved the others for later, knowing the promise of more words from his wife would sustain him through a whole day's march. Whether in tedious times or before a battle, Kurt would read and reread letters from home at every opportunity. When the letters were first placed in his hands, he would hold them to his face hoping to smell a trace of his wife's perfume.

A reddish hue from explosions on the ground rimmed the clouds on the northern horizon. The ever-present sound of artillery fire penetrated the calm and occasionally small arms fire would crackle closer by. As Kurt opened his letters from home, all those things vanished. To him his wife represented purity and goodness that could penetrate even the darkness of combat. He savoured every reminder of her. He pulled the string, which bound her second letter, and the guns in the distance silenced. He could no longer feel the mosquito bites that covered his body, and sweat no longer ran over his brow. He took a deep breath and read.

Chapter 8

Dearest Kurt,

I spend every day wishing that you could come home soon. I have not heard from you since the letter you wrote about your base moving, so I wonder if you are involved in all the fighting that is happening. I pray always that you are safe.

Kurt was in heaven. Even the fact that Eva had not yet received several of his letters could not poison the experience of hearing from her. The delay in replies was often over a month, and she would write many letters before receiving a batch of his. He looked back to the page and continued.

I have certainly had interesting times since moving in with your family.

When I first met your parents they were very nice, but I did not feel as much a part of the family as I do now. With you gone I think that they can really feel your absence from their life, even though you have not lived with them for years. Your old room in the house seems now as though it was made for me. I almost sat at your place at the dinner table yesterday, but we all agreed that it should be left empty until you return. On Sunday we had a beef stew, like your mother made before the war! Of course the ingredients have been in scarce supply lately, so the meals have not often been so rich. I think Mother wanted to make something special for the first Sunday that I would be living here, so she used all her best meat.

I thought of you especially yesterday after an unfortunate incident at the bank. That always one of my favourite buildings that you designed. The entryway was very beautiful, but now I am afraid that it is not what it once was.

Kurt's brow furrowed. Although his wife had communicated in benign words that would not be caught by government censors, he knew from experience that she was describing something very sinister. The bank must have been reduced to rubble by a bombing raid.

When I hear others complain, I reassure them that when you are home all the buildings will be better than before. I would love to see an entire city all as beautiful as the bank was.

Kurt almost tore the letter then. It pained him to hear about bombing in Düsseldorf. It was not so much because of the building that had been destroyed, as because he hated to hear about the war involving Eva. He found it physically painful to associate the mud, insects and death that surrounded him with his wife. To him she represented purity and happiness. He did not want to hear her talk about destruction. He did not want her to experience it.

He looked up from the letter to regain his composure. Hans and the other paratroopers had crossed the field between him and the nearby farmhouse. One of them was circling around to the back while the others rapped on the front door. Kurt wondered if anyone would answer. His concentration was briefly pulled back into the present time and place as he considered the interactions he and his men had had with the French. There were strict regulations against looting and other such unseemly behaviours. Kurt was glad that looting had never been an issue with his men. While on duty, the men of his platoon had always been very professional in their interactions with the locals. While off duty, when they had been training in the south of France, a few of them had had French girlfriends. That had been in a part of the country combat had not touched, where the locals were receptive to friendly inquiries. Now, with the war making its presence felt, his men were behaving equally courteously. Although they certainly intended to requisition a portion of this house for the rest of the night, it did not hurt to ask politely after knocking on the door like gentlemen.

We all went together to church on Sunday. I got a new blue dress, which was perfect for the occasion. The dress itself was not the finest quality, but your mother and I adjusted it and it looked wonderful. I can hardly wait for you to see it.

Kurt made a quiet, satisfied sound. This was what he longed to hear from his wife. Stories about a place where priorities were different and something as clean and simple as a summer dress could make a marvellous difference to the day.

You would not believe who we saw holding hands in the street on the way home from church! It was Helga from the grocer's and young Heinrich Brenner! Mother says that ...

Kurt could not care less who Helga from the grocer's had been seen with, but he enjoyed every one of his wife's words. Every taste of local gossip, every description of who was wearing what and what they had eaten for supper. Especially what they had eaten for supper. Army rations were occasionally in short supply, sometimes hearty but always monotonous. He could lose himself in a description of the food that was being eaten back home even though that food was a shadow of what was available before the war.

I'll write some more shortly, but next I have sent along letters from your family.

Kurt thought of skipping ahead to the next portion written by his wife, but he enjoyed his letters too much to risk missing even a single word.

My young hero,

It was still written in his wife's flowing script, but the words now had to be those of his grandfather. His grandfather's salutation was always the same.

I am again filled with pride to imagine you winning glory for the Reich on the battlefield. Once again, the young are riding into battle to defeat the enemy and we old men can only envy them the power of their youth.

Kurt sighed, but then chuckled. He could picture his wife taking dictation from his grandfather. Surely she would have reminded him once again that Kurt does not ride a horse, but once again Grandfather would not remember. A hero of the Franco-Prussian war, at least in his own mind, Kurt's grandfather had never stopped reliving the glory of his teenage years. At eighty-eight years of age, he had been the individual most insistent that Kurt should join the army.

Reading his grandfather's letter reminded Kurt of the many dinner table debates over the benefits of military service. No doubt, with his training in architecture and practical experience in civilian construction, Kurt could have obtained work in the many military construction projects that were ongoing. Instead he went straight from civilian work to the armed forces. He had trouble remembering now why he had made that decision. It had not been his grandfather's words that had convinced him, especially with his father and uncle in the background. His father had never served in the armed forces and expressed little enthusiasm for Kurt's participation. Kurt's father had always been more interested in him winning success at a trade rather than learning skill at killing. Kurt's uncle Friedrich was the most silent on the subject. As a veteran of the war of 1914, he had perhaps the most experience to speak from. When Kurt thought back now to the dinner table conversations where his grandfather had shouted for glory and his father had urged caution, he could not remember uncle Friedrich's opinion. Uncle Friedrich had only silently smoked his cigarette in the corner seat. Thinking of his uncle's quiet contemplation, Kurt thought of the events of today. He thought back to Schuler bullying the young infantry on the road and remembered the looks on the faces of the young recruits and on that of their lieutenant. He remembered the boastful expression on Schuler's face. Then he remembered the bland look on his corporal's face. Hans's expression was his uncle Friedrich's. While those new to combat bragged to the inexperienced, the men who had truly known all that war could do were silent. Kurt and Hans had looked on the younger men with that silence. Their expression revealed not indifference, but a respect for the inevitable.

Now Kurt could picture his uncle Friedrich smoking at the

dinner table with that look in his eyes. Surely Friedrich had cared deeply what happened to his young nephew, but he would not participate in the debate. He was the man who knew that war had changed. While Grandfather still imagined cavalry in their finest attire charging the enemy with sabres in hand, Friedrich knew the new horror mankind had created. Knee deep in septic trench water, crawling with lice, he had learned of that horror just east of a town called Ypres.

Uncle Friedrich would live his whole life and never share the story of a Christmas spent in the trenches singing *Stille Nacht*. The British in their trench had wept and responded with a song of their own, which masked the sound of the cough Friedrich had suffered since inhaling poison gas in no-man's land. Friedrich would live to be seventy-four years old, but no one would ever ask him what it was like.

Kurt looked back down at his letters. Following the brief words of encouragement from his grandfather came a note from his parents. He read briefly but was distracted by shouts from the farmhouse. An old French farmer had emerged from the side door of the house armed with a hunting rifle. Hans and the two men at the front of the house were yelling for the man to drop the weapon while the remaining soldier returned at a run from the rear of the house where he had been scouting. Crisp German words were mixed with mangled French from Hans, who knew only a few words of the language. The farmer was silent, his rifle still pointed harmlessly at the ground. His face expressed confusion at all this activity, but with a threatening countenance as though he expected to defeat the entire Wehrmacht himself. Kurt's gaze returned to his letters. Hans and the men could easily handle one old man with a rifle. The other soldiers seated on the grass around Kurt had tensed when the old man emerged. Now some of them stood and walked towards the house, but they all visibly relaxed when they sensed Kurt Doering's calm.

Kurt turned a page and his wife's words again greeted him.

One night I spoke with a young woman I had never met before.

Your parents were not with me then. The young woman was very frightened and I tried to console her.

Letters between Kurt and his wife contained many implicit understandings that would not be evident to another reader. No words that detailed military matters would pass through the web of censorship that enveloped Nazi Germany, but he knew immediately that her story of meeting a frightened stranger at night could only take place in a bomb shelter. His parents must have been taking shelter in another bunker.

I sensed that the events of the night were nothing new to her, but still she remained almost inconsolable. When I spoke with her a little longer, I realized that the present danger was not the only source of her fear. It seems that her cousin had been reported missing in the fighting in the East. She was understandably concerned for his safety, but the reason she was now so frightened had to do with her fiancé. He was in the Wehrmacht and now that her cousin was missing, it made her more aware of his danger. She told me that her fiancé was in France, and that now she was very worried for him. It was then that I realized that she was much younger than me. She was probably only eighteen years old.

I sympathized with her worries, but I must say that my heart swelled with pride as I remembered the things you said when you joined the Luftwaffe.

Kurt himself had a difficult time remembering what he had said, since it seemed a lifetime since he had been a civilian. He looked up from the page again and saw that the yelling by the farmhouse had stopped, and Hans was gesturing to the old French farmer to lower his weapon. The man just stood still. He seemed stunned. As Hans continued gesturing, and the men at his sides kept their weapons trained on the old man, the remaining paratrooper from behind the house crept quietly towards the farmer from behind. It was obvious that they were going to disarm the man one way or another, so Kurt kept reading.

I am sure that you remember the story of the day you enlisted as clearly as I do, but I must tell you that it was exactly that story that I told the young woman to calm her. I still remember that it was a sunny day, but you were inside working on your drawings. From outside came the sound of marching and you turned to look out the window. I remember well that you paused and watched the new recruits go by. You were very quiet after that. When I asked you later what you were thinking about, you said that you could not stand to see all those children go off to war. Thinking of you as a fairly young man yourself, I had to look out the window myself to see all the teenagers looking proud in their field grey. Still, I was not sure what was going on in your mind.

It was three days later when you told me that you planned to enlist. I had not fully understood the reason you gave me until I spoke with that young girl. You told me that all those children needed someone to look after them. You told me that you could not sit and do your work at home knowing that young men were dying and that you could help. We all know of the glory of fighting and dying for the Reich and for the Fuhrer,

Kurt raised his eyebrows and realized that this would not have escaped the notice of a censor with a sense of irony.

... But you are the only person I have heard say that he was going to fight for the children. Not the children at home, but the children you would be joining on the front line.

That was not exactly what I told the young woman that night. I only told her that someone would be looking out for her fiancé. I told her that it was someone I love and trust very much. I think that made her feel a little better.

A shot rang out and Kurt looked up from his letters. Hans stood with his weapon pointed at the back of the now dead old farmer. Apparently the old farmer had turned quickly to face the man approaching him from behind, and he must have raised his rifle then, because Kurt's men felt the need to shoot him.

Idiot. Kurt thought about the old man. *Why would he do something so foolish? He should have dropped his gun. Did he think he could fight the entire army?* Kurt tucked his letters back into the pocket of his tunic. The remaining men who had been comfortable in the grass around him had now grabbed their weapons and jumped to their feet. Kurt slowly picked up his kit and stood. His eyes were focused in Hans' direction, and Hans was now looking straight at him with a question in his eyes.

"What else could I have done?" Hans' eyes asked. Kurt just nodded back in his direction. The affirmative gesture calmed Hans. Kurt picked up his pace and marched promptly to where Hans and the remaining men were standing, then instructed some of the men to scout a quick perimeter around the building, while the remaining men were to prepare to occupy the house for the night.

An old woman, apparently the farmer's wife, burst from the building and ran towards the body that now lay in the yard. The men ignored her as they went about their duties, and Kurt stepped forward to speak with Hans.

"What was that old fool doing? I don't think you had much choice in what you did." He scowled as he went on. "The French I've met have generally been sensible people. I don't know what was the matter with him."

Hans just nodded in agreement, and then changed the subject as they walked together up the stairs into the house. "Do you think we'll be in the fighting soon?"

Kurt paused on the step. "Yes. I think we will."

Hans seemed thoughtful for a moment, and then asked the question that remained on his mind. "I'm worried it's true that we're being encircled. Are we going to have to fight our way out of a pocket?"

"I'm not sure." Hans put his hand on the knob of the door, but paused, holding his weight against the door for a moment. "Either way, I think the big battle is coming. Just by listening to the shellfire in the distance, by the number of British aircraft we have seen lately, and by the way the roads are getting more and more crowded with men, I would say that the big one is coming."

Hans hardly seemed reassured by his answer, but did seem to agree. He changed the subject again. "How are your letters? Any good news from home?" He pointed at Kurt's breast pocket, which had been left open.

"Some news," Kurt paused. "Unfortunately, things seem to have taken a turn for the worse. Now my wife is always telling me about bombs dropping on our neighbourhood."

"That's terrible." Hans shook his head.

"It's intolerable. It's damned barbaric. Can you imagine? Bombs dropping on civilian neighbourhoods all over Germany?" Hans and Kurt stepped through the heavy wooden door at the front of the house as Kurt gritted his teeth and completed his thought one more time. "It's absolutely barbaric."

As they entered the farmhouse, he hardly noticed the old French woman weeping over the body of her dead husband in the yard.

Chapter 9

"I want to get married."

Dr Darren Johnston found himself searching the hallways of the hospital for a place to sleep. Beds surrounded him in enormous wards that stretched into infinity. Running from bed to bed he would try to pull their covers back to climb in and make himself comfortable, but would always find a sick patient sleeping there. His search became more and more frantic until he was desperately running through an eternal white room. The walls were covered with large windows, but through them were more rows upon rows of beds.

"Darren, I said I want to get married." Now Courtney's voice roused Darren more completely.

Courtney's day had started early when she woke up alone. It took a moment for her to realize that Darren was still on call. He had been up early yesterday, and she had only seen him for a moment at breakfast, so today was the second day she had not spoken a sentence with him. Since she was not starting work until tomorrow, her schedule remained open for the day and she enjoyed a leisurely breakfast and read the newspaper. Stories about sensational trials, government policy, even local crimes and municipal affairs left her craving details and accuracy she would never find in a document written with an absence of specialized knowledge. During law school she had always longed for time to read the news, but now she was realizing it was not the news she enjoyed, but discussing it with friends. Calling a friend to go for coffee seemed like the natural thing to do as she cleared the table, but she had no friends in town yet, so she went for a walk by herself through the still unfamiliar neighbourhood.

The lights atop the football stadium could be seen from their house, and she recognized that the university hospital was on its far side. On her left she could see the silhouette of downtown's high-rises, reminding her of the many opportunities for articling positions for next year, many of which heralded the hard route to partnership in a prestigious firm. She walked past a small park and spoke with a young mother who was pushing a small child in a stroller. After a brief conversation beginning with pleasantries and ending with stories about a negligent husband who worked in the Northern Alberta oil fields, Courtney spent much of the morning thinking about her life, her priorities, and about the terms of the contract she had made with herself. When Darren arrived home in the early afternoon and lapsed immediately into insensate unconsciousness, she only started thinking harder. Now it made little difference where lay the breach of trust, because Courtney was feeling like an injured party.

She shook Darren lightly again. "Are you awake? Are you listening?"

Darren blinked his eyes twice. They hurt. His vision remained blurred and his head swam as he regained his orientation. Later, fully awake, he would appreciate the irony that when he finally had a chance to sleep at home, he had dreamt of sleeping in the hospital. Still silent, he turned his head and looked at the clock radio on their bedside table. The clock read "7:02", but it took him a few moments to decide whether it was morning or evening. Regaining his senses, he spent several seconds considering Courtney's statement. Unfortunately, his answer lacked the thoughtful, succinct prose he was aiming for.

"What? What are we talking about? Do you know how tired I am?" He sat himself up in bed and leaned back against their headboard. He had to untangle himself from some of the sheets as he did so. Courtney was seated on the edge of the bed to his left.

Her hand had rested lightly on his leg as she spoke, but now she pulled it away in frustration.

"That's your excuse for everything. You're always too tired. You're too tired to help out around the house, you're too tired to go out in the evening, and you're too tired to talk to me for a few minutes about what's on my mind. Just when were you planning on talking to me again?" She had seemed only mildly hurt as she began, but by the time she had finished, her fists were clenched.

"What?" Darren struggled to piece together a few coherent thoughts. "Listen. You know I just finished working a thirty-four-hour stretch. I didn't get a minute of rest the whole time. Now the only time I've got to rest is tonight, because at 7 a.m. it's all going to start again. I'll be working another thirty-some hours before I get to sleep again. I just can't start tomorrow's shift tired. I don't know how I'll survive one of these nights if I'm tired when the day starts." Darren could almost feel tears welling up in his eyes. He felt so desperate about getting some sleep that the subject was painful to discuss.

The sympathy returned to Courtney's face, and she reached her hand toward him again. Their eyes locked and Darren felt about to say something tender when his memory returned to the reason he had been woken up. He decided to end the conversation.

"I'm just too tired to talk about an old subject that we've already discussed." He gave her hand a squeeze and stood up from the bed then headed out of their room and towards the bathroom sink.

Courtney had always been well atuned to Darren's feelings. Yet today, despite her sympathy for his fatigue, she was hurt by the fact she had been ignored. She had spent her recent days so bored, and so lonely, she needed to feel at least the relationship for which she had made sacrifices had remained viable. She had been trying to strengthen her connection with him and he had turned his back on her without letting her finish. After a moment's astonished pause, she followed him into the hall and spoke through the open bathroom door. As he had turned on the tap and splashed some water on his face, Darren did not hear all of what Courtney said next.

"It's not an old subject. I've been giving it a lot of thought. Just because you thought the plan to get married in your third year of residency was perfect, doesn't mean that everything will stay the same for both of us. You've been gone for most of the last week, and when you are home, all you want to do is sleep. It's been like I have to tell you what's going on in our lives, but now you don't even want to listen. I just need something from you to let me know that ..."

"What?" Darren raised his head from the bathroom sink. Although this indicated he intended to listen to what she had to say, it was not a calming response for Courtney. Muscles tensed over her eyes and her upper lip tightened in a human vestigial response to frighten an enemy by bearing one's teeth, and while her teeth were not completely visible, her anger was. She turned her back and rounded the corner through the kitchen into the living room. Darren was stunned enough that he remained still in the bathroom doorway. Unaware that Courtney had been hurt by his inattention, his mind emptied. Like distant drumbeats, the sound of drops of water hitting the floor reached his ears, and he realized that they were dripping from his face. Before reaching for a towel, he noticed the hall was still empty, with its plain white walls standing out and reminding him he and Courtney had long delayed plans for them. Darren and Courtney had intended to decorate the walls with pictures from their trip to Mexico.

Feeling suddenly very thirsty, Darren finished drying himself with a handtowel, then tossed it on the bathroom counter. He walked into the kitchen and opened the fridge. He was surprised at its bare shelves. Courtney was usually very good at stocking up on healthy snacks like fruit, but he was often pleasantly surprised by cookies as well.

"There's nothing in the fridge." As soon as the words left his mouth he regretted them. Courtney's furious visage appeared in the door between the kitchen and living room. A pit filled Darren's stomach as he remembered they were still probably in the middle of an argument. *Why was he having so much trouble paying attention?*

Courtney disappeared around the corner again and Darren paused to think, but couldn't formulate clear intentions. His thoughts kept wandering back to the notion of going to bed, but all this excitement had temporarily roused him past the point where he would be easily able to fall back to sleep. Darren further realized he and Courtney had exchanged hurtful words and that he had better rectify the situation. His thoughts swimming, he could hardly remember if he was angry with her, or, more importantly, why she was angry with him.

He took a step into the living room adjoining the front door of the apartment, but she was not there, nor had she left. The door to the second bathroom was closed and the light was on. Darren never understood why a one-bedroom apartment should have a half-bathroom as well as the master bathroom, but Courtney had thought it a useful feature and they had both liked this apartment's layout as a whole.

He blinked twice, cleared his head with a shake and took a few steps towards the bathroom. A few steps hopefully towards a humble reconcilliation, but his journey towards a truce was interrupted when the phone rang. He paused a moment, then walked to the small table where the phone was placed, and raised the receiver to his ear.

"Hello?"

"Hi, Darren. It's me, Al. I'm going to be in town for the day on Thursday because I have some stuff to do at the University. I thought maybe we could get together for dinner. I haven't seen you or Courtney since you became a doctor, so it's about time we did some visiting." Al was a friend of Darren's from school. He and Darren had been very close when they did their first two years of university together in Saskatoon. They had spent many a sunny Friday afternoon enjoying beers on the patios of their favourite watering holes, but had drifted apart when Darren began the intense studying that was required for medical school. He had less time to carouse with friends after his grades became crucial. Of course, when Darren and Courtney had moved out of town, Darren and Al had lost touch a bit. They had never entirely been out of contact, though, and now Al was continuing a mutual pattern of making an effort to get together whenever reasonably possible.

"Oh, no. I'm sorry, Al. I'm working in the hospital on Thursday night," Darren lied. "I wish I had known that you were going to be around – I might have been able to switch my schedule." Thursday was two days away, meaning Darren would be home from another thirty hour shift that evening. He knew he was exhausted now, and the way things were going, he was not going to be well rested by tomorrow morning. He could not just now bear the idea of any further demands on his time – social or professional. He felt guilty for blowing off his good friend, but it was necessary for a measure of sanity.

"Geez, I'm sorry to hear that. Sorry I couldn't let you know earlier, but I only found out this morning that I would be driving through. Any idea when you'll be back in Saskatoon?" Al sounded genuinely disappointed, so Darren felt even worse.

"No, I'm not sure. You'll be the first one to know. I'll give you a call."

"That would be great. Sorry we couldn't get together, but I'll talk to you soon. Bye for now."

"See you." Darren hung up the phone and felt terrible. He thought for a moment about what he had been doing before the phone rang, then took a step towards the bathroom door, bracing himself for the tough conversation ahead.

The telephone rang again.

"Fuck!" Darren cursed under his breath. Not only was the telephone interrupting him when he needed some concentration, but the constant ringing of his pager at work had given him a new hostility to devices designed to demand his instant attention.

"Hello?"

"Hi, Darren, it's Mom. How are you doing? You said you were

going to call me this week, but I haven't heard from you."

"Hi, Mom." Darren was choking back anger now. He could not stand that everyone wanted to bother him when all he wanted was some sleep. "I've been really busy."

"I didn't realize that it took so much effort to pick up a telephone for a few minutes and call your mother. Your father and I have been wanting to hear some news about your work, and all we can do is …" Darren had stopped paying attention and begun looking longingly at the bathroom door. Talking to Courtney and sorting out their difficulties had seemed like an unenviable chore just a few minutes before, but now that he could not get to it, it seemed an absolute necessity. His mother was still speaking, "… so we told your uncle Jim that you would talk to him about his sciatica."

"Mom, can I call you back in about an hour? Courtney and I are just working on something important."

"Well, okay, but you make sure to call me back."

"I will, Mom. Bye for now." Darren hung up the receiver and took a few deep breaths. He reached down to the wall outlet and unplugged the telephone before he resumed his slow, purposeful strides towards the bathroom door. The door opened a crack, but before Courtney could emerge and speak Darren thought that he had better make a preemptive strike. As the wedge of light shining through the bathroom door widened, he spoke. "I'm sorry." The bathroom door opened and Darren's eyes locked on Courtney's tear-streaked face.

"Maybe you should have been sorrier before you decided to ignore me and treat me like I don't exist."

Darren always felt that a sincere apology was a mark of maturity. Now he was not pleased that his was not immediately accepted. "I'm not ignoring you. I love you, but you can't expect me to think straight when no one will let me get even a few hours' sleep."

"You keep complaining like you think you're the only person in the world. Moving here wasn't easy for me either, you know!"

The tears that streaked Courtney's face had begun to flow again. Darren knew from experience he was physiologically incapable of resisting her tears, and now he could feel sympathetic tears well up in his eyes.

"I didn't realize that being a doctor was going to be like this," he answered. "I can't stand being tired all the time. I can't stand not knowing if I'm ever going to be able to go to sleep. I really can't stand everyone demanding that I make all the decisions on the spot and take all the responsibility, but still treating me like I don't know what I'm doing." He was not looking at her now. He looked down as his emotion spilled out.

There was a long silence before Darren returned his gaze to Courtney, and in that time her face had changed. Darren recognized the frigid, logical clarity that could grasp her when emotions had taken hold. Her gaze became penetrating and Darren's breathing accelerated.

"What are we giving up and what are we gaining?" Courtney's voice was measured, professional, even as she began wiping the tears from her face.

While Darren was sleeping this afternoon, she had telephoned friends from law school who were articling in Saskatoon. Of course, she could only leave messages because they were at work and were almost as busy as Darren. She had called her sister, who was home with a new baby and could not talk long because she was busy changing a diaper and making lunch. Courtney had the time to read that she had wanted so badly while she was busy, but somehow the pleasure of a solitary activity was lost when the solitude was not of her choosing.

This had been the plan all along. Courtney's career would be briefly delayed, and she would be able to apply for positions next year. That had been the plan, but now she was standing on the median of a busy but silent freeway while the traffic of life drove by and ignored her.

"I was willing to delay my career, but the reward was that we would be together, and the purpose was that your residency was here." Darren was glad the yelling was over, but Courtney's suddenly analytical air could be frightening. "What have we gained, now that you're killing yourself at work every day?" When Darren did not answer, she spoke more loudly.

"Tell me why you want to be a doctor!"

"Because my father was a doctor." The answer came quickly, and it surprised Courtney. It seemed to surprise Darren as well. Darren took a slow breath and his chest trembled slightly as he released it. They stared at each other with wide eyes and in dumb silence before either of them moved. Courtney took a step towards Darren and hugged him, realizing that her analysis had been flawed, her assumptions incorrect. He held her tight. She was almost as tall as him, so he only had to bend his neck a bit to bury his face against her shoulder. She had been so frustrated with him just minutes before, as she waited for him to validate her sacrifices, but now he seemed so helpless, the product of external forces. Her long dark hair cascaded over his head. She brushed it aside.

"You've never told me that before." A long pause had elapsed before she spoke.

"I didn't know it. I'm not sure I meant it." He raised his head slightly to answer. "I'm sorry I haven't been paying you enough attention. I really do care about you. I've just been overwhelmed."

"I know." They moved together to the couch and sat leaning against each other. They took each other's hands as they continued talking.

"I hope you do," Darren said. "Because I don't know what I would do without you." He laughed slightly as he continued. "I can still hear my Dad saying 'Back when I was an intern ...'" They both laughed at Darren's very realistic impression of his father's voice. "He used to tell me stuff like, 'We would be on call every second night for a straight year. You think the patient loads are heavy now? You should see the number of sick patients we looked after back then!'" Darren laughed again. "I guess the tales have gotten taller because he has never looked after patients since he was an intern. What does he know about looking after sick people? He's a bloody medical microbiologist. He only looks after bacteria!"

Courtney laughed, then stroked his hair and stared deep into his eyes. Darren realized that he had diverted the subject back to himself again. "I guess I haven't thought about how hard it is for you," he offered. "Putting your career on hold for a year was a tough thing to do."

"Oh, I'm sorry too," she replied. "My days aren't so tough. I'm actually appreciating having some free time for once. When I was in law school I never had time to worry about where the future was taking me, because I was always chasing it. Now, I guess I just need to know that you haven't forgotten about me."

"Did you want to talk some more about marriage plans?" he asked.

"Not tonight, maybe after we have thought about things a little more. Tell me some more about what's so stressful and frustrating at the hospital. It must be scary to be around sick and dying people all the time." Now she laid her head on his shoulder and cuddled up to him. Darren could hardly resist an offer like that to talk about his day, even if he was still reprimanding himself for ignoring her.

"That's not it, really." He paused for a moment, finding it strange that indeed the morbidity that surrounded him everyday could be a reasonable source of stress, but had not been one that came to mind. He tried to articulate what was bothering him. "It's all these bizarre little things that you never learn as a medical student," he began. "Like sometimes we round all day on our inpatients, and only need to see one or two people in the Emergency Department. Then I'll get twelve consults from the emergency doctors between midnight and five a.m. Most of the people will have had problems that have been going on for days, or even weeks. Why am I seeing them in the middle of the night?" he grinned. Courtney had become quiet and thoughtful, but now he felt like he was on a roll.

"In fact, of all the really exciting things that have happened since I started, I can't remember any that were during the day. Not a single one when there was lots of more senior people around that I could ask for help. They were always in the middle of the night when I was all alone." He paused. Courtney was comfortable in his lap, and now she closed her eyes. Her frustrations remained, but she was enjoying being with him, even if he was talking about himself. After all, surely the reason she had come was so that they could be together.

"And people who come in with chest pain. We have a much better chance of figuring out what is causing it if we see them when they are actually having the pain, but it seems like everyone's pain gets better in the ambulance on the way to the hospital. It doesn't matter if they have been having the pain for twenty minutes or three days, it always gets better in the ambulance. What are we supposed to do with them then?" Darren was shaking his head. He felt like he was seeing things with greater clarity now that he was away from the hospital. He could suddenly appreciate the humor in situations that had been frustrating him to no end just a few hours before. He wondered whether he had truly attained a new clarity of thought, or whether he was hallucinating from sleep deprivation.

As Darren stopped talking, Courtney opened her eyes. She wrinkled her forehead and recalled something she had heard from a surgical resident at a recent barbecue.

"I heard once that you're not truly a doctor until you have been glad that someone died so that you could get some sleep."

Darren picked at a loose thread on the couch. Intrigued by his silence, Courtney returned to their earlier subject.

"Did you mean that? About only going into medicine because your father was a doctor? I've been thinking about this. I'm sure that I've asked you why you wanted to become a doctor before, but now that I think about it, I can't really remember you ever giving me a simple answer."

"I'm not sure that there is a simple answer any more. If there was one, I've forgotten it."

"Maybe there is no simple reason for anything we truly want."

Now Darren cuddled up to Courtney and they each dozed on the couch. Darren gave Courtney a squeeze and she felt warm, but still unsettled. The power of his fatigue hit him when he laid his head down. As soon as it hit the cushions on the couch, he was caught by a brief sensation of the room spinning. The darkness unfolded and he drifted into slumber.

In the morning, Darren awoke. He was back in bed but did not recall how he had gotten there. Although he had gotten eight hours of sleep, his body still ached with a need for more rest. Fatigue was a physically painful sensation as he pulled himself up and out of bed. As he walked to the bathroom and splashed water on his face, he dreaded the fact that he was facing another thirty hours in the hospital. That and the fact that he had forgotten to call his mother again.

Chapter 10

A tiny white whirlpool swirled before Darren's eyes. The sight was hypnotic. It was almost enough to make Darren forget about the stresses of his day until another customer of the coffee shop jarred him from behind and interrupted his reverie. The collision forced Darren to move out of line to finish stirring in his cream. He headed for the wards. Having already seen most of his patients, he had found time before rounds with Dr Smith to grab his daily caffeine fix. Now he would have to hurry and finish before the boss arrived.

He stepped into the elevator and was surrounded by other people wearing white coats and clinging to their Styrofoam cups. He unconsciously counted the people around him and reached a total of two respiratory therapists, one nurse and two residents. As an undergraduate science student at the U of S, Darren had always resisted the urge to join the trend and take up coffee drinking. Now he somehow found himself part of the majority.

Back on the ward, Darren steeled himself for the most unpleasant part of his day. No patient he had yet seen was quite as frustrating to deal with as Kurt Doering, and although Mr Doering's delirium was slowly improving, Darren wished that the old German would just stay disoriented. When Darren had sat Mr and Mrs Doering down together on the third day of Mr Doering's admission, he had truly hoped that sensitive communication would provide perspective. He had put aside enough time to answer all their questions and had prepared the data from Mr Doering's medical workup. While Mrs Doering listened patiently to the grim prognosis Darren offered, and even asked several pertinent and insightful questions, Kurt Doering's response had been hostile.

"Lung cancer? I can't possibly have cancer! That is the most ridiculous thing I have ever heard. You're just trying to collect a big fee from me." Mrs Doering tried to calm her husband, but he was inconsolable. "You're going to listen to this nonsense? These quacks don't know what they are talking about."

Darren's suggestion that Mr Doering's long and intense history of cigarette consumption might have something to do with his illness only resulted in even more aggressive and insulting comments. Mr Doering looked ready to fly into a rage when Darren suggested this was a disease seen almost entirely in heavy smokers. Darren had tried gently to explain why the tests they had were now irrefutable, but had eventually realized today was not the day Mr Doering was going to come to grips with either his medical prognosis or his mortality. He had accepted that Mr Doering was still not quite himself and concluded that perhaps bringing up the topic later would be worthwhile. This, unfortunately, did not prove any more productive. Mr Doering remained equally immobile in his conviction his diagnosis was either a hoax perpetrated by the doctors or simply a terrible mistake. While frustrating, that was not the worst thing about him as a patient. He was demanding and abusive to the nursing staff, and as a result Darren was frequently called to deal with his many petty complaints. Worse still was the fact this was all intensely distressing to Mrs Doering. Darren had wanted very much to help her since the first night she arrived with her sick husband in tow.

Darren wished he could just discharge Mr Doering. There was no law someone had to accept his or her diagnosis before going home, and Kurt Doering's diagnostic workup was already complete. There was no definitive treatment option to be pursued while he was in hospital, so the main goal was to get him home with his symptoms controlled. Unfortunately, Mr Doering's blood oxygen level was slightly too low for him to get by without therapeutic oxygen, so Darren and the rest of Dr Smith's team were stuck with him for now.

As Darren approached Mr Doering's room, he could hear the man's distinctive growl of a voice from a distance. Now he was complaining loudly and bitterly to the hospital staff that his food was of inadequate quality. Darren wondered if Mr Doering had spent his entire life yelling. The notion of being quiet, or even just speaking in conversational tones, certainly seemed alien to the old man. Darren took a deep breath and walked towards the door before being intercepted by Dr Smith.

"Have you seen your gentleman with the lung cancer yet?" Dr Smith inquired while keeping his eyes firmly on the clipboard in his hand.

"Not yet. He's the last patient I have to see this morning."

"Very well. Why don't you skip him for now and we will see him together on rounds. There is a patient I would like you to go have a look at in Casualty." Dr Smith used the European term for the Emergency Department.

Darren had never been so glad to be handed more work. After getting the details on the new patient from Dr Smith, Darren left Mr Doering's ward and marched downstairs purposefully. Unfortunately, the gentleman he was about to see was a man named William Sutherland with cancer of the esophagus. With this diagnosis, Darren's interactions with the man were liable to be grim, but somehow he felt certain that anyone would be more pleasant than Mr Doering. He did not realize how right he was.

On his arrival in the Emergency Department, Darren found Mr Sutherland's chart. As he had on the ward, he heard the sound of a patient with a strikingly loud voice, but this time the gentleman was relating a humorous anecdote rather than complaining. Darren dodged a team of paramedics who were furiously working on a trauma patient as they wheeled a stretcher into the department, and approached Mr Sutherland's curtain. The sound of people laughing emanated from behind the curtain, and as Darren pulled it aside, he found himself in a small crowd. In the centre of the curtained area was an elderly man who was clearly ill. Darren was trained to recognize signs of malnutrition and he noted them here immediately. Mr Sutherland had thinning of the muscles around his cheeks and on the sides of his head. His arms were thin and his eyes were sunken. Inside those eyes, however, burned a light so bright it drew people like flies to a candle. In the middle of his wasted face, Mr Sutherland's lips formed a smile that was indefatigable as he related what must have been a fascinating tale. A nurse, busy inserting an intravenous into one of his thin and brittle arms, paused frequently to smile back at Mr Sutherland and appreciate the twists and turns in his story. Two respiratory therapists stood at the bedside, clearly unnecessary for this patient's well being at the moment but taking a break and enjoying the work of a master storyteller. Also present were people of ages varying from teens to octogenarians. These were Mr Sutherland's family members.

"I'm sorry to interrupt," Darren interjected, "but my name is Dr Johnston."

Mr Sutherland flashed his winning smile and introduced himself. "Bill Sutherland!" He reached his frail hand towards Darren's, and shook vigorously with a force that seemed impossible for such a withered limb. Another hand touched Darren's shoulder.

"Hi, Dr Johnston." One of Mr Sutherland's family members, a middle-aged man well dressed in a dark blue suit, took Darren aside. "I'm Bill's son, Craig. I can probably answer some of your questions."

"That would be great," Darren answered and stepped outside the curtain with Craig.

Craig turned to speak with his father. "Dad, I'll talk to the doctor for a moment. Okay?"

"That's fine. Now let me tell the rest of you about the time my daughter ..." Mr Sutherland started back into a story. The crowd around the bed gathered closely again in anticipation. A woman's voice interjected playfully: "Oh, Dad! They don't want to hear about *that*." But clearly they did.

Outside the curtain, Craig gave Darren the history. His voice had a soft pitch but a purposeful tone. "We were at Dr Smith's office first thing this morning and he suggested we come in. He had been willing to see us on short notice after we called him last night because Dad has been getting weaker and weaker. You see, Dad has cancer of the esophagus. It was diagnosed four months ago. The doctors told us that there was no specific treatment for him, so they would focus on treating his symptoms." Darren and Craig sat down at one of the desks doctors used for paperwork, and Darren took a few notes as Craig went on. "Dad was doing really well until lately. He saw the doctor initially because he threw up a tiny bit of blood. The doctors did some kind of X-ray and then looked inside his throat with a scope and told him it was cancer. Then he went home and went right back to his work. He has been slowly losing weight, but it's just recently he has started to look so sick. That's probably because he hasn't been able to eat or drink anything. He was pretty sleepy and nauseated when he first got here, but the doctors down here put in that first IV and gave him some fluid about an hour ago. Now he's acting like his old self again."

Craig paused as Darren finished writing. Darren smiled as he completed his notes and said: "He certainly does look pretty energetic now."

"I'm sure he thinks he could conquer the world," said Craig with a laugh. His face became more serious as he continued: "I'd like you to know something. He is a very stoic guy. In the past he would never even take an aspirin. Now I'm afraid he's having some pain and not telling anyone about it. He keeps a smile on his face while people are around, but if you catch him when he thinks no one is looking, he is often grimacing. I hope you can convince him to take something if he is having pain."

"I'll certainly try," said Darren, "but for now I'm going to need some more specific information about his medications and past history."

Darren got some further details from Craig, then returned to Mr Sutherland's bedside and asked him some questions. As Craig had predicted, Mr Sutherland denied having any pain and waved away suggestions from his son it was an issue. Aside from Craig, the rest of the family went to the coffee shop while Darren conducted his physical examination. The exam proved fairly entertaining as Mr Sutherland jokingly flexed his muscles like a bodybuilder when Darren tested his strength. It was then that Darren noticed an old tattoo on Mr Sutherland's shoulder.

"Where did you get that?"

"Get what?" Mr Sutherland feigned innocence.

"Your tattoo. It looks like it's been around a while," Darren answered. Although questions about tattoos might be part of a medical history while inquiring about needle-acquired diseases, Darren in this case just thought that Mr Sutherland might have an interesting story to tell.

"A tattoo?" This time Mr Sutherland acted surprised. "I must have gotten drunk one night and tried to impress the ladies."

"Dad!" Craig smiled at his father. Mr Sutherland laughed back, and Craig decided to volunteer the story himself. "Dad was in the army during the Second World War. He got the tattoo then."

"Is that right?" Darren nodded as he continued his exam by checking Mr Sutherland's reflexes.

"Yes, Sir." Mr Sutherland had a note of pride in his voice. "Sixth Brigade, Second Canadian Infantry Division." He almost barked the identification of his former unit in a loud, crisp voice. Darren paused and looked in his direction, startled by Mr Sutherland's sudden increase in volume. Mr Sutherland's face softened, his lips parted in an enthusiastic smile, and he softly added: "And at your service."

After Darren had finished his physical examination, he returned to the workstation to write more notes. Mr Sutherland's family returned to his bedside, but Craig again emerged to speak with Darren. "So you'll bring my father into hospital?"

"It looks that way," Darren said, looking up from his paperwork. "Even though he looks so well now, he would just get dehydrated again if he went home and couldn't swallow."

"That's my concern, too," said Craig. "I just hope we can get him home again. Since he doesn't have much time left, it would be nice if he could enjoy his last days."

Darren nodded, but at that moment he was struck by the thought that Mr Sutherland's family members were not at all distraught. Unlike poor Mrs Doering who was becoming progressively more overwhelmed by the combination of her own grief and her husband's denial, Mr Sutherland's son seemed prepared for the worst but enthusiastic to enjoy his remaining days with his father. Now Mr Sutherland was interacting with his family in a way that seemed to put them all at ease. Darren could hear him wrestling with his young granddaughter and jokingly calling for help as he pretended to be tangled in his intravenous tubing. The family was in stitches enjoying his antics.

Darren worried momentarily that Mr Sutherland's sense of humour was another form of denial, but his worries dissolved as he spoke at greater length with Craig. It seemed that Mr Sutherland had been making careful preparations ever since his diagnosis of cancer. Craig spoke with great reverence about his father and noted that Bill was a central figure in a large extended family. Bill Sutherland was apparently the man who got the family together for reunions, intervened when family members were having disagreements, and looked out for the least advantaged members of the family. Apparently Mr Sutherland's preparations had focused on them first. He had called his lawyer and made sure that his will was in order. Craig explained that he made sure that his assets would be distributed equitably but also in a manner that would benefit those who needed the money most. Mr Sutherland had also been at work making sure that his other projects did not go to waste. He had been organizing a family reunion that was to occur in Winnipeg, and within days of his diagnosis he was making sure that others would take up his preparations where he left off.

As Craig continued, Darren was sure that Mr Sutherland's intense work on preparations must have meant neglecting his own needs, but on the contrary, he had found the time to go on a trip to Australia, which had been a longstanding dream of his. Now Darren was shaking his head in amazement. It seemed that Mr Sutherland faced his own impending mortality with such confidence and organization that he inspired his family with the same confidence. They seemed to know their cherished family member would die soon, but that his legacy would continue and he would have gotten everything he wanted out of life. Never in his four years of medical school or his brief residency training had Dr Darren Johnston ever encountered a person who could make his sudden exit from life with such quiet yet active dignity. Now his thoughts returned to Craig's initial concern.

"When we admit your dad, we'll do two things. First, we'll ensure that he stays hydrated, using the intravenous. We'll also see what we can do about any other symptoms he has. Second, we'll see what can be done in terms of placing an esophageal stent. That's like a little tube we can put into his swallowing tube to hold it open for him. It is only a temporary solution, but as you said, he will want to enjoy his time at home with his family, not here in the hospital."

Craig smiled and returned to his father's side. Darren looked briefly at Mr Sutherland's name and hospital identification number and had the feeling that he was in the presence of a hero.

After finishing with Mr Sutherland's admission, Darren returned to the internal medicine ward upstairs. The ward spanned two hallways, each on one side of the central nursing desk. Thinking that he should rejoin Dr. Smith and the rest of the team on rounds, he took a quick look down the first hallway. Although he did not see any sign of the other doctors, a nurse with some concerns immediately cornered him.

"Mr Doering is having a very severe cough. He looks terribly uncomfortable, and I thought you may want to give him something for it." She pointed to Mr Doering's room, and the sound of his hacking cough penetrated the otherwise sterile quiet of the ward.

"I'll go talk to him. I haven't seen him yet this morning." Darren walked towards the sound, and on his way asked the nurse if she knew whether Dr. Smith had already seen Mr Doering. She thought he had not.

As Darren entered the room, he was struck by the appearance of the people surrounding his patient. Mr Doering was in a large hospital room containing four beds. One of the beds was occupied by a very old man who was productively spending his time grasping at nonexistent insects in the air around his head. A second bed was empty, its current tenant sitting in a wheelchair and picking over a tray of hospital food. The third bed contained a middle-aged obese man in no apparent distress whose wife and two daughters sat on the bedside around him. What these people all had in common, save the man grabbing at bugs, was that the intense cough emanating from Kurt Doering's throat made them wince in discomfort at such an unnatural sound being expelled from their neighbour. As Kurt hacked away, his wife fidgeted at his bedside with a box of tissues. She reached them towards him when he looked as though he might need them, but he only batted them away. In a further attempt to be helpful, she reached to massage his shoulders, which were tensed as he expelled more purulent phlegm. He shrugged off this attempt at kindness as well.

Darren approached closer and Mr Doering clasped his sides in pain as he began another coughing fit. Darren inquired about his cough and about his pain, and Mrs Doering, who wore an expression of extreme concern, supplied most of the answers. Mr Doering was of little additional help, as he only looked up from his spasms with an expression of impatience. As Darren reassured her that a dose of codeine would control the cough, he felt satisfaction that at least he had relieved some of her suffering.

Darren left the room after a brief and sincere acknowledgement of Mrs Doering's gratitude. In the hallway were Dr. Smith, Layton and Eddy. Darren was somewhat reassured that he was not the only target of Dr. Smith's academic questioning when he noticed that Eddy was wilting under one of the consultant's onslaughts as Layton looked on. "Dr Bofors, it astounds me that as a resident physician in the field of diagnostic radiology, you should be so uninformed about the appearance of interstitial lung disease on a computed tomography scan." The sum of the formality with which he issued his condemnation and the number of large words in his sentence made Dr Smith's comments truly biting. Eddy seemed to decrease in physical stature. It was as though he was trying to slouch into a hiding place within his white coat. It was not surprising that he could not summon the energy to explain to Dr Smith that he had not yet had a single day of radiology training beyond medical school.

Layton and Dr Smith turned to Darren as he approached. "We're done rounds," Layton said blandly. "Since you're on call tonight, you should talk to Eddy about the unstable patients on the ward. I'll be in the hospital tonight because I'm covering the Coronary Care Unit, so you can give me a call if you want."

Dr Smith bid his team farewell with a slight nod and Layton went to the Coronary Care Unit to receive sign-over. That left Eddy and Darren to discuss their patients, but Darren quickly recognized that Eddy needed a few moments to recover. They had a seat together at the nursing desk, and after Eddy had regained his composure he proceeded. "The patients aren't too bad today. In fact, I feel sicker than most of them look. I don't think that anyone will give you trouble tonight."

"Of course they're okay now," answered Darren, "it's still daytime. Nobody crashes until after the sun goes down."

"Ain't that the truth?" answered Eddy. "I'd better go home. I'm on call tomorrow night and I need some rest."

They walked a short distance together towards the locker room. In the corridor, they looked past a teenaged girl with leukemia to see whether the candy machine had been restocked, and when

Eddy dropped his stethoscope and stopped to retrieve it, he was bumped by a woman who had just learned of her husband's death. Darren noticed a subtle change in the arrangement of plants near the hospital cafeteria and Eddy paused to listen as a speaker of the hospital's overhead system quietly clicked to life but deactivated without transmitting an announcement.

The hospital that surrounded them had been designed to avoid a large and impersonal impression. Open areas replaced the suffocating corridors of the traditional hospital, and patients' rooms were positioned to receive more natural light from windows.

University students walked near the building's front entrance, finding shortcuts home from classes, and a helicopter took the most direct route through the open sky to the building's roof.

A few kilometres away, Courtney was preparing an early dinner alone, with only the television for company. Looking at the television listings, she realized that there was a one-hour time difference to Saskatoon.

Chapter 11

Dinnertime arrived late because Darren had been hard at work admitting patients from the Emergency Department. He spent a long time heating his leftovers in the microwave oven, because he was interrupted several times by pages from the wards. When he finally found the time to sit down and enjoy his meal, Layton entered the residents' lounge, not quite bearing his usual appearance of controlled tension. Somehow he seemed more worried and distracted. As Layton sat next to Darren and began unwrapping a sandwich, Darren inquired about his change in countenance.

"It's this stupid code pager." Layton pointed at the pager on his belt next to the one he usually wore. "Whenever I'm covering CCU and have to wear this thing, I'm always sure it's going to go off and I'll have to run to a cardiac arrest. I feel like I can't even go to the bathroom." Layton took a big bite of his sandwich. It was made with peanut butter and jelly. Clearly it had been thrown together in a hurry this morning.

"Didn't you have the same kind of sandwich for lunch today?" Darren asked, smirking.

"Shut up," answered Layton. "I wish I had your common sense to make something that would leave me some leftovers." He looked longingly at Darren's warm meal.

They ate together in peace for a few minutes before Darren's pager rang. This time it was a nurse calling to tell him that a patient had been received on the ward from the Coronary Care Unit who would need to be reviewed. Darren took down the patient's name and sat back down to finish his dinner. Layton had been watching while he spoke on the phone.

"Was that about Mr Jensen?"

"It sure was. I guess he was sent out from the CCU. Do you know much about him?"

"I guess so. You must be the only resident in the hospital who doesn't know him." He paused as Darren looked at him questioningly. "He's a guy with severe heart disease. All three of his major coronary arteries are blocked, so everything he does gives him chest pain. The surgeons have looked at him for a possible bypass, but the vessels are too narrow for them to do the procedure. Now he's on every medication we have for heart disease, but he still has chest pain all the time. Of course, after so many years of having angina, he and his family have learned that chest pain is serious so now he comes into the hospital all the time."

"So what did you do for him in the CCU?" asked Darren.

"Nothing," answered Layton. "There's nothing we can do for him except reconfirm that his chest pain is from his coronary artery disease. So he spent a day in the CCU and now he's back out on the internal medicine ward."

"Well, there must be something we can do for him," Darren said.

"That's exactly what his family says every time they bring him in." Layton laughed to himself at the frustration of the situation. "But like I said, we're out of medications to try. He's on them all. All that's left is painkillers, and he doesn't like to take those because they make him tired."

"So why was he brought to the Coronary Care Unit if there is nothing to do for him?" Darren had trouble imagining that he was taken to such a high intensity facility just to be offered painkillers.

"When somebody comes into the hospital with chest pain that represents an exacerbation of coronary artery disease, nobody wants to turn them away at the door. He always gets brought into the CCU, we always tell him that it's his heart, we always tell him there is nothing more to do unless he wants painkillers, he always goes back out to the ward, and then he always gets discharged home." Layton swung his index finger back and forth in the air like a metronome keeping time with Mr Jensen's hospital stays as he described their inevitable course.

"And I suppose that he 'always' comes back again when he realizes he's still having chest pain," Darren completed the chant.

"Thirty-three times this year alone. Now you're catching on."

Darren sighed. "I guess I'd better go meet him," he said, packing up the plastic container of his now-finished dinner.

"I guess you had," said Layton. "Who knows? When you're covering the CCU next year, maybe you'll be looking after him there too."

Darren began to leave, then paused. He turned his head back towards Layton. "If he has such bad heart disease that he has constant chest pain, and there's nothing we can do about it, you wouldn't think that he'd live a year."

"That's what I thought a year ago." Layton took another bite of his peanut butter and jam sandwich. "But who knows? Maybe his next cigarette will be his last. Somehow I doubt it. His nicotine cravings are the only thing keeping him alive."

Darren continued out the door.

His pager rang again as he reached the ward. The nurse at the desk addressed him. "Oh, Dr Johnston. I just paged you. Mr Jensen seems to be getting worse."

"I'll take a look at him." Darren headed for the room. As he entered, he noticed that the room had two beds in it, and the occupant closer to the door was none other than William Sutherland. Mr Sutherland seemed to have made himself quite comfortable. The pole that held his intravenous solution was decorated with several pictures, some of his family members, but others of Mr Sutherland in far away places, often with important people. At a glance as he went past, Darren thought he saw a picture of Mr Sutherland with Pierre Trudeau. Mr Sutherland's face lit up as Darren entered the room and he waved casually.

"Good evening, old chap." He looked away, as a telephone on his bedside table rang. He answered it with a brisk: "Sutherland here!" A young lady was sitting at his bedside, and Darren recognized her as one of the family members who had been present when Mr Sutherland was admitted. She looked apologetically at Darren.

"Grandpa's going to be a handful. He insisted on having a telephone with him so he could do business from the hospital."

Darren just smiled back, and continued on to see Mr Jensen. He thought as he went past that Mr Sutherland was such a pleasure to speak with, that he wished he had met Bill before he came to hospital. The sound of Mr Sutherland's animated telephone conversation in the background brought a further smile to his face. For someone who was dying, Mr Sutherland certainly seemed filled with a contagious vitality.

In the next bed, a man who looked almost as cachectic as Mr Sutherland was in obvious discomfort. He was moaning and clutching at his chest, while a distraught elderly lady wearing bulky clothes and holding a cane stood at his bedside. Darren introduced himself and learned that the woman at the bedside was Mr Jensen's wife. She explained that Mr Jensen came to hospital because the chest pain that had been plaguing him during minimal activity was now present even at rest. She further described that his pain had been worsening ever since he left the Coronary Care Unit. Mr Jensen seemed barely able to respond for himself. Darren felt this must be due to his pain, but the patient also seemed quite disoriented. Darren needed a moment to collect his thoughts and obtain more information, so he excused himself to review Mr Jensen's chart, assuring Mrs Jensen that he would return momentarily.

Back at the nursing station with Mr Jensen's chart in hand, Darren discovered exactly what he already knew to be the case, that Mr Jensen was already taking every medication that was even remotely likely to benefit his heart. The best that could be hoped for now was to make him more comfortable. Darren was far from satisfied at having made this discovery. Part of him had hoped that he might find a way to help Mr Jensen – a way that the dozens of other doctors looking after him had missed, but now he had to return to Mrs Jensen to tell her what she surely must know.

As he re-entered the room, Darren remained slightly uncomfortable despite his confidence that he was only giving Mrs Jensen old news. It was not easy to see the trust in her eyes and have to admit powerlessness. She looked hopefully towards him as he approached.

"Mrs Jensen, as you already know, your husband has very severe heart disease. The heart specialists have seen him and have done everything they can to fight the disease. Unfortunately, he is still having pain, so I think you would agree that it is reasonable to give him something to make him feel better. I think that his obvious discomfort and confusion are from his pain, so I would like to give him some morphine." Darren found that he was twisting his stethoscope tubing back and forth in his hands as he spoke. He noticed a company logo on the stethoscope and realized that the company also produced the container in which he had brought leftovers for dinner. Darren forced himself to look up at her eyes as the long pause dragged on, but Mrs Jensen only stared at him blankly when she spoke.

"He always says that morphine makes him too sleepy."

"I understand, Mrs Jensen, but our only alternative is to leave him the way that he is now. Do you agree that for now we should try to make him feel better?" Darren leaned forward slightly while awaiting her response. She stood with the same blank expression on her face that made it difficult to tell if she was lost in complex thought or just cognitively vacant. Darren tried hard to see what was behind her eyes, but found he could only see his reflection. He continued to wait for her response, sure that eventually she would see reason. His eyes swept the room for a moment and he noticed the many get-well cards and flowers that adorned the nooks and crannies around the bed. A card coloured in bright crayon hues read, "I hope you get better, Grumpa."

Darren continued to wait patiently until Mrs Jensen finally answered. Mr Sutherland continued his brisk telephone conversation in the next bed as she began: "I suppose so. Does this mean he will go back to the CCU? Maybe he should get stronger medicine through his IV."

This stopped Darren in his tracks. He had not expected to think about sending Mr Jensen back to the Coronary Care Unit. They had not been able to do anything for him when he went there the first time. What were they going to be able to do now? Nevertheless, Darren did not feel confident telling her that her husband would have to stay here.

"I'll talk with one of the doctors who looked after him there and see what they have to say." Mrs Jensen smiled and Darren quietly left the room. On his way out, he saw Bill Sutherland starting an animated game of checkers with his granddaughter. After leaving an order for morphine at the nursing station, Darren proceeded back to the residents' lounge in search of his senior resident. Layton was not there, so Darren went to the Emergency Department. As it happened, he was not far out of his way, because on the way down he was called to see another patient there.

Before seeing the new patient, he walked around the department and found Layton. Layton was busily reading the electrocardiogram of a patient whom Darren judged to be quite ill by the number of hospital staff scurrying around his bed. Darren tapped Layton on the shoulder. Although Layton seemed deep in thought about the heart tracing in his hand, he smiled on recognizing Darren and said: "What's up?"

"Mrs Jensen asked me if her husband should go back to the CCU."

Layton's smile vanished and he set the heart tracing down on the table next to him. "And what did you tell her?"

"I told her I would talk to the doctor from the CCU. That's what I'm doing now."

"Okay, look." Layton sighed as he spoke. "We talked about Mr

Jensen already. There is nothing to do for the poor guy. Just make him comfortable. He's had pain constantly for a year."

Darren thought he would feel a little better telling Mrs Jensen that the CCU doctor could not take him back rather than telling her it was just a useless idea. At the same time, he did not feel good about taking responsibility for Mr Jensen's declining status. He tried one more approach. "How about a nitro-glycerine drip?" He referred to the strongest medicine for Mr Jensen's chest pain. It was a medication that could only be given back in the Coronary Care Unit.

Now Layton's face became hostile. "You know as well as I do that IV nitro' is a temporary measure until starting definitive treatment. What definitive treatment would you like to start? He's not getting surgery and we can't unblock his arteries. If we put him on a nitro' drip, he'll just sit rotting on that same drip in the CCU until he dies. Just give the guy some painkillers, because he's not coming back to the CCU on my watch! Now excuse me." Layton turned back to the heart tracing he had been studying and gave some instructions to the nurses looking after the patient in front of him. Darren quietly left.

Later in the evening, Darren found himself more and more frustrated with Mr Jensen. At eleven o'clock the nursing staff changed shifts, so he received a battery of calls about Mr Jensen's condition from the new nurses. They were obviously uncomfortable that their patient looked so ill, and they had not been present earlier when Darren had seen the patient and pronounced that morphine was their only option. At midnight another call about Mr Jensen's chest pain resulted in some unpleasantness. The nurse at that point had not yet seen Darren tonight and was indignant he should state there was nothing they could do, given that she thought he had not even come up to see the patient. Darren made the trek upstairs to the ward in order to see Mr Jensen once more, review his chart once more, and once more admit defeat by saying he had no magical cure for the patient.

Having been repeatedly beaten by his patient's disease tonight, Darren found himself more and more hostile to the idea of visiting Mr Jensen again and again. He started to wish that Mr Jensen's heart condition would finally claim him, since it had already clearly robbed his life of any quality. Back at the nursing desk, Darren took another look at the long list of medications that were undoubtedly keeping Mr Jensen alive by a thread, and considered the notion he was doing Mr Jensen a disservice by allowing those medications to continue while the poor man's body had clearly decided it was time to die. Darren looked up from the chart as Mrs Jensen left her husband's room, and he found himself angry with her as well. If she could only admit defeat, as he had tonight, perhaps she would allow this torture to stop. Instead of being kept alive in constant pain and constantly under the humiliating scrutiny of nurses and doctors, perhaps her husband could die at home with his dignity intact. Darren's body began to feel very heavy as he considered one more variable. Was he truly thinking in the best interest of his patient, or was he hoping that Mr Jensen would die so that he could get some sleep?

Darren rested his head in his hands and took a deep breath and a nurse bumped the back of his chair as she walked past. The nurses who were going about their work on this ward seemed to have stopped noticing his presence, as though he had become a constant fixture. Some of them flitted in and out of patient's rooms, while some sat and diligently recorded notes on their patients' progress. As Darren began to close the chart, he flipped past the pages of notes written by the nurses and noticed his name. He looked more carefully at the page and found himself frantically scanning the pages of notes that had been written in the last few hours.

23:25 Patient seems more short of breath – Dr. Johnston aware.

23:53 Patient having increasing chest pain – Dr D. Johnston informed; stated he does not need to see the patient at this time.

0:55 Dr Johnston reviewing patient's condition. States no

change in management required despite patient's obvious deterioration.

Darren's eyes widened. He reached for the charts of other patients he had been called about and reviewed the nurses' notes. He found similar notations on many of the charts.

23:45 Patient has had no bowel movement for two days – Dr. Johnston aware.

15:23 Patient inadvertently received incorrect medication – Dr Johnston aware.

Suddenly Darren had chest pain himself. He looked at his watch. It was almost two o'clock in the morning, so he was going to be covering these patients alone for another five or six hours.

He realized he had not done a single thing that would improve Mr Jensen's possibilities of survival. It seemed that here, in the middle of the night, making a little over minimum wage, he was only being used for the assignment of responsibility. Many doctors had helplessly done their best with Mr Jensen, but now only Darren was here in the middle of the night, taking full responsibility for his impending death.

Looking back at his watch, it occurred to him tonight had not even been a bad night, and there were no patients for him to see in the Emergency Department, so it was possible he would get some sleep. Before returning to his call room, he walked past the room housing Mr Sutherland and Mr Jensen. Remarkably, Mr Jensen seemed to have fallen asleep, but unfortunately, he was still moaning. Bill Sutherland winced once as his neighbour moaned, but smiled and waved to Darren in the doorway.

"Good evening, Mr Sutherland. Shouldn't you be asleep by now?"

"No time, my young friend," said Mr Sutherland, pointing to a small pile of paperwork in his lap. "Too many things to get done."

They said their goodnights and Darren returned to his call room. He was still lying awake when he received a call.

"Hi, Dr Johnston. I just thought that you would like to know that Mr Jensen's oxygen saturation has dropped a bit."

Darren thanked her for the news and tried again to go to sleep. He could sense his name being written as "aware" of Mr Jensen's condition. He ruminated for some time before finally drifting off to sleep, thinking mostly of Mr Jensen and wondering about the role he was playing in the man's care. His final thoughts before drifting off to sleep were of Mr Sutherland's face at hearing his neighbour's groans.

Chapter 12

On a warm dry evening in August of 1944, Corporal William Sutherland of 6th Brigade, 2nd Canadian Infantry Division, listened to the cries of a wounded comrade across the street. A cloud passed in front of the moon, leaving him in near total darkness. He covered his ears and hummed an old tune to himself in order to drown out the incomprehensible moans that haunted him. Curling himself up into a ball and leaning his head against a wooden beam in the rubble he had been using for cover, he reflected on this day, the worst of his life, and played out in his mind the events that led him into his current predicament.

The day had started like any other in this forsaken month, with him and the men of his section clearing buildings in one of the small hamlets on the outskirts of Caen. Bill had trouble recognizing where one city stopped and the other began. As far as he was concerned, they could still be in a suburb of the large coastal city. Unlike the endless prairies of Manitoba back home, there were few places in this part of France where a person was not surrounded by human construction.

Shading his eyes from the sun, Bill looked up at one of the steeples that dotted the French landscape. He continued walking, and looked down at the cobblestone street at his feet, then kicked a piece of loose stone and realized that he was not being as cautious as he should. On his way towards the next building in his day's work, he had walked out into the middle of the street. Although the platoon often went some time without encountering a trace of the enemy, it did not pay to assume that the next building would not hold enemy soldiers.

Two thumps, like sacks of flour dropped to the ground, echoed suddenly from a nearby house. Clouds of dust poured out of its windows. The ground trembled slightly with each explosion and then the reports of automatic weapon fire could be heard. All was quiet again after the last few shots. Other men of Sutherland's platoon had likely 'cleared' another unoccupied building.

"How many more blocks to Berlin?" asked Private Ender from behind Sutherland. Bill, Ender, and Private Friesen each laughed, but Bill began guiding the men towards the shelter of the roadside, keeping in mind that he was responsible for their well-being as well as his own. He hated that responsibility and wished he had never become a corporal. His own safety was quite enough to keep him occupied, and he could not even recall why he had been promoted, but it was fitting that his increase in rank had taken place while they were still training in England, when he had never even encountered the enemy. Bill had been efficient enough at drill and routine but was quite out of sorts here in France. He wished he was together with the sergeant and free from making any decisions, but for the time being, he and these two soldiers were on their own. As someone who did not much appreciate taking orders, he was not particularly fond of his sergeant, but at least when the sergeant was around there was a tangible organization to their activities. Bill knew the men at his side had no respect for him, even though he had one more stripe on his sleeve than they did. He, in his turn, chose not to respect them. If the three of them were to come under fire right now, Bill Sutherland was certain he would have no useful orders for the men, and equally certain the men would pay him little attention anyway. At least they got along fine while things were calm and no one was trying to order anyone around. Bill appreciated that peaceful compromise as he gratefully accepted a cigarette from Private Ender. He had smoked all of his – all the ones he had not lost playing poker.

Sutherland had never asked Ender his age, but he only looked about nineteen years old. He was the youngest of the three, but also the biggest. At well over six feet, he had to reach down slightly to offer Sutherland the cigarette. Despite his size, no one who met Ender would doubt that he had been a gentle, innocent soul back in Canada. Now he carried a rifle. Bill thought he recalled that Ted Ender had grown up on a farm, but he could not remember where. Maybe near Winnipeg, maybe not.

An old park bench was at the roadside, and scrapes on the cobblestones leading to it testified that it had been recently dragged there.

"I guess the sergeant wanted to meet us about here," said Sutherland. "Why don't we grab a seat?" Bill lit his newly acquired cigarette. Looking back in the direction they had come, he almost spit out the cigarette as he burst into laughter, then snorted and regained his composure.

"Can you believe we attacked that mess?"

The other men looked back and chuckled as well.

Across the road behind them to the north stood the building they had finished clearing earlier in the day. The cautious routine had been the same as with the many other buildings they had recently attacked, and began with a suspicion that the building was a likely location for the enemy sniper who had harassed them over the last few hundred metres of advance. From the north side of that target building, they made their preparations, then leaving their previous cover, the three of them ran as fast as they could across the street towards the target building, while their colleagues covered them with submachine gun and rifle fire. Not taking even a moment to slow down, Bill hit the wall next to a doorway with a painful thump of his shoulder. As soon as they were there, Sutherland and Ender removed the pins from their grenades while Private Friesen placed himself squarely in front of the door. The door was a sturdy looking wooden structure, so Friesen shot the lock with his rifle before kicking it in. With that done, he smoothly rolled to one side as Sutherland and Ender tossed their live grenades through the entrance. There was a momentary pause as they waited for the inevitable blasts. The covering fire from behind them silenced as their comrades across the street waited as well. Bill Sutherland had cleared innumerable buildings this way, and every time his bowels clenched as he waited for the blasts. Until those grenades exploded, he spent crucial seconds in terror at what he would find around the corner.

As always, the grenades exploded, filling the building with fire and shrapnel, then with suffocating smoke. The certainty of complete destruction evident from the settling dust eased Bill's dyspepsia, even as he and his comrades burst through the open door, weapons at the ready, and eyes darting about to identify targets. This time something was wrong. Instead of rushing into an enclosed room charred by the blasts of their grenades, they had run through the door into open sunshine. They paused and looked up and around. An artillery shell had long since demolished much of the backside of the building they had just stormed, and little remained of what had once been the front room. Above them, the upper floors of the building remained fairly intact. Ironically, Bill felt claustrophobic at the thought that much of the remaining building was dangling precariously over his head, supported mostly by the wall on the building's north face. Looking to his left and right, he saw little in the way of support structure left, and wondered what was holding up the ceiling above him.

At the time Sutherland, Ender and Friesen had still been too dazed to laugh. No stairs remained from which to access the upper floors, and as they looked around it was obvious this was not the hiding place of the sniper they sought. They might have appreciated the humour of attacking such a fragile structure at that point, had a bullet not ricocheted against the wall on Bill's left. The three soldiers looked for an instant at each other before rushing back through the door the way they had come. The 'building' that a moment ago was a possible hiding place for a sniper, became their cover against fire from that same sniper.

Now, an hour later, comfortable on his park bench, the sniper since found and captured by another section, Bill took a moment with the men to savour the humour in their situation. Now that they could see it from its south side, the building had a comical yet tragic appearance. Part of the second story remained, its floor jutting precariously out into space. It seemed remarkable it remained intact, particularly because a grand piano sat on its horizontal surface in the corner formed by the still standing north side, and a small remnant of the east wall. That piano reminded Bill that people had lived peacefully here only weeks ago. A photograph framed on the wall at the piano's side strengthened the image. The picture was too far away to make out, but Bill imagined it was of a cherished daughter, perhaps one who had diligently practiced her chords while seated in that corner which now hung perilously over a pile of rubble. Moments in which Bill recognized that this present ruin had once been a charming town were sad ones. Now the buildings were all dusty from the debris kicked up by artillery, and what were once people's prized possessions were strewn about the street. Scenes of normality, like the grand piano, were superimposed on a background of carnage. Across the street to the west from the bench in which Bill and the other men sat was a small park with a ravine running through it. Bill imagined that children must have recently played there. After another long drag at his cigarette it occurred to Bill that children here likely did not play "Cowboys and Indians", but perhaps they had played at being victorious French soldiers repelling the Germans in the Great War.

A book carefully marked with a small piece of leather rested at the foot of a tall tree in the park. It was images like that one that reminded Bill how many people had left here in a hurry. Suddenly the streets seemed very empty. Bill wondered what the town had looked like days before as its inhabitants realized that the storm of battle was approaching. Had townspeople fled in such a hurry that one might have forgotten about the book he was in the middle of reading, or had that book been sitting there for weeks, only catching a Canadian soldier's attention now by coincidence?

Having reached what may have been their intended rendezvous point, Bill would have been quite satisfied to while away the afternoon smoking if no further orders arrived. Ender took a drink from his canteen, and Friesen sorted through several crinkled photographs from his breast pocket. A small, dark-haired man with thin wire-framed glasses, Friesen offered an interesting contrast to Ender's hulking blond frame. As with Ender, Bill realized that he knew little about Friesen personally. He thought he had heard something about the rest of Friesen's family being spared military service for religious reasons, but was not interested enough to pursue the issue now.

He thought of wandering across the street to see the title on the book he had been staring at, when the sounds of nearby fighting interrupted his thoughts. Gunshots echoed from the south. Bill took a look in that direction and noticed a couple of large buildings on the edge of what must be the town square. About fifty feet south of him was a pile of rubble that had fallen into the street when a small bakery collapsed, so he and his men ran for the cover, Ender still closing his canteen and Friesen stowing his pictures. They collapsed behind the rubble and took a closer look towards the town square. On its south side, looking down on the soldiers was a church steeple. Two other tall buildings formed the east side of the square. Any one of those buildings would make excellent cover for a sniper, but the sounds of battle that echoed through the neighbourhood now suggested that more fighting was going on than could be caused by a single enemy soldier. Rifle fire was mixed with the sound of grenades, then an explosion that could have been one of the Germans' traps. The sounds seemed to be coming from a building on the near side of the town square, but neither Sutherland nor his men could make out its exact location. The sporadic sounds of fire continued for several seconds, then briefly stopped and were punctuated by a man yelling, apparently in English, but undecipherable at this distance. The sounds were abruptly cut off by blasts of automatic weapon fire.

Although not under fire, Bill took a moment to appreciate what excellent cover he had found. The pile of twisted stone and wood was approximately four feet high and was easy to lean up against while surveying the town square. He found a nook he could rest his rifle in and point it towards the square without exposing himself. As he remained alert in his ideal spot, he felt Friesen's gaze.

"Do you think we should move up there, a little closer to the action?" Friesen indicated another suitable position from which they would likely be in a better vantage to offer supporting fire to their comrades, but Bill was too satisfied with his current cover to agree.

"I don't think so. We should probably sit tight until the sergeant lets us know where he wants us." Friesen and Ender looked disappointed but stayed with Bill. More grenades were used in the nearby building, close enough that their explosions could be felt as well as heard. Not visible enough, however, that Bill and his men were in any position to help. Suddenly the distinct clanking sound of a man in full battle gear running approached the three men. From their left, Sergeant Whalen arrived at a sprint and dove behind cover with them.

"What the hell are you guys doing sitting back here?" The three looked at him dumbly as he continued. "Look, some of our guys were ambushed in that building up there. There was some hand to hand fighting, and now I think there's a couple of guys pinned." He pointed to a building only partially visible on the right. "I sent some men left to try to flank the Krauts and cut them off. Chances are they wanted to hit our guys and then get out of there. Our men pinned in there are probably keeping the Germans from getting out cleanly, so we have to get up there and help them. From here we ought to do a stepwise advance towards the building while the rest of the guys flank them. We should also let the lieutenant know what's going on." Now he sneered a bit at Sutherland, knowing who had kept the men in this useless position until he arrived. "Sutherland, why don't you run back to the restaurant there where the officer-types are looking at maps? Let them know we've hit a snag here." He gestured with his head and Sutherland began to stand to run back.

Bill felt slighted that the sergeant was so unhappy with his performance. In part he agreed that they should have moved to a better position, but found himself trying to justify his decision. As he stood up, the ground behind him was raked with machine gun fire.

"Shit!" exclaimed Sergeant Whalen. "Where the hell did that come from?" He peeked over the pile of rubble he now shared for cover and took a look towards the town square. His eyes narrowed and he looked back in Sutherland's direction. "You guys were all tucked in here while the Krauts set up a machine gun position in that bell tower. It's looking right down on us now!"

Now Bill felt nauseated. In his mind he reviewed his rationale for staying where he was, and his reasoning still seemed sound. While sure he had not erred, he could not shake the feeling that Whalen's criticisms might have some justification. The sounds of more grenades echoed down the street.

"Jesus," said Sergeant Whalen. "We've got to get into better position." He leaned back behind cover and removed his helmet momentarily to mop sweat from his brow. "Friesen, you come with me. We're going to get ourselves up closer to the action." Whalen worked the action of his rifle and checked his belt for more ammunition as he spoke. "Sutherland, you and Ender can stay back here in your precious hideout." He flashed a sarcastic smile at Sutherland. "And cover us as we advance. If any Germans try to move forward in support across the square, you should be able to harass them from here." He nodded to each of the men, and then grabbed Friesen's shoulder.

"Ready?" Friesen nodded and the two of them sprinted across the open ground towards their next cover.

Sutherland and Ender had been tasked with firing at enemy positions, but Bill realized he had no idea where those positions were. Ender was diligently discharging his rifle at an open window that could possibly hold enemy soldiers, but as the machine gun that fired in their direction earlier now declined a second opportunity, its position remained occult. Looking towards the steeple across the town square, Sutherland fired twice at the weather vane on its summit. While his fire could not possibly do any useful damage, at least Friesen and Whalen would have the comforting sound of supporting fire to their rear.

After firing, Bill leaned closer against his cover and hid almost entirely behind the pile of debris. Ender was still diligently watching the town square for signs of enemy soldiers, but Bill doubted they would emerge. He suspected they had already caused the havoc they had intended and then invisibly withdrawn, since that had been their disciplined pattern for the last two or three days.

Ender's eyes darted back towards Sutherland with a look of disapproval, a look of which Bill would not have thought Ender capable. Sutherland voiced the explanation that had been circling in his mind in answer to Ender's silent look.

"The sergeant told us to get up to that corner and wait for him. If we had gone charging ahead, he wouldn't have known where we were."

"I know." Ender turned his eyes back to his job of careful surveillance.

Bill wished he had another cigarette. He had lost the one that Ender had given him when they had run for cover. Now he felt frustrated. As more sounds of nearby combat resonated in their direction, Bill became aware of what a useless position they had occupied. He could not see where Whalen and Friesen had gone, because they had rounded a corner towards the fighting. Minutes passed. Bill thought of asking Ender for another cigarette but stopped himself, remembering Ender's aura of disapproval. He focused on Ender's face, the skin so young that it had hardly yet needed a razor, but rather than the innocence of youth, he could sense only the blame that oozed in his direction, as though through the younger man's pores.

As he looked back towards the steeple holding Ender's rapt

attention, he noticed the sun starting to set in the west. As shadows began to cast across the street, the sounds of nearby battle reached a crescendo. Whalen's voice could be heard barking instructions and then the sound of more grenades ripped through the evening air. The machine gun that had pinned them came to life again in a window on the church steeple. This time its fire was in the direction of the hotly contested building on the right, and now its muzzle flashes made its location obvious. Ender and Sutherland each fired careful shots in its direction, but its crew was well covered in the old stone edifice. Its fire may have had the desired effect, because cries of a wounded Canadian soldier could now be heard. They aroused a new intensity in Private Ender.

"We've got to get up there and help the sergeant!" Ender reloaded his rifle and made ready to run in the direction Whalen had gone.

"No!" snapped Sutherland. "Sit tight. The sergeant told us to stay here so that we could keep the square covered. We should be pressuring that machine gun."

"They're in trouble up there and we're entirely out of the battle," answered Ender. "Anyone can tell that they need help. I'm not going to stay back here like a coward!" He looked at the ground as he finished, but the implication was obvious. Bill calmed himself before answering.

"Look, Ender. We're pinned down here. That machine gun has us in its sights."

"The machine gun has better targets. Nobody has been bothering to shoot at us lately, because we're not even in the fight. I'm going." He gestured with his head to encourage Sutherland to come with him, but there was no doubt by Sutherland's crouched stance that he was not about to run anywhere.

Sutherland thought of turning to fire at the steeple but found he was just staring dumbly at his young colleague. Ender tensed his muscles and launched out from behind their cover. He had not even taken his second step when fire from the machine gun raked across the rubble and violently tore the life from his lungs. The machine gun's bullets ripped the already demolished building and sent chips of stone bouncing off Sutherland's helmet. Still in disbelief this had happened so suddenly at his side, Bill licked his dry, chapped lips and tasted Ender's blood where it had splashed on his face. His legs buckled under him and he slumped against the rubble, unable even to sit himself in a position that would allow him to face the enemy. Shadows continued to spread across the street and their fingers pawed at Ender's lifeless form when the sound of the machine gun again screamed out. More bullets splashed into the cobblestones around Ender's corpse and some tore off pieces of his flesh. Bill watched in horror, wishing that the machine gun crew would stop, but could not drag his eyes away from the large youthful body's mutilation. When the bullets finally stopped, he turned and vomited.

Darkness seemed to arrive quickly, and Bill wished the recent hours had been spent searching for a suitable sleeping place rather than fighting a battle. He did not know how many minutes or hours had passed when he noticed that the sounds of battle had died away. He was clutching a piece of stone in his hand and turning it round and round. He wondered why in near total darkness objects seemed to take on a blue hue, noticing that Ender's blood on the ground at his feet looked black as coal. He no longer perceived the smell of the blood that was such an affront to his nostrils earlier. Fascinated for a while with his changing sensation of sights and smells, the cries of an injured soldier from the contested building reached his ears. Sutherland sat up slightly, carefully remaining behind cover. The moans continued.

Bill returned to staring at his piece of stone, but a profound fatigue hit him. It had been some time since he had had a reasonable night's sleep. With the battle dead around him, his body made a claim for rest. He dropped the stone to the ground and sleep washed over his body like dipping into a warm lake. He laid his head against a piece of timber and felt relaxation embrace his feet and legs. When it reached his eyes he let go of wakefulness and slipped in.

The wounded man's cries pulled him back. Moans and whimpers emanated from the burnt out battlefield and woke William Sutherland of 6th Brigade, 2nd Canadian Infantry Division. For a fleeting moment Bill thought of running over to help the wounded man, but as he raised his head slightly to look in the direction from which the cries came, those thoughts came to an end. The sound of the machine gun screamed out into the now silent night air as it lashed supersonic metal towards Bill's cover. His breath quickened and he wondered how the German crew had seen the top of his head in this near total darkness. He clutched his rifle tight and stayed down behind his cover.

Now the wounded man's cries goaded him. He could neither offer assistance nor ignore their pleas. A sense of helplessness fell over him like a heavy, constricting blanket. His desperate feeling of wanting to help was tempered by his clear inability to do so. He felt a certain relief he was in no position to run out and try to save the day, but that relief left him with an uncomfortable guilt that gnawed at his stomach and pushed bitter bile into his throat.

He listened carefully but could not make sense of the cries. They sounded like English. Did that mean that the battle was won by Canada and only one brave wounded soul was left to claim their prize of a nondescript French building? Perhaps. Or perhaps the Germans had tactically withdrawn, leaving only dead Canadians and a single wounded man in their wake. Bill puzzled for a moment as he realized that until now he had not thought of matters of victory or defeat in this battle. Ironically, now he had considered them, he realized that he could not easily tell the difference whether they were winning or losing their battles for these cities. If they captured the city, he supposed they had won, but what did it mean when the Germans left Canadian casualties in their wake, but escaped unscathed themselves?

Bill's body relaxed and demanded sleep. He was comfortable enough with his timber for a pillow, and fatigue was becoming physically painful. More cries from the wounded man were all that kept him awake. He continued in that state for hours. The sun could not yet be seen on the eastern horizon, but Bill was sure that morning was approaching and still the man wailed. Bill could stand it no longer. He yelled in the direction of the cries.

"Shut up!" But the man's desperate cries continued. Bill's voice deteriorated to a quiet whine. "I need to get some sleep, would you shut up?" The cries went on.

Bill's body kept screaming at him for sleep. Having not left his cover during the many hours since the battle began, he stood up into the night air and fired a shot in the direction of the wounded man's cries. He was not sure where they came from, and had he taken time to think, he would have realized he was likely not even in a line of sight to the building from which they came. Amazingly though, the cries stopped after his blind shot in their direction. Bill fell back to the ground and laid his head down. Sleep snatched him immediately.

He awoke a short time later with the morning sun searing his eyelids. His body trembled after being taunted with such a short respite. Still there were no sounds of combat. The sounds of the wounded man also remained absent. He looked around and saw no one. While the barrel of a heavy German machine gun had so recently covered him, he somehow knew that the machine gunners had long since left their position. He stood up and surveyed the scene. No shots were fired as he emerged from his cover and revealed himself to the world. The Germans had silently left in the night. Sutherland looked back at the nook in the rubble where he had been hidden all through the battle and all through the night. There was a pool of drying urine where he had relieved himself, so he kicked dust over it, some of which blew onto Ender's lifeless form. Bill quickly turned away.

He began to search for other soldiers of his unit and thought of walking to the scene of the night's battle. Perhaps he could learn who that wounded man had been. He chose instead to walk in the opposite direction, and met soldiers of a different platoon. It turned out that he was one of his platoon's few survivors.

He never truly believed that his random rifle shot had killed his fellow soldier, but as years passed he revisited that night in his dreams many times. While he had spent the night believing that he could not comprehend the man's cries, he later knew with certainty on some level he had understood. From behind his cover, he had spent the night listening to the sounds of a dying man, alone and far from home, crying for his mother.

Chapter 13

The man's pain was evident at a glance, but even more so was the fact that he was nervous about his abdomen being touched. Darren sensed the unease and very gently pushed his hand against his patient's belly. The man winced as Darren touched him, but almost jumped from the bed with a howl of pain when the hand was pulled away. Dr. Johnston had learned what he needed to know. He apologized to the man for the necessary suffering he had inflicted and turned to the nurse who was watching intently over his shoulder.

"Would you please order a set of abdominal X-rays? We'll need to get them done portably up here." She promptly turned to execute his instructions. As she left, he added, "We'll need them stat." The Latin word for "instantly" rarely truly applied to the way things happened in a hospital, but was thrown around liberally and optimistically.

Darren strode confidently out of the room, assuring the man that his condition would be promptly dealt with, and made his way to the patient's chart where he wrote a note and requested some blood work. Although he felt constantly in a state of near exhaustion, the many nights he had recently spent in hospital gave him a much greater sense of confidence in dealing with sick patients. Mr Howland, the man he just examined, had arrived in hospital several days earlier with an exacerbation of his emphysema. His shortness of breath was now improving, and earlier in the day he was deemed, "Ready to go home tomorrow." Unfortunately, this afternoon he had developed abdominal pain that had worsened for several hours, and while weeks ago Darren might have been nervous about managing this new problem himself, he now felt that he had things well in hand. The man's abdomen was definitely painful and his history suggested he was at risk for peptic ulcer disease. His physical examination suggested a surgical abdomen that would need attention. A less experienced Darren Johnston might have called the surgery residents in a panic at this point, but he now knew that they would inevitably need more information. Mr Howland's blood pressure and heart rate were stable, so taking the time to obtain X-rays and important blood work would help the surgeons, when they arrived, decide what needed to happen next. Obtaining the information now would help save them time.

Darren looked at his watch and realized that it was nine o'clock and he had not stopped for dinner. There were no patients waiting for him in the Emergency Department, so he decided it would be a good time to grab a bite to eat while awaiting Mr Howland's results. The residents' lounge was on the far side of the hospital, so Darren spent several minutes on his way there before his pager rang. He answered the call from a house phone in the hallway.

"Johnston."

"Hi, Darren. It's Unit 62 calling. Just letting you know that Mr Howland's X-ray is done and on its way to processing."

"Wow, that was fast!"

"The X-ray team were doing a film on 63 when we called, so they came right over."

"Thanks." Darren hung up the phone and decided to delay dinner a little further. Everything was falling into place quickly with this patient, so he imagined that he would quickly have Mr Howland off to surgery and then he could relax and enjoy his dinner. He turned to the nearest stairwell and walked downstairs to the radiology department, then waited a few minutes for the portable X-ray to arrive, and watched the technicians develop the film. He took the hard copy, still warm, out of the developer and put it on a nearby view box. His suspicions were confirmed. Sure enough, the film showed free air in the man's abdomen. Normally there is no way for air to enter the abdominal cavity, so its presence indicates that there must be a rupture of the bowels, which do contain air, and Darren suspected that this rupture was from a perforated ulcer. He had no doubt that Mr Howland would continue to get sicker in the upcoming hours, so he decided that he would call the surgical team before waiting for the blood work. The X-ray was evidence enough that the man needed surgery quickly.

Darren returned to the ward where Mr Howland was suffering and made sure that adequate painkillers were ordered, then, with the chart in front of him so that he would have all the necessary information at hand, he paged the surgery resident. While he waited for his surgical colleague to answer his call, the nurses on the ward offered him a chocolate, which he accepted gratefully. He again became aware that he had not eaten since lunch, as he enjoyed the candy and watched the telephone. Twenty minutes went by before he decided that he had better try calling the surgery resident again. He telephoned the surgical suite and learned that the two night time operating rooms were functioning at full capacity because there had been a motor vehicle trauma somewhere nearby. The surgery resident and attending surgeon were both in the middle of a case. Darren left his number and asked to be called as soon as someone was scrubbed out.

His feeling of confidence began to wane. Just minutes before he had been satisfied with the notion that he had addressed Mr Howland's problem, made a diagnosis, and decided on the management, but now the necessary management, surgery, was not immediately available to him. He returned to Mr Howland's bedside and found the patient looking a little worse. Despite painkillers, Mr Howland was in acute distress. He was looking pale and starting to breath harder. His vital signs were still stable, so Darren decided he could wait until the surgical team assessed him. Hoping to get their call soon, Darren started to make his way back to the lounge to get his dinner.

After making his second trip across the hospital, Darren was greeted in the lounge by the sound of cheering and hollering by Chris, who was once again covering the Intensive Care Unit.

"What's going on?" Darren made his way to the refrigerator.

"See for yourself!" Chris, his white coat draped over a nearby chair and his stethoscope discarded on the floor nearby, had made himself very comfortable on the couch. His feet were rested on the coffee table and he brandished a remote control with his eyes fixed intently on the television screen.

Darren turned to see for himself, and saw that the focus of Chris's interest was a beauty pageant of some kind that was being televised. "You're covering the ICU and this is the best thing you've got to do with your time?" Darren laughed as he pulled his frozen dinner from the fridge.

"I just have two things to say about that." Chris paused to jeer again as a contestant modeled a swimsuit. "The first is that the ICU has been really quiet tonight, so I'm taking advantage of an opportunity for a much needed rest. The second is that this is a fabulous way to spend my time. Besides, what are you complaining about? You seem to have time to eat dinner. Although I can't say it looks all that appetizing." He gestured at the frozen dinner that Darren was now reheating in the microwave.

"Are you kidding? What makes you think this stuff isn't fabulous?" Darren removed the plastic-wrapped package from the microwave and then rapidly tossed it from one hand to the other to avoid being burned. "Besides, I'm only taking a momentary break between looking after a guy crashing on the ward and trying to get a hold of surgery."

"Good luck with that," said Chris. "By the number of patients they have us alerted to in the operating room, I'd say that they're pretty tied up."

Darren kicked at discarded napkins on the floor on his way to the coffee table and got ready to sit beside Chris, when his pager rang. He went to the phone and was informed that Mr Howland's blood pressure was dropping. He left his dinner and the sounds of

Chris further cheering on the pageant to hurry back to the ward. He hoped intensely the situation was not too bad so he could get back to his lukewarm dinner. As he hurried up the stairs, Darren mentally scolded himself for not ordering a lipase level – the test for damage to the pancreas, which can happen when an ulcer perforates. Darren mentally scolded himself before arriving on the ward. He asked the unit clerk at the desk to add the lipase level to the blood work that had already been drawn as he turned a sharp corner into Mr Howland's room. Mr Howland's nurse was busy taking his blood pressure.

"I'm just repeating the B.P., Dr Johnston."

"Thanks." Darren stood in the doorway and thought about dinner as she finished. He noticed that Mr Howland was looking a little paler and was breathing even faster.

"It's 125/82. We called because it had dropped to 90/55, but it seems to have come back up. In the meantime, his temperature has gone up and he looks a lot worse."

Darren strode across the room and felt Mr Howland's forehead, then checked his pulse. Sure enough, he felt like he was on fire and his pulse was racing. Darren felt increasingly uncomfortable because he had already called surgery and was not sure what he should do next.

"I guess we should cover him with antibiotics to prevent infection. And why don't we increase his IV rate to 250cc/hour?" Darren checked the dose in his pocket manual and ordered the medications. The nurse looked to Mr Howland's arm.

"We only have the one IV. Do you think that's okay?"

A chill ran through Darren. His earlier feeling of control had fled. He could not believe he had gone for dinner while a patient who was becoming unstable had only one tiny IV in his arm. Mr Howland should have had at least two large IV's in case he needed emergency transfusions.

"Would you put in a second one, please?" Darren tried to maintain a calm exterior, but his skin was crawling. First he forgot the lipase, and then he left a patient with inadequate intravenous access. He could not believe they left him alone in the hospital. Meanwhile, he could still not get hold of the surgical team. He stood with a blank look on his face for several seconds until he realized that the nurse was looking in his direction and waiting for him to say something. He just turned around and walked out of the room, hoping that he maintained an air of competence.

Darren walked slowly back to the residents' lounge, no longer sure if the gnawing sensation in his gut was hunger or guilt at his poor performance. His pager rang and he felt like curling into the fetal position on the floor. When he checked the number he saw it was his home number. Courtney was trying to call him. As he re-entered the residents' lounge, he was not greatly impressed by the raucous sounds of laughter still emanating from the neighbourhood of the television set.

"That was great!" spouted Chris. "You should have seen this contestant, Darren. She said that she wanted to cure world hunger by …" he paused as he got a better look at his colleague. "Why are you looking so glum?"

"Oh, I've just got this patient upstairs who's getting sicker and sicker, and I keep screwing up."

"What happened?"

"Well this guy came in with crappy lungs, but today he developed an acute abdomen with free air under the diaphragm. He's getting unstable. So I called surgery, but they haven't called me back yet. I can't believe it – I didn't even order a lipase."

As Darren paused, Chris stared silently. He turned his head towards the television and smiled in appreciation of one of the contestants and then returned his attention to Darren, his face serious again. He waited another moment, as though expecting Darren to continue, then spoke quietly but forcefully.

"That's what you did? You forgot to get a lipase? What the hell does it matter what his lipase is? Tell me this. If his lipase was normal, what would you do?"

"I guess I'd just keep waiting for surgery."

"Okay. What would you do if his lipase was high?"

"Well, that could indicate pancreatitis. In this case, I'd say it was from his ruptured ulcer." As Darren carefully phrased his response, Chris gestured for him to hurry up, his body language indicating that he wanted to his attention to the television. "So I guess I would just have to wait for surgery."

"Fine," said Chris, looking exasperated. "So it sounds like that little blunder didn't exactly cost any lives."

"That's not all, though." Chris's eyebrows rose as Darren continued. "I didn't even make sure he had enough IV access!"

Chris only grinned. "Do you want me to help you put in a central line? Then he'd have a ton of access. Why don't we go up and thread his jugular?" Chris's expression turned into one of excitement at the prospect of carrying out an invasive procedure. Now Darren was exasperated. Chris had not even blinked at the mistakes he had made.

"No, I don't want to put a line in him."

"Why not? Maybe it would cheer you up."

"I don't want to put a line into him because he doesn't need a central line!" Darren stood up and looked down at Chris. It was not difficult because Chris was slouched so low in his chair. "The patient doesn't need a central line," Darren repeated. "What the patient needs is to go to the operating room!"

Chris looked away from Darren for a moment and reached for a can of root beer on the coffee table. He picked it up and adjusted his straw, then took a long drink before he spoke. Darren's anger was rising.

"Do you want to do the surgery?"

Now Darren was furious. All Chris wanted to do was ask foolish questions while someone's life was at stake. Darren spoke slowly and in measured tones for fear that he would start screaming if he lost control. "No I don't want to do the surgery, because I am not a surgeon. I have called the surgical team, but they have not gotten back to me. That's what I just told you."

The two of them stared silently at each other for a moment. Chris took another drink from his straw, and after a moment the sound of the straw sucking against the bottom of an empty can filled the room. He set down the drink and then returned his gaze to Darren. A wide smile illuminated his face. "Well, there you go! You're living the dream!"

"What's that supposed to mean?" Darren was on the verge of losing control again.

"The guy needs surgery. You can't do it. You have to wait for the surgical team. It doesn't matter what his lipase is or how many IVs he's got. He needs to go to the OR. You have nothing to get excited about. Now, if you wanted to put a central line into him, then you'd have something to get excited about. You'd have to put in the line. But as it stands, all you can do is wait for surgery, so you're living the dream. You can sit down here, enjoy your dinner, and watch the lovely ladies strut their stuff on TV." He gestured to the television, but frowned. A commercial was on.

Darren's anger faded, but the overwhelming sense of powerlessness did not. His shoulders visibly sagged as he asked, "Why the hell won't the surgery resident call me back?"

"The surgery resident is in the OR with a trauma." Chris paused and Darren slumped into his seat. "She's busy, so what can you do? Enjoy the show." Chris picked up his pop can again but grimaced when he remembered it was empty. His eyes returned to the television and he slouched even lower in his chair.

Darren stood still for a moment. Unable to relax to the same extent as Chris, he did muster enough calm to take a seat by his dinner that had been left on the table. He took a bite and found that it was cold. On his way to the microwave oven, his pager rang. He set his dinner down again and hurried to the phone. To his relief, it was the surgical resident, Dr Berry. She apologized for the delay and he gave her a summary of the patient's problems. She asked where she could find the patient. Darren checked the list in his pocket for Mr Howland's name, and she was on her way.

Darren hurried out of the seat to leave for the ward.

"Where are you rushing off to now?" asked Chris.

"That was surgery. She's on her way to look at my guy with the perforation."

"Does she need your help?" Chris was rummaging through his pocket looking for change to buy another pop as he spoke.

"No, but I just want to see what she has to say."

"Eat your dinner first, man." Chris paused and smiled as he removed a quarter from his pocket, then winked in Darren's direction. "You'll be much easier to get along with if you've eaten." Darren grudgingly took his seat again and wolfed down his dinner, still cold. Then he hurried towards the door. As he passed the pop machine on his way out, Chris called to him.

"Hey, would you grab me a root beer?" He threw change, one coin at a time in Darren's direction. On catching the third coin, Darren responded.

"How can you cover the ICU if you're too damned lazy to get out of your chair for a drink? Have you left that couch all evening?" Darren put the coins into the machine and punched the button for root beer. As he pulled the can from its slot, Chris answered: "The last time you left here, I had to run up to the Unit and intubate someone. I hurried back down because I didn't want to miss any important action on TV."

Darren just stared at Chris for a moment, wondering if he could be serious. The last time Darren had left the lounge, he had only been gone for a few minutes. Now Chris was telling him that he had run to the Intensive Care Unit and put a tube in someone's throat to help her breathe, while she must have been in severe distress to require that treatment, but not only had Chris made it back to the lounge during the course of a commercial break, he had regained his semblance of complete calm as though he had never been interrupted.

Darren did not say anything, but a questioning look must have been written all over his face, because Chris chose to explain.

"What can I say? I'm a machine."

Darren tossed Chris his pop and left for the ward. When he arrived, a resident he presumed to be Dr. Berry was talking on the telephone. He looked towards her nametag in the hopes of catching her first name, but it was behind the lapel of her white coat. She was apparently on hold because she kept the telephone cradled between her chin and shoulder as she reached her arm out to shake Darren's hand.

"Hi, Darren? I guess I talked to you on the phone."

"Hi."

"I'm Veronica Berry, the surgery resident." She did not look like the stereotype of a surgeon. While laypeople might immediately think of a confident elderly Caucasian man when asked to picture a surgeon, Darren's personal surgeon gestalt reflected the group of people who had most intimidated him during medical school. The last female surgeon with whom he had worked had acted as though she might break him in half at any moment, and had looked as though she could. Perhaps the new breed, the female surgeons, had only survived a male-dominated specialty by being tougher than their superiors. Perhaps only the most intensely driven women would try to enter a field where decisions must be made immediately, without hesitation, and with lives at stake. Perhaps the intense responsibility, pressure and sleep deprivation had an especially hardening influence on women. Perhaps Darren did not care either way, so long as he could avoid their wrath.

"I took a quick look at your patient," Veronica gestured towards Mr Howland's room. She was a short, slender young woman with dark hair that was folded into her operating room cap. Her demeanour was not physically intimidating, and she already seemed socially pleasant, particularly for someone who had no doubt been working flat-out in the operating room since six in the morning. Darren found her quite lovely, even in operating room scrubs, which are not flattering. She wore no makeup, likely because she had to wake up at four-thirty in the morning to be at surgical rounds on time, but she possessed a natural beauty.

"I'm just talking to the attending surgeon on call. He's answering another page at the moment." She gestured to the phone as she spoke. She looked as though she might continue speaking, but paused as the surgeon came on the line. "Hi, Dr Steen ... Yes, that was my impression ... Sure, I'll ask." She looked in Darren's direction and covered the phone with her hand. "Darren, who is the internist in charge of Mr Howland's care?"

"Dr Jenkins." Darren had not felt so comfortable all night. Finally someone was going to take over Mr Howland's care and he could stop worrying.

"Yes, Dr Steen? It's Dr Jenkins ... Okay, I'll wait for you to call me back." She hung up the telephone and looked back towards Darren. "Dr Steen wants to talk with Dr Jenkins directly about Mr Howland's other medical conditions. You said he has emphysema, right?"

"That's right," answered Darren. He was enjoying talking with Veronica. The way she smiled as she spoke was warm and charming. "I guess I'll go check on him again."

They walked into Mr Howland's room together and found him still breathing rapidly. He did not look as uncomfortable as before, because he had taken more painkillers, but he still looked septic.

"His abdomen is still pretty rigid, even though he has had morphine," said Veronica as she touched Mr Howland's abdomen. I think you're right that this is a perforated duodenal ulcer." She nodded and smiled again. Darren beamed at her praise, and his new sense of freedom at relinquishing responsibility for this clearly surgical case augmented. The phone rang at the nursing desk, so they left the room together. The charge nurse had answered the telephone and held the receiver in Veronica's direction.

"You were waiting for a call from Dr Steen?"

"That's right, thank you." She took the telephone from the nurse. "Yes, Dr Steen ... Okay, I understand. The medicine resident is here with me now. I'll let him know. Bye." She hung up and turned to Darren. "Dr Steen and Dr Jenkins agree that Mr Howland's emphysema makes him too much of an operative risk. Dr Jenkins wants you to continue with the antibiotics and morphine, and we'll just have to see how he heals up on his own."

Darren had smiled slightly as Veronica began speaking to him, but his smile was rapidly fading. He had been desperate to get Mr Howland off to surgery; now he was stuck looking after this critical patient all night with nothing he could really do to help. He was still looking in Veronica's direction, but his eyes had focused into the distance, as he comprehended the mess he was in. A second later, upon regaining conscious thought, he found himself focused on a bulletin board on the wall behind Veronica. A large poster with a picture of a smiling nurse washing her hands read, "YOU can help prevent the spread of antibiotic resistant bacteria."

Darren regained his concentration as Veronica continued speaking. "Wow, I've got an hour before I have to be back in the OR. I should grab some dinner. Maybe this would be lunch, because I missed that too. Nice meeting you, Darren." As she turned away, she pulled off her operating room cap and her long dark hair spilled out over her shoulders. She turned back towards him where he stood silently watching her leave. She smiled. An awkward smile formed in return on his lips and he kept staring in her direction until she turned the corner into the stark white hospital corridor that led towards the stairs. A patient was seated in the hall where he could be seen from the nursing desk. Perhaps the patient had been unsafe to leave alone in his room, but now his chin rested against his chest and he snored loudly. The sound was a harsh contrast to the corridor otherwise deprived of sensory stimuli.

Darren felt so deflated that he could not imagine feeling worse, until the next thought crossed his mind as Veronica left his line of sight. "Oh, shit! Courtney paged me over an hour ago and I never called her back." He looked at his watch and the time was eleven-thirty.

He was busy wondering whether he should call Courtney back at this hour or talk to her in the morning when a voice from over his shoulder asked: "So what are we doing with Mr Howland?" Darren turned and saw the charge nurse holding a clipboard and awaiting his response. His body had all the will of a wet noodle to stand up straight since hearing that Mr Howland was not going for surgery, so the nurse seemed to tower over him even though he was four inches taller than her.

"I guess nothing."

"His breathing is very fast," she replied, as though that summed up the whole problem.

"I know," said Darren, "but the directive comes from higher up than me." He felt sure that this brief explanation of his troubles would satisfy her, but had no such luck.

"So what are you going to do about his breathing?"

"I don't know." Darren was out of ideas. "Let's give him some more morphine. Maybe his breathing will settle down if he's more comfortable." He took Mr Howland's chart and wrote that notion in the form of a medical order, then began to leave the ward. He felt sure that there was something else he should be doing for the patient, and even thought of going to ask Chris's advice. Although Chris was consistently either annoying or obnoxious, he certainly seemed to have all the answers. The most ridiculous things he said always turned out to be the most true.

On his way back to the lounge, Darren remembered again that he had to return Courtney's call. He had once before made the erroneous decision to hold off calling her until morning, and had regretted it ever since. Halfway through his journey, he saw a nursing station that seemed fairly inactive and went to use their phone.

Courtney was still awake when he called. "Oh, hi, I'm glad you called back. Listen, I was thinking today about repainting the hallway, so I thought I'd ask you what colours you like best. If you had a few minutes, I also wanted to talk to you about something really interesting I read today."

Darren had trouble paying attention because Mr Howland was still on his mind. He remembered Chris telling him there was no point in worrying if you have already done everything you can, but he was not confident he was not missing anything. The sensation continued nagging at him until his pager went off.

"Oh, damn."

"What is it?" He had interrupted Courtney in mid-sentence.

"I just got a page from Emergency. I'm sure there's a patient down there for me to admit."

"Okay. Will you think about what I asked until I see you tomorrow?"

"Sure, goodnight. I love you," he replied, hoping that he could remember what it was he was supposed to think about.

Down in the Emergency Room he was fifteen minutes into taking a history from his newest patient when he got a page from the ward.

"Hi, this is Cindy on Unit 62. I just came on shift and I'm looking after Mr Howland. He seems to be breathing very quickly."

"I know," answered Darren. An awkward pause followed, with neither participant in the conversation having anything further to add. Darren had nothing more to say. Once again he had lost the battle.

Chapter 14

The following morning, as Darren bought himself an unappetizing Danish and a cup of watery coffee, he contemplated the continuous string of discomfiting nights on call and gruelling post-call mornings that had led him to this day. Ironically, he found he no longer relished the thought of going home. He knew when he saw Courtney again there would be another confrontation regarding his constant absence. He emptied some change from his pockets at the cashier's desk and then rubbed his tired eyes before quietly walking to the ward. On his way upstairs in the elevator, he cradled the coffee between his hands and quietly sipped. Looking down at his drink seemed to protect his thoughts from the people crowded around him in the elevator car, but he felt as though they would all sense his dismay if he so much as looked in their direction. When he did raise his eyes momentarily, he found himself looking at the back of a short man's head. The man wore hospital scrubs, but from behind it was difficult to tell what his job might be. Above him, a sign proclaimed a maximum number of occupants for the car. Darren could feel the weight of people behind him, but did not want to turn his head and count.

Darren continued to slowly sip his hot coffee as he walked onto the ward, turning his head slightly back and forth to look into the open doors of patients' rooms as he navigated the corridor. He was in mid sip as he saw something that surprised him. Mrs Doering was seated at the side of her husband's bed. It was no surprise that she should be there. In fact she had spent many hours there every day since her husband's admission. The surprise was Mr Doering.

It took Darren only a moment to see the change. Although he had not spoken a word, something about Mr Doering's demeanour announced he was thinking more clearly. While Mr Doering had recently recovered from a state of delirium, something had remained that was still not right about him. Darren almost spat out his mouthful of coffee, so unexpected was this pleasant turn of events.

At the time it was not evident to Darren exactly what visual cues led him to the diagnosis of recovered sanity, but had he paused to contemplate, he would have been able to identify several points. First, Mr Doering was sitting up straight in bed. Until this time Darren had always seen him in a dishevelled state with the bedclothes tangled about him like a hungry constrictor snake hoping to starve him of oxygen. Furthermore, his hospital gown was adorned with a housecoat, obviously brought from home, which had been carefully fastened about his waist. Perhaps more obvious was the fact that he was reading a newspaper. The Kurt Doering Darren had known until now would certainly not have been in a state to read the newspaper with any insightful comprehension; in fact, he would have been unlikely to think of faking it. Finally, Mr Doering's breakfast tray was neatly put away on his bedside table, with the cutlery carefully stashed under a plate cover. This had been the work of a man with some quiet dignity, a virtue that Mr Doering's illness had heretofore robbed him of.

Junior medical students have an incredible ability to miss simple cues and physical findings like these. People spend their lives learning how to be socially appropriate, but doctors must relearn the way they see other people. An obvious deformity is often missed in a novice's report of a physical examination, since the trainee has learned not to comment on such things. They feel foolish when it is pointed out, and think: "I knew that was there. Why didn't I say anything?" A couple who spent an evening in a restaurant studiously avoiding the gaze of a man in a tin-foil hat talking to himself at the window might not recall the disruption if asked whether their meal was remarkable. Was the confused and unkempt person on a downtown street homeless or lost? Maybe they were just drunk. Maybe they were lapsing into a diabetic coma. Darren had spent his whole life learning to not notice things, but could now be proud that after four years of medical school he could step outside of polite society.

"Good Morning, Dr Johnston," Mrs Doering called out to the hallway. "Kurt is much better today! He does not remember very much of what you told him before, so I hope that you can explain things for him, because I have not been so good at remembering the details you told me."

When Darren entered the room, Mr Doering extended his hand in Darren's direction. "Dr Johnston," Kurt nodded his head politely and gripped Darren's hand in a firm, confident grasp, "I hope you will excuse me for not feeling as though we have formally been introduced until now. The last few days are fairly hazy to me."

Darren smiled and returned the handshake. He did not feel it necessary to tell Mr Doering just at the moment he had in fact been hospitalized for over two weeks. Nor did he feel it necessary to elaborate on the many silent battles he and the rest of Dr Smith's team had fought on the chart and in the laboratory reports against Kurt's many and serious electrolyte abnormalities. The abnormalities had only resolved completely in the last few days. Mr Doering's level of consciousness had apparently been close behind in its improvement.

Now Darren found himself the focus of questioning glances from the Doerings. No doubt he would be expected to provide a brief synopsis of Kurt Doering's medical issues and progress to date. Far from feeling frustrated at having to explain Kurt's medical problems again, he was enthusiastic to have a more sensible audience. Unfortunately, he found himself suddenly at a loss for words, his sleep-deprived brain fumbling for the details that he knew were in the chart. It was further down the corridor at the nursing station, so he decided to give it his best shot.

"Mr Doering, by now I am sure that your wife has informed you that you have lung cancer." He paused and stumbled in his speech for a moment. Mr Doering's eyes were focused on him with a severe concentration. He tried to elaborate. "You see, your bronchoscopy showed a neoplasm with undifferentiated cells suggestive of ..." he realized that he had fumbled his way into "med speak", and had likely stopped making any sense to the Doerings. Latin root words are powerful tools for professionals to communicate because they can be used to describe diseases or treatments in detailed and unambiguous terms. The precise language of medicine is as useless as Swahili, however, to someone who does not speak it. The term "water on the lungs" is a wonderfully descriptive phrase that patients can visualize, but is useless among doctors, for whom it could describe any of several pathologic conditions. The term "cardiogenic pulmonary edema" fares no better when describing to a retired carpenter why he is short of breath.

Mr Doering's intense gaze remained on Darren. At the word "cancer" Mr Doering's eyebrows had raised slightly, but he had otherwise remained immobile. Darren found himself still struggling for words. "What I mean, is that the diagnosis is fairly certain and all that is left for us to do is to resolve your remaining biochemical abnormalities and consider palliation." Darren winced inside. That had been awful. He was not sure exactly what useful information he had conveyed, but he waited for Kurt to respond.

Kurt gently set down his newspaper before swinging his gaze back up to meet his doctor's. He had not looked towards his wife who was reaching a supportive hand in his direction. He licked his lips and then began loudly. "Well, this is the first I have heard of this! What have I been doing in hospital all this time if all you can do is tell me these ridiculous speculations?"

Darren's heart sank. For a moment he had believed that the new and oriented Mr Doering might take a reasonable approach to his illness, but he was just as irrational. His only improvement was in his diction, articulating his unreasonable complaints. Mr

Doering's tirade continued. "How on earth would I have gotten cancer in my lungs?"

Darren was at least reassured that this was a question he could answer. "Well, Mr Doering, the main risk factor for lung cancer would be your smoking." Darren was immediately sorry he had chosen that moment to answer. The stern look in Mr Doering's eyes evolved into rage.

"You don't know what you are talking about! I've read on this subject, and doctors do not have one solid piece of evidence that smoking causes cancer." As he continued to rail against Darren, his wife tried to calm him, but was too timid to catch his attention. Darren felt the need to make a tactical retreat.

"Why don't I give you a few minutes to absorb this news? I'll see you a little later to answer any questions you have." Darren turned an about-face and exited the room. Mr Doering was still bitterly complaining but Darren could not muster the energy to understand what he was saying.

What the hell is his excuse for being a jerk now that he's not even confused anymore? Darren asked himself.

He walked to the back room of the nursing station where he could review the charts on his patients before going to see them, and found Eddy Bofors hard at work, perched over a pile of his own charts.

"Having a rough morning?" asked the radiology resident as Darren entered.

"You could say that." Darren looked around as he suddenly wondered where he had put down his cup of coffee. "I just had a run-in with Mr Doering."

"I heard," answered Eddy. "I could hear him from back here. He was pretty pissed off."

"Yeah. It's days like these I wonder why I ever wanted to do internal medicine."

"It's every day I wonder why you wanted to do internal medicine," answered Eddy. "I can hardly wait to get this year over with. Then it will be smooth sailing." Eddy leaned back in his chair, fantasizing of a happier time to come. "After my rotating year, I'll spend my days looking at people's X-rays. There will be no obnoxious patients wanting to yell at me, like your guy there." He gestured vaguely out the door in Kurt's general direction. "More importantly, there will be no body fluids to get spilled on me. No nurses to tell me that I'm doing everything wrong. No late nights by myself wondering if my patients will survive until morning."

"A lot of boring days in a dark room looking at pictures, though," Darren interrupted, thinking of dampening Eddy's enthusiasm.

"Boring days in the dark, you say?" Eddy acted horrified at the suggestion. "Let me show you something." He threw an empty doughnut box from the table into the trash and pushed his office chair off against the table to propel himself across the room. There, he reached from his seated position for a folder of X-rays. He carelessly knocked one of the many coats that were hung over the shelf that held the films. "I took a look at your lung cancer guy's films. What's his name?"

"Kurt Doering."

"That's right. Mr Doering." Eddy was leafing through the X-rays in search of the one he sought. When he found it, he removed it from its bag with a flourish, and placed it on a conveniently located view box that was on the wall of the back room. "What do you see?" Eddy turned back towards Darren and pointed to the chest X-ray.

The X-ray looked awful. Darren remembered it well from the middle of the night when he had admitted Mr Doering. He remembered knowing with a single glance at that X-ray that he would have to tell nice Mrs Doering that her husband had cancer. "I see a bunch of splotches all over his lungs. They're cancer." Eddy kept looking quietly in his direction. A questioning look crossed Eddy's face and Darren felt he had to justify his conclusion. "I could tell they were cancer, because that was consistent with his symptoms."

"Consistent with his symptoms!" Eddy repeated in a high-pitched sarcastic, mocking voice. "I guess that's the way an internal medicine guy has to look at the film: 'What might I see that would explain this guy's symptoms?' But in my dark room, do you know what I see when I look at this?" Darren shook his head and Eddy continued. "I see areas of tissue density surrounded by the lung's normal air-density. I see interfaces between air and water." Eddy spoke more quickly as he went on. He also spoke in a more confident voice than Darren had yet heard him use. He swung his hand back and forth across the film to draw attention to its highlights. "These are only shadows and borders but they have so much to say. Those 'splotches' are increased densities in the lung's parenchyma. What could they be? You see the fluid he has accumulated in his pleural space? Again it is only a shadow but it hints at inflammation. Put all of these findings together and the pieces of the puzzle fall into place." Darren's head was swimming. He did not want to go into a complex explanation of pathophysiology right now, he was too tired. As if on cue, Eddy's tone of voice mellowed. He spoke more slowly and more deliberately. His hands dropped to his sides. "It's all just shadows and borders, but it tells us so much. It's like appreciating a fabulous painting, but instead of an artist's impression of a possible universe, it is an inside look at life itself. An inside look that needs to be interpreted with all the tender nuances of a sonnet. It's beautiful."

Eddy definitely seemed to derive something deeper than Darren could about chest X-rays. Darren thought he could afford to learn a little more.

"Would you go over your technique for reading chest films with me some time?"

"Sure, what the hell," answered a suddenly more prosaic Dr. Bofors.

Darren found himself looking at Mr Doering's X-ray again. He could appreciate that a radiologist would see a lot more subtlety in a chest X-ray than he could, but beauty was not something he could appreciate here. All he saw was gross distortion of life's form that transformed normalcy into an ugly mess. Suddenly the sound of Eddy's head falling to the table in despair filled the room.

"What's the matter?" asked Darren.

"All this talk about radiology has just reminded me of how long I have to last until my radiology rotation starts."

"You only have a few weeks of medicine left, don't you?" asked Darren.

"Sure, but then I have to do two months of general surgery." Darren slumped into the chair behind him thinking of the horribly long hours that Eddy would have to endure, with work starting at six in the morning, and thirty-six hour shifts the rule rather than the exception. Eddy seemed to be thinking on a different tangent. "Cutting into people's abdomens is the most disgusting thing I have ever been a part of. I don't want to see that stuff!"

Darren laughed out loud at that, and Eddy raised his head off the table. "What's so funny?"

"Nothing. Good luck in surgery."

"Thanks. Did you want to go through this X-ray together for a few minutes now?" Darren looked back up at the X-ray, and was about to answer when Eddy interrupted him. "Actually, never mind. Your eyes are all bloodshot. We should do this some day at lunch when you're not so tired. I want you to get a full appreciation of my chosen field."

They finished their work in the back room, and then rounded quickly on their patients before Dr Smith arrived. On rounds with Dr Smith, sounds of Kurt Doering loudly making demands of a nurse emanated from his room as they approached. Kurt could be heard speaking angrily to his wife in the intermissions between his barks at the nursing staff.

"What's all that about?" Dr Smith gestured towards the door from the corridor.

"I talked to the Doerings about his diagnosis again," answered Darren. "I think this was the first time he understood what's going on, but he still didn't take it well."

"Fine." Dr Smith reviewed Mr Doering's much improved laboratory results in the hallway. His team of residents stood quietly next to him while a delirious elderly patient tied to her chair in the corridor quietly said: "Help, help me, help me." She did not turn her eyes towards any of the people in her immediate area. Darren looked in the patient's direction occasionally, then towards the nursing desk, where the patient's nurses smiled in response. Dr Smith made no notice of the patient. When he had completed his review of laboratory results, they continued on rounds without entering Mr Doering's room. Darren was glad.

Rounds were mercifully brief, so Darren soon packed himself up to go home. Conveniently, he now no longer had to wait for the bus because he and Courtney had bought a car. On his way home he remembered the fiasco they had experienced at the used car dealership. Courtney was well read on the subject of used cars, as she had been carefully researching their purchase. Courtney would say things like: "Based on last year's figures, the resale value on this vehicle shouldn't drop more than ten percent in the next three years." Darren would then mumble something incoherent about being hungry. The dealer would pat him on the back and say: "It's a pleasure to work with consumers who know exactly what they want." Clearly addressing Darren, he would then say: "Now let me show you a nice model that …"

As he drove, Darren knew that the situation must have infuriated Courtney, because she had clearly and precisely been planning the purchase. He hoped that her memories of the car salesman's rudeness might deflect her ire from his recent absence. He slowed down at a red light and closed his eyes momentarily, relishing a moment when no one could bother him. Alone in the car, he knew his pager would not ring, and Courtney did not know where he was. He felt pure freedom for a fleeting moment.

The hospital's overhead pager system emitted a loud, shrieking, unfamiliar alarm. He would have to leave his call room at a run, but to where? Why was he unable to move? An angry vehicle sounded its horn again and revved its engine behind him.

The light was green. He had fallen asleep at the intersection. Darren put the car back into gear and continued home.

Chapter 15

Darren awoke with a mild headache from sleeping away most of the day. He rolled onto his back and took in the room around him as he continued to enjoy the warmth of his bed. New pictures adorned the walls. One was a nice enlargement of a portrait-style photograph that he and Courtney had had taken the year before. There was also a framed print of a mountain he did not recognize. He wondered how long the pictures had been there, and specifically if they had been on the walls the previous night he was home. He worried that Courtney would be offended at his failure to notice her successful attempts at affordable décor.

From the kitchen came sounds of Courtney chopping vegetables, so Darren rose and went to see her after a stop in the washroom. "I like the pictures you put up."

"Oh, you noticed, did you?"

"Uh, oh," he thought. She must have hung the pictures some time ago.

"I guess you were too tired to see them when you got home earlier."

They must only have gone up in the last day or so.

"That looks like quite a dinner you're putting together." Darren reached for a piece of green pepper she had chopped and then paused in mid bite. The table had been set formally with candles and napkins. Something was going on.

"Don't you remember what today is?"

He paused again, this time in terror, hoping that it was not an event for which he was supposed to have bought her a present. "Uh ..." he started.

"My parents are coming into town, silly. I told you last week."

Darren finished the piece of green pepper he was holding as the relief set in that he had not forgotten anything that would get him into serious trouble. "Oh, of course." Their conversation from a week earlier found its way back into the conscious centres of his brain. "Did they decide if they would stay with us?" He hoped they would not. He had not had much time to spend alone with Courtney recently, and her parents in the apartment would not remedy the situation.

"They said they were staying in a hotel because this is really just a stopover. They made a big deal about how they weren't really flying here to see us, but were only on the way to their vacation. We're really not even on their way from Saskatoon to San Francisco. I can see their route stopping over in Vancouver, but it's pretty obvious they booked an extra flight and didn't just get a connection here. I'm not sure why that was such a big deal to them. I think they just really wanted to come, but felt sure they were going to cause us great inconvenience." She spoke quickly with the tone of a little girl ready to show her parents an excellent report card.

A little guilty that his first thoughts had, in fact, been of inconvenience to him, he reached for another piece of chopped vegetable and took a closer look at what Courtney had done for dinner. There was a large salad, almost completed on the counter top, and she continued to work away at its ingredients. The oven emitted some warmth in the direction of his legs and made him conscious of the fact that he was still only wearing his boxer shorts. Also wafting from the oven was a rich odour that could only be a succulent roast beef. Some pots bubbled on the stove to complete the picture.

"So, how was your shift last night?" Courtney continued working on dinner with an expectant energy, but despite the intensity of her chopping and slicing, she engaged Darren with her eyes as she spoke. Unfortunately, she made him realize that he had quite consciously avoided thinking about the previous night until now. His bitterness bubbled towards the surface.

"I guess it was a frustrating night," he answered. "There was this guy who should have been taken to surgery, but instead I had to look after him all night." Darren took a breath but sighed before beginning his next thought. Courtney paused at her work and looked towards him, quietly raising her eyebrows. His eyes absently searched the kitchen counter and then returned to Courtney.

"So, what was that book you mentioned on the phone last night?"

"What?" She was surprised by the change of subject. "Oh, the statistics I was reading. Yeah, I thought you might find that interesting." She gently set her knife down on the counter. During her exams in law school, Darren had cooked many wonderful meals that helped take her mind off the stress. She had bought him the chef's knife at the end of one semester and now she knew he treated its fine edge with delicate care. "Do you know how many lawsuits were filed against doctors in the University Hospital last year?"

"Probably tons," he answered too quickly. "Everyone expects things to work out perfectly in the hospital, but the only fact of medical care is that every single person will die eventually, even if they have the world's most perfect doctor. Every one of those deaths is a potential lawsuit." His face flushed.

Courtney returned her attention to the countertop and reached for the stainless steel blade. Her hand stopped. "Your patient last night – what did he need surgery for?"

"It was a perforated ulcer." Darren picked up another piece of raw vegetable, but his hand stopped just short of putting it in his mouth. "I can't believe that the internist wouldn't back me up and insist that the surgeon take him to the OR."

"Why did you say that they didn't want to take him to surgery?"

Now that he was feeling flustered, Darren took Courtney's request for clarification as a sign that she had not been paying attention. "They said that his lungs were too crappy for the operation and it would probably kill him."

"I'm listening." She recognized the tone of his voice, and reassured him, but her eyes were still fixed on her chopping board.

Darren opened the refrigerator and poured himself a glass of juice. His tension diffused and the air softened as he drank. Courtney slid her fingers along her knife's blade, and diced onion cascaded into the salad bowl. "Were they right?" She paused to taste a sample of salad dressing from the tip of her spoon. "Or do you think that surgery was the best option for him?"

"That's not the point," Darren answered hotly. "It's easy for the attending doctors to say he's too sick for surgery while they're on the telephone at home!" Darren continued at perceptibly louder volume. "I'm the one who gets called by the nurses every five minutes and has to tell them again and again that there is nothing else I can do for the guy."

"Maybe in a way, that's what the surgeon was telling you."

Courtney had always been an excellent poker player, and her skill at reading subtle changes on the faces of her opponents was going to make her an excellent lawyer. At parties with friends from school Darren would often relax and enjoy the spectacle of Courtney nimbly eliciting an emotional response from an unsuspecting conversational victim. She took pleasure from the use of subtle means to discover people's passions. Well rested, on a good day, Darren would never have dreamed of finding malice in her verbal games.

"What did you just say?" Darren demanded.

Why should his body have chosen that moment to bring him to such a state of emotional arousal? Perhaps he detected that Courtney's argument had unquestionably defeated a premise that he needed to hold true. Perhaps the decision from higher up the chain of medical authority that led to Darren's horrible night, had been in the patient's best interest after all. Perhaps there was no one he could blame. Perhaps that night would be typical of his job – no better, no worse.

Courtney's eyes locked his. "I'm just saying you're all frustrated at having to tell the nurses you couldn't offer anything, but you seem pretty upset that the surgeon told you they couldn't fix the patient." She reached to take Darren's hand, but he suddenly backed away.

"Damn right I'm upset! That should have been their patient and they left me holding the bag. Now that guy is still sitting in pain, and it's all because they wouldn't do their job." He turned to leave the kitchen.

"Are you arguing for the patient's best interests, or for what's most convenient for you?" Darren immediately turned back to face her. "If you had let me finish a moment ago, I would have agreed with you that the number of lawsuits against doctors in the hospital is huge, but that most of them have nothing to do with medical ability, and everything to do with bad communication. Doctors who tell their patients about risks rarely get sued when things go sour. Right now I'm thinking you should have been listening more closely, because you have a thing or two to learn about communication." Courtney was all business, but now Darren perceived her defense of her feelings as a verbal dissection, an attack against his abilities.

"You don't know what it's like being left all night with these crashing patients! Every night I'm there is another exercise in forcing me to take responsibility for things I shouldn't have to."

"Will you listen to me? How can you accuse me of not knowing how you're feeling when you won't communicate with me? Even when I'm trying to help, you get defensive." It was her turn to raise her voice, her controlled, clinical demeanour cracked and spilling sorrow. "You're always complaining about how tough your work is, but you don't take even a moment to acknowledge everything that I have been doing here for you."

Darren wilted, wondering how he always managed to get himself in so much trouble. Why had he let a conversation that began with her pleasantly asking him about his night turn into a big argument? "Look, dinner smells great and I love what you've done with the place." It still stung that she had questioned his medical judgment, but he knew it was time for damage control. He tried to go on but Courtney was checking her watch.

"No. We don't have time for this now. I've been making this big dinner and my parents will be here any minute. You go get dressed." Darren left the room in silent obedience as Courtney furiously completed her preparations.

Back in the bedroom, Darren could hear cutlery rattling as Courtney finished setting the table. He sat on the bed and pulled a pair of cotton slacks over his legs, but paused as he pulled them on. He realized that he had found this latest confrontation impossibly draining, and slumped limply onto the bed with his head hanging over his chest and his pants sliding back down around his ankles.

The sound of a knock at the door surprised him, and he reached out his half dressed legs and kicked the door to the bedroom the rest of the way closed. Dreading having to make conversation with Courtney's parents, he reluctantly finished dressing but remained in the bedroom. Outside, he heard their guests as they entered the door.

"Hi! So where's the new doctor in the family?" Courtney's father had a booming voice that echoed around the apartment.

"I'll take your coat, Dad." Courtney's voice was dry. Darren smiled to himself slightly, finding humour in what must be going through her head. After a frustrating argument about Darren's work, it was the first thing that her Dad thought to bring up, even to the exclusion of inquiring about his own daughter. Her parents had only arrived seconds before, and already her thoughts had turned from anticipation to tedium.

"You'll never guess who just announced their engagement." Courtney's mother added her voice to the sounds of Courtney putting away coats in the hall closet.

Still hiding in the bedroom, now Darren dropped his head into his hands, acutely aware of Courtney's seething aggravation. This had been the worst of all possible moments for her mother to indulge a blatant attempt to pressure Courtney and Darren to formalize wedding plans. Now, with their argument done, his sympathy for Courtney rapidly returned, as he recognized that this evening she had been looking forward to was already ruined beyond repair. She was doomed to spend the evening in a state of resentment.

Darren spent several more solitary moments of contemplation and took a few deep breaths while preparing to join the fray. He tried to think of things to do or say that would salvage Courtney's evening. As he stepped out into the hall, he saw that Courtney's father had already found himself a beer and a comfortable seat on the couch, while Courtney's mother was looking over the apartment. "Dinner smells just wonderful!" she was saying as she noticed Darren's entrance. "Oh, hello Darren. Hank, Darren is here."

As Courtney's mother sent Darren a warm glance, and Hank moved towards him for a firm handshake, Courtney's glance was cool and demanded, "How could you leave me out here alone with them for so long?"

After their handshake, Hank slapped Darren on the back with one of his large, powerful arms. "We brought you a little something. We haven't had a chance yet to congratulate you on starting the new job."

He went back to the front door and removed a wrapped package from his shoulder bag. The package was clearly in the shape of a bottle. Darren accepted, and removed the wrapping. It was Scotch. Darren hated Scotch. He looked thoughtfully at the label for a moment, trying to conjure up suitable words of thanks. He suspected that it was a pretty good bottle, for someone who liked Scotch, as its date indicated that it was twenty years old. It had a fancy sounding name: Glen-something.

"Mmm, thanks …" he began, as though keen to savour this new beverage, "I'll bet it's really … smoky." He was sure he had heard somewhere that smoke was somehow a desirable quality in Scotch. All the while he reconciled that at least he would have a fancy-sounding drink to offer guests.

"You bet it is!" said Hank. "Now you put that away for an important occasion."

"Oh, Dad!" Courtney chided. "Darren doesn't like Scotch."

"Sure I do," answered Darren feebly, knowing that not since 1914 at the time of the Archduke Ferdinand's assassination had any attempt at diplomacy been so thoroughly throttled.

"Ha, ha!" Hank's large laugh matched his stature. "Men all like Scotch," he answered confidently. "Those who say they don't are just being diplomatic to their wives." Hank winked in Darren's direction and Courtney visibly rolled her eyes. Darren smiled meekly and wondered why diplomacy seemed suddenly to be such an important fundamental of almost all family interactions.

"Why don't we sit down for dinner?" Courtney's suggestion received a general agreement. Despite Hank's boisterous remarks and his wife's compliments of the food, dinner remained an extraordinarily tense affair for Darren. He did not miss the more subtle hints at marriage his would-be mother-in-law threw in Courtney's direction, and even more obvious were the covert return signals from Courtney that the hints were inappropriate. Darren felt terrible about the whole situation and wished Courtney's mother would leave her alone on the subject. Unfortunately, the ongoing pressure seemed only to harden further the stares Courtney sent his way. Darren began silently applying his efforts to soften those stares. By covertly smiling when she looked his way and when he knew her parents had said something that would annoy her, he gradually tried to create an understanding that they were on the same team.

Courtney remained stern but remembered that these small things demonstrating his affection were what drew her to him so much. Unfortunately, her interaction with her parents remained strained. Hank seemed the only person to remain oblivious of the tension at the table, and continued to question Darren about how work was going, while occasionally barking out another burst of laughter or offering an inappropriate question or anecdote.

"So, Darren, just what the hell are doctors trying to get at when they shove a finger up your …"

"Dad!" Courtney interrupted him.

"Hank! Not at the dinner table." Her mother joined in the protest.

At that Darren laughed. He laughed hard. While the question seemed only to magnify the tension being experienced by poor Courtney, it was the first conversation that managed to put Darren at ease. As Darren finished laughing, Courtney and her mother kept their heads down and their eyes focused on dinner. For a moment Darren was able to catch Courtney's eye and they smiled at one another. It was a subtle signal that Darren's efforts to soften her were starting to work, and Darren hoped that their argument would soon be officially over. He continued chuckling as he set his knife back to work on his roast beef, and Hank, apparently immune to social discomfort, leaned way back in his chair and took another drink of his beer.

Chapter 16

It was a pleasant evening with a sky full of stars and a mild breeze blowing as Unterfeldwebel Kurt Doering found time to sit and talk with Unterfeldwebel Gerhard Schwerin, a sergeant from one of the other sections in their platoon. Gerhard was enjoying a relaxing smoke and talking about home. Kurt was simply savouring the quiet evening air and doing a lot of listening. Having finally completed their rendezvous with the rest of their platoon, Kurt felt more comfortable that they were part of an organized plan, but worried that most of the soldiers must be aware of the turn the war was taking.

"I have a beautiful German Shepherd at home named Hermann," Gerhard was saying. "Do you like dogs?" Kurt only nodded, but the subtle smile that crossed his lips betrayed him as a fellow dog lover. This was how their conversation had been going. Kurt was not an enthusiastic storyteller, but he sincerely enjoyed participating in Gerhard's reminiscences of home. Gerhard stepped on his cigarette butt and lit another before continuing. The light from the match made Kurt suddenly conscious of how alone they were. They had walked a small distance down the road as they talked and were now sitting on the ground and leaning against a decrepit stone wall.

Most of the men in the platoon were getting some crucial hours of sleep before resuming their trek. Marching during the day had come to an end, as enemy aircraft were becoming more and more prominent in the daytime skies. Signs of fatigue were starting to show in Kurt's men. They spent the night hours moving and something always kept them awake during the day. Whether it was nearby enemy troops or aircraft, or just tasks that had to be done when it was light, only the brief hours of dusk were left for the men to sleep. Combined with a gruelling schedule of marching, their limited time for rest left them exhausted. The men's morale suffered further when a long night's march was ordered in the opposite direction from the previous evening's journey, and they were becoming acutely aware that confusion had begun to reign in their command structure. With their regiment fragmented and partially destroyed, it was rumoured that now little was left of it but scattered platoons. Conversation subjects alternated between sore feet and disparaging comments regarding the Wehrmacht officer core.

"As I have risen in rank, I have found little satisfaction in giving more orders," Gerhard was saying as he began working on his next cigarette. Kurt had been looking up and enjoying a celestial view. Now he turned to his colleague, who had paused. "Back at home I used to love to give Hermann commands. He learned very quickly, so I taught him lots of tricks. That was very satisfying because he just loved to take orders. He seemed to feel so good about himself when he did what I told him." He paused for another long drag from his cigarette and looked off into the darkened countryside of Normandy. "Of course, that was the only authority I had at home, because my wife wouldn't listen to a thing I said." They both laughed, but Kurt looked back up towards the night sky when he saw tears moistening Gerhard's eyes on mentioning his wife. Gerhard shifted his weight on the ground and switched his cigarette from his right hand to his left.

"Back home it seemed so simple to be happy." He paused again and then turned to Kurt. "Do you worry about the bombing at home?"

Kurt looked down at the ground and picked at some tiny weeds, then brushed dirt off his hands. "Yes, I do." They sat in silence for a few moments and then Kurt began his own story about home. "When I built buildings, I felt like I ruled the world."

Gerhard smiled at that comment and Kurt smiled back. "Not literally, of course, but I really felt like nothing could stop me when I had contributed something to the city skyline. All I had to do was plan very carefully what I wanted a building to look like, and at the end of the project it was like something had been pulled right out of my imagination and turned into reality."

"I know exactly what you mean," said Gerhard. "Not that I have actually built any buildings, but I've always loved little projects. I built a doghouse for Hermann once. At the time it seemed like a frustrating and pointless chore to get the thing done. I hit my thumb with a hammer more than once that weekend, but it was a great high when I finished. For once I felt like the master of the house. Of course, then the dog wouldn't sleep in the stupid thing." They laughed again. Gerhard was still chuckling at his remembrances as Kurt took a drink from his canteen. "Now my wife puts her gardening tools in the doghouse, as though it was a tiny shed." Gerhard shook his head, and then suddenly dropped his voice to a whisper.

"Someone's coming."

Indeed, they realized they could hear the faint sound of boots crunching on the gravel of the nearby road and it was increasing in volume. Although Kurt and Gerhard were not doing anything wrong, they each felt compelled to sit very still and avoid notice. Maybe they did not want their solitude disturbed, or maybe something newly instinctive about being quietly approached at night suppressed their usual military response of standing and addressing the individuals. Whatever the reason, they simply sat quietly and listened to a half dozen approaching pairs of boots.

The road was about twenty feet from the grassy spot where Kurt and Gerhard were seated, and looking to their right, the two sergeants could only see a small stretch of it. The wall they were seated against framed a small yard, and the portion that made up their backrests ran perpendicular to the road. The footsteps approached the yard, but the owners of the boots were still hidden from Kurt's view by a copse of trees. Gerhard put out his cigarette and they continued to wait in silence until the first two pairs of feet came into view. Kurt and Gerhard each stirred slightly as they noticed the khaki uniforms worn by "Tommy"-soldiers of the British army. They relaxed when they saw that these two soldiers held their hands above their heads and were followed by three rifle-wielding soldiers of the Wehrmacht regular army. Gerhard looked in Kurt's direction and raised his eyebrows in a silent sign of relief. Kurt's face remained impassive, but it was reassuring to see some enemy soldiers taken prisoner. The group did not notice the Luftwaffe sergeants seated in the darkness.

On closer inspection of the men, Kurt noticed the insignia on the uniforms of the prisoners. They were not, in fact, British. Kurt had always thought of those khaki uniformed individuals collectively as "Tommy", but wondered whether that was an appropriate moniker for these soldiers who, it turned out, were Canadian. Thinking to himself, Kurt realized he knew little about the large and distant country of Canada. He did recall, from stories of the first war, that their soldiers had been known to fight like demons, so he was reassured at the thought that these soldiers' fighting days were over.

Kurt leaned back against the wall with a new found comfort as he watched the procession pass, but his eyes suddenly widened and anxiety gnawed at him when the sixth man came into view. Following the two Canadian soldiers and their three Wehrmacht guards was a Lieutenant of the 12th SS, recognizable by his characteristic dark green camouflage. Gerhard and Kurt shared an uncomfortable glance.

Since the previously invincible Wehrmacht had begun losing battles, a new policy had been instituted of adding small groups of SS soldiers to units of the regular army. As far as Kurt knew, this had not been done in the Luftwaffe, and he was glad for it. In theory, the duty of the SS soldiers was to strengthen morale with their fervent patriotism and toughen up weaker units with battle-hardened veterans. Rumours from the Eastern Front spoke of a more sinister motive, with stories of SS soldiers shooting their own comrades who attempted to retreat.

Now feeling more than ever the need to remain silent and observe what was about to happen, Kurt and Gerhard crouched behind the cover of the fence, and watched as the Canadian prisoners were led into the isolation of the yard it surrounded.

Kurt recalled the American prisoners he captured in Africa, green soldiers of the United States. While ineffective in battle, those particular soldiers were pleasant to talk to after their capture. Kurt fondly recalled how frightened they had been, but how their fear had changed to a kind of wary acceptance when they realized that no horrible mistreatment awaited. Kurt had improved his English when he traded commodities that were in excess among the Germans for those that the Americans could part with. He had managed to trade some cigarettes, easy to give up since he did not smoke, for food, of which the Americans had plenty. Now, no doubt, those timid but smiling Americans were somewhere in a prisoner of war camp. Nevertheless, the interactions he had had with them epitomized to Kurt the way that prisoners should be treated.

Until now Kurt had only known little about the SS beyond their reputation. He had never been enthusiastic to learn first hand of what they were capable, and in a nation with secrets, both hidden and open, it did not want to confront about itself, it was easy to avoid the subject.

The SS lieutenant was barking orders in English at the prisoners. Behind the wall, Kurt and Gerhard remained shrouded in shadows, quietly watching. The prisoners put their hands behind their backs, and at an order from the lieutenant one of the Wehrmacht soldiers bound their hands. Gerhard's eyes widened, and he turned to Kurt with a look that seemed to beg the question:

"What is going on here?"

Kurt felt an overpowering urge to leave, to walk away and never know the fate of those enemy soldiers. Somehow an insurmountable force that held his feet glued to the ground balanced that urge. The knowledge that Gerhard was also silently watching beside him made him feel he could not move. Later, he wondered if Gerhard also felt the urge to flee the scene.

As they continued watching in silence, the lieutenant gave more orders in English. The Canadian soldiers, facing now away from their captors towards the empty, dark yard, looked at each other briefly before obeying. The Canadians had been ordered to drop to their knees, and they silently complied. Now the lieutenant turned to the Wehrmacht soldiers. One of these three young men in grey uniforms had a helmet slightly too large for his head hanging over his smooth, young face. There was clearly no doubt left in the German and Canadian soldiers' minds of what was about to happen, yet the Germans still looked slightly bewildered as they received the order to load their weapons. Perhaps they had until now cherished the unrealistic hope they would not be ordered to commit this atrocity. Perhaps they had hoped beyond all reason that the tall blond lieutenant in dark green camouflage, whom they had never met until an hour before, would remove his sidearm from its holster and dispatch the helpless prisoners himself. Had that been the case, the three soldiers of the Wehrmacht could someday have returned home with the self-respect of men who only harboured the memory of witnessing something terrible. Instead the war would leave them a far heavier burden.

Two of the three soldiers of the German army loaded their weapons with the efficiency of men who have spent disciplined hours at practice. The third fumbled slowly. His hands shook, and his breath raced in and out of his lungs in short, irregular gasps. His eyes darted away from the task at hand to the impassive face of the lieutenant, then to the two men kneeling on the ground before him.

From behind the wall, Kurt began to notice small details about the scene before him. As the two Wehrmacht soldiers finished loading their weapons and waited for their slower comrade, the face of the lieutenant remained expressionless. He said no words to hurry the young soldier in his task, but watched with clear interest, as though he savoured the young German's discomfort. Kurt wondered for a moment whether the SS had been assigned to army units in order to toughen them up or to break them.

Kurt's eyes turned from the German soldiers to their prisoners. He noticed the two Canadians were now leaning against each other, and he wondered why. Then he noticed that behind their backs they had joined hands. They had also begun speaking in quiet phrases. Kurt's English was inadequate to understand their words, but he noticed that they were reciting the same phrases together and wondered whether it was a prayer, or perhaps a song. There together on the ground, any vestiges of male bravado had been shed. Their last inhibitions were lost as they held hands and shared those words together while awaiting their death, which was now so clearly upon them.

On Kurt's left, Gerhard was beginning to frantically look left and right, as though for the messenger who would deliver the last minute stay of execution. Kurt remained staring straight ahead, his arms at his side. For a moment his hand brushed against the Luger pistol he wore. Years later, in his nightmares, he would wonder whether he had considered firing at the SS lieutenant. He would wish with all his heart that the thought had crossed his mind. He would rationalize that fear for retribution against his wife and family were the only things that prevented him from killing the cowardly man in the yard, an authority in a contingent moment who could kill with an accident of power. The truth was different for Kurt. The truth was he had never thought of intervening in the events taking place in that yard. There was no fear of retribution. Discipline alone was enough to keep him standing still, but only a profound sense of helplessness kept his mind so clear. He had not intellectually calculated he could do nothing to change the events before him, but rather held an unshakable belief what happened in the yard was beyond his power.

The lieutenant gave the order in German for the soldiers to raise their weapons. Two rifles snapped into position while the third lingered. The lieutenant repeated his order with quiet force.

Perhaps had he screamed the order in anger at the man's delayed obedience, he would have demonstrated his latent lunacy to the world. Instead his quiet, carefully enunciated words demonstrated only a sense of inevitable calculation.

Finally, all three rifles were aimed. The tip of the third rifle quivered slightly but held its aim. With another quiet and purposeful order, the lieutenant instructed the soldiers to aim for the man on the left. A pause ensued. Only three seconds long, it was a small eternity. The Canadian soldiers closed their eyes tightly and their hands gave each other a final squeeze.

"Fire!"

The Canadian on the left fell forward to the ground.

"Reload!" The lieutenant's next order followed the first immediately. In an instant of bolt action, three chambers each filled with another lethal round.

"Aim!" The order came too quickly for second thoughts.

The remaining prisoner opened his eyes to witness his fallen comrade, then again squeezed them tightly shut.

"Fire!" It had concluded.

Gerhard had clutched at Kurt's sleeve as the first prisoner was shot. As the second man fell, his eyes were wide, but facing the ground in front of him. Perhaps from his lateral vantage point, Kurt was the only man present who noticed that on each order to fire, one of the three bullets hit the ground harmlessly, several feet from its intended target.

Kurt and Gerhard each took a step back, deeper into the shadows. They were now more than two sergeants enjoying a few moments of privacy away from their men before resuming a march. They were witnesses. Silent accomplices. The thought ate at Gerhard, who now fidgeted nervously. Kurt, however, remained impassive. His stolid countenance was a tribute only to the strength of the cords of helplessness that bound him to inaction.

"Bury them." The next order from the lieutenant broke the silence, but there was a delay. While two of the Wehrmacht soldiers retained a strict air of professionalism, the third broke down. The tip of his rifle touched the ground as his arms fell limply to his side and he began to cry. The other soldiers might quietly shed tears to themselves in future solitary moments, but he lost all control. Huge tears streamed down his face into puddles at his feet as he shook perceptibly.

The other two soldiers stood silently. One rechecked the action on his rifle while the other made a poor show of concentrating on some distant point in an abandoned field. Even the lieutenant seemed surprised by this unexpected display, and began carefully cleaning dirt from the sides of his boots. Their gazes averted for the requisite period of time, they were now capable of ignoring the sniffling man in their midst. The lieutenant turned his back and walked out of the yard. The two composed soldiers began silently digging, ignoring, but uncomfortable with, their sobbing comrade.

Gerhard and Kurt remained very still in the obscurity of darkness and the sound of the lieutenant's boots receded into the distance. Before they began to move, something new caught their attention. Two soldiers of the 12th SS had silently moved into the shadows across the road as the executions took place. Now, on a signal from their lieutenant, they joined him on the road. Previously concentrating on the events in the yard, Kurt had not noticed the men, but he did notice them leave, and now wondered at their function. Perhaps this whole show was a test of the Wehrmacht soldiers. Perhaps it was to disgrace them, or to force them to share some blame. Perhaps the lieutenant, a graduate of the Hitler Youth, amused himself by observing those who were not as hardened to the sight of death as he had become. *He certainly got a show*, Kurt thought, wondering for a moment whether the man who had cried was the same man whose bullets had intentionally missed their mark. Seeing a momentary wince on the face of one of the digging soldiers, he suspected it was not.

Gerhard fumbled with a cigarette as Kurt completed his silent reflection.

"Do you believe the stories?" asked Gerhard, afraid to light a match under their blanket of darkness. "I mean the stories that we are already almost surrounded."

"I'm starting to. Let's go. The men have napped long enough."

Emerging from their cover, Kurt and Gerhard walked the same road the SS men had just taken.

"Do you know where we're going tonight?" asked Gerhard as they walked.

"Our orders are to take the road south towards Falaise." Both men were speaking in quiet, subdued voices. Kurt now felt amazed that he even had the energy to walk. He wanted to curl up in a ball and lie on the ground, and was not sure how he would make it through the night's march.

"Falaise ..." Gerhard's thought trailed off and then he resumed. "Isn't that French for a cliff?"

"I guess so," answered Kurt. "What's your point?"

"Has it occurred to you that we seem to be getting herded in that direction?" As Gerhard turned towards him, Kurt smiled wryly. He did find their unit's recent and often inexplicable movements disturbing, as they were always moving towards and then away from allied advances.

They walked further, and beyond a turn in the road began to make out the area where the platoon had set up temporary camp. It had been dark for over an hour now, and they were due to begin marching.

"I need to find our lieutenant," said Kurt. "We should get moving."

"Wait!" Gerhard shouted and then paused for a moment on the road. "Do you think the men know that we are being surrounded? What should we tell them?"

"Hold on!" Kurt raised a hand and Gerhard stopped speaking. "First of all, you don't even know that we are being surrounded. That is only a rumour." Kurt felt his energy returning. "Second, the officers will tell the men whatever they want. You and I are nobody's information source."

"But I heard rumours that the Americans were making a move to our south." At Gerhard's comment, Kurt again raised his hand.

"You haven't let me finish," he said calmly with his hand still raised. "The third point is that the Wehrmacht's grand strategy is not your concern."

"But …" Gerhard again tried to interject.

"In fact," said Kurt, "the whole issue is really none of our concern."

"None of our concern?" Gerhard challenged, but Kurt had already turned and begun walking back towards the camp. He left Gerhard standing alone in the middle of the road, knowing that Gerhard must have some of the same feeling of leached energy that was plaguing him.

Normally Kurt knew he was important to his men not only because of the instructions he gave them and the valuable experience he contributed to the platoon, but because his confidence was infectious. Now he had left a junior sergeant standing alone in the middle of the road with little sense of hope. Tonight, he could not make himself care. Tonight, the same feeling of helplessness that had infected him earlier persisted. Tonight, German soldiers burying their prisoners plagued his thoughts on the entire war.

Chapter 17

On the evening of Monday August 7, 1944, as Kurt Doering prepared the men of his section for a long march, Corporal Bill Sutherland was only a few kilometres away. Unlike the Germans to their south, who for fear of allied aircraft attacks were resorting more and more to foot traffic, the camp where Bill found himself was a flurry of vehicular activity. Near where Bill was seated, two soldiers were pushing hard to dislodge a small truck from the roadside mud, while jeeps and trucks roared past in every direction. Bill looked up from his mail to watch the men push for a moment, and was relieved when they were successful. That meant his help would not be solicited. Looking side to side before resuming his reading, Bill was rewarded with a beautiful view of the French countryside. No longer surrounded by the tall hedgerows that had plagued their advance further north, Bill and his unit had emerged into much more open ground. Lush green hills rolled off in each direction, and the sight of small farmhouses memorialized a more peaceful past.

In Bill's nearer surroundings were the other soldiers of his battalion, engaging in their pre-combat routines. Sutherland's platoon had been in this attack position for a few hours. Their orders were to remain in position, so he tried to relax and catch up on his letters from home. Anxiety showed in the men, but revealed itself differently in each soldier. Some men compulsively joined small groups to play cards or dice. Others isolated themselves. A few spent time in prayer. Some shared a song with comrades. However they spent their time, none were spared from tachycardic apprehension since the news had arrived that they would be leading an attack tonight.

Earlier in the day Bill and a small group of soldiers had passed enormous stacks of white crosses being readied as makeshift grave markers. Two men diligently unloaded them from the back of a truck and added them to a growing pile. Bill and his comrades wondered at their large numbers.

One soldier asked: "Who do you think all those crosses are for?"

Most of the men only shrugged, but uncomfortable silence followed. Eventually another man remarked: "They're for us."

In the hours before the battle, Bill returned to his personal solitude and began reading a letter from his mother. The smooth lines and vivid loops of her handwriting evoked a vision of her face and he wished she were there talking with him. As he read, he perceived sights, smells and sounds of the Canadian prairie. Instead of France's tall churches on the skyline, small houses of worship were dwarfed by huge grain elevators. The smell of wheat fields on a hot August afternoon melted into the crisp freshness of a sheet of ice during a December hockey game. The sounds of artillery were gone and only children's laughter was on the wind.

As she often did, his mother began by sending wishes from his father.

Your father sends his best. I asked him to write a few words himself but you know how he is.

Yes, Bill knew how he was. No doubt when this letter had been written, Dad had been quiet and sullen, offering nothing to a letter that would make its way around the world. Bill smiled as he read. He had been far from home for so long that even his father's melancholy was recalled with the fondness afforded a treasured memento.

Bill's father, Ronald Sutherland, prayed daily for his son's safety, but as a solitary sufferer, never made his feelings known. Not his positive feelings that is. His negative feelings on the subject of the army were well recorded at the dinner table or anywhere else a captive audience might be made to learn of his disappointment with a government instrument that carelessly discarded its loyal but no longer useful servants.

Ronald had served as a soldier in the Great War, and although he had not seen combat, he had been in Europe for almost two years. He had returned to Canada proud of his involvement and had even remained in the army for several years after the armistice. The army was rapidly dwindling in size and administrative non-commissioned officers like young Ron Sutherland eased the army's transition to peacetime by keeping the paper flowing. It was in those years he and his wife had a son, and with the work of preparing for peace almost done, and his days starting to feel less productive, Ronald decided to find civilian employment. Working for a small publisher doing clerical work agreed with him, but having joined the army fresh out of school, he had little education.

When his company folded in 1933, he had terrible difficulty finding work. Sure his job experience would help him, he tried not to become frustrated as the savings dried up, and spent every day in an intensive search for work. Jobs had all but vanished for men, but women and children, expected to work for less money, could occasionally find something. Ron lost heart when his wife took a job in a department store. For a man to whom pride in one's accomplishments had always been a driving force, that socio-economic distortion was too much to bear. Forced to accept that his wife was the family breadwinner, Ronald had all but given up and become increasingly bitter. While the target for his bitterness varied from day to day, he finally decided that his ill fortune was the army's doing. Having served in "the war to end all wars", Ronald felt entitled to something when he returned but although he had enjoyed office work at the time, that clerical job left him minimally skilled and unprepared to adapt under pressure of the Great Depression. Like the ubiquitous automobiles pulled by horses for lack of gasoline, Ronald felt obsolete. Unfortunately, the army seemed to feel little obligation to a man who had donated much of his youth before retiring to a civilian job.

When Bill was growing up, his father intermittently worked at casual labour jobs, but with none of the pride or energy characterizing his earlier life. Bill's attitudes towards work were coloured by this pernicious influence, and he had never been instilled with much internal urge to make something of himself. He had never worked hard in school and had not given much thought to the future. When the war began, and the job that everyone was off to do was available for the taking, Bill uneventfully followed the other young men of his generation to the recruiting station. Now, reading his letters from home on the night before a big attack, Bill wondered once again why he had joined in the first place. It was certainly not at his father's suggestion. He recalled that when he returned home with the news of his enlistment, his father only commented that, "I hope they treat you better than they treated me."

It certainly seemed to Bill that joining the army had been the natural, if not sensible, thing to do. He had just been born in the right time and in the right place for the job. But he still did not feel at home.

His mother's letter went on to cover all the gossip from home.

I was surprised yesterday when I saw a young couple on the road walking hand in hand and realized that it was David Peters and Helen Thiesen.

Bill scowled as he read – he had always hated Dave Peters, a local boy who had been afflicted with polio as a child. The disease had left him with some mild weakness in his left leg but instead of a telltale limp he had a characteristic swagger. That cocky walk and air of supreme confidence gave him popularity with women that Bill envied. Besides his arrogant personality, Dave seemed to have everything else going for him. Good in school and an expert card player, he had a way of humbling you no matter what your game was. Now he was strutting his stuff, thousands of miles from the war, with the prettiest girl in town on his arm. It only added to Bill's resentment that of the many girls Bill had tried to land with the same story about leaving for war soon, and, "who knows if I'll come back", Helen Thiesen was perhaps the one who had most firmly repelled his advances.

I understand that David has started a business together with ...

Bill sneered again at the mention of Dave Peters, and firmly resented the free roam he had of their hometown to make his fortune and get his pick of the ladies. It was not that Dave had not tried to enlist. When all the young men had taken their turns, he appeared at the recruiting station no less than four times, the last time yelling about his raw ability to soldier so loudly that people thought he was having a breakdown. Each time it was his leg that got him turned away. A smile came to Bill's face to imagine that Dave had also tried to join the navy, particularly since they lived in the middle of the prairie, thousands of miles from the ocean. That had not stopped a few of the young men back home from finding their way into that service, but Dave had had no more luck with the navy than with the army.

When I spoke with David and his mother at church, he sent his best and said that he wished he could be there with you.

I'll bet he does. Despite all Dave's apparently honest efforts to join the service, Bill found no sympathy for him. Now that he was thoroughly disenchanted with the military life, Bill was more angrily suspicious at Dave's degree of effort to enlist. It may have been just another well-acted show. Unfortunately Dave Peters was one of those guys who always managed to say something friendly, even if he must have known that you hated him inside.

Soldiers newly arrived in Europe from Canada told Bill that women in Canada carried white feathers in their pockets. Those feathers were reserved to pin on the coat of a young man seen without a uniform, and thus mark him as a coward. Those white feathers would stand out like a Star of David on the streets of Berlin, and it made Bill laugh to think of Dave Peters wearing them.

Bill lowered the letter into his lap and looked around. More men were crowding into the area, so it would not be long before they were ordered to move out. Vehicles raced back and forth with even greater urgency, and games of cards heated up around him. With his concentration off his letter, the noise of his surroundings became stentorian. On the horizon, the sun began to sink and darkness approached. Frustrated after reading about Dave Peters, Bill decided he would quickly finish this letter before the sun went down. He made himself comfortable where he sat at the base of a small tree. Sitting at trees nearby were other soldiers who had chosen solitude. Contrary to a short time ago, when most had been reading letters, now it seemed that many of the men were busy writing. These letters were written with the emotion of knowing they could be any writer's last, and would often be entrusted to a close friend to mail their special messages in the event that the writer did not survive tonight's battle.

Bill continued his mother's letter.

Nice Sarah Halverston from down the street always asks how you are doing when I talk to her ...

Bill had learned to read between the lines of his mother's letters. Better than the clumsily encrypted meanings she never managed to conceal in her dinner table conversation, she had learned to use the written word in a subtler manner that conveyed more than it obviously said. Sarah Halverston was always "that nice Sarah Halverston." Somehow that extra word conveyed so clearly that Bill's mother was sure Sarah harboured feelings for her son. Bill unfortunately found the situation much more complex. Sarah was a member of the proud cadre of women who had balked at the chance to spend some of Bill's "last few days in Canada" with him. He was embarrassed to have attempted that unscrupulous, last minute manipulation with her, because "that nice Sarah Halverston" really was genuine. She did seem to think well of him, even if not well enough to fall for his pathetic line. Considerately, she had rebuked him much more gently than the others. He could not help wondering if he had approached her more sincerely and tactfully, whether he would now be exchanging letters with Sarah instead of exclusively with his mother. On second thought, he had no regrets about his coarse approach. He had been in a hurry, after all, and despite the legion of rejections he had sustained, he had managed a couple of successes. Unfortunately, the very fact of their acquiescence made them seem not the type with whom he would care to exchange letters. The knowledge of friends and brothers dying overseas gave a country's youth a certain neediness. Eager to explore carnal possibilities, Bill never took the time to find out what those lonely girls wanted from him, but perhaps they found it. Bill was as repulsed by their longing as by the whores on the streets of burnt-out French towns.

After completing the last of the neighbourhood gossip, and some comments about the family, his mother's letter closed as they always did:

... So we are still praying for your safety every day and hoping to see you soon. With love, Mom.

The letter was crinkled and slightly torn from its long journey across the Atlantic. Bill folded it with tenderness and precision. Once compressed into a perfect little rectangle, he added it to his pile of letters from home, which was tied with a piece of string. The daylight retreated behind the horizon, so Bill stretched out his now stiff muscles and stood from his comfortable nook. Walking a few steps, he noticed other men finishing their reading, and one soldier handing a letter to a comrade for safekeeping. The constant racing of vehicles was dying down now, as most of the battalion was in position.

Butterflies that preceded every battle stirred in Bill's chest. Distracted until now by his letters, he realized anew that his unit was about to attack. Pacing did not help relieve tension, so he wished that the sun would set and the battle would start. Men often questioned their odds at this point, but Bill did not like this sort of reflection. Through close observation, he had noticed that the odds makers fell roughly into two camps. One camp diligently recalled every set of numbers they had heard about combat casualties, and applied them to the upcoming battle. Bill arrived in France shortly after D-Day, but he had heard of men who landed in the early waves of attack saying things, things not easily forgotten.

"The first wave will have about thirty-five percent casualties. That means that a two-thirds chance that I'll make it, but the odds are less than half that me and my buddy will both make it."

This first group of probability theorists seemed to want to imagine themselves as dots on a set of dice. There was no intrinsic comfort in their calculations, except the mind's merciful distraction.

The second group of soldiers believed in destiny.

"You won't hear the shot that gets you. If it's your time to go, you'll just get it and never know what happened. There's no point in worrying about it. Ever." This group became absolutely detached before battles, but their stance was finally solipsism and rarely saved them any anguish when shrapnel filled the air. Their cold reasoning always had a hole. A hole which left them fearing the bullet they would hear an instant after it had shattered their leg and left them dying of blood loss on the battlefield.

Bill fell into a silent third group. This group carefully avoided talking about death, as though mentioning a demon would surely summon him.

Walking further, Bill noticed Howard, a private from his section, cross-legged on the ground reading a letter in his hands. The light was now too dark to read by, and as Bill approached, he noticed the letter was partly crumpled in Howard's hands.

"Are you all right, Howard?" Bill approached and put his hand on his comrade's shoulder.

"I just got a letter from my girlfriend back home." He paused to catch his breath and then went on. "She says she's leaving me. She's gone off with some other guy."

"I'm sorry," said Bill. He really was. Home was not supposed to change while you were gone. Bill read every letter from home as a reminder of a different world – a stable one – waiting for him when he returned. In Howard's case, the letters had been literal reminders.

"We were going to get married when I got back," Howard finished, as though that said it all. Maybe it did. Bill sat down next to him, and as they sat quietly next to each other, Bill began to reflect on his own situation and in a sense, he was sorry he had never found a woman to make promises to, a woman that would ground him to the reality back home. Only his mother was awaiting his return, but his mother's love did not give him an aching desire to be home, only a sense of not belonging here. He felt the sudden absence of something, and realized that Howard's situation had so affected him that he had lost his pre-battle jitters. As though summoned, the uncomfortable feeling in his abdomen returned. After a moment of silence, Howard asked: "What should I do?"

"What do you mean?" answered Bill, not sure to what he was referring.

"I mean, do I write her back?" This was a question Bill had not considered until now. Letters to and from home were lifelines for one's sanity. No doubt returning his girlfriend's letters had been as important to Howard as receiving them, and now, to leave the letter unanswered would be like leaving a crucial thought uncompleted.

"I don't think it could hurt to send her a letter and tell her what you're thinking." Bill, thinking of Howard's need to respond more than about the content of the letter, gave what he thought was the necessary answer.

"I guess you're right. Maybe I'll write her back tomorrow." This thought left Bill concerned. Only in moments of supreme or boisterous optimism did soldiers talk about what they would do the day after a battle. Letters of consequence were always written before the battle. Again, Bill was not so concerned about what Howard put in the letter, as he was about what the act of responding signified. Had Howard lost hope? Bill did not wait long before Howard confirmed his suspicions.

"I just don't know how I'll make it through without knowing that she's waiting for me," said Howard quietly.

"I know." It was all Bill could answer. He wanted to stay there with Howard a little longer. He thought there was something he should say that would make him feel better, but his time ran out.

"Fall in!" The order came from the Company Sergeant Major.

Men grabbed their equipment. They rushed into line. The order was repeated and embellished by the sergeants to their platoons. The clamour as everyone assembled was the beating heart of a single massive organism of which the soldiers were a part, but in the instant after they had formed up, the night seemed suddenly very silent.

Chapter 18

The gentle breeze swept a few hairs across Bill's face as he stood at ease. He looked forward at two rows of Sherman tanks packed together more tightly than he had ever seen on the battlefield. The metal beasts sat silently, their commanders perched in their turrets, only occasionally quietly speaking to the men in the vehicles beneath them. Behind the tanks were infantry carriers known affectionately, if not sacrilegiously, as Defrocked Priests, because they were ordained by removing the turret from a Priest M7 tank. Infantrymen of Bill's platoon were assembled in parade ground formation behind the vehicles on the reverse slope of a hill that overlooked French farmland. During the day, that farmland could be seen stretching lazily into the distance, dotted by haystacks and small collections of trees and bushes. Tonight it seemed that it would not be seen at all. A short while ago the sun had set, there was no moon in the sky, and only starlight relieved the oppressive darkness, but the stars provided little to see by, as the sky was filled with low-lying clouds. Unfortunately, if any of the soldiers saw the picturesque scene visible during the day, it would have given them no comfort. The haystacks dotting the countryside were favourite hiding places for German tank-killer teams, and the apparently innocent copses of trees often concealed machine gun nests or field artillery.

Bill began to wonder just how this attack would proceed. He had never been involved in night attacks on a large scale. That did not mean the night was a time of peace and quiet for him, on the contrary, small teams of soldiers often used the darkness to carry out deadly raids. Tonight, Bill found himself assembled with what must have been his entire battalion lined up shoulder-to-shoulder and ready to march over a hill. This seemed like an appropriate formation for being reviewed by the Prime Minister, but far from a realistic way to walk into battle. He thought back, mostly to involuntary memories, to stories he had heard from the Great War. In those days, thousands of young soldiers were often walked in pristine formation into a steel wind of machine gun fire. When a division was massacred, an entire town could be robbed of a generation of youth within minutes. Bill chose not to believe that he and his comrades were about to be moved forward in an officer-assisted suicide, but uncertainty screamed in his mind.

A moment of quiet passed, and the silence made him conscious of the sound of his breathing. This self-consciousness was dangerous in war – the self under pressure was dangerous in war. Awareness of the self could hurt morale, motive. With the upcoming battle drawing closer, his breaths became rapid, and in the quiet, he could now hear the men beside him breathing. He felt his hearing magnified in the darkness. Bill realized he had seen the tanks pull in some time ago, but now he could hardly see shapes just fifty feet ahead. He raised his hand in front of his face to confirm he could still see anything at all as a soft rumbling in the distance broke the silence. Behind the men of Bill's battalion the sound of aircraft engines grew.

"That sounds like our signal," said the platoon commander, who happened to be standing near Bill Sutherland. He had spoken in an almost hushed voice, speaking to himself. Now he spoke louder, but still in a tone that suggested he was only addressing the few men in his immediate vicinity. "We're about to be part of a very unusual attack tonight."

Bill had no doubt he was correct, but still wondered what to expect. This attack had apparently been planned in hurried fashion with no time for rehearsal by the troops. The sound of aircraft engines continued to build until it was impossibly loud. Its pitch was so low that Bill felt it building from within his viscera. He tried to guess how many aircraft were coming, but as the sound increased to incalculable volume, his guesses rapidly became underestimates. Even experienced men around him began to crane their necks and look skyward, but still nothing could be seen in the pitch black above. None of them had any model in their heads for such an assembly of planes. The din of the aircraft was finally so loud that Bill doubted he would be able to hear his orders, but was proved wrong as he made out the shouts of tank commanders ordering their crews to start their engines. When the tanks contributed to the racket, Bill wanted to cover his ears. This din rivalled the sounds of nearby artillery in its intensity and the suffocating smell of diesel fumes added to the sensory barrage. As he thought of artillery, Bill realized the thunder of guns was strangely absent at the moment. A long barrage from the many rows of howitzers before an attack seemed an offensive staple before sending the troops forward. Tonight all this was notable in its absence.

The men remained standing at ease, but in tight formation, and the tanks idled motionlessly in front of them as the cacophony built. Bill thought of the bombers high above them. Unlike artillery, which could pre-site landmarks during the day, the bombers would now be flying in the dark over unknown ground. Bill wondered how much room for error the bombers had without dropping bombs on their own men.

Suddenly the darkness fled in panic from massive beams of light around the battalion. Thousands of dilated pupils painfully squeezed at the startling change. Anti-aircraft spotlights had been recruited and were shining onto the scattered low clouds. Bill had never before seen what some of the troops referred to as "Monty's Moonlight", but it was a strange and impressive sight now. The sky was filled with spotlights so that reflection from the patches of broken cloud resulted in an eerie glow over the landscape. Orders were yelled and the tanks began roaring forward towards the hilltop, and the infantry was ordered forward behind them. Bill was relieved that their formation was loosened somewhat as they began marching, but he still felt that they were advancing in an impossibly tight group.

Bill was looking down at his feet, wondering whether Monty's Moonlight would be enough to prevent him tripping over stones on the ground, when the sound of an airplane streaking low over his head alarmed him. He ducked in preconscious fear and then twisted his neck to look up. By the reflection of the spotlights he could see that the sky between the clouds had filled with heavy bombers at high altitude streaming out of the north, and flying low over the men's heads were spotter aircraft locating suitable German targets for the bombers.

Ahead of the infantry the tanks had now crested the hill. Bill's nerves reached a heightened state as he imagined what might be facing them on the other side. Perhaps the hilltop was already sighted by German machine guns that were now preparing to mow down the first Canadian infantry coming into sight. Bill was clearly not the only man affected.

"What the hell is that smell?"

"He's done it again!" laughed one of the other soldiers.

Bill could not help smiling for a moment. One of the best sergeants in the battalion was a man of about thirty-three years old named Keller. He was a combat veteran who had seen a lot of action and was universally respected for his bravery and solid leadership. Something that had always distinguished him when a battle approached was his habit of soiling his trousers. As a more junior infantryman, he suffered under the great embarrassment, but it was something he had learned to live with. If asked, he would say: "I always feel terrible with nerves right before a battle. It builds up and builds up inside me until I finally shit my pants, then I feel better. It used to bother me that I always had to fight with a load in my pants, but I got used to it." Now Sergeant Keller seemed not even to mind when his subordinates made snide remarks about his habit. It never stopped them from following his orders.

Nearing the top of the hill, Bill heard anti-aircraft guns firing on either side of his formation. He wondered what they were doing, given that the sky was filled with their own aircraft.

Cresting the hill, some of the infantrymen crouched, expecting a hail of bullets, but something about marching in a row of men in formation made them stand back up as though they must be safe if everyone else was willing to continue advancing. Bill crouched for a moment too, and then blinked his eyes as he observed the scene of the battle. Thankfully, there was no hail of enemy bullets, not yet in any case. As the French countryside beyond the hill became visible, Bill saw a lot of strange things by the light on the clouds. Across the valley, bursts of yellow were rising from the ground. Smoke canisters had been dropped by spotter aircraft and marked German targets for the bombers. Clusters of bombs were beginning to fall over those sights and their powerful explosions added to the glow from above. On either side of the Canadian advance, Bofors guns were firing tracer bullets parallel to the ground towards the Germans. Now Bill understood that the anti-aircraft guns were not firing at enemy planes, but marking an avenue of advance for the tanks that were driving forward through the dark.

What Bill did not know was that his superiors had identified this valley as a junction between two German divisions, where a narrow seam was left in their defences. In this surprise night attack, the Canadians were moving in strength down a very narrow corridor in hopes of breaking the German line in two. A surgeon's blade cuts by virtue of motion, not pressure, and likewise, this attack could only be successful through rapid, unimpeded movement.

Bill could always feel the movement of his innards at the beginning of a battle, when he was not yet sure what he was up against. It seemed almost to ease his nerves when the bullets began to fly and he could identify enemy targets. Those bullets were what he was anticipating when he topped the hill. He did not know where the enemy was, or when they would start shooting, and that was indisputably the most frightening thing about the entire battle.

Now, although there were few enemy bullets in the air, he felt strangely dissociated. The panorama before him was terrifying in its destruction, but he regarded it almost as a circus. Bright plumes of yellow smoke in front of him, green tracers streaking by on the left and right, and orange explosions from the bombs ahead, all under the greenish glow of Monty's Moonlight, with so much noise of tank engines, aircraft and explosions that Bill found he could suddenly ignore it all. He felt that he was walking through this colourful landscape in a bizarre silence. His thoughts of enemy bullets disappeared as he looked up and around at the strange colours. He laughed out loud as he saw a soldier nearby trip and fall trying to look up at the sky, but his laughs were drowned out by the surrounding white noise.

The sounds grew to a new height as artillery shells began to fly overhead and crash into the Germans' presumed positions. Apparently there had been no preliminary barrage, in the interest of maintaining surprise, but the guns were now joining the fight with a vengeance.

Despite his dissociation, Bill identified a new sound, a sound he had always dreaded. It was the sound of German Nebelwerfer mortars. They had a distinctive scream as they sent shells hurling against an enemy, such that the British often referred to them as "Moaning Minnies". Bill did not know why, but he had always preferred the nickname given to them by the French: "La Vache". Bill hated those stupid cows.

Despite the enemy announcing their presence with flying, screaming, crashing explosives, Bill still walked forward with his relaxed sense of dissociation, not believing that all the madness around him could be real. Rather than an assault on his senses, the noise became a comfortable womb that enveloped his body. Surely nothing could touch him. On his right, several men had crowded behind one of the Sherman tanks that provided cover for the advancing men. Their lips were moving as instructions were shouted back and forth, but Bill was untouched by the sounds of their voices. Frantic hand signals were exchanged between the men, who were obviously also having trouble hearing each other. They ducked for a moment as the sound of a Nebelwerfer shell screamed overhead, but another explosive landed right in their midst. Bill watched human forms dissolve into a horrible collage of blood and severed limbs, but maintained his emotional distance. He turned his head forward and saw more clusters of explosions from the Royal Air Force's ruthless carpet-bombing of its enemies. As one explosion blended into the next, he could envision the birth of a new star, immeasurable in its beauty and power.

Now Bill felt almost as though he were floating, even as he carried a heavy pack and a rifle. His legs carried him across the battlefield without any conscious thought. He was one among an army of khaki-clad leaves being swept forward on a gentle breeze into a bonfire.

Bill lost his balance on a piece of uneven ground. He had a sense of hanging in mid-air as he fell. Time moved slowly and the dirt gently embraced him. His eyes focused on his hands beneath him and he realized he had cut them when he landed on a thorny bush. No longer focused on the hypnotic sights of approaching battle, he concentrated for a moment on his discomfort. Someone tapped him on the shoulder.

"We've got to call for help."

"What?" Bill stood up and brushed the dirt from his uniform.

"This won't do. We've got to call for help." Howard, the soldier who had so recently read bad news from home, was staring intently at Bill and clutching at the arm of his uniform.

Bill's auditory world instantly resolved itself from white noise into a thousand crystal clear sounds. Bombs were crashing on enemy positions. Friendly artillery ripped through the air over his head. The sky was filled with aircraft. The tanks were still rolling forward, their engines keeping up a steady pace without outracing the infantry. Few, if any, had needed to slow or stop to fire on enemy positions. Nebelwerfer shells were filling the air, but few were yet hitting close to the mark. Most reassuringly, there was scattered small arms fire in the vicinity, but no sound of emplaced enemy machine guns ripping into the mass of Canadian soldiers. The attack had apparently achieved its goals of locating a weak point in the enemy line and taking it by surprise.

"What the hell are you talking about, Howard?"

"It just gets worse and worse." Howard grasped at Bill's sleeve and tried to stop him, his eyes wide and his thoughts not consciously directed. Bill responded by hauling Howard forward to keep up with the rest of their section. It was important to stay behind the shelter of the tank in front of them. Howard kept talking.

"I was at the riot in Winnipeg. I saw a man get knocked down. Someone had punched him and he fell in the middle of a crowd." Through the noise it was difficult to hear what Howard was saying, but Bill concentrated on keeping them both moving forward. Howard was still talking. "They just kept kicking him and kicking him. What good could it do? He was already on the ground. The police were around but they couldn't get through. I think they might have been hitting someone else. What good could it do to just keep kicking?"

Bill was now dragging him along by his collar. Howard's rifle dangled loosely in one hand. He paused and raised his head to look at Bill, as though struck by a realization.

"We've got to call the police!"

Bill had only heard bits and pieces of Howard's monologue, but found himself suddenly angered by this nonsense, now that Howard was starting to impede his forward momentum.

"Jesus Christ, Howard! We're not in Winnipeg!" He slapped Howard hard on the back of his head and pushed him forward. Howard's rifle fell from his hands and he looked back and forth with panic in his eyes. He took two rapid steps to his left and looked like he might run away. Sergeant Keller, taking cover behind the tank on their left, interpreted Howard's intentions and yelled at him.

"Pick up that weapon and keep marching!"

Howard only stared in incomprehension. When he did not look

like he was going to reach for his rifle, the Sergeant cocked his pistol and swung it in Howard's direction.

"He's coming, Sergeant." Bill hurriedly grabbed the rifle from the ground and continued dragging the stunned soldier by the collar. Keller rejoined the half-section he had been advancing with behind the cover of a lumbering tank, but took several rapid glances back in Howard and Bill's direction.

Bill found himself dragging Howard for some distance before Howard was walking under his own steam. Bill reprimanded him along the way.

"You're going to get us both killed, you idiot! If not by the Germans then by our own fucking NCOs! I'm not going to help you again!"

Bill released Howard's collar and took stock of their situation once more. Looking behind them, he realized they had covered several hundred metres of open ground. Looking from side to side it seemed that they had still taken only very light casualties from a few lucky mortar hits. Now a short distance ahead, they were coming to a more wooded area that would provide better cover and relieve them of the obligation to crouch behind the tanks. On either side, section commanders were alerting their armoured comrades to enemy targets, then scattering around their covering tanks to make section attacks towards the tree line. With the battle apparently going well, Bill realized that he had become more aggravated by Howard's ineptitude than by the prospect of being shot at.

For God's sake, he thought, *if that idiot would just stay focused.* Bill reflexively worked the action of his rifle and felt at his belt for extra ammunition as tank treads splashed mud onto his uniform.

Chapter 19

Kurt Doering intensified his efforts at digging as a distant rumble of enemy bombers caught his ears. He was not at all happy that the sun was setting and his men were still entrenching, but at least it seemed after all their marching, they had finally reached a position where they would set up defences to meet the enemy. He shouted a few instructions to the soldiers nearby and warned them that trouble must be brewing. The bombers were audible to everyone now.

The ground was hard and Kurt's gloves were torn from constant friction against his entrenching tool. In the long tradition of infantry on the move, he and his men were digging hasty slit trenches for cover where they would spend an uncomfortable night. He paused to wipe the dripping sweat from his brow to keep it from running into his eyes and surveyed the scattered trees on a fairly flat plain that surrounded him and his men. Behind them, two tank crews were camouflaging their vehicles. Unlike the infantry, the tankers were forced to think of their vehicles first. After covering up the tank with foliage, they had the choice of cramming themselves into a tight corner of the vehicle for respite, or lying on the ground underneath it. The infantry often resented the panzer crews because they drove while the infantry walked, and it only added to their resentment that the tankers might have luxury items like heaters to make tea inside their vehicles, even if they would often heat some for the *landsers* outside. Lately, Kurt was not so sure he would like to be in their shoes. It had been a long time since he had seen any Luftwaffe aircraft, and with the western Allies ruling the sky, the panzers were utterly vulnerable. Unlike the infantry in their trenches, panzers were often caught driving across the open ground. Crews could only hope their luck would hold up against aircraft that chose to unleash their rockets, but the Allies were particularly ruthless against tanks on the move. If tanks were caught traveling on narrow French roads, the Typhoon rocket bombers would first destroy the lead and rear tanks. That left the remaining tanks effectively immobilized, wedged between the burning wrecks that had become their comrades' fiery tombs, with a difficult task of pulling off the road while the aircraft took their time and circled for more prey. Even Hitler's prized Panzer Lehr Division had been reputedly massacred on a charge across open ground. The elite armour division had hardly fired a shot at the enemy before aircraft had ruthlessly finished them off.

In contrast to the tanks, infantrymen who dug in, maintained their composure, and stayed under cover were well protected against bombs and artillery shells. In a foxhole a shell or bomb needed to land right on top of a soldier to get to him. Even near misses would send their hail of deadly shrapnel harmlessly over his head. It was in this situation that psychology became particularly important. Under heavy fire an inexperienced soldier was often tempted to flee his cover and run into the open where he would stand little chance.

With all that in mind, Kurt continued the mechanical chore of digging himself a deeper hole. His men sometimes vented thinly veiled complaints when ordered to keep digging, but he knew that their foxhole would be their only chance when bombs started falling.

Finally deciding his hole was deep enough, Kurt did a quick inspection of his men's work. They were spread out along a tree line that overlooked an open plain. Kurt suspected they were very close to the British front lines now, but in the increasing darkness he saw no enemy activity across the field. While a few men were instructed to keep digging, most could now make themselves comfortable in their holes. Paired up, one partner would have to stay awake and keep watch while the other soldier could take the first shift sleeping. Kurt was satisfied with their position, but worried when an enemy spotter airplane flew close overhead. He noticed that one of the tanks remained incompletely camouflaged, and hoped they would not draw fire on the position.

Sitting himself down into his own foxhole, Kurt remembered, not for the first or last time, the comfort of the French farmhouse they had so recently requisitioned. Earlier in the war he had often spent his time thinking of home, but these days even his imagination seemed more firmly rooted in the present.

The sound of bombers in the distance now grew to a loud roar, but to his surprise Kurt saw anti-aircraft spotlights in the distance towards the northwest. The sound of anti-aircraft machine guns could be heard from the British lines in the north, and Kurt again felt optimistic. He wondered if the Luftwaffe might actually be on the attack, but concluded he had been overly optimistic when he saw swarms of bombers approaching his position. An eerie glow from the spotlights lit the sky that had so recently been a comforting blanket of concealing blackness, and Kurt tried to piece together what was going on.

He was no closer to a conclusion when another spotter airplane raced low over the treetops. Some of his more optimistic men fired their rifles in its direction, and the nearest tank commander cocked the turret machine gun on his vehicle. As the aircraft circled for a second look at their position, an order was yelled and he fired a volley of bullets in its direction, but, unhindered, the aircraft circled back towards the north, dropping a small object in its final pass. Kurt ducked as the canister skipped along the ground nearby, but took another look when it began to release bright yellow smoke. He sensed this was not a good development.

"Everyone take cover!" Most of the men were in their slit trenches, but a few who had been carrying supplies hurried for shelter.

The roar of enemy bombers built until they were directly

overhead, and then the scream of bombs falling from open bomb-bay doors filled the air. Sounds of distant explosions from the west came first, but moved closer and closer, until the ground shook as a bomb landed about fifty feet behind Kurt's position. A proud old tree crashed to the ground. It almost landed directly on top of a tank whose crew were now buttoned up inside and hoping for the best. Dust and smoke filled Kurt's foxhole and the ground shook more violently as bombs fell all around. Soon he felt that the ground was continuously pitching him up and down, and he began to hurt from the continuous jostling. Desperately clinging for the ground at the bottom of his hole, Kurt felt himself once more thrown up towards the deadly hail of shrapnel overhead. As a bomb's shockwave passed over him, the air was forcefully sucked from his lungs and his chest collapsed in on itself. He tried to keep his thoughts clear, but his ribs ached and his head was filled with desperate, instinctive longing for a deeper hole.

His ears rang with a high-pitched whining from the auricular trauma of nearby explosions and his mouth and nose became filled with the dust that was now continuously showering him. He spat dirt and blood from his mouth, realizing that the pressure changes from nearby blasts had given him a nosebleed. He longed for a sense of what was immediately coming so that he could shout useful orders to his men, but he doubted if anyone could hear him. He chanced a quick look over the rim of his slit trench to see if any enemy were nearby, but could see nothing but flying smoke and debris.

Some light was shed on the dark situation when a tree burst into flames. Looking again out from his foxhole, Kurt could see the short trench nearby where the platoon lieutenant and radio operator were stationed. There was not a hope he could approach them, or even hear what they might have to yell in the current mayhem, so he clung to the bottom of his hole and kept trying to endure the concussion of nearby explosions.

As though the assault had not yet been intense enough, a new weapon joined the fight. From the far distance, shells of heavy artillery could be heard whistling through the sky towards unfortunate soldiers' positions. When they came close, a man in his foxhole experienced those shells as the sound and sensation of a freight train passing directly overhead. Even in the pandemonium surrounding him, Kurt immediately recognized when the enemy added their high calibre artillery to the mix.

Only a cool-headed and experienced soldier can take a moment for reflection while death is raining down around him. As someone with both qualities, Kurt managed to think about what might be coming next.

When spotter aircraft had flown nearby, Kurt had initially expected the beginning of an artillery barrage or perhaps an attack from dive-bombing aircraft. Only an enemy confident that they own the sky could afford to send a fleet of heavy bombers to carpet bomb an enemy about to be engaged in battle. An artillery barrage might proceed all night before a morning attack, and then suddenly stop as soldiers were sent into action, but Kurt had never before encountered the use of heavy bombers on the front line. He found it particularly surprising, since in this complete darkness they would not be precise enough to avoid their own nearby troops.

Kurt spat thick, clotted blood and gritty dirt from his mouth and then tried to look again over the rim of his foxhole. Intent on maintaining communication with his men, he attempted some hasty hand signals to nearby soldiers. Another close explosion threw him roughly against the side of his hole, but he persisted in his attempt to make some sense of the destruction. There was still no sign of nearby enemy soldiers, and the strange lighting against the clouds was centred further northwest. It occurred to Kurt that surely he must be on the flank of the attack – that this intense bombing was designed to keep nearby German soldiers from moving towards the centre of the battle. It also occurred to him that it was working. As the ground continued shaking and the air became so thick with the smell of spent explosives and dirt that Kurt could hardly take a breath, he accepted he could not communicate with his comrades fifty feet away, let alone march to resist an advancing enemy. The British must be making a bold move down a narrow line of attack and pitilessly bombing to protect their flanks. Kurt's only consolation from his deep thought was that this bombing was not likely to herald a sudden wave of British tanks approaching from across the field to his front.

Kurt thought of his men and hoped that they were faring well in their holes. He thought back to times when he had seen the Luftwaffe bomb an enemy. Then it had been the Stuka dive-bombers that had attacked with ruthless efficiency. Screaming down out of the sky, they would drop their bombs with fine precision. The psychology of bombing was used with great effect by those German marvels of engineering. A siren could be mounted in their undercarriage, which would howl as the airplane swept down at its target, and then the airplane would rain down not only bombs, but also terror on the pitiable soldiers underneath. Fear was the Luftwaffe's greatest weapon. In the early stages of the war, French soldiers would throw away their weapons and run when they heard that awful siren heralding their impending deaths. In doing so, they sacrificed their cover, which had been their only hope of surviving. Thinking back to the scream of the Stukas that he occasionally heard over the British or American lines in the desert, he realized that as much as it terrorized the enemy, it heartened the Germans, who knew their enemy was being softened up for them.

Although he was now trying only to sink as low in his foxhole as he could, Kurt could not help but notice the sight of legs running near his foxhole. They paused as the soldier stopped, hovering indecisively over Kurt. As Kurt looked up in disbelief, he saw that the legs belonged to a young and very frightened looking Wehrmacht soldier, likely belonging to the unit on the paratroopers' right flank. Kurt was impressed that the man had actually survived running about in the open, but focused on forcing the young man to take cover.

"What the devil are you doing? Get down here!" The young

soldier only looked around him in confused disbelief, apparently not realizing that Kurt was speaking from the level of his feet.

Not wanting to expose himself by climbing out and hauling the man into his foxhole, Kurt reached up just enough to punch the man in the back of the knee. The young infantryman collapsed beside the foxhole, and Kurt dragged him in, his weight fully on top of Kurt. The young man began thrashing about, yelling incomprehensibly, but Kurt overwhelmed him with an easy roll and was suddenly on top of him. Initially holding a tight grip on the man's neck, Kurt gradually relaxed when the Wehrmacht soldier seemed to be near losing consciousness. Given a chance to fill his lungs with air once again, the young soldier again began to yell wildly. His eyes were wide with fear.

"Do you see what's happening? Do you see what's happening?"

Kurt tried to calm the man, but still needed to hold down the young man's hands to keep him from flailing. Kurt released the soldier's left hand and again took a death grip on his throat. Kurt was strong and his young companion could only grasp helplessly against that large paw at his neck while his right hand was still pinned to the floor of the foxhole.

"Now you listen to me!" yelled Kurt. He lowered the tone of his voice. "That's enough of this nonsense. If you want me to let go of you, you're going to have to calm down." The ground shook from another nearby explosion and a cloud of dust fell over the two men. Since the younger soldier was pinned beneath Kurt, he was mostly sheltered from the fallout and it was obvious that his eyes were filling with tears. "Now are you going to calm down?"

The young soldier nodded as he bit his lower lip. When Kurt released his grip, the infantryman curled up in the side of the hole, wrapping his arms around his legs.

"Now what the devil are you going on about?" The bombs had stopped falling, but the artillery barrage continued. Between the sounds of nearby blasts they could only hear each other at a yell.

"They're all coming to kill me!" He choked back sobs as he said it.

"Yeah, I see that." Kurt looked up into the sky filled with explosive death.

"They're all coming to kill me!" Kurt stared at the young man who looked so desperate before him. A moment ago he had been wide-eyed and crazed, now he had the look of a dog that had been beaten for no reason. The young man sat quietly looking down, but now it was Kurt who was wide-eyed. He stared back at the man sharing his hole and thought about what had just been said. Despite Kurt's initial response, the man's comments had hit home. Of course those bombers were coming to kill them. It had never occurred to Kurt to take it personally. He found the implication terrifying.

Another blast hit nearby and startled the young man from his calm. He stood up in the foxhole, exposing his head and shoulders over its lip.

"You sit down!" Kurt yelled, his voice pushing through air that was viscous with noise. This time he found himself furious at this idiot endangering his safety. The young soldier started to reach over the ground to scramble out of the foxhole. Kurt reflexively grabbed for the knife he kept on his belt and drew it. With his left hand he hauled the man back down by the back of his shirt. His knife went to the man's throat. "You'd better be sitting absolutely still or I'll kill you myself." Kurt hissed through clenched teeth. The boy again curled up on the floor of the foxhole.

Regaining his calm, Kurt reassured himself that they were effectively pinned. Through the bombing there would not be a British attack coming this way. He lay down on the floor of the foxhole. Beside him the younger man lay shaking. Kurt held him and after a seeming eternity they drifted off to sleep together, suddenly unaware of the intense noise around them.

Kurt awoke with a start as the first glimpse of dawn appeared over the horizon. He shook his head and knew the feeling of a man who has just slept about two hours and has a long day ahead.

Quickly taking in his situation, he noticed the nearby explosions had all but disappeared, and the rumble of guns was now off to their left, in the west. It was a cloudy day with a cool breeze. The ground around was littered with debris. One of the tanks nearby had exploded, obviously hit by a bomb or heavy artillery shell, and large trees were blasted to the ground, their huge trunks making obstacles for the few men venturing out of their foxholes to help wounded colleagues to the rear.

As Kurt looked around, he noticed with little surprise the phenomenon that was a principle of infantry warfare. Despite the carnage above ground, the Germans in their foxholes remained. Mighty trees, generations old, had fallen, but from every foxhole peered an attentive rifleman or a machinegun crew ready for action. Kurt stared with derision down at the man sleeping soundly at his feet. Under his breath he cursed his superiors for allowing such inferior troops to be along the flank of the mighty paratroopers. He gave the young man a light kick and forced him to his feet.

"What's the plan, Herr Unterfeldwebel?" Yells came from the foxholes on his right.

"Stay where you are," he answered back.

"Herr Oberleutnant!" he yelled to the nearby trench on his left where his immediate superior struggled with a radio operator to get a signal.

"Yes, Herr Unterfeldwebel?"

"I'd like to review the men's positions, but I have an infantryman here who will need to go back to the field hospital. I was thinking of sending a small group of men to …"

"Never mind about that. I'll have Unterfeldwebel Rogosch check on your men. Why don't you take him back to the hospital yourself? That gives you a chance to check out the situation at headquarters. The radio is down and the only message I got back from the runner was that we were to hold the line for now. I need someone with some experience to get a sense of what's going on."

Kurt suspected he had an idea of what was going on already.

He only hoped their line had not been broken where the brunt of the allied attack had hit. He hauled the still whimpering and incoherent infantryman out of his slit trench and began marching him along the track to their administrative area. To the calls of his men in their foxholes, wondering what they were to do next, all he could answer was: "Hold your positions."

Kurt walked at a leisurely pace behind the lines with his young protégé slowing him up significantly. Occasionally paratroopers from Kurt's unit who were following the same dirt road would gesture as though to ask what was the story with the confused young man, but Kurt only shook his head in reply. When Kurt finally approached the nearest field medical unit, he took a moment to observe the small clearing that housed it. All around the makeshift tent, wounded soldiers lay on the ground awaiting medical attention. The tent was still only partially erected. Some debris nearby suggested that its predecessor had been obliterated in the previous night's attack. A large red cross painted on its fabric had given it little protection from above in the dark night.

Soldiers were walking this way and that, so Kurt grabbed the one dressed like a medic. "This guy's from the army unit over that way." He gestured vaguely in the direction from which he thought the man had come. "I'd leave him here with the rest, but I have a feeling he'd just run away."

"What, did he snap or something?" The medic looked appraisingly at the young soldier.

"You could say that."

"I suppose the doctor will see him when he gets a chance. Maybe this guy's lucky. Dr Muller has sort of an interest in neuro-something. That's what he calls the cases of battle fatigue. There he is now."

A doctor walked by, wearing a white coat stained with blood and dirt. He paused as the medic called to him.

"Herr Doctor! I've got another case of that neuro-whatever for you."

"Fine, fine another neurasthenic," said the doctor. "I'd like to chat with him, but you can see that things are a little hectic right now. Give him this. It will calm him down for now." He handed the medic a syringe filled with clear liquid. The medic administered it into the soldier's shoulder, and then sat him down on the grass.

"He won't be running away now. That's the sedative that Dr Muller likes to give."

"I see." The young army soldier was already contentedly sleeping on the ground so Kurt thanked the medic and began to walk towards their Abteilung headquarters.

"Are you okay?" the medic called after him.

"Of course I'm okay. What do you mean?" Kurt responded.

"You look kind of on-edge yourself. Like you need a cigarette or something."

"I don't smoke," Kurt answered, wondering why he had suddenly become a subject of interest to the medic.

"You should," answered the medic. "Dr Muller says it's good for the nerves." He pulled a package of cigarettes from his pocket as he spoke. Walking towards Kurt he handed him two of the crudely rolled army-issued smokes. "Take them," he said, and followed up the cigarettes with a package of matches. "We wouldn't want you to become like that guy back there." He gestured at the young soldier sleeping on the grass.

Kurt mumbled a few brief words of thanks and continued his walk towards headquarters. Looking back, he saw men who were carrying supplies stepping over the wounded, including his so recently abandoned colleague. Grabbing a young paratrooper who looked like he belonged at the field hospital, he asked, "Are these wounded going to be transported further back any time soon?"

"No," the man said, continuing to walk past on his business. "The SS stole our ambulances so that they could drive around in vehicles with a red cross during the day." He then turned back over his shoulder and said: "To be safe from the airplanes."

Well that's just wonderful, thought Kurt as he began the walk to headquarters. *The whole Wehrmacht is walking at night from battle to battle but the SS are driving around in ambulances during the day. Wonderful.*

After a walk down a dirt road through thick woods, Kurt found himself at headquarters, but instead of a Fallschirm-Jäger Abteilung, these headquarters belonged to a battalion of the 89th infantry. It was little more than one truck, very carefully camouflaged and tucked under the boughs of some trees, and a small group of officers furiously working away in a tent, sending runners out in every direction.

"You, Unterfeldwebel!" An Oberleutnant called from inside the tent. "What's your name and unit?" Kurt identified himself and his platoon and was then told, "Good! Stay right there until we call for you!"

Kurt had heard that from officers before. This was not even the first time today he had heard soldiers told to, "Hold your position for now." He stayed looking alert for ten or fifteen minutes, and then sat himself down and got comfortable in the shade of a tree. It no longer bothered him his platoon seemed completely disconnected from its parent unit, but he did spend a moment trying to remember what he had heard about the 89th infantry. From what he could recall, it held a lot of Eastern Front veterans. Now he was satisfied as long as someone was in charge. The guns still boomed in the distance, but with a nice breeze and some pretty trees, the spot he was in right now was not at all uncomfortable. He became aware he had not eaten yet this morning, and reached into his pocket where he had a stale biscuit. Now munching contentedly, he began to look through the pile of letters from his wife, and the two he had written but not yet sent.

Carefully removing an old stump of a pencil from his pocket, he began to write. He wrote and wrote. Never before had he written with quite such fervour. Normally he savoured every word and tried to imagine his wife's face as she read them. Today he wrote with a sudden passion to express everything that was on his mind. He wrote about the bombing of the night before. He wrote about the soldier he pulled into his trench. Most importantly, he wrote about his fear. He wrote about the terror that filled him when he realized that it was possible to take all those bombs as a personal attack against oneself. Never before had he wanted to tell his wife about all the horror that he saw everyday. Never before had he wanted her to be touched by the war. Today he could not help it. He simply needed to tell someone what was happening.

Kurt paused for a moment and wondered why he was suddenly struck by the visceral need to write it all down, then realized it had not been his memory of the bombs that triggered it. It had not been his memory of the terrified soldier. It had been the ambulance. Despite all the death and pain he had seen, the knowledge that men had stolen a vehicle needed to transport the wounded set him off. He had been feeling numb all morning, content not to take personally Tommy's attempts to kill him. That young soldier had taken it personally, but Kurt had never even learned his name. Perhaps some of those wounded would take it personally when they lost their leg because someone pinched an ambulance.

He fumbled in his pockets to try to find another pencil, since the stump he was using was worn down to almost nothing. He stumbled on the two cigarettes in his pocket and drew one out. Deciding to give them a try, he lit one of his matches and put the cigarette between his lips. He took a deep breath as he lit his first smoke and then erupted into a fit of coughing. He immediately threw the cigarette to the ground and decided it had been an awful experience. He spat in an attempt to get the taste of nicotine and tar out of his mouth and stepped on the discarded cigarette.

"Unterfeldwebel!"

Kurt startled as he realized someone was yelling at him. He absentmindedly returned the second cigarette to his pocket. "Yes, Sir?" He stood quickly to his feet.

"Hurry back to your platoon and take this message to your officer in charge. See to it quickly."

Kurt took the message and started back at a run for his unit. It occurred to him only briefly that running a message was work that did not require an experienced non-commissioned officer like himself. When he returned to his lieutenant, he handed over the message. It was as he had suspected. They would be withdrawing again. Doomed to forever be on the fringe of this attack, his platoon was missed by the British assault and now they would be falling back to try and form a new line.

The letter he had written to his wife had not gone in the pile of letters he was planning to send her. It was tucked in his back pocket by itself. He was not sure when he would find time to burn it.

Chapter 20

Bombs crashed harmlessly around as heroic American soldiers saved the day once again.

"This movie sucks," commented Chris, "and I've seen it about a hundred times before. Switch the channel already!"

"We haven't even gotten to the part with the girls in bikinis yet," insisted Denny, an obstetrics and gynecology resident relaxing in the lounge.

"I don't care about the bikinis!" Chris did not look convinced at his own words and Denny stared briefly in his direction before he ventured another comment. "I just want to watch the hockey game, okay?"

"Well, if you had just given me a good reason in the first place." Denny leaned forward to change the channel and spilled a half full bag of chips from his lap. His rear end protruded out of his one-size-too-small scrubs in Chris's direction as he bent over.

"Keep that to yourself, big guy!" protested Chris.

From a nearby chair Darren just sat back and watched the human comedy unfold before him, as these two residents who never seemed to feel the stress battled against one another for control of the sofa. He was finishing his dinner, knowing just one more patient was waiting for him in the Emergency Department. Every few moments he looked nervously down to his belt where the cardiac arrest pager dangled.

"What did I do to deserve another night with this thing?" he silently asked himself as he wolfed down the last of his pizza. It was not too bad, almost fresh, and had clearly been under the heat lamp in the cafeteria for less than the critical hour. It was that crucial time threshold that the residents referred to as, "The Golden Hour."

"Hey, guys! How can anyone ever take our advice about healthy diet knowing that we eat this crap?" he asked no one in particular. Chris looked back from the hockey game to respond.

"Are you kidding? You've got two food groups there, cheese and grease. I think you're doing pretty well."

"My stomach doesn't seem to agree with you," Darren protested.

"Hey guys, did you know that in Vietnam, the Americans could get a wounded soldier out of the bush by chopper and into an operating room faster than we can get someone from a car-crash by ambulance to an OR in downtown Edmonton or Calgary?" As Denny flipped past channels on the television, a familiar war movie graced the screen.

"That's 'cause we suck." Chris shifted in his seat and potato chips could be heard crunching underneath him. "And speaking of sucking, how long is it going to take you to find the hockey game?"

The unmistakable ringing of the cardiac arrest pager interrupted the last bite of Darren's dinner. He choked down a swallow and ran for the door, grabbing his stethoscope from the back of a chair as he went and stumbling on an empty pop can.

"Sucks to be you," he heard Denny mutter as he left the room.

The sound of the overhead page filled the air: "Code Blue, Unit …" He struggled unsuccessfully to hear which nursing unit he should be heading for. The person announcing the cardiac arrest might as well have been speaking with marbles in her mouth. Jogging down the corridor he noticed the nurses with the crash cart making a sharp turn and thought that following them would be a good idea. As they wheeled into a patient's room there was a crowd of people obstructing their passage.

"Everyone who doesn't need to be here get out of the way!" an enormous nurse who had been pushing the crash cart yelled into the room. Her voice was even more impressive than her muscular frame and people scurried out of the room to avoid her wrath.

Now the scene cleared and the patient's bed could be seen on the far side of the room near the window. The patient was a very old lady with a waxen complexion, and a surgical resident furiously heaved on her chest. Darren knew that, as the code team leader, his place was by the bedside with his hand feeling the top of the patient's leg for her femoral pulse. He tried his best to get there, but found himself jostled out of the way by a nurse putting ECG leads on the patient's chest, then by a nurse starting an intravenous drip, then by a respiratory therapist taking equipment to the head of the bed. Darren felt that perhaps he should announce his presence or say something, but now the surgical resident took charge.

"What's our rhythm? Check a perpendicular lead. All right, do we have IV access? Give an amp of epinephrine." The surgical resident confidently pointed people in the right directions and always commanded the situation. Darren wanted to shrink away into the corner and just watch him at work, when suddenly the surgery resident asked: "Who's the code team leader?"

Darren meekly raised his hand.

"Well, get in here then. This isn't even my patient. I was just walking by." The surgical resident asked a nurse to take over chest compressions and stepped away from the bed. He looked at the monitor that was set up and announced to Darren what was happening. "The patient's rhythm is asystole. Take it away." He stepped back and looked at Darren, waiting for him to take over.

Looking around, Darren saw the patient in front of him, with the respiratory therapist at the head of the bed with a bag mask. All around him, nurses were poised to do what came next, but they were waiting for his order. One nurse was perched over the intravenous site with a full syringe, ready to administer it immediately. Darren wished he knew what was in that syringe so he could tell her to go ahead. The whole room seemed to have gone silent and motionless, waiting for him to say something. The monitor showed a flat line when the nurse was not giving compressions, so Darren felt that he had better work quickly. But what was in the syringe?

"Epine…" Darren began to say.

"Are you sure you want to give that *again*?" asked the enormous nurse. She added, "Doctor."

Darren felt about three inches tall. Here he was in a life and death situation and he had completely frozen. Of course! The surgical resident had already given epinephrine, so the next drug was … "Atropine!" He nearly screamed. "One amp, IV-Push!" he added for good measure. The nurse who had been poised and ready to administer the syringe gave it without hesitation and the room erupted into sound and fury once again.

Twenty minutes passed as Darren tried everything in the book to restart the lady's heart, to no avail. The surgical resident Darren had thought abandoned him had in fact remained in the room, knowing he was terrified. "That wasn't so bad, was it?" He patted Darren on the back when they finally concluded their efforts. Darren thought that yes it had been so bad, and in fact someone had died, but he remained silent on the issue. All through the cardiac arrest protocol, he had felt sure that everyone in the room knew exactly what to do and he was only slowing them down. He felt very small as he walked to the nursing desk to call the patient's attending physician and inform her of the death. He heard the nurses, including the tallest and most intimidating one, laughing in the hallway behind him. He knew it was only paranoia, but part of him was sure they were all laughing at his ineptitude.

As the nursing staff finished cleaning up their equipment, he made the phone call. The attending physician's voice was obscured by static and Darren had to listen carefully to understand her. "Oh, hello, Darren. Yes, I guess we should let her family know. Would you mind giving them a call?"

Darren thought it was not at all fair that he should have to call the family of a patient he had only met post mortem, but went ahead and called them anyway. He finished the necessary paperwork before informing the family of the passing of their loved one. As he spoke with the patient's son he was interrupted by the ringing of his pager, but he waited for an appropriate time to pause the dialogue and checked the phone numbers while the sound of quiet sobs emanated from the receiver. It was the Emergency Department requesting two more consults. With the nagging feeling that he was sinking further and further behind, he began walking to the Emergency Department but was interrupted by the ringing of the cardiac arrest pager. His heart skipped a beat and he ran for the new site of all the excitement.

On his arrival at the patient's room, this time he encountered someone in a white coat who looked even more junior than he did. That was hardly possible, since he was a first-year resident, but on closer inspection he realized that it was a medical student who had called the cardiac arrest. Now the young student was standing nervously at the bedside of a young woman, who was clutching her chest. Darren had beaten the nurses with the crash cart to this emergency, so he had time to ask a couple of questions before they came crashing into the room behind him. "So what's going on?"

"I'm sorry," responded the young medical student. "This isn't a real cardiac arrest. Mrs Hamilton here has a history of PSVT and now her heart is racing."

PSVT refers to a condition where the heart's electrical signals speed out of control and the heart beats very quickly. Mrs Hamilton seemed aware of what was going on.

"This has happened before," she began, "but it always went away on its own before. The palpitations are getting very uncomfortable."

Darren checked her pulse and confirmed that it was an incredible 200 beats per minute. A team of nurses arrived in the room behind him, and again he heard the familiar shout, "Anyone who doesn't need to be here ... *get out!*"

Darren winced as the enormous nurse manhandled people out of the way. This time he felt moderately more confident because he had arrived first and was pretty sure he knew what to do, but this time there was a more complicated choice of drugs to use. As the nurses attached leads and monitors to the patient and started an intravenous, he took a few deep breaths and prepared to order the medication. He wanted to sound like he knew what he was doing this time, so he went over all the algorithms he had memorized in his head until once again a nurse stood poised and ready to give a drug. This time the syringe was not preloaded. She was not sure what drug he would choose. The room seemed silent and motionless for a moment until he said: "Adenosine." The nurse poised by the intravenous line reached for a syringe.

"Adenosine," repeated the huge nurse who now towered over Darren's shoulder. She did not sound disapproving, but did sound like she wanted him to be sure.

"Adenosine. Six milligrams IV-Push." This time he said it with authority.

Mrs Hamilton looked expectantly at Darren. What she did not realize was that he had just ordered a medication that would briefly stop her heart and allow it to reset its electrical rhythm. Darren was sure it was the right drug, but he had never seen it used before, and he was starting to wonder what its effects would look like.

On the heart monitor, Mrs Hamilton's heart was still beating at a rate of 200 per minute. As the nurse with the syringe injected it into Mrs Hamilton's IV, Darren looked at the patient. "This may make you feel a little ... funny."

"Okay," she answered. She was satisfied with his answer because he seemed to know what he was doing. Darren appreciated the sentiment, but deep down he was wondering exactly what she really would feel in the next moment. He focused his eyes on the monitor. The medication reached Mrs Hamilton's bloodstream and in an instant her heart tracing went from 200 beats per minute to a flat line. Darren continued watching the monitor intently. Mrs Hamilton heard the whine behind her that is so frequently used on television to indicate that someone has died, and she turned around. Seeing the flat line, she turned back to Darren with a questioning look in her eyes. Darren's face remained impassive, and he continued watching the monitor. Now, seeing that his eyes remained fixed on the monitor, Mrs Hamilton turned around again. Her heart monitor still showed a flat line. All this took only a couple of seconds. Once again, the room around Darren seemed silent and motionless. All except for Mrs Hamilton's eyes moving back and forth from him to the monitor that indicated her cardiac arrest, but her mind was not racing nearly as fast as Darren's.

Oh my God, he thought. *Any second now she's going to pass out and die. What if I've killed her?* Mrs Hamilton looked back in his direction. Making a feeble attempt at a smile, he nodded. Despite his outwards show of confidence, he thought: *When the hell is her heart going to start up again?*

"Beep." A heartbeat appeared on the monitor. "Beep, beep, beep …"

Darren closed his eyes for a long second and took a deep breath. He opened his eyes as Mrs Hamilton said: "Thank goodness, my palpitations are finally better."

The monitor showed a nice, normal rhythm at a rate of 65 beats per minute.

"Good old adenosine," said Darren, as though he had seen it before many times and not just in a textbook.

He took a moment to talk with the medical student, and suggested she talk to her attending physician about what had happened. She thanked him and he began to make his way out of the room past the inevitable crowd of people that accumulates at cardiac arrests.

"Way to stay calm." The huge nurse slapped him on the back on his way out of the room and nearly knocked him over. "My name's Tina, by the way."

Tina, thought Darren. *That must be the equivalent of a gigantic Hell's Angel named 'Tiny'.*

"Thanks," he answered. "My name's Darren."

"You're having a fun night already and it's still only seven o'clock," she added.

"I know," he answered, and began to head back to the Emergency Department.

Darren had only walked a few steps when he realized he had better stop to take a breath. Partially relieved that everything had gone well and partially triumphant he had saved a patient from a life-threatening condition, he stepped into the nearest staff washroom and splashed cold water on his face. When he looked back up in the mirror and assessed how he was feeling, he found he was almost as excited at the approval he had won from the nursing staff as he was about the medical care he had been executing.

He had only just finished calming down and heading for the Emergency Department when the code pager rang and the familiar claxons sounded overhead once again. He ran.

That long night became longer and longer. At his third cardiac arrest of the night, he had to put in a central line and an endotracheal tube. He finished some of his work in Emergency after that, but it was not long before he was running to a fourth cardiac arrest.

At about four o'clock in the morning his work was done and he headed for his call room. He had been nearly spent when he started his day some twenty-one hours earlier, and now he was so exhausted he probably could not sleep. He stared at the ceiling from his call room bed and noticed his shoes were still on his feet. He felt the only thing keeping him alive was adrenaline. He could not remember whether he had eaten dinner, but he did not care because he was nauseated anyway. His medical school days of reading crisp, detailed textbooks and studying for standardized exams seemed a thousand years distant. The only thing standardized about medical emergencies was the terror they produced, and the crucial detail in every case was always an exception to the rule. Multiple-choice examinations were feeble preparation for a world where the educational technique for invasive procedures was most often described as: "See one, do one, teach one."

He had only been lying down for about fifteen minutes when the code bells sounded again. It was the fifth cardiac arrest of the night. Earlier he had been afraid to go to the bathroom for fear the code pager might ring. No matter what he did he could feel its weight at his side as a constant reminder of a terrifying responsibility. This time, it was starting to seem routine. Not routine in the sense that he felt in control and knew what was going on, but routine in that his feet just carried him out of bed and raced him there without his consciously willing it. The halls sped by him as though in a dream. People's voices seemed far away as he ran down the hall. The next morning when asked how many cardiac arrests had been called, he had to think hard to remember if the fourth and fifth had been real or imagined.

When he arrived at the scene there was a form in the bed, but not a person. Its skin was waxy and its eyes held no vitality. Darren could not truly believe that this body had ever held life. It was only a practice dummy, waiting for him to take his turn putting in central lines and arterial catheters.

Darren's instructions to the nurses were concise and clear. They worked with crisp efficiency, always knowing that his next order would be correct. Darren was working with the confidence of a person who does not feel connected to the world around him. While never physically looking at himself from across the room, as described in out-of-body experiences, Darren felt freed from the perception that everything around him was real.

The nurses made friendly remarks again as he left the scene, and this time he knew all their names and could spout some amicable comments. On his way back to the call room, he saw that it was six o'clock. Just about time to shower and get ready for morning rounds. He no longer had the euphoria he had felt after the second code of the night, but he did have the casual confidence of someone who had correctly followed all the algorithms. What did it matter if he could not remember whether the patient had lived or died? That seemed inconsequential.

Hot water from the shower hitting his face felt good, but only so long as he imagined that that warm, safe feeling meant that he was going to bed and not starting a new day. In the locker room he encountered Chris, who inquired about his night.

"I sure heard a lot of code bells last night. They made it hard to pay attention to the hockey game. How many codes were you at, anyway?"

Darren had to think. Somehow in the light of day the world seemed to be resolving itself back into reality. Even though he had not been to sleep, the night began to feel like 'yesterday'. Confident that he had not imagined some of the images racing in his head, he answered. "Five, I think."

"Five? Wow, I think you have the record. I heard of a guy who had four, but five! How does it feel to be the record-holder?"

"It doesn't feel at all." Darren thought that sentence about summed up the way he felt about the whole world at that moment.

"I'm sure it doesn't," answered Chris, as he went to his own morning rounds.

Chapter 21

Darren felt pasty as he woke up and realized that he was sleeping in all his clothes. Opening his mouth, he felt dehydrated, as though suffering from a punishing hangover, but he knew that he had not been drinking. Could it be morning already? Was another day at the hospital beginning? Regaining his senses, he turned to his alarm clock and saw it was six o'clock in the evening. He felt a sudden and overwhelming relief that he was only waking up from his afternoon nap after that long and punishing night in the hospital. As he put together his thoughts, he felt an even more significant joy that today was Friday and he was not scheduled to work this weekend. Tomorrow would be his first day off in three weeks and the promise of sleeping late was the greatest feeling he had been rewarded with in months.

He peeled off his clothes and stepped into a steaming hot shower, fully savouring the warm comfort and letting his mind go peacefully blank. By the time he was finished – it felt like a mental and physical cleansing – the room was heavily steamed up and his skin was wrinkled. He put on his most comfortable but unattractive tracksuit and a cozy pair of wool socks and headed for the couch. There he found Courtney, curled up under a blanket and reading a heavy textbook.

"Good evening, sleepy head." Normally he might have responded to her gentle jibe by calculating the scant number of hours of sleep he had in the last week, but now he would not be bothered. All that mattered was that he had two beautiful days off, an unimaginable vista of unstructured time. She went on. "Maybe the sleeping beauty would like to go for a walk with me?"

"Absolutely." Free movement, unscheduled, undirected – this sounded like an expression of greater joy than he had ever before appreciated. Darren was not sure that he was publicly presentable in his well-worn tracksuit, but he put on a jacket and headed quickly for the door, surprised at his new energy.

"I feel like I haven't seen you in ages," Courtney commented as she tied her shoes.

"I feel the same." He had done little at home but sleep for the last couple of weeks, but now that he had the promise of a weekend off, he felt he could regain his normal life, re-enter its usual rhythms and shapes. "What's that huge book you're reading?" He gestured at the coffee table.

"It's on the Nuremberg trials. You asked me about it the other day." She finished buttoning her coat.

"Oh, yeah." Darren had never shared Courtney's love of history, but often enjoyed her synopses of themes she had teased from daunting texts on long-forgotten eras. He rarely thought to ask her about legal texts she was reading, and was not sure he would find much interest in this new combination of her favourite interests. He tried anyway.

"How is it?"

"Fascinating. It's a great mystery of human nature what people can make themselves believe that they haven't heard," she paused and looked down at the text, "or didn't know." She looked up to scrutinize Darren's attentive expression, and a smile passed between them. "I'll let you know if it has any car chases." Even a joke at his expense relieved him, given that he would be spared a discussion of Nazi war criminals.

They stepped out of the apartment together and began to walk at a relaxed pace, down the street to a small park where people liked to walk their dogs, both knowing without speaking that this was where they wanted to go.

Now fully roused from his deep slumber, Darren refreshed his memory about recent events. He thought about his cardiac arrest protocols, and reanalyzed his decisions in retrospect. Courtney knew immediately that the 'here and now' was still not the centre of his attention. She held her gaze on him for several seconds, and when he continued to stare forward without acknowledging her, she spoke. "Even when you're at home, you're at work."

"What are you talking about?" Darren knew immediately what she was saying but found himself startled, without a reply.

"What am I talking about? Why don't you answer your own question and tell me what you were thinking about just now?"

Although he had systematically rehearsed the events of the previous night in his head, Darren found that he could not easily recall his thoughts as a coherent explanation for Courtney. After a moment's pause, he decided that he might do better with a different approach.

"I'm not really thinking at all. I guess I'm just enjoying not having to worry about anything right now. Thanks for taking me for a walk. This was a nice idea." He smiled at her and she softened. Although she did not really believe that his mind had been at all focused on them, she gave him the benefit of the doubt.

"Well, you should be enjoying yourself. You've been working hard, but now look at what a beautiful day it is. The sun is still shining, the leaves are falling, but it's warm for autumn. What a gorgeous day for a walk." She linked her arm in his and leaned her head on his shoulder as they continued.

Darren looked up to appreciate the facts. He was amazed to see the leaves were already falling. They were not only falling, but they were magnificent. He began to wonder how this new season had escaped his notice. Large trees overhung a road bordering their street and now, as Darren and Courtney looked on, there was an arch of boughs leisurely raining their colourful cargo onto the pavement. There were infinite shades of yellows, oranges and reds around them, and each was a delight.

Courtney's mention of the sun made Darren acutely aware of it. How long had he been working inside and missing out on the sun's warm touch? Like his luxurious shower earlier, he felt the sun, already going down, bathing him in its warm and comforting rays. He closed his eyes and raised his face towards a sun he had never enjoyed as much as he did now. He realized how long he had been without it.

Courtney pulled gently on his arm. Opening his eyes, Darren saw that they were crowding another approaching couple. After they bypassed the other pedestrians, Darren appreciated Courtney's comment about just how warm it was. He took off his jacket, threw it over his arm and found that he still felt warm. A gentle breeze brushed across his face, and he enjoyed it with the same sense of rediscovery that he had savoured with the sun.

"What are you thinking about now?" The question Courtney frequently asked and which Darren always had trouble responding to, this time he found himself very well equipped to answer.

"I was just thinking about the sun and the wind and the leaves. I feel like I have been missing out on really simple things lately. Who would have thought that I could enjoy the sun's rays so much?" Appreciating the openness and simple pleasure in his answer, Courtney squeezed his arm a little tighter. He turned to face her and their eyes met. "I guess I feel like I haven't seen enough of you lately. You're so beautiful."

They almost stopped walking to look into one another's eyes, but Courtney resumed their pace as she blushed and lowered her eyes. Her expression showed pure satisfaction, but she lightly tickled Darren in the ribs and teased him. "You smooth talker. You're just hoping for something special when we get back from our walk."

"No," he replied. Courtney raised her eyebrows in surprise at his answer. "Well, yes, maybe I was, but I was also just appreciating being with you."

They walked a little further until they reached the nearby park. It covered the area of about two city blocks and was dotted with pretty trees and bushes. Still arm in arm, they walked as far as a park bench where they sat down together and enjoyed the view.

"I spent the morning on the internet looking at articling

positions for next year." Courtney brushed an insect from her leg. "Luckily, it looks like there will be lots out there next year. It's kind of scary to realize how hard I'll be working and how much more responsibility I'll have. It sure won't be like law school anymore."

"I'm sure it won't." Darren knew little about work in the legal field but was quite confident on this point.

They talked for a while and appreciated each other's company, but as the conversation faded, Darren found himself once again lost in introspection.

Looking around, Darren was unexpectedly surprised to see people walking about. Some were walking their dogs; others were out for an after-dinner stroll. A group of small children were enjoying a game of tag while their parents looked on from a bench. Darren found that he could not truly believe that all these people were real. It seemed impossible that this layered world outside the hospital was going in such smooth but complex fashion every day. People went to work, fulfilled their duties, spent time with their families, sorted out troubles and lived their lives, all outside the hospital. Darren knew this was the case, but felt that at the moment he could not wrap his mind around the magnitude of the world that he did not realize he had forsaken. It simply did not seem possible that outside the hospital people might have so many places to go.

Shocked by his feelings of dissociation, Darren felt sure that all he needed was a good night's sleep to set him right, but still, he remained disturbed that he felt so distant from the immediate public world around him.

"Maybe we should go home," he said to Courtney.

"Sure, let's go." Courtney pulled him close to her as she took his arm. Thinking about next year brought her insecurities to the surface.

They had walked about halfway home when Darren noticed that Courtney was talking to him. Once again he had become caught up in his own world.

"… So Saturday is okay with you?"

"I guess so." As he fumbled his response, Courtney stopped walking and looked towards him.

"Darren, pay attention. Next year when I'm focused on my career, how do you think we'll get by if I'm as distractible as you are now?" A sense of satisfaction had vanished from Courtney's face. She was not angry, but concerned for him, for them both. When he did not immediately answer, she continued: "You know, you used to be able to pay attention to a whole conversation. Earlier you seemed so happy to walk with me, and now you're preoccupied again. Why won't you tell me what's on your mind?"

"It's really nothing important. It just feels like I've been in the hospital forever."

"What happened last night? Was it that bad?" Sometimes Courtney seemed to see through to what the problem was, even when Darren could not recognize it himself.

"No, it's not last night that has me all preoccupied." Darren may have been lying, but he was not sure. "I just need a good night's sleep tonight. Why don't we rent a movie and just relax."

Courtney agreed and they walked for a while in silence. Suddenly Darren remembered Courtney had been trying to ask him something. "What was that about Saturday?"

"I told you, I made some new friends and wanted to have them over for dinner tomorrow."

"That sounds great, I'm glad you're meeting people." Darren was glad that at least Courtney might have a social life, and was keen on the idea of meeting new, non-medical people. Perhaps he would not feel so locked in the world of the hospital if he got out a bit. Still, it was the prospect of sleeping in tomorrow that had him even happier.

They picked up a video and returned home. Traditionally their debates in the movie store were such drawn-out affairs that only a system of taking turns allowed them to make timely decisions. Tonight it was Darren's turn but he conceded the choice to Courtney. He felt positive and optimistic about the whole weekend. Unfortunately when he woke up on the couch at two o'clock in the morning, he wondered if Courtney would tease him about falling asleep in the middle of the movie. He could hardly remember even the opening credits. He was in his clothes and Courtney had thrown a blanket over him.

Chapter 22

The touch of sunlight through the bedroom window gently woke Darren from his deep slumber. He savoured the sensation of his body waking of its own accord in a fully rested state, and then, rolling on his side, he checked his alarm clock and saw that it was 12:06 in the afternoon. Including his time on the couch, he had slept for over fourteen hours and it felt marvellous. Wonderful scents were wafting out of the kitchen and his nose soon led him in their direction as, invigorated with new energy, he hopped out of bed and walked towards the smell of food.

In the kitchen, Courtney was hard at work at the stove. She looked up as he entered. "I didn't want to wake you in case you were still tired after just fourteen hours of sleep, but I suspected that bacon might draw you in here." There was more than bacon on the stove. In fact there was a veritable feast, with bacon and sausages in a frying pan, eggs in second one, and a selection of toast and fruit laid out all around. Realizing by the grumbling of his stomach that he had forgotten about dinner last night and had not eaten in over twenty-four hours, Darren could not help reaching his arms around Courtney and squeezing her tight.

"You're the best! This smells so good."

"Let go of me, you goof!" She laughed out loud as she answered him. She wielded her spatula like a sword as he began wrestling her to the ground. When she playfully smacked him with it, he realized that it had been coated with grease. The grease was now in his hair, so he gave her a kiss and they agreed that breakfast should be served after he had gone for a shower.

Darren emerged from the bathroom feeling even more wonderful than he had when he awoke. He was rested, he was fresh and clean, and the prospect of a long, lazy day seemed almost more than he dared ask for. He sat at the table in his housecoat and began enjoying a cup of coffee and the newspaper as Courtney put the finishing touches on breakfast. He grunted with interest several times as he read, so Courtney inquired as she set the table.

"What's caught your attention?"

"There's an article in here about a patient I'm looking after. It's a little biography."

"That sounds like an article I noticed earlier. Is it the one about the soldier?" Courtney set salt and pepper shakers and two glasses of orange juice on the table.

"Yeah, it looks like he was a soldier in the Second World War." Darren paused and thought for a moment. "I think I knew that already. His name is William Sutherland. The article talks about a platoon in the 6th Brigade of the Second Canadian Infantry Division. It looks like they were right in the middle of things in a lot of battles. The article says: 'William Sutherland, a corporal during the unit's hard-fought battles in France and Holland, is now one of only four men remaining from the platoon that distinguished itself in the Battle of the Falaise Gap. Sergeant Sutherland is now fighting a new battle against cancer.'" Darren paused and reached for his juice.

"What else does it say? That sounds really interesting." Courtney sat now, having set down two plates of hearty breakfast. Darren folded the paper so that he could continue reading between bites.

"It goes on a bit about his family being at his side, and then talks about what he did after the war: 'Bill Sutherland remained active in the military for eleven years after the war and later championed a movement for Veterans' rights.' There's a quote from his son here about how he was always looking out for the other soldiers he fought with." Darren paused to chew a large mouthful of sausage and then continued. "It looks like he did well financially after the war, but he was a real hero to guys who got the short end of the stick. The quote from his son goes on here: '... although Dad does not often talk about the specifics of battles he fought in, I am sure from his work later in life that he was always a leader to those around him. I can't think of anyone more likely to risk his own neck to help out one of his buddies in trouble.'"

"So what is he like now?" Courtney interjected. She had barely touched her breakfast and was listening with rapt attention.

Darren lowered the newspaper and slurped a mouthful of coffee before answering. "I guess you could say that he's a hero now, too." He looked down at the picture in the newspaper of a young and vigorous Bill Sutherland before reading further. "I've never seen anyone handle being really sick quite as well as this guy does. He just seems to be a constant comfort to his family. He really has it together."

"I wonder if we can really appreciate the kinds of things he must know and perceive after all he has lived through. He survived an incredible period of history."

"You haven't even heard his whole story yet," Darren added. "There's even more about him. Listen to this," he ruffled the newspaper and cleared his throat. "'William Sutherland's greatest contributions to his country may be those from the 1970s. The diplomatic skills he gained in his years as a lobbyist were perfectly suited to his eventual posting with the United Nations.' Isn't that interesting?"

Courtney was obviously impressed. "I guess it's no surprise that he is such a strong individual, having been through so much."

"Yeah," answered Darren. "He's exactly the opposite of this other guy I'm looking after. He's a German guy who was in the war too. He's a complete nutcase to his family and to the nurses. I bet in that famous battle, Sutherland was leading guys on to victory while the German was running for his life."

"Darren, have you even thought about the kind of life that the German man may have lived?"

"Oh, I'm just joking. The German guy is a frustrating jerk,

though." He reached for his juice but paused. "Wait, you're reading that book on war criminals, right?"

"It's about the trials that took place at the end of the Second World War. I'm mostly reading for the legal precedents that were set. Maybe you should be taking advantage of the living history you have in front of you at work. Have you even asked these men about their stories?"

Darren stood up and cleared the breakfast table as Courtney finished her last few bites. "No, we don't have much time to chat, and besides, the German guy has been pretty confused most of the time." He did the dishes as she took her turn with the newspaper and read more of William Sutherland's biography. While scrubbing a burnt piece of sausage from the bottom of a frying pan, he reflected on what she had said.

"What was it that you said about legal precedents?"

"I just meant that the Nuremberg trials are fascinating, both legally and psychologically, because international law was developed to cope with the horrible atrocities that had happened over the previous years."

"Wasn't the Geneva convention already written by then?" Darren rinsed the frying pan, pleased with its clean surface and with his recollection of history he had learned in high school.

"The Geneva convention deals with appropriate treatment of prisoners of war. It has nothing to do with occupied civilians." Courtney put down the paper as she walked to the counter and poured herself some coffee.

"So why weren't there any laws about civilian atrocities?" Darren started rinsing their plates, and Courtney set down her coffee cup.

"There were no laws dealing with crimes so horrible that no one had dreamed of them yet. I wonder what your German patient's memory of those days is like."

Darren kept washing, realizing that he had drawn Courtney into a more serious conversation than he wanted to contemplate on his day off. When he finished the dishes he went to the living room and made himself comfortable. He reached for the remote control to turn on the television.

"Don't turn the TV on yet," said Courtney as she hurried into the room and cuddled up next to him. "Let me tell you about the people we're having over tonight."

"Sure."

"I met Charlene at the bookstore. She's a Master's student in political science and she works part time at the store. She's been writing about North American monetary policy."

"Don't even get me started on that." Darren rolled his eyes in mock boredom and suffered a jab in the ribs from Courtney as she went on.

"Her fiancé's name is Keith. I think you'll like him because he's interested in a lot of the same things as you. He follows college football and he's really into mountain biking."

Darren liked the sound of Keith already, but he was disheartened to realize that he had not watched a single game of football all season. It occurred to him that this afternoon would give him a chance to catch up. Courtney laid out the plans for the afternoon.

"I'm going to get some groceries so that I can make something nice for dinner. You can relax for now, but whenever you feel like it, would you mind walking down the road for a bottle of wine and maybe some flowers for the table?"

Darren responded that it sounded like a manageable assignment, and in the meantime he would make himself comfortable on the couch. Having done most of their cooking himself while Courtney was busy with law school exams, Darren was not sorry that Courtney was now taking over that household task, particularly since she was the better cook. He leafed through the television guide and found a selection of football games that would make for excellent viewing.

Darren watched football for some time, and found he was flipping channels from game to game because he had no idea how any of the teams were doing in the standings. After her return from the store, Courtney worked in the kitchen preparing several tasty dishes. At first she gently reminded him of his task, but her reminders gradually increased in intensity before she finally tossed his jacket on top of him and insisted that he get moving out the door. Their guests would be arriving in under an hour.

Darren took his time and enjoyed the walk. At the flower store he picked up a bouquet of flowers he hoped Courtney would like. Having not recognized the names of any of the flowers he was trying to choose, he looked for nice colours. The ones he selected had petals the shade of pink … he thought it was called coral … that Courtney liked. He spent even longer at the liquor store. He quickly chose a bottle of wine he remembered having before, but also decided that he should stock the fridge with a half dozen beers. It was in that last choice that he spent most of his time, noticing there was a large selection of local ales he had never sampled.

While Darren was getting dressed in some tidier clothes after his return home, the telephone rang. Darren winced, realizing that the frequent uninvited ringing of his pager when he was on call had sensitized him to the sound of even the telephone. Even knowing that no one would be calling for his medical assistance here, he could not entirely shake his fear of the cardiac arrest pager. He wondered how many days he would need to be off work before ringing noises would stop startling him, and considered unplugging the telephone.

Courtney came into the bedroom and began putting on earrings. "That was Charlene. They'll be here in about ten minutes."

Darren could tell that Courtney was excited about this evening. He felt momentarily guilty that she been alone so often since they moved here. He had at least made acquaintances at the hospital, if no close friends, but she had little opportunity to associate with her own crowd. At least next year, when she began articling, that would no longer be an issue, and now the bookstore had provided an opportunity to meet someone with similar interests.

There was a knock at the door a few minutes later, and Courtney invited in Charlene and Keith. They had brought a bottle of wine, which Keith handed to Darren before they shook hands. Courtney surprised Darren by taking two beers from the refrigerator and offering one to Charlene. He had never known her to like beer, but now she seemed to be enjoying one while she showed her new friend some pictures from Mexico. Darren offered Keith a beer, now worrying that he would run out, and a seat on the couch. Football was still playing at low volume on the television, and Keith immediately started up the conversation.

"So what do you think of the Lions' chances this year?" He gestured towards the screen.

"Oh, I don't know …" Darren struggled to think of anything informed to say, but he had simply lost touch with sports. Knowing he had not seen them in a game all year, he tried to remember how they had done the previous year and could not. Thinking about football, he realized that he had not seen much last year either because he had been studying.

"I think they've got a pretty good team." Keith said when he saw that Darren had nothing to offer. "But you know who's going to be the team to beat?" He began informing Darren of his foolproof picks for the Grey Cup, but slowed down when he noticed Darren was offering only polite nods.

Darren felt frustrated with himself. Usually the first person to expound on sports statistics, he was quite unused to being at a loss. Keith began to probe deeper for areas of common interest. "Do you follow hockey?"

"Yeah, but I guess I haven't seen many games lately. I turned on an exhibition game at the hospital the other night and I didn't even recognize one of the uniforms." They both chuckled, but now Keith looked like he wanted to change the subject again.

"So, Courtney told us you're a medical resident."

"Yeah." Darren was relieved that a subject had come up on which he should easily be able to comment. He did not notice that he was most comfortable now that the subject was himself.

"How's that going?"

"It's okay, I guess. It's pretty busy. I don't get much sleep." Now Keith was politely nodding. He leaned forward very slightly and raised his eyebrows in expectation, but Darren felt absolutely at a loss. He could not think of anything else to say. What would people want to know about the hospital? Keith leaned back in his seat when Darren trailed off. After a brief pause, Keith tried again to establish common ground for a conversation on anything at all.

"Charlene and I went to see a movie that was pretty good the other day. Have you seen *Sudden Refusal*?"

"No, I haven't been to a movie in a while." Darren thought he might have seen a television commercial for it this afternoon, but could not remember much about it. He listened while Keith described the film and summarized that it would be a good choice if he had time. Darren's mind was racing but he was coming up short of anything interesting to say. He wondered when he had been robbed of his ability to use conversational platitudes. He thought of commenting on the weather but did not bother. Finally they sat back silently and watched the football game without the distraction of speaking to one another. Their quietude was only interrupted when Keith inquired if he could have another beer.

Thankfully, the painful silence was relieved when Courtney invited everyone to take their seats at the table. Keith complemented Courtney on the lovely presentation of the food as Charlene helped her set it out and Darren quietly unfolded his napkin into his lap. Courtney smiled warmly at her guests when the table was set and Keith politely took his chair after she and Charlene were comfortably seated. They began enjoying dinner and Charlene and Courtney continued talking enthusiastically about people they knew from work, current events, prospects of Courtney's legal career and anything else that came to mind. Keith sighed, almost inaudibly, before taking his first bite, then contributed occasionally to the conversation. Darren mostly ate in silence. Seeing the asymmetry of the conversation, Charlene tried to lure Darren in.

"So, Darren, Courtney tells me you have been working really hard at the hospital."

"Yeah, I guess so." Darren made sure to smile politely, afraid that his complete inability to think of anything to say might seem unfriendly.

Charlene was not deterred. With a warm smile, she went on. "You must see some really interesting things."

Now Darren was suddenly struck by just how much he had to talk about. Somehow he had assumed that no one would want to hear about his work, but now his mind was filled with amusing anecdotes. "Yeah." He smiled widely as he began his story, "like the other day a patient died on the ward. There was a medical student there, so I asked the student to make sure he was dead. The student leaned over him to listen to whether he was breathing, and while he was leaning over he put his hand on the dead patient's chest. Well, when he put his weight on the guy's chest, all the air came rushing out of the guy's lungs, and the medical student felt air blown in his ear." At this point Darren acted out the dead body blowing a large gasp of air as its chest was compressed. "The student must have jumped ten feet in the air! I couldn't help laughing. I'm just glad the dead guy's family wasn't in the room because I practically had tears in my eyes I was laughing so hard." Everyone had been smiling, and Keith had laughed until the point in the story when Darren mentioned the dead man's family. At that point Courtney gasped slightly and put her hand to her mouth. Charlene and Keith suddenly quieted. Darren was on a roll now though. Obliviously, he began another story. "Actually, one of the most exciting cases I've dealt with was two or three days ago when this diabetic lady came into the hospital with pneumonia. She had all this fluid around her lung, and she was really sick." Looking into their faces, Darren realized his guests' discomfort at his previous anecdote. He quietly turned his eyes towards his dinner and reached for a bite. Charlene and Courtney also turned their attention back to the food, but Keith remained motionless, staring at Darren. Finally he broke the silence.

"So, what do you do about that fluid?"

The animation returned to Darren's face and he began speaking with his mouth still full. "When that happens with pneumonia," he swallowed a large piece of potato, "you have to drain the fluid out, so I put a chest tube into her. It was really gross."

Darren picked up his knife, which he had placed beside his plate, but halted the motion when Keith again broke the silence. "What was so gross?"

"This senior resident was helping me, but when I got the chest tube in, pus just started pouring out of it. We couldn't get the tube attached to the container it's supposed to drain into, so this pus just kept flowing all over the floor." Now Charlene and Courtney had stopped eating and everyone was listening to the story in silence. Charlene was pale. Courtney loudly set down her knife on her plate but Darren did not notice. "Well, a nurse came into the room and asked us what the hell we were doing making such a mess, because pus was literally spraying out of her chest. When the nurse came up to us she slipped and fell on the mess on the floor and the stuff sprayed out on top of her." Darren paused because he was now laughing at his own story.

Keith chuckled and said, "You were right, that is really gross."

"We were still trying to get the tubes hooked up, and I think pus sprayed into the nurse's hair. You wouldn't believe it, there was litres of the stuff and the nurse just about puked!"

"Darren! I think we've heard enough of that!" Courtney's voice arrested both Darren and Keith's laughter. Charlene looked socially uncomfortable and nauseated. Courtney's beautiful dinner was aesthetically ruined. Darren was still laughing to himself, but slowed to a stop rapidly as he looked at the people around him. He quieted down and began finishing his dinner, but Courtney had put down her cutlery and Keith stopped eating after a sharp glance from Charlene.

Darren offered to clear the table when he was done, and Courtney tried to resuscitate their dinner party. She suggested to Charlene and Keith that they go out for a drink, but the guests politely declined, saying that they had to be up early.

On their way out, Charlene and Keith each told Darren that it had been, "nice to meet you," and he reciprocated. Charlene told Courtney that she would talk to her later at work, and the guests were on their way.

"Well," said Courtney after they had left. "They certainly went home early."

"What do you mean?" Darren was not too dense to see Courtney's obvious anger.

"You know, I haven't had much chance to meet people since we've been here, and this dinner was important to me."

"I know it was …" Darren tried to empathize but was sharply cut off.

"So why couldn't you be nice to Keith? Even if only so that I could enjoy myself with Charlene."

"I don't know what you mean. I was being nice."

"Oh, come on." She looked at him like he was an insect. "He was already sending Charlene signals that he wanted to go home by the time we sat down for dinner."

"But he was … I didn't see that." A desperate pleading note was starting to enter Darren's voice.

"Of course you didn't." Courtney's tone was aggressive. "And then those terrible stories."

"But they asked about …"

"Nobody asked to hear stories about body fluids at the dinner table. That was revolting. Now maybe in the future you could pull together what's still left of your social skills, and try to be a little more sensitive about what's important to me."

Courtney turned and stormed into their bedroom, and Darren could only stand in stunned silence. Part of him wanted to go to the fridge for another beer, but he decided that he would get more points in the long run by doing the dishes instead. Arguments are so often stoked, he knew, when each party becomes defensive. Darren was not convinced, as he moved to the kitchen, that he knew enough about what had just happened to want to defend himself.

Courtney spent the rest of the evening in the bedroom, and she was already asleep when he came in late and went to sleep beside her.

Chapter 23

On Friday it would never have occurred to Darren that he might be glad to return to work on Monday. Yet here he was starting rounds and thinking it was not such a bad place to be. He was not on call tonight, so a brief ten-hour workday was all the hospital had in store for him. Compared with the icy mood at home on Sunday, this was practically a holiday.

Now the team approached Mr Doering's room. Dr Smith stopped in front of the door and faced his young apprentices with a stance suggesting a barrage of questions was impending. "Mr Doering's biopsy has now proven beyond any possible doubt the presence of a small-cell lung cancer." He addressed the team with this blunt statement of fact. He did so in order to preface his first question, rather than because his team was unaware of the diagnosis. Samples of tissue had been taken from Mr Doering's lung through a fiberoptic scope in a procedure known as a bronchoscopy. An experienced pathologist had concluded with certainty that the cells she saw were cancerous after looking at them under a microscope. Dr Smith's team had been contacted with the news, and Dr Smith had informed Mr and Mrs Doering personally. The news should not have been a surprise, since the team had already told the Doerings they thought Mr Doering had cancer and all that had been left was to determine exactly what kind. The news had not gone over well, and Kurt Doering could now be heard arguing with his wife. His raised voice sounded in the hallway and Darren had trouble concentrating on what Dr

Smith was asking. "Who can tell me about the prognosis of small-cell lung cancer? Dr Bofors?"

Eddy visibly squirmed at the question. "Um, it's not good."

"Dr Leigh?" Dr Smith curtly redirected the question as though Eddy never existed.

As Layton concisely summarized recently published data on several thousand lung cancer patients, Darren was struck by a sense of irony. If Mr Doering were reasonable, his first question to his doctors would be the same one as Dr Smith's, but in stark, plain language, the language of need, not expertise. It would not include fancy Latin root words or medical mumbo jumbo, but would be a plea to know what to expect in the language of the land, the language of the person before him.

"How bad is it?" English was not Kurt's childhood tongue, but the language of a Canadian patient shared meaning with words that might be spoken in German. Medical jargon, precise, lacking ambiguity, bound forever to the structure of dead languages, could exclude a listener from any country.

Although his answer had not been detailed, Eddy's answer, "not good," was what the patient would want to know. Had Eddy offered his answer to Mr Doering, the patient's next question would almost inevitably be some variation on duration: "How long have I got?"

That was the question that Layton was starting to reconnoitre. He was busy describing statistical measures of how long people would live with lung cancer. Unfortunately, what those measures always obscured was how doctors never really know how long anyone will live. Layton might eloquently summarize data about lung cancer patients by describing a 'median survival' of six months with a 'five-year survival' of two percent and a 'one-year survival' of fifteen percent, but unless his patient was a statistician that message was an empty vessel. When given an answer masked in a statistical smokescreen, the patients would invariably say to their friends and family, "The doctor gave me six months to live."

As Darren heard the statistics, he wanted very much to be sure the Doerings would get an answer they would understand. He decided to talk to Mrs Doering later in the day and tell her the answer in plain English. Without any statistical nonsense, all those median survivals and one-year survivals could effectively be summarized in comprehensible human discourse. It might go something like this:

"Mr Doering has a disease that has affected many people in the past. We don't know how long he will live, but of those people in the past, only half of them lived for more than six months and only fifteen percent of them lived for a year. He could develop a fatal complication at any time, but in all likelihood it will probably be only a matter of months. The thing to remember is that he will need to be prepared for the worst at any time."

Darren was satisfied that he had mentally summarized the data into a form that would be understandable to the Doerings, and most importantly to Mrs Doering, whom he very much wanted to keep informed. He suspected they would not get such a clear answer on rounds this morning, but was proud of himself for the clear statement he had formulated. Unfortunately, experience in medical school had taught him that after such a concise and understandable explanation, anxious patients often still came away with, "The doctor gave me six months to live."

Layton finished his answer and Dr Smith nodded in satisfaction.

"All right, Doctors, let's see how the patient is doing." Dr Smith swung around and took a step into Mr Doering's room. Mr Doering's raised voice suddenly silenced. From Mrs Doering's tear-stained face it was obvious that she was not only saddened by her husband's illness, but that he had been saying hurtful things to her.

"Good morning, Mr Doering. You know the members of your medical team." Dr Smith greeted his patient formally as though unaware of the obvious tension in the room. He gestured to Darren, Eddy and Layton as he spoke.

"I want a second opinion." Doering ignored Dr Smith's

formalities and spoke as though suppressing rage. His wife raised her hand to her mouth, and then leaned towards her husband to put a hand on his arm. She obviously felt he was being rude to his doctors for the sake of rudeness and hoped he might mellow somewhat under her influence. He only shrugged off her attempt at tenderness.

Smith seemed completely unaffected by Doering's sudden statement of dissatisfaction. He responded in his usual, emotionless, businesslike fashion.

"I understand, Mr Doering, but I need you to be more specific. You understand that a biopsy was taken from your lungs by bronchoscopy. Would you like the bronchoscopy repeated or would you like the biopsy examined by a second pathologist?"

"What I want is to know why you think that I could have lung cancer. I want answers and all I get is your medical nonsense." Kurt was beginning to raise his voice again. His wife looked distressed but did not reach out to him a second time.

Dr Smith again responded emotionlessly. "Mr Doering, the primary risk factor for small-cell lung cancer is a history of smoking. Because you have a long history of smoking, we know, as any doctor would, that you were at risk for the disease."

"That's ridiculous!" Kurt was not quite yelling, but he was beginning to sound flustered. "You have no evidence that smoking causes cancer. In fact, it was a doctor who told me to start smoking in the first place."

"That is all beside the point now, Mr Doering, because the biopsy has medically proven small-cell lung cancer."

Darren was wondering how Dr Smith remained so completely unaffected by all this. He realized once again that he had preferred the previous Mr Doering, the patient too confused to speak coherently. He, Layton and Eddy continued to stand silently in the background.

"All I want is answers, and all you give me are more lies," Kurt's complaints continued. "First a doctor tells me to smoke, and now you're telling me it's bad. Does advice change over time?

You don't even know what's going on here obviously, because I felt fine before I came in and now you're telling me that I'm sick." Darren realized he would find this contradictory diatribe sad if he did not find Mr Doering so dislikeable. Dislike, surprisingly like patience, goes a long way with professional demeanour. As it was, he was beginning to find the patient offensive. His feelings were only magnified when Doering was rude to his wife after her attempts to help.

"Dear, I think the doctors are only trying to …"

"Nobody asked what you think!" he snapped at her.

Dr Smith stood motionless through all this, as though thinking of something else. Now he once again gave an answer that suggested he had ignored everything that had been going on.

"All right, Mr Doering. We will have another pathologist look at that biopsy for you. Goodbye for now." He led the team out into the corridor. "Who is next on our list?"

"That would be Mr Sutherland," responded Eddy, quick to answer this one manageable question.

The team followed Dr Smith into William Sutherland's room. As always, the atmosphere was much different than that in Mr Doering's room. Darren felt a palpable difference in the air. Mr Sutherland was seated in bed and two young women were in the room with him. His daughter sat at the foot of his bed and his niece, whom Darren had met on rounds once previously, was in a chair near the door. As the team entered, the niece excused herself, saying she would let them talk in private because she needed to get a coffee anyway. Mr Sutherland's telephone rang twice, and he answered with a forceful, "Sutherland here!"

The doctors all paused as they entered the room, and looking in their direction he spoke into the receiver.

"I'll have to call you back shortly. There's some blokes with important business here to see me." He winked in the direction of his medical team as he spoke, and Darren thought he had never seen anyone who could be so charming and socially engaged from a hospital bed.

On Bill's bedside table was a pile of file folders filled with letters, pictures and documents. Darren imagined that Mr Sutherland must have been working on a journal or diary, and he looked more carefully at a map that extended from one of the files. Darren recognized that some of the text represented names of French towns, but could make little sense of the numbers and symbols over much of the terrain. Some symbols represented military units, long since disbanded, and some the headquarters of officers, now dead. A hill featured prominently near the middle of the paper, and had even been given a name, marked in bright red. It was a hill that had been bulldozed in 1972 to make room for a new road.

"What can I do for you lads?" Sutherland asked the team. Darren smiled, realizing that from Bill Sutherland's perspective and experience, Dr Smith was almost as young as the residents in his charge.

"The question is, 'What can we do for you?'" answered Dr Smith.

"Oh, I'm doing just fine," answered Sutherland. "No need to go out of your way for me. I won't interrupt your business if you leave me alone to mine." He looked out of the window and then turned back. The smile that Darren anticipated was absent from Sutherland's face.

"Are you eating and drinking?" asked Layton. That was the question that got to the heart of Mr Sutherland's admission to hospital. He was still requiring hydration by intravenous because the cancer in his throat made it too difficult for him to swallow.

"A little bit," answered Mr Sutherland.

"Oh, Dad," interjected his daughter. "You've hardly had anything at all."

"Well, I don't want to complain," Bill responded. "After all, the food here is better than the army." Darren found conversation with Sutherland strange and disquieting when Bill's perpetual smile was not evident. The intern's breath returned to his lungs when Sutherland's lips twitched upwards. Bill spoke in a quieter tone, as though revealing a secret. "But it's not exactly the Ritz."

"Well, what do you think is the next step in our management here, Dr Leigh?" Dr Smith turned to his senior resident.

Layton silently accepted the transfer of command, and explained his plan directly to their patient. "Mr Sutherland, maybe it would be helpful for you if we went ahead with the stenting procedure we talked about. The procedure can be done tomorrow. A stent is placed in your swallowing tube to hold it open and help you swallow. It won't make the cancer go away, but it will make it easier for you to get down some food."

"Whatever you chaps think is best."

"I think this will make you feel better," Layton answered. The team members excused themselves, and Eddy quickly reviewed the patient's temperature chart on the wall while Smith made a show of returning his stethoscope to his hip pocket and his gold pen to his breast. Mr Sutherland's daughter touched Dr Smith's shoulder before the team entered the hall.

"Could I speak with you for a moment?" She left the room with them and spoke when they were out of Mr Sutherland's earshot. "I think my Dad is having more pain than he is letting on. He never asks the nurses for painkillers because he doesn't want to bother them, but he's always uncomfortable." Her impression of her father was impeccable, but Darren wondered at Mr Sutherland's refusal of analgesia. Might he be afraid of relinquishing his independence? Perhaps his choices were tainted by vanity or denial.

"I asked him this morning if he had any pain, and he said he didn't." As Darren spoke she turned, affording him a view through her pupils at the light reflected from her retina. Examining his own reflection, dressed in a sharp white coat, he contemplated the subtle interpersonal interactions within the Sutherland family.

"He's always been very stoic, but I hate for him to be in pain just because he won't ask for painkillers," Sutherland's daughter continued. As she spoke, Darren leaned back to give himself a line of sight into Mr Sutherland's room. Bill was dialling his telephone, a look of obvious pain across his face. Obviously, he had been suppressing it while others were in the room.

Layton once again took charge. "There are painkillers ordered for him if he asks, but we can't give him painkillers if he doesn't want them. Why don't you keep encouraging him to ask for some if he is uncomfortable? Dr Johnston here will come back this afternoon and do the same thing. Maybe if he gets the same message from different sources, he'll start to listen."

She returned to her father's room unconvinced, after thanking all the doctors for their help. The next patient the team was scheduled to round on was on a different ward, so they talked together as they walked.

"That wasn't quite as painful as Doering's room," said Eddy when Dr Smith stepped away to wash his hands.

Darren did not return Eddy's gaze. He wondered if Mr Sutherland's good nature was as genuine as they all found it easy to believe.

Chapter 24

Darren regretted that he and Courtney had not spoken much the night before. He knew from her distance she was awaiting an apology. Because he was still not exactly sure what he should be apologizing for, he had put it off, but he was on call tonight, so he would not see her until Wednesday afternoon. He cleaned his tray of a greasy lunch and considered calling her just as his pager interrupted his train of thought.

The call was from an emergency physician who explained that a lady had arrived with a stroke, so Darren headed for the department. Even before finding her chart, Darren recognized the person he was looking for. Near the nursing desk, a lady about seventy years of age lay on an outdated hospital stretcher that continued its tour of duty despite advanced age and rusted wheels. Her distressed husband was standing at the bedside and speaking to her, but she stared past him with no apparent comprehension. The right side of her face drooped down, letting saliva dribble onto her chin, and her right arm hung useless at her side. As Darren approached she smiled in her husband's direction in response to a hand he laid on her arm. His speech still did not arouse any interest from her.

"Good morning, Sir. My name is Dr Johnston."

"Don Fleming."

"I'm with the Internal Medicine Department. The emergency physician has asked me to come and see your wife because he feels she will need to come into hospital. Can you tell me what has been happening?"

"I think she must be having a stroke." Mr Fleming stopped as though there was nothing more to say.

"What did you first notice?"

"When I got up this morning, she just stayed in bed. I talked to her and she looked at me, but she didn't seem to have anything to say. I thought maybe she didn't feel like talking, so I left her for a while. When I went back to talk to her, it seemed like she couldn't hear me. Then I noticed that her arm was hanging limp." He pointed at her arm, which remained flaccid.

Darren asked a few more questions to complete his medical history. He discovered that Mrs Fleming had an irregular heart beat, which he knew to be associated with stroke because the irregularly beating heart can launch blood clots to the brain. Together with her other symptoms, there was not much doubt of the diagnosis. He began to examine Mrs Fleming, and as he did so he marvelled at how much he could tell about her with his physical examination. By knowing the paths of nerves from the brain to the face and limbs, he could pinpoint exactly where the blood clot was that had robbed her of the use of her arm. He knew also that the area of the brain dedicated to speech sat right next to the area he had pinpointed, and that was why Mrs Fleming could not talk. He prepared to order a CT scan, but knew that it was unlikely to tell him anything he did not already know. He felt proud of the power that his knowledge had given him, but as he looked back at Mr Fleming he also felt powerless because he knew there was precious little he could do to help her. Powerful medications that break apart blood clots can only be used within three hours of the event. Mrs Fleming had awoken four hours ago with symptoms, and may have had the stroke at any time during the night.

Darren finished his examination and Mr Fleming's eyes began to fill with tears. Darren, who had been about to ask more questions, handed the man a tissue and gave him a moment to dry his eyes.

"Why can't she hear me?" pleaded Leona Fleming's husband of fifty-one years.

Darren thought it ironic that his greater understanding of what was happening only made the story seem more tragic. While Mr Fleming believed that his wife was not responding to him because she was unable to hear what he said, Darren knew that this was not the case. Mrs Fleming's hearing was unaffected. The part of her brain necessary to process language was lost. That meant not only that she was unable to understand English, but also that the whole concept of communicating with other people was something now outside her comprehension. She continued staring forward, oblivious to the conversation around her. Darren thought for a moment of the right response to Mr Fleming's question.

"I think she can hear you," he answered. There was a moment of silence, and then Mr Fleming nodded. Perhaps he had understood the double edge of what Darren had said and perhaps he had chosen a different way of understanding. "I'm going to talk to the nurses so we can get a few tests. I think you're right that she's had a stroke, but we will get a scan to help confirm it. Then we will do everything we can to help her. Do you have any more questions for me?"

"Could I talk to you again when the tests are finished?"

"Sure. I'll be around." Darren smiled warmly and excused himself.

After he wrote orders for Mrs Fleming's admission, he strolled to the resident's lounge. The day had not been too busy so far and he was enjoying a relaxed pace. He decided that he should let Layton know he had admitted Mrs Fleming and then maybe he could get some studying done.

"Layton here." Layton answered Darren's page in his usual way.

"Hi, Layton. There's a lady down in the ER. She's a seventy year old with a left middle cerebral artery CVA." He described her diagnosis using the medical abbreviation for a stroke. "She's too late for clot busters. The diagnosis is pretty clear, but I'll still need to check her CT scan. I just went ahead and ordered her admission to Dr Smith's team."

"Sounds good," answered Layton, "I'll take a look at her when she gets upstairs. What's her name?"

Darren paused. He was struck by the irony that he could remember exactly which blood vessel in her brain was blocked, and even her exact age, but he could not remember her name. He struggled, trying to recall how her husband had introduced himself, but had no luck. "I can't remember."

"That's okay," Layton continued. "She'll show up on our list in the computer when they get the paperwork done down there. Any more business down in Emergency?"

"Not for now."

"All right. I'll see you later."

Darren paused for another moment after hanging up, but could still not remember the lady's name.

He sat down and opened a textbook. Not sure exactly what he should read about, he began on a chapter about stroke management. It was a depressingly thin chapter since so little could be done for patients who were not seen very quickly after suffering their stroke.

Ten minutes into his reading, his pager interrupted him once again. Really busy days were often less frustrating than these days when he was constantly teased with the promise of time for studying or sleeping but was intermittently interrupted by a call. The afternoon was punctuated with more of the same, and he admitted three more patients before a break for dinner. As he finished and realized that once again he had a free moment, he again decided to give Courtney a call to try and smooth things over. His hand was on the telephone receiver when his pager rang again.

This time he was being called to see a patient with pneumonia. The emergency physician apologized that this was a complicated patient, and said she would explain why when Darren arrived in the department.

Back downstairs, Darren found Dr Williams, the emergency physician who had consulted him. She was an outgoing and relaxed young doctor, young enough to remember what it was like to be a junior resident. Whenever she called a resident with a frustrating consult, she always seemed apologetic, and that was certainly the case this time.

"I'm sorry about this one. We hoped to be able to send her home. In fact, she's been down in the ER since yesterday morning. She has a pneumonia." As she spoke she held up a chest X-ray with an obvious white patch in the left lung. "But she's not all that sick from it." Darren nodded knowingly as he looked at the X-ray, but began to wonder what Dr Williams was getting at. "The point is that she has this chronic pain problem. Ever since she came in, she has been complaining of pain in her legs. It's exactly the same pain she has had for the last twenty years, but since she complains about it so much it has been hard to get her back home."

Darren was not sure what facial expression betrayed him, but Dr Williams seemed to read his thoughts. "I know what you mean." She smiled.

Grabbing his list of patients from his pocket, he added the new consult. He also noted that he still needed to check the CT he had ordered on "the stroke lady," as he had begun calling her to himself. "I'll see her in just a moment. I just need to stop in radiology."

"Thanks a million," said Dr Williams.

The stroke lady's CT scan revealed nothing surprising, so with minimal enthusiasm, Darren went to see his new patient.

"Hi. My name is Dr Johnston. I understand you have not been feeling well." He entered the curtained area around her bed. The patient was a thin lady, about fifty years old. She did not look terribly uncomfortable.

"No. I have this terrible pain in my legs."

"How long have you had the pain for?"

"About twenty years. My family doctor gives me painkillers for it."

"Who is your family doctor?"

"Dr Sterns."

"I don't know him. Where does he work?"

"He just moved to practice in California."

"Okay. How about the pain? Is the pain any different now than it has been for the last twenty years?"

"No. It's always terrible."

"I'm not sure I understand. What brought you into the hospital yesterday?"

"My daughter said I should come in."

"Why?"

"I don't know."

"Is your daughter here now?"

"No."

Darren could feel his frustration building. He decided to change the topic and ask about the pneumonia. "Have you had any other symptoms lately?"

"Yes, I have felt terrible."

"In what way?"

"Oh, it's hard to say."

Darren still sensed that he was getting nowhere. If he was going to get to the bottom of this, he had to ask some closed questions. "Have you been coughing?"

"Not really."

"How about any fevers or chills?"

"Maybe."

"Pain in the chest?"

"Not exactly."

Darren had hoped for at least a few definitive answers when he asked about symptoms of pneumonia, since she obviously had that, but he had had no luck. After working for a while on the paperwork accompanying her admission, he looked at the clock on the wall and saw that it was now after ten o'clock at night. He decided there and then that he would admit her and start treating her for the pneumonia. At least he would be able to fix the pneumonia, even if it did not seem to be what was bothering her. There was no chance he was going to be able to fix her leg pain miraculously if she had had it for twenty years. While she was in hospital, he could get some more answers about what else had been going on. Perhaps he could contact her daughter and her family doctor the next morning.

Having decided how to approach this case, Darren finished taking his history. That took him a very long time because she was extraordinarily complicated. It turned out that she was now taking two hundred milligrams of morphine a day, enough to kill most people, and even most large livestock. She had been slowly increasing her dose for many years. She also had a host of other medical problems, like an irregular heartbeat that required blood thinners. He was careful not to forget to order her blood thinners, remembering the lady who had had a stroke earlier in the day because of her irregular heartbeat. He also ordered the same painkillers that his latest patient had been taking at home, thinking that the team could start working on the leg pain in the morning.

"What about my pain?" she called to him from her bed as he finished writing.

"I'm ordering you the medicine you get at home, so the nurses will get that for you shortly."

"But I'm in agony."

"Well, let's get you this medicine and then see how you do." He was getting fed up with her. He had seen other patients in serious pain today who managed to behave like adults. This lady's pain had not even changed in twenty years and now she was yelling at him like it was the end of the world. She did not even act like a person in serious pain. Maybe she was just addicted to painkillers. Either way, he was not going to be able to solve the problem tonight, so he went back to the lounge to call Courtney.

Sterile white hallways offered a backdrop for introspection, and Darren considered the thought of living with constant pain. Pain derived from internal organs is dull and ill defined. Doctors refer to it as visceral. The body has no motive for pinpointing its exact location, since we cannot defend ourselves from our insides, so patients with pain from their stomach or bowels will vaguely gesture at their abdomen when asked what hurts. Visceral pain is distressing, though, since problems with the internal organs may hearken serious illness. Parietal pain is pain that comes from cutting the body's surface, and occurs more often in the limbs. It is sharp, and since it may signal an attack requiring urgent defence, it is exquisitely localized. Darren thought of specific causes of each type of pain and realized that chronic inflammatory diseases could cause longstanding pain. Two examples are rheumatoid arthritis, where the joints are inflamed, and Crohn's disease, an inflammatory bowel disease. Patients with rheumatoid arthritis and patients with Crohn's disease each have chronic inflammation caused by the same general process, even requiring the same medications, but patients with Crohn's disease have distressing internal pain of their bowels, whereas patients with rheumatoid arthritis might have just as much pain, but their joints cause a more parietal pain that lacks the distressing quality of visceral pain. He had seen patients with Crohn's disease present with pain to the Emergency Department in the middle of the night, but never patients with rheumatoid arthritis. Now he felt even more sceptical of his patient's leg pain.

Darren noticed that it was getting quite late, so once again he decided he would put off talking to Courtney until tomorrow. He changed course and began to walk to his call room in the hopes of getting some sleep before he was called again.

His luck did not change, and he was called the instant his head hit the pillow. It was three o'clock by the time he got to bed, and his pager rang again. This time it was not a new consult, but a call from the wards.

"Hi, Dr Johnston. Sorry to bother you, but this lady you admitted earlier, Mrs Henry, is complaining of a lot of pain in her legs."

Darren had started to look at the list of patients he had just seen to remind him who Mrs Henry was, but did not need any help once he heard about the legs. "Okay. Mrs Henry has had that pain for twenty years. Did she get the painkillers that she usually takes at home?"

"Yes. She says it's not enough."

"Okay, would you give her five milligrams of morphine, please?" Darren knew that his order would not make much difference. He did not want to give her much more morphine, in case she was an addict. The pain in her legs had been present for twenty years, so it was not going to kill her tonight. Five milligrams was a big enough dose that the nurses would figure they were helping their patient, but was small enough that it would not make a damn bit of difference to someone who was used to taking two hundred milligrams a day.

"Sure, Dr Johnston. Thanks."

Hoping for some sleep, Darren lay down and was rewarded by merciful loss of consciousness. Two hours later he was roused again. Dreading that he might have another consult to see in the ER, he was almost relieved when it was the same ward again.

"Sorry to bother you again, Dr Johnston. Now Mrs Henry says she has a terrible headache."

Darren sat silently for a moment as his sleep-deprived brain regained function. When it did, all he could think was: *It's probably from taking too much morphine.* He kept that thought, and noticing that his clock now said five o'clock, he said, "I'll be by to see her shortly."

"Thanks, Dr Johnston."

His plan seemed a good one. He could grab another hour's nap, have a shower, grab a coffee and see her quickly before morning rounds started. The plan was successful, too. He did not feel much better rested at six, but he dragged himself out of bed and had a quick shower. On his way down to get a coffee, the plan came apart. His pager rang again from the same ward.

"Hi, Dr Johnston. Now Mrs Henry has vomited, and she's not waking up."

This sounded more serious than the stupid pain in her legs. Someone who threw up without regaining consciousness could choke to death. Why wasn't she waking up? Darren set off at a run for Mrs Henry's ward. On his way up, he began thinking about what could be going on. "Did I give her too much morphine? Maybe she's overdosed." It did not make much sense, given that she was accustomed to two hundred milligrams a day. Nevertheless the idea frightened him.

When he arrived, Mrs Henry was unresponsive, staring at the ceiling. There was vomit around her mouth. He knew she was in immediate danger of choking, so he turned her on her side and asked the nurses to call for the Intensive Care team.

Now that it was morning, all the residents who had not been on call overnight were in the hospital. The first fresh and chipper looking individual to arrive was Chris. Recognizing Darren, he smiled and stopped in the doorway.

"Good morning. How are you doing?"

Darren looked down. He was leaning over Mrs Henry's bed to hold her on her side. The vomit from in and around her mouth had spilled onto the bed and was dribbling over his leg. His patient was taking only gasping breaths and was starting to turn blue.

"Not so good, Chris."

Chris looked momentarily concerned, but did not rush to his aid at the bedside. Instead he leaned on the door jam and asked, "Really, why? What's the matter?"

Darren gestured with his head to the body he was supporting. "Having a little trouble with this patient."

"Oh, the patient! You had me worried about you there for a moment." Now Chris came and offered help. As the respiratory therapists arrived, he intubated the patient to keep her windpipe clear and got ready to take her to the Intensive Care Unit.

Darren began to summarize her medical history for Chris. He had just finished telling Chris about her blood thinning medication when he noticed that one of her pupils was growing very large, and the other was very small. He immediately recognized the sign of someone who has increasing pressure inside their head. He pointed it out to Chris, and they agreed that she had likely spontaneously bled into her brain as a result of her blood thinning medication. It was a rare complication, but one that was well known.

Nurses had arranged monitors around Mrs Henry's bed and now, together with Chris, they were ready to start wheeling her to the Intensive Care Unit.

"Well, it's been nice talking to you. I guess I'll see you later," said Chris on his way out of the room.

"Yeah," said Darren, wondering how Chris remained so calm through such emergencies. Despite his apparently unconcerned attitude, Chris had proficiently intubated the patient and had been very organized when they began treating her. He exerted real leadership for all the support staff in the room, and his confidence quickly seemed to rub off on them.

Suddenly a realization struck Darren. His jaw dropped as the nurses and Chris left the room. His legs felt weak underneath him, and as Chris was just getting out of earshot down the hall, Darren spoke a few words in a feeble voice: "She had a headache."

"I'll bet she did," answered Chris, thinking of the bleed they had diagnosed in her head. Chris carried on, not knowing what it was that had just struck Darren.

Darren was now standing alone in Mrs Henry's room. The other staff had left several minutes ago, and it was now emptied even of the hospital bed that usually occupied it. Darren had just recalled the phone call he had taken about Mrs Henry's headache. He thought back to the way he had stalled the nurses to buy some time for a nap and a shower. A nap and a shower he had enjoyed while Mrs Henry slowly and painfully bled into her brain.

Chapter 25

Wagon wheels rumbled over the torn cobblestone road. Unterfeldwebel Doering was once again marching with a single section of men, once again making his way to a rendezvous point. The frustration of marching in perpetual confusion had long since ceased to bother Kurt, but the fear of defeat hung more closely around him. Now Kurt and his small group of men were walking on a narrow road bordered on the right by a stone fence and on the left by a farmer's field. The wall was three feet in height, and did not give the same claustrophobic sensation as the enormous hedgerows in more northern Normandy. The road was a jumble of men and material with horse-drawn wagons making up their most mobile force. Kurt tasted bile at the thought that the once invincible Wehrmacht was reduced to using wagons, stolen wagons, to transport its men to a new defensive position. Kurt's section was identifiable only by their paratrooper uniforms amongst the crush of Wehrmacht soldiers marching west on the road. A Feldwebel marching with his army platoon had been talking with Kurt as they marched the last few miles.

"My father-in-law had some connections, so he got me an office posting in Kiel, but I requested transfer back to France when the invasion came."

"Why would you do that?" Kurt could not understand the man's desire to join this failing army.

The man had just finished telling the story of his combat experiences earlier in the war. He had fought in the invasion of Belgium and after the fall of France had been posted on the French coastal defence. His family had been concerned that he might be transferred to the Russian Front and had intervened to have him moved to a non-combat posting. Although he had been successfully returned to Germany, he was apparently not satisfied there.

"I suppose I had been fighting for years, and I suddenly could not picture myself behind a desk. I had to go somewhere, but going to the Russian Front never appealed to me."

Kurt smiled at this extreme understatement. The Russian Front was a terrifying prospect not only because of the intense fighting, the harsh cold and the hopeless situation. In the East, the German Armed Forces faced an enemy that might take no prisoners but would certainly show no mercy to those it did take. The soldier continued to talk. "I could not resist fighting in the west. Of course, I could not leave my men to fight here without me."

Kurt nodded. Veterans felt no responsibility more strongly than the need to protect their comrades from abandonment, and when they returned from the battlefield, they would find that their old home no longer satisfied them with its security. Many experienced soldiers were also unable to live without the continuous adrenaline infusion of battle. Why should they be so uncomfortable with a return to normalcy? Perhaps they could no longer face their family and friends with the shame of knowing what they had done and witnessed.

"Walking during the day is a nice change." Kurt rarely felt the need to fill a silence when conversation lulled but today he could not help sharing his enjoyment of the daylight, muted as it was by heavy cloud cover.

"It's overcast," the other sergeant agreed with the sentiment. "No visibility for their aircraft." He looked behind them, and then squinted to look back at the road ahead of them before he continued. "Not that we have any tanks around for their rockets to burn."

Kurt took a look in each direction as well, and again silently nodded. The sergeant was no doubt thinking, as Kurt was, just how disarrayed the army seemed at this point in time. Kurt and his small group of paratroopers were marching among the army, far from the transport planes that were intended to drop them deep behind enemy lines. This other sergeant was part of a mechanized infantry unit, but the only vehicles supporting them were French wagons. The assembled collection of men on the road looked more like a column of refugees than an organized fighting force.

The conversation the two soldiers had been sharing was different from that of any German soldiers on the move so few days ago. Then, it seemed that every soldier wanted to talk about the rumours of an impending massive encirclement by British and Americans. Every man had an opinion about how the counterattack should proceed and how Tommy should be routed back into the sea. Now encirclement was their grim reality. The Allied attack that smashed through the line so near Kurt's position two nights ago was the northern prong of a vast pincer movement. Canadian and Polish armour advanced down from the North, while the Americans swung to the south and steadily closed the ring. Although Kurt had no way of knowing how the foreign armies in northern France were situated relative to one another, the soldiers on the road said that they were now almost directly between those vast pincers and were rapidly retreating east to avoid entrapment and slaughter in the ring.

Ahead the road forked into two branches. The long column of retreating German soldiers snaked along the right branch, but checking his map Kurt noted that he and his men were to head left. Kurt waved to his men to signal they were turning and bid farewell to the other sergeant. He had never learned the man's name and had no interest in it. In the past, men had often made parting comments like, "See you back in Germany." Today, nobody wanted to envision what he would be returning to. No one wanted to speculate on circumstances.

As Kurt and his men left the main road, shouts erupted behind them. A field artillery piece, pulled by horses, had fallen off the roadside into the ditch and men were struggling to return it to the road. Kurt turned to look, and when he returned his eyes to the road ahead of him, he noticed three men in the distance. A few men had turned from the main road and were continuing ahead like Kurt's section, but the three were the only men coming towards them. As they approached, Kurt's fears were confirmed. They wore the dark camouflage of the 12th SS. Kurt walked carefully along the right side of the road, giving the Hitler Youth graduates plenty of room to pass. He kept his face down, avoiding all eye contact. Although he rarely had dealings with the SS, his contact with them always gave him a sense of discomfort, a sense of seeing human faces as facades for more sinister and ruthless beings. He thought of some SS soldiers who had been on the road near them earlier. They had yelled patriotic slogans, insisting that victory was near. Many of the men retreating on the road were exhausted, many had born the brunt of the harsh fighting that had so closely missed Kurt and his unit; they did not want to hear patriotic slogans today. Kurt reflected, not for the first time, he had joined the armed forces too late to experience victory. While he had been a part of some victorious exchanges in Africa, the Germans were still driven relentlessly from the continent. No longer would the Third Reich's tanks spew diesel fumes across rugged and granular expanses south of the Mediterranean. Never again would Kurt dip his filthy fingers into his coffee to skim sand from its surface. Now he was here in France living one military disaster after another, a paratrooper never to be dropped into combat.

The officer and two soldiers stopped as Kurt was approaching. Kurt paused and squinted, rubbing his thumb and index finger together. They were filthy, but only with Europe's smooth, cultured soil, not Tunisia's coarse grit. The officer was an SS untersturmführer, and he gestured to Kurt as he approached.

"Unterfeldwebel, what is your name and unit?"

Kurt told him. "Excellent. You are coming with us. We have been tasked to collect remnants of other units for use in a counter-attack."

"Sir," answered Kurt, "we are not a remnant. Our unit is intact, but we were temporarily separated from our platoon during a brief assignment. We have been ordered to report to a rendezvous point a few kilometres down this road." Kurt pointed down the road and prayed that his explanation would suffice.

"The enemy is that way, Unterfeldwebel." The untersturmführer gestured down the road from which Kurt and his men had just come. He was a young, tall and powerfully built man with auburn hair. He had smiled almost amicably when informing Kurt of his task, but was now absolutely stone-faced. The two young men with him seemed formidable as well. Each had a submachine gun at his side.

"Sir," Kurt began in a quiet, measured voice. "We have orders."

"Your orders are cowardly, and it is your duty to disobey." Now the SS officer raised his voice. His two men stepped closer to his side. "In fact, I want the name of your officer who told you to march east in desertion of your duty, and in direct violation of the Führer's order that there was to be no further retreat."

Kurt stood dumbfounded as the officer took a pen and notepad from his pocket. There was a moment's silence before the SS man yelled in his face: "The name!"

Kurt recited the name of his superior, thinking this a useless exercise, but only later beginning to wonder if repercussions would fall on officers in his unit for their common-sense orders. Would a kindly Captain, always a father to his troops, be named on a flimsy slip of paper that would guarantee a 3:00am knock on the door at the home of his wife and daughters? He told his men to meet at a rendezvous point. Who would pay the price?

"Now that the unpleasantness is out of the way," continued the untersturmführer as he replaced his pen and notepad in his pocket. He paused while he stared down at Kurt, and his crisp utterance hung like a second threat in the air. "You can come with us without any concern that you will be violating orders." The smile suddenly returned to his face and he gestured down the road, back towards the west. Kurt and his men remained standing motionless. Kurt was not sure why the SS man was so sure that he would now disregard the orders from his captain, but he had no intention of doing so. As the untersturmführer took a step forward, it was obvious that Kurt was not going to budge. The SS lieutenant shook his head, as though in grave disappointment, and casually drew his pistol. As he pointed it in Kurt's direction, Kurt heard the actions moving on guns behind him. He turned his head and saw that the nine men with him had drawn their weapons and were facing off against the men of the 12th SS. The two soldiers with the untersturmführer had their submachine guns aimed in readiness. Kurt was the only man without his weapon drawn.

Facing the SS man opposite him, he locked eyes and paused for a moment's thought. Rather than think about the gun pointed at him, he thought about the men behind him. Some of them had served with him for many months, some for only weeks. Moments like this made him realize the intense loyalty he inspired in all of them. While soldiers generally took orders from their own sergeant, under usual circumstances an officer of another unit who made forceful commands would quickly be obeyed. Today was different. Perhaps the calm that Kurt seemed to exude under this moment of brinkmanship made his men more confident in his righteousness, but he had not earned their trust in these last few moments. He had earned their loyalty by the way he had treated them every day. He had treated them with sincere respect and with unflinching confidence in their capabilities. Now they were standing behind him, making him proud of his identity and theirs. He decided not to risk their deaths today.

"The Führer's orders, you say?" He smiled an ironic smile, his words dripping with sarcasm. "I suppose that we had better turn around." He continued smiling, but the untersturmführer remained impassive.

Kurt turned and gestured to his men to lower their weapons. The SS soldiers did the same. As Kurt and the paratroopers began marching west, the untersturmführer made one last comment from behind him, to have the last word.

"Wise choice."

Kurt had been outwardly emotionless until now, but the officer's Parthian shot infuriated him. Until now he had gone without any fear of the death that was staring him in the face, without any anger at the aggressive and deluded men of the SS and without any despair that they would be walking back into the enemy's ring. His body discipline seemed to have suppressed his emotions completely, but now the final insult made them all return to his racing mind, and he was forced to bite back rage that swept up like a storm at sea. Nevertheless, he walked on stolidly. His men remained clustered around him, occasionally looking behind to watch the SS following.

Kurt once again controlled emotion with self-discipline and pushed his emotions deep inside. A sense of futility began to dominate his thoughts, and he found himself thinking despairingly.

None of this matters. The war is lost anyway. How many sons need to die because their fathers wanted them to be soldiers?

Perhaps the fact that they were not retreating to a tenable line was not important. Perhaps the loss of another battle was not important. What Kurt could not make himself believe was that the loss of his men was not important. By confronting the SS, his men had placed their loyalty above their own lives. Yet they would lose their lives if they proceeded in a futile counterattack from an encircled position. Kurt began to wonder how he could protect these men from such wastefulness. For now he would have to wait for a moment of opportunity.

Kurt despaired as they walked. He wondered if the men would lose respect for him because he had bowed to the SS, or if they would recognize that he had sacrificed his pride to give them a better chance later. He continued to think that the war was already lost and he thought of his wife. He wished he could return home to her, because he was concerned for her safety. At the same time, he began to wonder just what he would return home to if the Allies won the war, but the general's maps were as far from him now as his home.

They reached the fork in the main road and began walking past the column of retreating German soldiers. The men of the 12th SS paused to speak with a Wehrmacht Captain and to insist he bring his men on the counterattack. Kurt wondered whether this might be their chance to blend back into the mass of retreating soldiers. Perhaps the captain would refuse and there would be a disagreement. Kurt sensed opportunity, but the SS Lieutenant seemed to know the right things to say to convince this man. The captain and untersturmführer exchanged rapid words and nodded agreement. Orders shouted. One hundred men on the retreat suddenly reversed direction. Crowded against each other like cattle, they returned towards the closing jaws of enemy encirclement. Kurt and his men walked. They moved now with the crowd instead of against it. Once again, they all blended into the anonymity of a large group. Kurt's corporal stepped out of the grey and green white noise to approach him.

"What happens now, Herr Unterfeldwebel Doering?"

"It looks like we have joined a popular movement."

"Where do you think we are going?"

"We are going to fight Tommy." A look of concern crossed the corporal's face and he added: "That was always the idea, wasn't it?"

They continued walking in silence. At one moment, Kurt turned to look back towards the east. He wondered if enemy tanks were closing the ring behind him. He wondered if the tanks would reach his wife before he would.

Chapter 26

"Mr Doering would like to speak with you."

"What does he want?"

"He says that his breathing feels worse and he is having a lot of chest pain."

"Fine. I'm really busy right now, but I'll get to him as soon as I can."

"Thanks, Dr. Johnston."

Darren rinsed his lunch container of leftovers and returned to the couch. It was a quiet day; he had taken his time eating, and now all he could think about was how little he wanted to talk to Mr Doering. The guy was rude to doctors at every opportunity, but worse than that, Darren feared having to watch him verbally abuse his wife. She had enough stress dealing with his illness without him berating her, but she never stood up for herself. Knowing he was dying while she was healthy, she felt deeply – and beautifully – obliged to put up with everything he threw at her. Darren wondered about the ethics of commitment. He wondered about his relationship with Courtney. What was the extent, the depth, of an abiding bond after romance had faded? Would Courtney stand by a hospital bed when he was elderly and delusional? When he was verbally and physically incontinent? Would he wait days for her to stop sleeping?

Darren sat down on the couch but felt guilty watching television when he had just told a nurse he was too busy to see a patient. He glanced at his 'to do' list for the afternoon and saw several scans and X-rays he knew he would need to attend. The films were unlikely to be completed for his review until later in the day, but he made his way to the radiology department anyway. At least while he was there he would not have to talk to Mr Doering.

In the radiology department, he found the results of some of his patients' chest X-rays, but neither the CT scan nor the ultrasound he awaited. At least he could check the X-rays. When he recognized Mr Doering's, he was forced to acknowledge that he was only killing time. Mr Doering's X-ray showed cancer all over his lungs, as it had ever since his patient-physician relationship with Darren began. No wonder he was short of breath. No wonder he had chest pain. If only there was anything they could do for him except treating his symptoms and telling him the diagnosis. If only Mr Doering would understand and acknowledge the diagnosis when they told it to him.

Darren sighed and checked his list of errands for anything else that could occupy his time, and for once he hoped his pager would ring so that he would have an excuse to go down to Emergency. He checked his pager. He double-checked his list of errands. Nothing. Finally he steeled himself to face Mr Doering.

On his way to the ward he encountered a lady who was having trouble getting her walker through the door of her bathroom. He spent several minutes helping her before resuming his journey, still avoiding his patient, and hoping he would find another good deed to occupy some time. There was no avoiding it. Finally, he arrived at Mr Doering's room.

"Hello, Mr Doering."

"Hello, Doctor."

"What can I do for you?" Darren was relieved to see that Mrs Doering was not around. His least favourite aspect of visiting Mr Doering would not be an issue. Time spent speaking with her was always rewarding, because she was sensible and made him feel that he could try to help. It pained him to see her with her abusive husband. Today, Mr Doering did not seem like his usual obnoxious self. He seemed nervous, as though about to address a difficult subject. He was not making eye contact with Darren, but was absentmindedly twisting his bed sheets in his hands.

"I guess my chest feels worse."

"Are you having more pain?"

"Not exactly pain I guess …" Mr Doering trailed off. He still avoided eye contact. Darren recognized the signs that his patient was trying to bring up a difficult subject and was using his illness as an excuse to have contact with the doctor. As a modern resident physician, Darren had been trained in effective communication and in other holistic approaches, but at this moment it was all out the window. He did not want to enhance the doctor-patient relationship with this man. He did not want to get to know him better. He just wanted to deal with whatever the current complaint was and get out of there.

"Not pain? Is your breathing worse?"

"I guess it hurts when I take a really deep breath."

"When you take a really deep breath?" Darren knew he was short with Doering, but he just wanted him to say what the problem was and move on.

"Yes, when I take a deep breath. I guess it is from all the smoking." Was Doering starting to take some personal responsibility? He had still never acknowledged he had cancer. This was the first time he suggested he had heard the doctors.

"Yes, it probably is." Darren checked his watch. "Have your symptoms changed at all?"

"I guess not really."

"Well, I'll let the nurses know you have been having some discomfort, and if you ask, they will get you some painkillers. Okay?" Darren turned to leave.

"I'm worried about my wife." Now Mr Doering looked up towards Darren. This was what he had wanted to talk about.

Darren paused and stood still, waiting for Mr Doering to explain himself. There was a long pause and a thought crossed Darren's mind. This was the first time he had spent any time talking to Mr Doering while his wife was not around. Could it be that all Mr Doering's obnoxious behaviour was part of a brave front for her? Darren could not imagine a much more pathologic way of coping, since no doubt his wife was hurt by his harsh treatment.

"In what way are you concerned about your wife?" Darren remained unimpressed with Mr Doering as a person, but he did care about Mrs Doering.

"I read that when a person who has been married for a long time dies, their spouse often dies soon after."

Darren was forced to pause by Doering's honest, vulnerable statement. Now Doering seemed to admit he was going to die. He was going to die and he was wondering what his wife would do without him. Darren was worried for her, and hoped that Mr Doering had a good insurance policy.

"I think that's true." Darren paused again. Mr Doering again avoided eye contact. Now he seemed deep in thought. Darren was fed up with him. "Is there anything else I can do for you?" He began to turn and leave.

"I guess," Mr Doering began a statement without any real resolve. He trailed off and ended his brief utterance, as though he had meant to express something different. "There must be some other tests you can do." His sorrowful eyes wandered to the picture of his wife at his bedside, then fell into a stare, seeing only his own strong, coarse, aged hands.

Darren was furious. He wanted to yell at Kurt, "You've got cancer! You're going to die! Just accept it and deal with it already. Don't keep insisting there 'must' be something we can do when there isn't. If you're worried about your wife, then help her instead of being an asshole." Instead, he responded in a quiet and measured tone, "We've done all the necessary tests, Mr Doering. We know the diagnosis." He turned and left. From the doorway, he heard Mr Doering speak quietly, almost in a whisper.

"I know. Thank you."

Darren paused for only an instant, and then stepped out into the corridor without turning back. He felt guilty now about the old man's pain and fear, but his thoughts turned outward when he noticed Mrs Doering coming down the hallway. If he could not help Mr Doering by curing his illness, he would help Mr and Mrs Doering by ensuring Mrs Doering knew what to expect.

"Good afternoon, Dr Johnston."

"Hi, Mrs Doering."

"How is my husband doing today?"

"He's okay." Darren paused. Part of him wanted to say Mr Doering was not acting like himself because he was worried about her. He thought of telling her she should reassure her husband that she was all right, even if she had trouble thinking of herself. He was much more concerned now for her than for her husband. He could read in a textbook the most likely outcome of Mr Doering's lung cancer, but he knew no way of predicting what lay ahead for this sensitive lady.

Darren did not want to overstep his bounds and interfere in this relationship. He hoped to say something she would interpret to mean all of those things without having to say any of them out loud.

"I think he's scared," he said. Mrs Doering's jaw tightened and her brow descended. There seemed to be an instant of comprehension, but when she answered, he realized that he had failed.

"My husband is hardly someone to be frightened. He may be stubborn, but he is very strong." She did not seem offended by his comment, but she did seem to feel a need to defend her husband.

"I'm sorry, Mrs Doering, I just meant ..."

"You don't have to explain, Dr Johnston. You have been very understanding and have answered all my questions truthfully. You have to understand my husband, though. You know he lost his first wife."

"Yes, you told me."

"He has always cherished me like he knew that every moment of my life was precious." Darren nodded, but thought to himself that he had never seen it in the way he had treated her here. "He has been through a lot, and this is only another chapter in his life.

He has seen more of the world, and known more of pain than you have, young Doctor."

"He is lucky to have you here with him," answered Darren.

"I feel lucky myself," she said. "Thank you, Darren." She turned and went into her husband's room.

Darren felt that perhaps his suspicions had been confirmed. Mr Doering might normally be a caring person with his wife, and now his apparent hostility was only a way of looking strong to her. Darren could still muster little sympathy for the man, particularly when he heard Mr Doering once again raising his voice. It seemed impossibly pathological. He could only watch, and wait, and hope that Mrs Doering would survive the abuse.

Darren was exhausted after those conversations. He walked to the nursing station and fell into a chair, needing to have a nap right there. The charge nurse was seated in the chair next to him, and was watching a group of people enter a room across the hall. She had a wide smile on her face. "What's going on?" asked Darren.

"That's Mr Sutherland's family. A big group of them has come in, they're getting ready to take him downstairs to the courtyard, and they look like they're going on a picnic or something."

She was right. There were small children laughing together, and adults with smiles on their faces carrying large books. Darren wondered what was going on. He walked to the doorway and peeked his head through the open door. "Hi, Mr Sutherland."

"Hello, young man!" Sutherland replied in such a jovial tone that Darren smiled. "Have you met everyone here?"

Darren replied that he had not, and enthusiastic introductions followed. Then Darren asked about the books. "So what are you all up to?"

"Going to get some fresh air, and look through old photo albums to relive old times, my young friend. By the way, have you any idea what happened with that procedure I was going to have done?"

"The stent, you mean?"

"That's the one."

"I'm sorry, Mr Sutherland. We had it booked for today, but it was delayed until tomorrow."

"Oh, no bother, no bother," replied Bill Sutherland. "I was just wondering when I'd be able to eat a nice juicy steak again."

"We'll see what we can do for you." Darren thought of joining the Sutherlands to look at old pictures, but left to review Bill's X-rays instead.

Chapter 27

Darren had just finished in the radiology department when he encountered Eddy near the cafeteria. Eddy looked even more shaken than usual, so Darren asked him what was wrong.

"You wouldn't believe it," Eddy began, "we just had a crazy time with one of the patients upstairs." Eddy paused for a moment in realization. "I think you admitted the guy. You know, Mr Sutherland."

"What happened?" Darren had the feeling of cresting a large wave on an unsteady boat.

"I was walking by the door to his room, when all of a sudden his daughter screamed. I took a look in and he was vomiting blood. It was a total mess. Luckily, Layton was on the ward too, and he helped me out."

"So?" Darren prompted him when it seemed that Eddy's story had finished.

"Oh, yeah." Eddy had absentmindedly begun looking towards the cafeteria counter. He had missed lunch in all the excitement. "He could hardly breathe because he was throwing up so much blood, so Layton intubated him. Then we called the Intensive Care Unit guys. At first they were like: 'Why the hell did you intubate a guy with terminal esophageal cancer?' But in the end they took him to the ICU. He seemed to stop bleeding after a few minutes, so I guess they'll take a look in his throat with the scope and then punt him back out of the ICU to us."

Darren stood momentarily silent, bathed in his patient's misfortune. Even though he had only spent a short time with Mr

Sutherland, he felt as though a cherished family member were in distress.

"Have you had lunch?" asked Eddy, once again preoccupied by food.

"Yeah," answered Darren.

"Do you want to grab a coffee and have a seat while I get something?"

"Sure." Darren needed to sit down for a few minutes. He tried to imagine Mr Sutherland's sudden deterioration did not concern him. After all, he had known all along that Bill was going to die. He paid for a small cup of coffee and found a seat while Eddy paid for a disgusting greasy mess. In a sense Darren realized he was now in a position to feel even less concern for Mr Sutherland. The Intensive Care Unit was, after all, like a hospital within the hospital. The intensivists would look after the patient, and Sutherland would only become Darren's concern again when and if he returned to the regular ward.

"Can you believe that we're almost done?" asked Eddy as he sat across from Darren.

"What do you mean?" Darren was lost in thought.

"We're almost done. General Internal Medicine, I mean. After this week I'm one step closer to bigger and better things. Radiology. I thought this rotation would never end."

Darren realized that Eddy was right. He had only a few days left of his rotation in General Medicine, and then he would be doing Pulmonary Medicine. He would be doing fewer nights of call on that rotation, which would be nice. Somehow, he was not as excited about the end of the week as Eddy. It was because Eddy would be finished with General Internal Medicine forever after this week. Eddy would have finished his mandatory medicine training and would then go on to complete his training in Radiology. Darren had months and years of Internal Medicine in his future. If he did not like what he was doing now, then there was little promise that things would get any better.

"I guess this rotation was only a chilling vision of the future for me," Darren said with a chuckle.

"Sucks to be you," said Eddy through a mouthful of French fries and ketchup.

The two of them sat down for a brief break while Eddy finished eating, and then they returned to their afternoon chores. Although he had convinced himself many different ways that Mr Sutherland was not his problem, he had already decided to stop by and see him after work.

Darren remained distracted that afternoon, but he managed to order all the right bowel routines and review all the appropriate test results before finally calling it quits. He dropped off his white coat in the locker room and made his way to the Intensive Care Unit. As he approached the large double doors to the unit, they swung violently open and Chris emerged. He was covered from head to toe in shaving cream and was laughing hard. The ridiculous sight made Darren smile. "What the hell happened to you?"

"Nurses," answered Chris. "You can't trust them for a second." He wiped a tear from his eye as he finished laughing and began walking towards the change rooms. Darren followed along.

"So was this some kind of practical joke?"

"Yes, just one in an escalating series. I'm almost finished my ICU rotation, so the senior residents and nurses are starting to give me a hard time. Today one of the nurses told me that there was a patient crashing, so I went running down the hall to get there. She was in on the joke. When I was almost to the room, suddenly my senior resident and another nurse tackled me at the knees and covered me in shaving cream. I thought at first it was whip cream, until I made the mistake of getting some in my mouth." Darren laughed, and Chris continued his story. "You wouldn't believe all the practical jokes that go on towards the end of this rotation. I've gotten my share, but they're only just getting started. My last day is Friday, so they'll really hammer me then. At least I've gotten my share of pranks in on the other residents."

"What did you do?"

"Oh, I've got some good ones." They were almost to the change room, where Chris intended to shower and get cleaned up, but he could not help sharing his exploits. He stopped walking and continued his story in the hallway. "When Dave was on call the other night, we put blue dye on the receiver of the phone in his call room, so he had a big blue circle on his ear for the rest of the night. We also put Vaseline on all the door handles, and by the amount of cursing and hand washing he was doing, I think he fell for it every time. The pièce de resistance was when we put clear plastic wrap over the toilet bowl. I'm not sure if he fell for that one, but I guess I don't really want to know."

Darren was laughing at the thought of how messy Dave's night must have been, but found that Chris was only just warming up. "Then there are the really serious pranks we've played. We got one of the nurses to page Dan when he was on call. We made it sound like a really official call from someone important. The nurse pretended to be a secretary and said: 'please hold for a call from Mr What's-his-name.' Then we made Dan think he was getting a call from a hospital administrator. I put on a phoney accent and played the administrator, and told him I was furious that such expensive treatments were getting used in the ICU. Dan got all flustered and kept saying: 'I'm not really the person you want to talk to,' but I kept telling him that I wanted all this stuff stopped right away. I think Dan really bought it until I told him that he had to shut down the burn unit. I think I said something like: 'Burns? Why don't you just put some lotion on them?'"

Chris's Texan accent was only moderately realistic, or maybe not even intended to be Texan, and the vigorous hand waving was unlikely to help convince a victim over the telephone, but nevertheless, Darren could not help imagining that the poignancy of the whole ridiculous call on its unsuspecting victim was supremely enhanced by fear of an unseen and furious hospital administrator. The overall effect was hilarious.

"We got Dave again last night, and this one is really good. Carl and I paged him from outside the hospital, and Carl pretended to be a small town doctor who was having trouble and needed help. Carl put on this crazy accent and started telling Dave that he was looking after a patient who had stopped breathing. Dave kept telling him what to do, but Carl kept pretending to screw up all his instructions and ask for more help. Dave would tell him to do something, so Carl would say: 'All right, I'll try that. Just a moment.' Then he would put down the phone for a second and say: 'Okay, that didn't work, what should I do next?' Pretty soon Dave was beating himself up trying to help this clumsy small-town doctor, but the ICU senior resident walked by, so he handed over the phone. When the senior introduced himself on the telephone, we just told him, 'Hi, it's Chris and Carl. We're playing a joke on Dave so pretend that we're telling you something medical.' On the other end of the phone, the senior resident just said: 'Okay … okay. Well, it sounds like my junior has been very helpful, so I'll put him back on the phone.'"

Now Darren and Chris were loudly laughing in the hallway as Chris went on. Chris got some strange looks from the passers-by, as he was still caked in shaving cream. "So Dave is still trying to give Carl instructions over the phone, when Carl tells Dave that the patient's heart has stopped. Dave says: 'Start chest compressions and give epinephrine!' Then Carl said: 'How should I give the epinephrine, our intravenous line was blown?' So now Dave was really stuck. He turned to the senior resident who helped us out and said: 'I'm talking to a doctor who has a patient in cardiac arrest and they don't have an IV. How should he give epinephrine?' Well, of course the senior knew that the call was all a prank, so he said: 'Tell them to give the epinephrine rectally.'"

"No way!" said Darren.

"Yeah, I'm serious. The senior told Dave to tell us to give the epinephrine rectally, so Dave repeats the order. I couldn't believe it. It was the funniest thing I've ever heard. I thought for sure that Carl would start laughing, but instead he just started speaking in a really measured way. 'Just a moment, I need to turn the patient on his side.' He put down the phone for a minute, and the two of us could hardly control ourselves. I don't know how Carl managed to keep from laughing for so long. Then he picked up the phone and started to say to Dave: 'The syringe was too large for the patient's rectum.' He couldn't do it, though. We both burst out laughing. When the senior resident heard us laughing on the other side of the phone, he burst out laughing too. It was a few minutes before Dave could laugh, because he was all wired thinking he was talking a guy through a cardiac arrest and the patient was going to die."

"So what did he do then?" asked Darren.

"He just told us that he was going to get us back. He sort of laughed, but he was still kind of shaken up. I hope he goes after Carl, because Carl's the one who was talking to him on the phone." Chris turned back towards the change room, still laughing to himself. Darren began to walk back to the Intensive Care Unit, but stopped as Chris paused in the doorway and called back to him. "When is your Intensive Care rotation?"

"Some time next year."

"You're going to love it. It's a lot of fun, and the ICU is about the funniest place on earth. I haven't laughed so hard in a long time."

Darren smiled and bid him good luck getting all the shaving cream out of his hair, then began walking back to the Unit. As he approached the large double doors, he began laughing to himself at the thought of Chris's ridiculous pranks. He pulled open the right-hand door just as the left one swung open. The grin faded from Darren's face as a young couple comforting each other through painful tears walked past him. The first thing Darren saw as he entered was the waiting room where families were seated. Some looked dishevelled, as though they had been there for days. Many were crying and most looked miserable. Darren recognized one small group of people as Mr Sutherland's family. Doleful eyes looked up in his direction. He tried to smile back in a way that looked positive but not too happy. Suddenly Darren felt horribly inappropriate that he had entered this area with laughter still on his lips.

He walked through a second set of double doors to the Intensive Care Unit proper and was struck by the mournful sound of respirator bellows rising and falling. Staff moved quietly and efficiently from place to place and myriad machinery spoke in a rhythmic language of electronic beeps and chimes. He searched through beds filled with patients so ill that it was hard to detect their humanity through the jungles of wires and tubes that regulated their lives.

When he finally found Sutherland, Darren sat by his bedside. A respirator worked to move the air in and out of Mr Sutherland's lungs. The old man was sedated and unconscious. The weight of the machines around him strangled the levity Sutherland usually wore like a cloak.

"Are you a family member of Mr Sutherland's?" a compassionate voice came from behind Darren.

"No, I'm the medicine resident who admitted him." Darren realized that he was not wearing his white coat. As he turned, he saw a senior Intensive Care resident standing over him. A demeanour that suggested confidence and understanding matched the compassion in his voice. Darren wondered if this was the senior resident who had participated in the cruel prank recently played on an inexperienced and nervous young doctor.

"I'm Kevin Turnbull. Mr Sutherland had a nasty bleed where his cancer eroded into a blood vessel. The gastroenterologists stopped the bleeding, so I hope he will be okay for now."

"Thanks." Darren appreciated the seriousness of the assessment. Kevin became more casual when he realized that Darren was a resident. His appearance of confidence was unchanged, but his carefully measured warmth was replaced by collegiality. "We'll be bouncing him back out to you guys by tomorrow, I hope. Normally we would hate to take a guy with esophageal cancer into the ICU, but I guess we can fix up this bleed and maybe get him a few more weeks with his family."

"All right." Darren turned his head to resume his silent vigil by Sutherland's bedside.

"You know this guy pretty well?" asked Kevin before leaving.

"Yeah. He's really nice." It seemed a pathetic understatement. Kevin left. Darren stayed for about half an hour and, when he left, he walked quickly through the waiting room hoping not to see Mr Sutherland's family. Darren left thinking about the added work that he would have to take on the next morning in order to accept Mr Sutherland back in transfer from the ICU. "Damn paperwork," he muttered to himself as he passed the hospital's chapel.

As he made his way back to the change room, where he had left his coat, he looked forward to relaxing at home for a few hours. Before he made it, he was stopped by one of the other junior medicine residents.

"Darren, I'm glad I found you!" Darren knew her name was Jody, but he had seen little of her while she worked with one of the other general medicine teams. "I tried calling you at home, but of course you weren't there yet. I have a huge favour to ask. You see, I'm on call this evening and I just got word that my Mom is sick in another hospital, so I want to go see her. If you cover for me tonight, I could take one of your calls on another day."

"I am really tired tonight," Darren answered. The idea of sticking around in the hospital for another eighteen hours was psychologically and physically repulsive to him, but he did not want to leave her in a difficult situation. He knew he would want someone to help if he was in her predicament. "If you can find someone else that would be great, but if you're really stuck, I guess I could do it. I'll go home, and if you can't find anyone, then give me a call. I'll just pick up my clothes and stuff and come back."

"Thanks Darren. I'll call around. I'll give you another call if no one else can do it."

"I'll talk to you later." Darren left, hoping that he would not.

Chapter 28

On the second day after the nocturnal battle known as *Operation Totalize*, Bill Sutherland and his colleagues were advancing again. Glad as he was that the heavy fighting had paused, Bill was not at all thrilled to be back at work clearing the buildings that made up another of the tiny hamlets between Caen and Falaise. There was a more relaxed atmosphere among the men today than there had been a few days earlier since, in this sector at least, the Germans seemed to have fallen back in disarray and had not been as diligent in their placement of snipers and booby traps as they had been prior to the recent Canadian advance.

Although the soldiers were feeling fairly confident, there were still signs of caution and unease. Walking along a sidewalk, Bill looked back and saw a major in the street a short distance behind him. No one unfamiliar with the individual soldiers of the battalion would have recognized the officer at a distance. He wore the same khaki uniform as the private soldiers around him, and wore the same flat British-style helmet that the German soldiers referred to as "straw hats". The major wore no distinctive rank insignia and even carried the same type of rifle as the enlisted men. Although unlikely to put the rifle to much use, the major carried it as protection against snipers. The protection was not gained by giving the major increased firepower, but by helping him blend into the enlisted men. Patient German snipers were known to stay motionless for very long periods of time, even watching enemy soldiers encircle their position, while waiting for an officer to reveal himself. A single shot would then ring out and hit its target, after which the sniper would slip quietly away or wait silently for another opportunity.

Officers protected themselves by more methods than just their choice of gear. While on operations such as this one, men were strictly forbidden from saluting, an action that could draw a sniper's attention to the man in charge. This regulation went over well in the Canadian ranks where a casual approach to seniority prevailed. With the British, on the other hand, there was often tension when an officer was not properly acknowledged. In these tiny French hamlets, even a Canadian general had recently been present among the men carrying a rifle and a heavy pack to blend into the crowd.

Bill scoffed as he thought about the officer behind him. Events of two nights ago had poisoned his thoughts about the entire chain of command. After his battalion had followed the armour through a gap in the German lines, they had reached their designated target and dug in. Bill had been horrified to see bombs from their own bombers landing among a group of Canadian troops on his far right. The soldiers had begun deploying yellow smoke, which the Canadian infantry routinely used to indicate to the artillery that friendly troops were under fire. Bill later realized that in the dark of night their smoke was indistinguishable from the yellow smoke that had been dropped by spotter aircraft to indicate German targets. The smoke had drawn more bombers to their positions. Over the next two days there had been a lot of talk among the rank and file about the stupidity of a chain of command where yellow smoke meant one thing to artillery and the opposite to bombers. Bill had never felt quite so distasteful about orders coming from the top as he did now.

A smile returned to Bill's face as he recalled other recent events. As his platoon had prepared for a night's sleep on the previous evening, a young private named Luke had decided to have some fun with his comrades. Bill had been seated in an outhouse while two other soldiers in the platoon were using the nearby bushes. Under cover of darkness Luke had quietly crept up behind the outhouse. He waited a moment and then screamed out in German (or a close approximation) for the men to surrender. Bill had jumped in terror inside the outhouse, realizing that his rifle was in a nearby building. One of the soldiers in the nearby bushes had urinated down his own leg in his hurry to close his trousers and arm himself. What Luke had not noticed was another soldier using the bushes a short distance away. Not wanting to wait for the outhouse, he had squatted in the undergrowth with his rifle at his side. He had not seen Luke creep up, but could see the lone figure yelling in German. Without thinking twice, he picked up his rifle and shot at the shadowy figure, knocking Luke to the ground with a bullet in the belly.

"Stop shooting! It's me, Luke."

The nearby soldiers had rushed to his assistance and found him in a heap on the ground. Each grabbing an arm or leg, they rushed their wounded comrade to the nearest aid station. They did not reach their goal, however, before Luke, clutching his bleeding abdomen, started laughing through the pain.

"You should have seen the looks on your faces." He began laughing, and the men carrying him laughed as well. In his mirth, Bill dropped Luke's left leg and Luke had a painful fall to the ground. Apologizing, Bill had resumed the comical portage. Luke had still been in pretty good shape when they stopped at the aid station, but Bill was concerned. He knew that belly wounds, even minor ones, were often fatal long after the initial injury and he hoped that Luke would be okay. The men who had carried Luke had promised to visit him in the hospital as soon as they could, and it was obvious that this incident would be a source of hilarity for years. Already, men could get some easy laughs with the recollection.

"Hey, remember when we shot Luke in the stomach?"

Still chuckling to himself at the story, but thinking again of the present, Bill came to a junction of two streets and joined four men of his section who had been walking on a road perpendicular to his. Further ahead on the road, scattered soldiers walked among buildings that had already been cleared. Now Bill and the other soldiers walked quietly together, seeing that their colleagues were some distance ahead. The sound of footsteps jogging up behind Bill surprised him and he turned around. It was Corporal Jennings from another section in Bill's platoon. Bill was not overly fond of Jennings, who always seemed to want to boss him around. Bill often thought that Jennings must have given himself a promotion to think he was further up the chain of command than he was.

"Sutherland!"

"Yeah, Jennings."

"Sergeant Whalen wants us to split up some men and head down these two roads, then meet at that little bridge." He pointed down the roads that divided into a V ahead of them, and leaned to his right to indicate a small bridge crossing a stream about one hundred meters further down.

"Why don't we all just head straight there?" Bill gestured to the road on the right.

It must have been obvious to the private soldiers with Sutherland and Jennings that an unnecessary debate was about to begin. As the two corporals spoke in the middle of the road, the other men took seats in two doorways on the right side of the street. Two of them lit cigarettes, while the others leaned their tired heads against anything that would support them, hoping that an extra minute or two of sleep would provide psychological sustenance.

"Sergeant Whalen wants us to have a quick look in that building." Jennings gestured to a small shop down the left road.

"Why bother? I just saw some guys check it out ahead of us a minute ago.

"Look, it doesn't matter. Sergeant Whalen wants us to check it out. I'll take two of these guys down the left, and you can take two on the right."

"Maybe I want to go to the left." Now Bill was being difficult, but he was tired of the chain of command. He was tired of following orders, and especially unimpressed with being told what to do by another corporal.

"Just take two guys down the road!" Jennings was clearly fed up with talking to him. The other soldiers, seated at the roadside, were trying hard not to pay attention.

"Jawohl, mein Führer!" Bill snapped to attention and threw his arm forward in a mock Nazi salute.

About to chuckle at his own childish joke, Bill suddenly felt a blast of hot water against his face. He blinked but could only see red. The sound of the bullet only reached his ears as Jennings' headless body fell to the ground. Bill rubbed his eyes and realized that it was Jennings' blood and brains that were coating his face. He dropped face down to the cobblestones.

On the right side of the road, the four private soldiers huddled into their doorways. Further ahead and behind on the road, the sound of men diving for cover was evident. There was an eerie silence as the last of the men found cover, but Bill remained prone in the middle of the street. All around, men looked left and right, up and down the street for the source of the bullet. Lying on the cool, dusty cobblestones, Bill began to squirm. He knew the sniper was looking at him. Afraid to stand up or move, he kicked his legs helplessly and rolled on the ground like a child having a temper tantrum.

"Aaaah!" he screamed, still lying helpless.

Calls began to come from each side of the road.

"Stay still!"

"Make a run for it!"

Haplessly rolling back and forth Bill could feel the sniper's crosshairs on his back. Like a dull knife pressing against his ribs he knew it was there. Rolling onto his back he desperately searched the nearby windows with his eyes. Most of the nearby buildings were one or two stories high, and old artillery strikes had damaged many. He knew it was hopeless. No one had any idea what direction the shot had come from. Besides that, the sniper was unlikely to be looking out from one of the windows overlooking the street. German snipers were skilled in a technique known as "cover in depth." The German might be several blocks away, looking through a hole in a damaged building on this street. By finding a site where he looked through windows or holes in more than one plane, the sniper would have a tiny "kill zone", perhaps only a square meter of street, but would be completely hidden from people near his target.

Bill wondered if by falling to the ground he had dropped out of the kill zone. He could not believe it to be true. He was too acutely aware that he was at the sniper's mercy. At the same time, he felt sure that if the sniper were going to kill him, it would have happened already. Still he could feel the invisible crosshairs taunting him with death. Why was the sniper mocking him? Perhaps he was not a good enough target and the sniper was relocating at this very moment to find new victims. Why, then, had the sniper shot another corporal? Then it dawned on Bill. It was the mock Nazi salute that had convinced the sniper he was looking at an officer. He suddenly felt the need to yell out to his unseen predator.

"That's not the way we salute, you bastard! You wasted a bullet on a corporal."

"Shut up and get out of the road, you idiot!" a voice yelled from a nearby doorway.

Now Bill felt more than the sniper's eyes burning into him. He felt all the Canadians were looking at him, knowing he had caused Jennings' death. Shots were being fired somewhere nearby, and still helplessly squirming in the road, Bill was once again face down. He continued screaming in frustration at his helplessness, not sure how long had passed since he had been in the road. It had likely only been several seconds or perhaps a few minutes when a boot tapped Sutherland in the ribs. He once again rolled over and looked up. The sun was shining down from behind Sergeant Whalen.

"Get up, Sutherland." Bill struggled to his feet. "Somebody saw where the shot came from and rushed the building." Whalen pointed to the right, gesturing as Bill had suspected, to an unseen building behind wreckage on this street. "The sniper had already relocated when they got there."

How long had Bill been lying in the road? He felt so ashamed he could hardly raise his eyes to face his sergeant.

"Fall in!" Sergeant Whalen yelled to the nearby men. They resumed their walk down the street and Whalen divided them into two groups, going down the left and right roads. "Keep your eyes open," he added unnecessarily.

Bill walked behind the sergeant with his head down. He looked briefly to his left and right and saw the other soldiers casting glances in his direction. He was not sure who had seen his mock salute to Jennings. He knew Whalen had not. The sergeant had been well behind Sutherland when the shot was fired. He felt confident, nevertheless, of what Whalen was feeling. It was pity for the coward who had been screaming in the street. The pity on Whalen's face stung more painfully than contempt.

Bill was not certain which he dreaded more, the notion that everyone had seen him salute Jennings and thought of him as the corporal who got his comrade killed, or the idea that no one had seen the salute. If no one had seen the salute, then perhaps the glances in his direction were all filled with the same pity that Whalen had exhibited. Perhaps there was no pity. Perhaps they were looking at the corporal they could no longer trust. No combat soldier can afford to pity a fool for long. Was Sutherland the one who was likely to let them down? Inadvertently signal the enemy? Start screaming when things got tough?

The other men did not talk to Sutherland very much over the next few days. Uncharacteristically, he followed orders to the letter, asked no questions, and spent much of his time trying to read his colleagues' gazes. He had difficulty doing so, because he could not bring himself to look them in the eyes.

Chapter 29

Glancing at his watch while waiting at a traffic light, Darren realized he would be home late. Precious as his few hours of personal time were, he cursed himself for his choice to sit at Mr Sutherland's bedside. "What was I thinking?" he asked himself on his choice to look in on a patient for personal reasons. "Why did I waste so much time? There's nothing new about his case that I'll have to know for tomorrow. Oh well, I guess talking with the ICU senior resident helped get me up to speed a bit."

Still feeling frustrated, he cringed at the thought that he might receive a request from Jody to return to the hospital.

Darren turned his car radio to a station playing a relaxing selection of classical music and tried to enjoy the rest of his drive. "Eine Kleine Nachtmusik," Darren's favourite example of Mozart's mathematical precision, gave him a brief feeling of control, the music's supreme discipline herding his unruly thoughts. The rush hour was now long gone, and he savoured his solitude in the confines of his vehicle. When he finally arrived home and stepped out of the car his legs were stiff. Walking to his front door he tried to calculate how many hours in the last week he had spent on his feet, but concluded that was useless. He finally fumbled for his keys at the entrance.

"Something important going on at the hospital tonight?" Courtney's voice greeted him as soon as he entered the door. Lost in his own thoughts and bending over to remove his shoes, he hardly looked in her direction.

"Not really."

He removed his first shoe as he said, "Just one patient causing all sorts of trouble." He removed his second shoe and slipped an arm out of his coat. "You know the guy," he added, making his way further into the apartment. "The old veteran in the newspaper the other day." Darren paused in a cold startle as he finally looked to see Courtney seated at the dinner table. Her hair had been styled and she was wearing his favourite red dress. Several candles, long extinguished, adorned the area around the table.

"Oh my God."

It was all he could get out. Before he could think about beginning to apologize, the simple realization of his own insensitivity struck him. It was his birthday and he had promised to be home by six. He had not just promised, he had promised more than once. Each time she had brought up this evening's dinner, he had responded with even more certainty that getting home on time would be no problem. He was so wrong. Not only was he entirely at fault for this oversight, but he had not even been doing anything important. He had been just wasting time sitting around in the ICU. He looked at the table for another moment and then looked at her, wanting so badly to tell her how sorry he was, but still too shocked at himself to get the words out.

"Tonight was very insensitive, Darren." Courtney remained calm. He began to speak, but she began again with slightly increased intensity. "What hurts the most is that our life doesn't seem to matter to you. It wasn't that you were too busy and called to let me know. It wasn't that there was an unforeseeable emergency. It was that you just didn't care enough to keep your promise."

Her words were starting to sting, but not as much as his shame. Darren once again opened his mouth but was not quick enough. The words to express how badly he felt were beyond what he could reach in the instants between her onslaughts.

"I've sacrificed a lot for our relationship, you know." She stood up now. Darren was even more concerned now because her words began sounding like something she had been rehearsing for hours.

Her monologue went on uninterrupted. "It wasn't easy for me to postpone my articling for a year for the benefit of your career. It wasn't easy but I did it because I thought it was worth it for you to be happy and for us to be together. We're not together though, are we? You don't seem to make any effort to be with me. Instead, you treat me like I'm invisible. It doesn't get much better when we're together and meet with other residents, either. When we get together with people from the hospital I might as well have leprosy for all the effort people make to include me in conversations. All you and your friends do is talk about medicine until we finally go home." Darren remained motionless, stunned. Courtney's verbal assault intensified. "You know Darren, I can't imagine how you could contribute less to our relationship. All I have done is give to this relationship and all you have done is take. You take and do not even acknowledge the value of what it is you are taking. I don't think you know how easy you've had it!"

Darren could hardly stand it. Filled with feelings of regret for his behaviour, he could not bear to hear that he had been having an easy time. "That's not fair," he replied. "You talk about how easy I've had it while I've been working one hundred and ten hours a week. What have you been up to all this time? I don't understand how you can complain that life is so tough when you've had all the time in the world to enjoy whatever it is you want to do." Tears were forming in Courtney's eyes as he spoke. Despite her anger, the tears represented sadness, not rage. It was too late. Now that Darren was defending himself the tears only inflamed him more. He felt every one of her tears hurled almost like a weapon against him. Still, he continued his argument. "I'm tired all the time, and you tell me how easy I have it? I can't believe your audacity. You knew I'd be working hard this year when we planned to move, but now that I'm out busting my ass all you can do is complain that I'm late for dinner."

Courtney started to answer, but now her voice sounded pleading instead of angry. Just minutes before, Darren would have melted at the sound of her sadness. He had wanted so badly to tell her how terrible he felt for what he had done. He had wanted so badly to make her feel better. Now he was on the defensive and any emotion she launched at him struck him as a noxious insult.

"What could you possibly do to make me feel less important?" she asked. "Why do I not exist as a part of your world?" She was giving him a chance to tell her she was important, and a very short time later he would wish he had taken it. He might also have told her then about the sad, quiet hours he had spent at Mr Sutherland's bedside, but as he was not ready to let himself believe he was mourning for a patient who had become a friend, he only continued as before.

"You're making all this up, it's crazy," he retorted. "I'm busy, and you've got all the time in the world to sit around and dream up that my hard work must be at your expense."

"I'm not crazy. I know it is at my expense. I knew that before we came here. Anything that is worth anything has a cost. That's why I did it." Courtney was crying now, and she had to stop and wipe her nose between sentences. "But I'm wondering now if I made the right decision. Maybe it was all a mistake."

Darren still felt about three feet tall, but now more afraid than he had been before. There was a pause in which he had an important decision to make. The decision was whether to continue the discussion or to run. Rationally, he knew that he had to sort things out with Courtney, but emotionally he could not bear to find out what she might have meant by "this was all a mistake." He decided to run. He knew immediately that this was the wrong choice, but somehow inertia carried him forward and there was no turning back. He walked to the telephone.

Courtney blew her nose again, but only stared in disbelief as he dialled. In the instant before he had fled, perhaps she had sensed the terror in his eyes. Perhaps through all her hurt and anger, she recognized that she had frightened him. Now she just waited.

"Hello, switchboard?" Darren was speaking on the phone. "Would you page the internal medicine resident on call for me, please? Thank you." Courtney had no idea why Darren had called the hospital, or what he might be doing. He stared at the wall as he waited and did not acknowledge her questioning stare. "Hi, Jody." He began again as a voice responded on the other end of the line. "It's me, Darren. Yeah, I can take call tonight if you want. Okay, no problem. I'll be there in twenty minutes. Talk to you later."

Darren hung up the telephone and walked into the bedroom. He picked up his toiletries and a change of clothes and packed them into his knapsack. He never made eye contact with Courtney all this time but cautiously avoided her gaze. She stood still in the same spot where she had been arguing with him just moments earlier and watched him. Her anger and sadness had given way to a morbid disbelief.

Darren put his coat and shoes back on, but paused in the doorway before he walked out. Courtney remained standing where he had left her. He knew he had a last chance at salvage, at some temporary reconciliation, and knew immediately he had failed again. All he could offer before turning to leave was an empty gesture.

"We'll talk later."

She did not answer.

The night was cold and the wind seemed to blow harder than when he had arrived home just minutes before. Darren ran to the car. He did not pause to wonder whether he was hurrying because it was cold outside or because he was in a hurry to get away.

He drove quickly for several blocks before stopping at a stop sign, and then he pulled over to the side of the road. He leaned his head against the steering wheel and banged it once, hard. Why hadn't he just apologized as soon as he got through the door? Why hadn't he apologized when he got the chance again? Why hadn't he told her she was important? Why had he run without fixing all the damage he had done? With each step it had been harder to face himself and admit he was wrong. And now that he knew so well what needed to be done, he was expected at the hospital and his pager would be going off soon.

He realized for the first time he was capable of hiding from the truth.

Trying to pull himself together, he mustered whatever optimism was left about tonight. At least Jody would cover what would be his next night on call. That made tonight his last night of call on his junior internal medicine rotation. Surviving tonight would be cause for a small celebration.

Chapter 30

Back in the hospital Darren really hit his stride. He was on a roll. Never before had he been able to solve so many problems so quickly, to cut through the nonsense and distil the essence of the medical issues he could resolve. He was fabulous. The night was busy, but the work never seemed to get ahead of him. Perhaps it was only the fact he was subconsciously avoiding thinking about Courtney that allowed him to focus more than ever before on the work at hand: the beautiful concentration that evasion often allowed. He didn't care. Tonight he was going to bask in the glow of his superhuman efficiency.

Darren was strutting the hallway with the confidence of someone who knows he will be able to handle whatever comes. His pager rang. He was passing a house phone on the wall, so his hand stabbed out and took it. He had hardly broken his stride.

"Johnston here."

"Mr Kelly's heart rate is too fast. It's one hundred and twenty."

"Give him fifty milligrams of metoprolol now and increase his twice daily dose to seventy five." He knew the patient. He knew the problem. He did not hesitate. The call had taken seconds.

"Thank you, Dr Johnston."

"You bet." As he hung up the phone, his pager rang again. He dialed the telephone instantly.

"Johnston here."

"Mrs Granger's heart rate is too slow. It's fifty-five."

"Hold her digoxin. Check her blood pressure every hour until her rate is back over seventy. Call me if the BP drops. Cheers."

"Thanks, Dr Johnston."

But he was already hanging up. One more problem had been solved. Eight more seconds spent.

Darren resumed his stride down the hallway. He strutted to the beat of a song he had heard on the radio. It occurred to him that on a night like this he needed a soundtrack. Movie characters always looked cool when they moved down the corridor to the tune of a new rock song. Tonight he felt that cool.

A patient was waiting in the Emergency Department and Darren made his way there. The little old lady was the first in a string of six admissions, and he nailed the diagnosis on every one. He was invincible.

"Hello, Ma'am. My name is Dr Johnston."

"Hello, Doctor."

"Can you tell me what brings you into hospital tonight?"

"Well, it all started when I was driving through Saskatchewan. My son was using my car, so I had borrowed one. I think that was the weekend that I needed to go to the farmer's market …"

It was obvious to Darren early that this answer was going nowhere. He had already started looking to his left and right. He spotted exactly the person he was looking for. "Is this lady your mother?" he asked of a middle-aged woman who was approaching with a cup of coffee. The confused little old lady went on with her story. "… and Gus told me that we would be needing some money …"

"Yes, she's my mother," answered the middle-aged woman. "I called the ambulance."

"How long has she had Alzheimer's dementia?" asked Darren. His confidence never faltered.

"It was diagnosed two years ago."

Darren felt like jumping in the air and yelling, "Yeah!" He wished there was someone nearby he could high-five. Nothing could stop him tonight. A patient only had to speak a few sentences and he could diagnose their cerebral pathology. Instead of the juvenile celebration he was contemplating, he elected to ask more questions in a calm and mature tone of voice. "Can you tell me what the problem is?"

"… and they were all out of pumpkins …" the little old lady continued.

"She began wetting the bed yesterday," her daughter answered. "And today she was very drowsy."

Darren was already leafing through the lab results obtained while this lady was in the department. The daughter had not finished speaking before he had found the answer he sought. Sure enough, the lab results showed a urinary tract infection, just as he had suspected. Another correct diagnosis and he had only been here a few minutes.

He asked the daughter a few more questions about her mother's medical history and medications, but it was all gravy now. He had already chosen the antibiotic he was going to use anyway.

"Your mom will be admitted to the General Internal Medicine service upstairs. We'll get her feeling better."

"Thank you, Dr Johnston."

He left the curtained area and strode over to the nursing desk. He wrote all of the admission orders before he realized he did not know the patient's name. He must have forgotten. No, in fact he had never asked. He had only ever gotten her bed number. Oh well, first goof of the night. He checked on the nursing computer to find out the name, and dropped his orders off with the charge nurse.

"Here's another one done. She can go upstairs."

"Thanks, Darren."

Darren paused.

The nurses in the Emergency Department had never called him by his first name before. He really was on a roll tonight, and everyone seemed to know it.

Before he knew it, he had been called for another consultation. Soon he was talking to a young woman with epilepsy that had stopped taking her medication and had come in with a seizure.

"I didn't think it was important any more. I haven't had a seizure in years," she said when asked about the medication. Darren reviewed her test results. Some were a little abnormal so he wanted to make sure he wasn't missing anything. Odds were she had just had a seizure because she was not taking her medication, but he made sure to check for any other possible causes. It was going to be a few hours to get the last results so he suggested that she stay in the Emergency Department until morning so he could discharge her when he was sure that nothing sinister was going on.

"I'm feeling fine. I think I should just go home now."

"I understand that you feel fine now," he replied, "but some of your test results are not quite normal. They might not represent anything important, but if you have another reason to be having seizures now, we should know about it before you go."

"I'll just go home and start my medication again." She began packing up her things and was preparing to change back into her street clothes.

"I've told you that I need to review some further tests before it is safe for you to go." Darren was speaking in measured, emotionless tones.

"Yes, that's what you said but …"

"Despite my advice, you still want to go home?"

"Yes, I think you're being too cautious. I'll be fine if I go home."

"Look, it doesn't matter to me whether you accept my advice or not," answered Darren. "I get paid either way." He enjoyed saying that, thinking that she likely thought he was a highly paid doctor in contrast to his meagre earnings. "Do you understand that if you leave now, you could have a seizure in the middle of traffic and die?"

"Well, I don't think that …"

"Do you understand that I have informed you of a risk of death if you leave now?"

"Yes, I understand that you said that."

"Super!" Suddenly there was a jovial note in his voice. "Here's a form." He reached behind him and out of her curtained area to grab a green sheet of paper from a nearby filing rack. "Just fill out this release form if you want to leave against my advice. Otherwise, you are welcome to stay. Then I will see you when all the tests are done and we can assess whether or not it is safe for you to go." He turned and left. She just stood stunned, staring at the green sheet. He spoke to the charge nurse on his way out of the department. "The young lady in curtain six may choose to leave. Otherwise we will reassess her when the rest of her labs are back."

"Did she get a green form?" the charge nurse answered without looking up from a stack of paperwork.

"She got it."

"Fine. See you later, Darren."

Darren checked his watch. It was ten-thirty. Tonight had been a terrific night so far. In fact, it made him impressed at just how much he had learned in a few weeks. A month ago if a little old lady like the one with Alzheimer's had come in, he would have spent an hour trying to get a history from her before realizing that she was not going to give him any useful information. Tonight he had bypassed her within seconds. He hardly needed to look in her direction. He had churned her through the assembly line with instant efficiency. The old Darren would have spent hours fretting over the lady who wanted to leave the department. He would have talked and talked to her, likely only to realize that she was looking for attention because she had been laid off her job or something. Tonight: boom! Another admission processed in no time. If she left, then it would be that much less work for him the next morning. As it happened, his rough approach seemed to have convinced her. She waited around until morning and was properly and efficiently dealt with by the team.

Darren's efficiency did not end in the Emergency Department. His pager was far from done with him.

"Dr Johnston, would you come by Unit 61? We're having a few troubles here."

When he arrived on the ward, he was led to the room of an obese man who was struggling for breath. The man had a desperate look in his eyes and lay clutching at his bed rails. The veins on the man's head were bulging out and each breath sounded like he was blowing tiny bubbles in his lungs. Darren, who had never met the man before, immediately grasped what was going on. While the man's nurse stood silent in the doorway and the man continued gasping, Darren proceeded promptly to the bedside and raised the head of the man's bed until it was in a seated position. The man's breathing miraculously recovered when his position was changed.

"My name is Dr Johnston."

"I'm feeling better all of a sudden, Doctor."

"I know. I'll take a look at your medications and see if there's anything else we can do." Darren quickly examined the man, but he had known as soon as he saw him that the patient was accumulating fluid in his lungs. He knew the symptoms would be much better in a seated position. He was still on a roll.

"Thank you, Doctor," said the nurse as he wrote a few hasty notes in the chart. "We have one more person for you to see. The man in the next room is having chest pain."

Chest pain. It was a challenging symptom, because it could come from so many sources and could represent such serious problems. A patient with a blood clot to the lungs classically presents with sharp pain that makes breathing difficult. An aortic dissection causes similar, tearing pain. Blood thinners are crucial for one patient and would kill the other. Darren marched into the next patient's room wondering what he would find.

When he entered, he once again seemed to know the answer the instant he laid eyes on the patient. The man was clutching his chest, but did not look short of breath. He did not look like a man in distress. His face wore a sour expression. Darren only needed to ask one question.

"Have you ever had pain like this before?"

"Every time I eat Mexican food," the man answered.

"Give him an antacid and call me if it doesn't work right away."

"Thanks again, Dr Johnston." She did not need to call him back.

Darren realized it was getting late and he had not eaten dinner. Still riding the wave of success, he went to the cafeteria and bought a meal that he took to the resident's lounge. Chris arrived a short time later to find Darren comfortable on the couch and watching a movie on television.

"It looks like you've finally learned how being on call is supposed to be done." Chris congratulated him. "Most of the time, you look like you're afraid that someone is going to die."

"But someone is often going to die. This is a hospital, after all."

"Yes, it is," answered Chris. "But you don't have to let that fact ruin your whole evening. Now, what's on television?"

Darren and Chris watched television and joked for a while before Darren finally decided that he should get some sleep while he still could. Back in his call room he was still feeling great about the evening. What an excellent way to end his rotation. He did not even mind the thought of being woken up later. All he had to do was make it through tonight and he would have completed all the overnight calls on his first clinical rotation. The worst of it had to be over. Maybe in future rotations he would have all the calm Chris seemed to carry around with him. Nothing would be able to stop him then.

He went to bed.

The pager rang and Darren checked his watch. It was four-thirty in the morning and he had gone to bed at just after midnight. He felt exhilarated. Even though it was the middle of the night and he was being woken up for who-knows-what, he had already had four hours of sleep. Now nothing could ruin his night. He went to the sink in his call room and splashed water on his face before answering.

"Johnston here."

"Dr Johnston, would you come quickly? Mr Doering can't breath."

Somehow Darren knew that this was going to be bad.

Chapter 31

Darren struggled into his clothes and hurried to Mr Doering's room. He was still trying to get his right arm into his white coat as he hurried down the hallway. On his way he fought both his coat and the complex problem of what might have happened to his patient. There were dozens of possibilities why Mr Doering might be having trouble breathing. The cancer might have caused fluid build-up in the lining around his heart. It might have made him prone to blood clots, and a clot could have blocked his lungs. Maybe he was getting pneumonia in a site blocked off by tumour cells. Maybe he was confused again and had inhaled some of his dinner.

By the time he arrived on the ward, Darren was seriously worried about what he would find and what he might be able to do about it. A nurse standing in the corridor gestured through the open door to Mr Doering's room, so Darren went in. He absorbed the scene. Mr Doering looked like he was in serious distress. Even from a distance his skin looked distinctly blue, and he was clutching at the bedrails with a look of desperation on his face. Each of Kurt's breaths seemed to require supreme effort and it was not hard to imagine that any one of these awful gasps might be his last. At the bedside a nurse was taking his blood pressure while another held an oxygen mask over his face. It was not an easy job since he was beginning to thrash back and forth like a man being held underwater.

Darren wanted badly to turn around and just leave the room, but felt himself taken prisoner by responsibility. As he took a step forward, he once again began running through all the possibilities in his head. Blood clot? Aspiration? Pneumonia? He placed his stethoscope lamely on Kurt's chest and heard a few breath sounds before deciding that none of this was of any use whatsoever. He clearly needed to act quickly.

"Well?" said one of the nurses, an obvious suggestion that a doctor ought to be doing something.

"Okay." Darren stood up and tried to assume an air of authority. He did not know what had happened to Mr Doering. He did not know what to do. He hoped that by simply acting like he was in charge, he might think of something. And he did.

Suddenly all his life support training returned to him. He had learned simple steps that could be followed to help a patient in extremis no matter what was wrong with him. It was an algorithm he could follow without needing a precise diagnosis. How had this not occurred to him earlier? He began to count through the steps in his head. They were named for the first letters of the alphabet:

'A' is for airway. Can the patient get air into his lungs? This step was easy. Darren had listened to his lungs and heard air going in and out. Unhelpful as it had initially seemed in making a diagnosis, that fact now got him through the first step in his algorithm. 'B' is for breathing. This was easy too. Mr Doering was clearly having trouble with his breathing. What to do now? Darren remembered the word 'OIL' from his classes. 'O' is for oxygen.

"How much oxygen is he on?"

"Eight litres by mask," answered the nurse who was fighting to hold a mask over the patient's face.

"Would you turn it up to fifteen, please?"

'I' is for intravenous.

"Do we have an IV in place?"

"No."

"Would you start a peripheral intravenous, please," he directed the nurse in the doorway and she hurried to her task.

'L' is for leads. He needed to get monitors on the patient.

"Would you please check his oxygen saturation?" he requested of the nurse checking blood pressure.

Now things were going smoothly. When he began taking action, the cynical looks disappeared from the nurses' faces and they seemed satisfied to promptly execute his orders.

Okay. In the alphabet he had gotten as far as 'B' for breathing, then he had gone to 'OIL'. Next on the algorithm was 'C' for circulation. Right on cue, the nurse who had been checking a blood pressure reported, "His blood pressure was 110/75 with a heart rate of 120." Okay, that was not too bad. The nurse continued speaking as she finished taking his oxygen saturation. "His oxygen saturation is 60%." That was very bad. Now Darren needed to go back to 'B' for breathing.

"Would you call the respiratory therapist, please?" he calmly asked the nurse who had now finished placing an intravenous line. "Please inform her that I will need to intubate this patient." She hurried to the telephone and Darren reached out to hold his hand on Mr Doering's pulse.

Everything had begun to go smoothly as soon as Darren had fallen into the carefully taught sequence for critical patients. It seemed ridiculous that he had initially thought of trying to make a diagnosis. The diagnosis would come later when he had time to think. For now, he would take care of the patient using training designed to serve him well when time was running out.

Soon the respiratory therapist arrived with the equipment Darren would need to intubate Mr Doering. Suddenly Darren recalled a conversation that Dr Smith had tried to have with Mr Doering. "In the event that you are unable to breath for yourself, would you want us to support your breathing using a machine?" Dr Smith had asked Kurt while his wife was present. Suddenly that conversation was of crucial importance. If Darren were to intubate Mr Doering, it would mean that he would need to send Kurt to Intensive Care to be on a respirator. Unfortunately, Kurt had never answered the question. He had only become offended and rude at the suggestion that he might become sicker. Did it really make sense to send someone with lung cancer to the Intensive Care Unit? The cancer would kill him whether he spent time on the ventilator or not.

Darren spent only a moment on these thoughts. Once again he realized that there was not time right now to make complicated diagnoses or explore philosophical issues. He returned to his algorithm. It was the algorithm that would spare him the need for conscious thought until he had bought himself some time. He looked towards the head of the bed where the respiratory therapist was readying the equipment needed for intubation. He was feeling confident now, and was ready to carry on, when suddenly the situation changed again. Mr Doering stopped thrashing. His gasps for air stopped. Darren could not feel his pulse.

"Call a cardiac arrest," he said calmly to the nursing staff. He asked the respiratory therapist to begin mask ventilating the patient while a nurse began chest compressions. Soon the cardiac arrest team arrived and Mr Doering was attached to a heart monitor.

Darren carried on without a care in the world. He felt much more comfortable than he had when he first entered the room. Now that he could revert to his life support training he felt absolved of responsibility for his actions. All he needed to do was remember the simple lettered steps from his textbook and he could not go wrong. There were no judgment calls.

The heart monitor showed the fast erratic rhythm of ventricular tachycardia.

"Get ready to shock him," Darren quoted with ease from his class notes. Doubts regarding the outcome of running an electrical current through the man's body remained absent so long as the unambiguous algorithm remained clear in his mind.

The room had filled with people as the nurses from the Coronary Care Unit brought in the heart monitors. More residents had responded to the cardiac arrest page, but Darren realized that he had somehow not heard it through the overhead speaker. It was odd, he thought, as a nurse prepared the paddles to shock Mr Doering. Usually the sound of a cardiac arrest page overhead seemed so obvious and terrifying, but now that he was actually here he had not even heard it. The nurse handed him the paddles.

"Everyone stand clear." Darren checked that he was not touching the bed, then double-checked that no one else was in contact with Mr Doering. Recalling his training where he had shocked a simulator, he double-checked that the heart rhythm was ventricular tachycardia and then discharged the paddles.

Bang!

Mr Doering's body rocked with the force of the electrical shock designed to reset his heart into a normal rhythm. Darren checked the heart monitor again. The rhythm was unchanged.

"Shock a second time," said the algorithm in Darren's head.

He proceeded without giving it a second thought. Mr Doering remained blue and limp.

"Everyone stand clear," Darren repeated.

Bang!

Mr Doering's body rocked. The monitor remained unchanged.

"Shock a third time," said the algorithm. This was easy.

"Everyone stand clear." Darren's fingers tightened. The electrical signal to discharged the paddles rushed from his brain to his fingers. In the instant before the paddles fired, something changed on the monitor. Had one normal electrical heartbeat appeared? Mr Doering's eyes opened.

Bang!

The shock again shook Kurt's body, which then remained blue and limp.

"I'll intubate," intoned one of the other residents. That was the right thing to do after trying three shocks unsuccessfully, but Darren was no longer enjoying the detached feeling of blindly following protocol that had sustained him just moments ago. What had just happened? Had Doering awoken only to be electrocuted to death by Darren? Suddenly Darren felt ambiguity creep into the room like a dangerous, uninvited guest. It seemed that Mr Doering had recovered for an instant before the shock designed to get him out of ventricular tachycardia had thrown him right back in.

Darren's eyes swung left and right. No one else had noticed. The efficient bustle of activity continued around the room, but Darren stood motionless and the blood drained from his face. The more senior resident who had just finished intubating looked in Darren's direction and said something. Darren did not hear him. For a moment the room seemed filled with an eerie white noise, but Darren slowly regained his senses.

"Are you going to give amiodarone?" The other resident was prompting him to resume the algorithm.

"Yes, please. Go ahead." A nurse was already poised with the drug at the patient's intravenous. On his signal she administered it.

"Get ready to shock again." The resident signalled to Darren. Darren looked down and realized that he was still holding the paddles. According to the rhythm on the monitor and the algorithm Darren had found so useful, this would be the next step. There was no time or need for second thoughts. It was all in the textbooks. But now Darren was having doubts and he was not sure he wanted to electrocute the old man again.

This was the moment Kurt and his men had been preparing for, and despite their misfortunes so far, he knew they were performing brilliantly. His section had recently been moving with a column of mixed troops towards Falaise from the east when the situation became difficult. They had been marching near dusk along a road sheltered from the north by three large hills when British tanks came crashing over the crests with their machine guns blazing. Many soldiers were mowed down as the tanks cut a swath through their ranks, then swung east to further maul the German column. This was a terrible example of the Germans' poor leadership in recent days. Imagine that an armoured strike force had completely surprised a marching column of men. It would have been unthinkable in Kurt's well-organized paratrooper battalion, where reconnaissance was always conducted conscientiously. Now that he and his section unfortunately found themselves among a disorganized rabble of infantry, engineers and headquarters troops ordered about by fanatical SS soldiers, anything was possible. Despite the horrible carnage around them, Kurt's men had distinguished themselves as disciplined soldiers. They had not lost their cool, and had effectively taken cover before reorganizing, as Sherman tanks sped past them.

Kurt took charge of the nearest men and ordered them over the crest of the hill from which the tanks had come. He knew that enemy infantry were approaching from behind to support this rapidly advancing group of tanks. He now surmised that taking cover and getting in good firing positions was the best, possibly only, course of action. What he could only suspect at this point was that he and his men were now in the crucial fulcrum of the entire campaign in northern France. The Canadian forces had enclosed Falaise from the north and the Americans had swung to the south. They were about to close a ring around the city that would encircle an entire army of German soldiers. Kurt and his men were at the closing point of that ring. The Canadian tanks that Kurt had mistakenly presumed were British were racing ahead of their infantry to slash a wound in the German line that would complete the encirclement.

Just over the crest of the hill was a forested area that would give Kurt a nice view of the enemy's approach. With any luck, he would be able to establish firing positions under adequate cover. With rapid hand signals, he indicated positions to the four men that remained of his section. There had been seven of them just moments ago, but one had been killed in the first hail of bullets and two, including Corporal Schultz, were pinned on the far side of the road. Kurt had confidence in their bravery, just as in the four men around him now. They dodged forward through the trees towards Kurt's chosen firing positions, alternately pausing to cover one another. To their right were several Wehrmacht infantry under the command of a lieutenant who had independently chosen to follow the same plan.

The sound of bullets crashing through the foliage suddenly

surrounded Kurt. Again his men behaved admirably. They each fired two quick taps in the direction of enemy fire and dropped to the ground. It was exactly as they might have done on the practice ground near Marseilles, and now when they needed to act in a hurry they could do so without the need for conscious thought. They behaved like precise machines. Firing two bullets from their submachine guns as they fell and rolled for cover, they instinctively looked left and right to identify targets. Kurt was lucky to find himself beside a shell hole, so he hastily slid into it. Looking right, he noticed that the novice infantry soldiers had not quickly found cover, in fact, one had already fallen dead, and two were crawling about like idiots searching for random shelter. Kurt thought clinically that he would not trade two of his paratroopers for one hundred of those poorly trained children.

Kurt fired a few shots in the direction of a thicket of trees where he saw some partially concealed British soldiers. On his left, one of the paratroopers fired a burst from his submachine gun to cover a comrade who threw a grenade. Kurt yelled a few instructions and fired more shots. At first he was heartened that the over-enthusiastic armour seemed to have outpaced its infantry support. If he and his men could hold up the British advance here, those tanks would be cut off from behind and, with any luck, might be destroyed by one of the tank-killer Panzerfaust teams on these roads.

The situation was darkening as Kurt noticed more British troops advancing to strengthen the ones the Germans had already engaged. Bullets flew more thickly over Kurt's head now, and he looked around to organize better fire from his men. Thankfully, on his right, a group of infantry moved forward a machine gun and was contributing additional firepower. The firefight was now well matched. Kurt realized that the best they could do was keep up the suppressing fire and hope that more Germans advanced from behind them before British reinforcements arrived.

Kurt reached for his belt for more ammunition and a letter fell out of his pocket. He had received it days earlier but had saved it for a moment when he could fully savour every written word. He opened it that morning in anticipation of an opportunity to read his wife's beautiful scrawl, but saw to his surprise that it was written in his mother's hand. No bullet could have hit him harder or done more damage than the horrible news that his wife had been killed in a daylight-bombing raid. Perhaps the letter had not been noticed, or perhaps some Nazi lapdog had thought it too cruel to hide the news from a soldier, but somehow it had reached him through Germany's web of censors. Strangely, coldly, he thought almost nothing of his wife's death today. It would affect him more soon, but this morning he was only numb. He thought all day not about his loss or her death, but of irrevocability: that she would never read the letters he had written for her. One unsent letter still sat in his back pocket, the letter that carefully, reflectively described his feelings about the war for her, so she could share this incomprehensible experience. When he had thought she was alive, he was sure that he would destroy it. Now that his wife was dead, he could not stop grieving that the letter would never be read by her, never be read by anyone.

A grenade exploded on Kurt's right near the novice infantry soldiers who could find no cover but were trying to participate in the battle. The British concentrated their fire on the machine gun position and now advanced towards it. Two small groups of British infantry on Kurt's front kept up fire that pinned the infantry, while others advanced on the Germans' right flank to find grenade range and expertly finish their business.

Kurt winced. The infantry on his right, manning the machine gun was pinned by only a few British riflemen and would soon be killed. If he and his men were to stand a chance they would need that machine gun to remain spitting. He swung his weapon right and managed to hit one of the flanking British soldiers, although they stood a distance from him and he shot with an imperfect line of sight. The other flanking British soldiers fell to the ground and added their rifles to the fire directed at the German machine gun position.

While the British focused efforts on the machine gun that had been rendered nearly impotent by mild suppressive fire and incompetent operators, very little fire held Kurt's position. Again he yelled instructions and targets to the paratroopers on his left. Hoping he might also improve the situation for the men on his right, he turned to reassess their situation. The two young men manning the machine gun could do nothing. They crouched in a hollow behind a fallen tree and while they found a useful firing position, the bullets around them so psychologically incapacitated them that they could not direct fire at the enemy. Kurt almost yelled something inspiring to encourage them to fire a few shots. Then he noticed a look in their eyes.

"God, no!"

They were going to run. They had in front of them a machine gun that, in the right hands, could hold a whole company at bay. Instead, the enemy bullets around them had frightened the rational thought out of them and they were tensing their muscles to leap from their cover and flee. The paratroopers on Kurt's left continued to fire calmly without evident fear. Normally Kurt might have been happy enough to lose the green soldiers as casualties. They were, after all, drawing fire away from his position. Today, though, he and his men were fighting alongside the dregs of the German army. He knew that if they lost his right flank, those young idiots would be responsible for the encirclement of his force. They were about to commit not only the stupidest error possible in the tactical situation at hand, but also the worst one for their own safety. If they kept working their machine gun, the firefight would remain balanced. If they stood to run, British soldiers would be delighted to see targets not taking cover and would immediately shoot them from behind. It would then be only a matter of minutes before those British soldiers advancing on the right flank would swing further to the rear to cut off the paratroopers.

Kurt fired another short burst and wiped sweat from his forehead. He glanced again to his right. Those soldiers were going to run. He knew it. How could he salvage the situation so that his men would not be encircled? What could he do to make sure that the machine gun position was not lost?

They were going to run any second. Thoughts raced through Kurt's head.

Those cowards deserve to die. They should never have been fighting alongside us. Maybe we can fight our way out of this without them.

Kurt gripped his gun tightly. He continued yelling directions to the paratroopers. Under covering fire by their colleagues, two of them were to fall back to a position behind him. From there they could fire on the flanking British soldiers who would inevitably be taking the machine gun position. The green infantry soldiers would be sacrificed and a new line would be held.

Kurt never finished yelling the instructions. As the first words left his mouth, he felt an old letter from his wife in his pocket. The words "I am proud of you" seemed to leap off the paper into his chest, as though she were sending him a final goodbye. There was no pause. Kurt never paused to think in battle. The paratroopers awaited the completion of his orders, but at the very moment the thoughts of his wife entered his mind, he tensed the muscles in his legs. His orders trailed off incomplete and the paratroopers resumed their suppressing fire. Kurt threw his body up and out from behind his cover. He was in the open with no protection from the British bullets and his legs were moving. From his new perspective he saw three British soldiers. Their guns had been trained on the machine gun position, but now they turned their faces towards him. Their eyes were wide with surprise.

Darren was working furiously in his attempts to maintain Kurt's circulation. No sooner would Kurt's situation seem to stabilize than his cardiac rhythm would revert to fibrillation. Again and again he administered defibrillatory shocks only to gain a temporary respite before the whole cycle would repeat. Darren felt numb. He knew that if he took a moment to think about what he was doing he would realize how much he hated and was frightened by administering the repeated shocks. He could not be medically faulted for his actions; in fact, everything he did was according to strict protocol. And yet he could not escape the perception he was shocking Kurt to death. Inside he knew perfectly well that the repeated shocks were likely all that was keeping Kurt's heart beating, but on an emotional level, he could not stand seeing the helpless body in front of him steadily beaten and battered by the trauma he inflicted.

Everything so far had happened in a hurry, but Darren had realized some minutes ago that he would soon need improved intravenous access. He had sent a medical student rushing to obtain a central line kit, and now the student returned with a broad smile on his face.

"I've got the line! Can I try to put it in?" Darren was struck by the inappropriateness of his young colleague's enthusiasm for experience, but realized that in the past he had occasionally seen doctors or students hurrying to a stressful situation with a joyous expression. He nursed a silent hatred for that young student now. He wondered if he had ever been so tasteless to exhibit such inappropriate attitudes towards learning while a man was dying.

"V-Fib again!" By calling out the abbreviation for 'ventricular fibrillation', the nurse signalled to Darren that Mr Doering's heart rhythm again required intervention. Darren winced. He placed the paddles on Mr Doering's chest but could hardly bear to discharge them. Mr Doering seemed so helpless lying unresponsive with his gown torn open and a room full of people poking and prodding at his body or shoving needles into him.

"Is everyone clear?" Darren closed his eyes and tensed his grip on the paddles. He paused for a long moment in fear that Mr Doering might suddenly awaken only to be killed again by Darren's ruthless intervention.

Bang! The paddles discharged. This time Darren loosened his grip as he triggered the buttons with his thumbs and sparks visibly flew between the paddles and Kurt's chest. Chest hairs singed and Darren could smell them burn. He felt nausea rise in his throat like rats scurrying up a tree to avoid a flood. He wished someone else would take charge and he could leave the room, but he knew he was running this code and was all alone. There was no time to transport Mr Doering to the Intensive Care Unit. The patient had never become stable enough. All Darren could do was continue this increasingly futile attempt to force Kurt's heart to keep beating against its own will.

The resuscitation continued with the heart rate often returning to a reassuring regular rhythm, but always for shorter and shorter durations. The electrical rhythm of Kurt's heart seemed to be willing itself always into the erratic and rapid spikes of ventricular fibrillation, and each time it returned, its pattern was coarser, weaker. The algorithm that had sustained Darren's confidence such a short time before now seemed only to trap him in this hopeless cause.

"V-Fib." The nurse who was monitoring Kurt's heart called out the rhythm.

Darren could hardly stand it. Again he tensed his hands on the paddles and reached them towards Kurt's chest. To anyone in the room, it would have seemed that he had remained completely emotionless through the entire ordeal, but now he closed his eyes hard for an instant to blink away tears.

Falaise. The road signs now no longer pointed to a distant end point of a long road, but to the adjacent town. Bill grumbled as his heavy pack jerked against his back with each step of his quick jog. At least now a tangible objective was within reach, and their commanders' optimism became clear when their supporting armour went racing ahead.

"They must figure they've got the Hun on the run," Bill commented to a soldier in his section, and he was right. Knowing that the ring around Falaise was nearly complete, and seeing that a large body of German soldiers was near the closing point of the ring, the commanders sent their tanks forward as a shock weapon to sever the encircled Germans from their colleagues who still had a chance to escape. *Why is it that no matter whether they think things are going well or badly, it always means more work for us?* Bill completed his thoughts on the increased marching pace they had to sustain in order to catch up with their armour.

Bill's battalion was crossing a lush valley dotted by French farmhouses and land marked by the ever-present church steeples that characterized this part of Europe. Ahead of them was a ridge shrouded in trees where the tanks were crossing over. The sound of their heavy machine guns filled the air. Orders were shouted and the pace of the soldiers was redoubled. The armour had apparently encountered an enemy infantry force and would need support. It was crucial that the Canadians reach the cover of the forested ridge before the Germans could attain a position. The sound of nearby small arms fire rang out and mortar shells began to land around the ridge. Bill could not even tell whose side had caused the explosions, but knew that he was approaching them.

On Bill's left was Sergeant Whalen. Bill took a quick glance in his direction and kept running. Whalen had remained civil towards him, but lately rarely left him unsupervised. Bill felt that his interaction with Whalen represented the discomfort he had been experiencing around all his comrades lately. He had not recovered from the humiliation of the day he had been pinned in the street by the sniper, and would never forget Whalen standing over him as he cowered on the ground.

Bill felt somewhat relieved as he and the men around him began to enter the cover of the trees. He was still frightened by what might lie ahead, but at least the Germans had not already fortified the tree line. Had that been the case no doubt he and his entire platoon would have been massacred in the valley. Scattered small arms fire was now closer as Bill continued running forward. Whalen took charge of the men around him.

"Sutherland! Take Kenwood and get in position by those

trees." He gestured ahead and to the left.

Bill and the private with whom he had been instructed to stay turned and sprinted to the cover indicated to them. They dove just in time, as a German machine gun added to the growing din. Joining them seconds later, Sergeant Whalen rushed into position on their left.

Their position was excellent. The group of covering trees was at the top of a short slope, so they could lie flat and peer over the crest. Undergrowth made their position even more difficult to see from the German line. Ahead and on their left, the muzzle flashes of the German machine gun position could be made out, but through the bushes the Germans themselves could not be seen. After taking several shots with their rifles in the direction of the machine gun, they took some fire from directly ahead, where some Germans with submachine guns were camouflaged. A grenade landed nearby, and Bill realized that they were facing heavy resistance.

Sergeant Whalen exchanged signals with men on their left. "Direct your fire on that machine gun position. We've got guys flanking it on the left, and then we should be able to roll up these Krauts ahead of us."

More Canadian soldiers got into position on their left and right, as Sutherland, Whalen, and Kenwood kept their rifles trained on the German machine gun. Occasionally submachine gun fire from their front would rake the ground nearby, but the Canadian position was well covered.

Now the German machine gunners were pinned, and grenades began exploding near their position. Whalen smiled at the success of the hasty plan that was being so well executed. "Sutherland, keep firing on that machine gun. We're going to keep those bastards pinned until our guys have dug them out of there. Kenwood, see if you can't get some fire on those guys in front of us."

Bill continued squinting in the direction from which the German muzzle flashes had come. He had still not seen the grey of

German uniforms, and began to wonder if the enemy soldiers had already been killed or had pulled back. He was filled with frustration at his unseen enemy. Most of his encounters with the Hun so far had been against snipers, none of whom he had ever seen. Now the Germans could only be seen as brief muzzle flashes through the undergrowth. Bill wished that just for once he could see what he was shooting at.

As if on command, his wish was granted. He worked the action on his rifle and took aim at the group of bushes he thought represented his target when a Wehrmacht helmet appeared above the foliage. He was adjusting his aim when the rest of the figure emerged from cover. A German soldier stood right up with his back to them and tried to run away. Bill had never had such a clear target, so he took careful aim.

"What the hell?" Kenwood exclaimed next to him. Submachine gun fire raked the ground around Sutherland and his two colleagues, as Bill turned away from his target to the source of the assault. A tall, powerfully built German paratrooper had also emerged from his cover in front of them to run in their direction. He was spraying bullets as he came and only paused for an instant to lob a stick grenade to his right. Supporting fire from two men behind him added to the assault. Bullets were landing so close in front of them that none of the three Canadians was able to turn his rifle at the approaching threat. They all dropped down further, their rifles uselessly pinned under them.

Bill had never been in a situation like this before. Generally the enemy was far enough away that ducking behind cover was a reasonable option until an opportunity arose to fire, but now an insane enemy was coming right at him. Bill buried his head behind his cover, but again experienced the feeling of helplessness he had known when an unseen sniper had trained a scope on him. Now he felt it because he knew the German might already be standing over him. Bullets rained around until the sound of the man's footsteps right in front of the Canadians overwhelmed all other noise. Then there was a pause. A silent eternity passed as the bullets abated and the footsteps stopped. Bill raised his head and saw that Kenwood too had been cowering at his side. Rather than ducking forward, Sergeant Whalen had rolled onto his back and pointed his rifle up at the approaching enemy. He had fired one shot but had missed his mark in haste. Now he pointed his rifle up at a German paratrooper who stood directly over them, blocking out the sun. A submachine gun was in the German's hands but was pointed off to the side. A blank expression was on his face. Sergeant Whalen was an expert rifleman who would need only an instant to work the action on his rifle and chamber another round, but with the German standing immediately over him, he just motionlessly stared back in disbelief.

Likely only a second or two passed, but they were the longest seconds Bill had ever known. The small arms fire from nearby positions seemed to have paused too, as though in anticipation. Then the German moved. He pulled the trigger of his weapon even though it was pointed harmlessly off to the side. It clicked. He had emptied all the bullets from his clip in his maniacal charge, and had only realized it during the last few steps towards the Canadians. He was not surprised when his weapon had not fired when he pulled its trigger. He had apparently done it only to signify its harmlessness to his enemy. Now he shrugged with a quizzical smile on his face and gestured at the empty weapon as though to say: "Oh well."

Another instant passed in stunned silence before Whalen reached forward and grabbed the German by the shirt. Whalen was a powerful man and could easily overcome the average soldier. This German looked as though he could be a match for the tough sergeant, but today he did not resist. He let Sergeant Whalen pull him down behind their cover.

"Give me that!" Whalen grabbed the empty gun from his German prisoner.

The German again allowed himself to be manhandled and wore an expression that seemed to indicate he had been resigned to his capture all along. Bill began to wonder whether in fact the man's intentions had been suicidal, but he caught the German turning briefly and looking back towards the machine gun position. No German corpses lay on the ground where the infantrymen at the German machine gun had stood to run. They had successfully fled because of the distraction afforded by this man who had made a suicidal charge. Sutherland turned to his prisoner and realized that he had just met the bravest man he had ever known.

The battle raged on for a short time longer, but its outcome was obvious now that the machine gun was out of action. A section of Canadian soldiers managed to flank two German paratroopers who put up tough resistance. Both of the Germans were killed, but not before they had taken seven Canadians with them. The remainder of the platoon managed to fight to the top of the ridge and link with the armour that had sped ahead to wreak havoc amongst a column of Germans that had been caught unaware.

Bill was assigned by Whalen to guard the German prisoner through much of the remainder of the battle, and Bill stood over him, making him lie face down on the ground with his hands behind his back. Only when the remaining enemy had been routed could Bill, as instructed, escort the prisoner behind the lines for interrogation. No words were exchanged between Bill and the German, but Bill could not shake the sense of awe he felt for this man who had until so recently been a faceless enemy.

Chapter 32

"I'm sorry to have to call you so early, but I'm afraid I have bad news. Your husband's condition deteriorated very suddenly this morning and despite our best efforts we were unable to save him. Mr Doering died."

Darren put down the receiver after he finished speaking with Mrs Doering. She had said very little after hearing the bad news, except to ask if she could come and see her husband. She had spent the night with a sister a short distance out of town, and wanted to telephone family members before coming. She would likely not arrive until early afternoon. Darren had responded that nothing would be done with her husband until she arrived. Part of him wanted to speak with her personally, but he found himself so physically and emotionally drained by the long night that he wanted to flee the hospital. Rounds seemed to drag on for an eternity, but they were done by noon and Layton encouraged Darren to go home and get some rest.

"I'll talk with Mrs Doering when she gets here." Layton's tone suggested that he knew how important it was to Darren that her husband's doctors see Mrs Doering personally.

"Thanks." Darren felt that he did not have the strength to stay much longer. He just wanted to go to sleep. He finished his last errands on the ward and made his way back to the residents' lounge to retrieve his coat. He did not make it far before stopping in the cafeteria for a cup of coffee. Although he had no intention of staying awake much longer, he felt like he needed a boost just to make it through the drive home. His fatigue transcended any mere need to sleep and called into question his desire ever to wake up again.

Realizing that he had left his stethoscope sitting on a chair at the Internal Medicine Unit's nursing station, he made one more trip back to the ward before leaving the hospital. Passing one of his patients' rooms, he noticed some familiar faces. Family members surrounded Mrs Fleming, the lady who had recently suffered a stroke robbing her of her speech and the use of her right arm. Darren smiled politely as her husband recognized him. Darren prepared to continue on his way, but felt an urge to stop as he noticed something in her room. Mrs Fleming's family had surrounded her with flowers and mementos from home, including pictures of friends and grandchildren. Until today, Darren had seen her everyday on rounds but had been unable to remember her name. He had referred to her as "the stroke lady". The nickname was easy to recall and summarized her predicament, but also implied that she had never been any different. Although he knew her presentation was acute, Darren had always sort of believed she had been born with a useless, limp right arm and no power of speech. Now she continued to stare forward with no concern for the verbal communication going on around her, but what struck Darren was a photograph at her bedside. In the picture, she was smiling a beautiful, symmetric smile, unlike the crooked, drooling expression she wore now. She wore a summer dress and was surrounded by grandchildren. It had never seemed possible that the uncommunicative individual Darren had known as "the stroke lady" could truly have been a real person, but now Darren admitted to himself that she had been.

"Oh, God," Darren said under his breath. How had he come to work everyday without realizing that he was talking to the family of a woman whose very essence had been stolen from them only days before. There she was in the picture, laughing and playing with children, and now her body was present, but her mind gone. Mr Fleming returned Darren's polite smile.

"Good morning, Dr Johnston." Despite his tragic loss, he

addressed Darren with respect and amicability, suggesting that he felt satisfied with his wife's care. Darren had not been able to do much to help, but Mr Fleming was confident that he had done everything in his power.

Darren wanted to scream out: "I'm sorry; I had no idea!"

He had not missed any important medical therapies, but somehow he had missed Mrs Fleming's humanity. Surely he had missed something important if not until now had he realized that she had been a loving and intelligent person for more than forty years before her doctor was born. Darren quietly continued walking down the hallway and retrieved his stethoscope from a chair. Now just wanting to escape from the hospital and go home, he walked quickly down the corridor towards the walkway that connected the hospital with the car park.

"Darren!" a voice called from behind him. Surely there could not be anything else worth keeping him here a moment longer. He turned and faced the speaker. It was Chris, emerging from the Intensive Care Unit. "I should just let you know that you won't need to take back that guy with the esophageal cancer. He died this morning."

On any other day Darren would have been touched by Mr Sutherland's death. Now he felt so numb that there was no more room for grief. His legs might have given out underneath him had he felt as if he was supporting his own weight, but he had the sensation that he was only a marionette on strings outside his control. Chris had told him of the death in a casual tone. Nothing in the hospital seemed able to touch Chris. It was a quality that Darren had so recently admired but, this morning, he found sickening.

"What happened?"

"He bled. Man, did that tumour open up. He started vomiting blood and it just poured. It was all over before we could do anything."

"Thanks." Darren turned to resume his walk.

"See you later, Darren."

"Yup." Darren did not turn to look back.

The drive home passed in a blur. Before he knew it, he was back at the door of his apartment. He turned the key in the lock and looked in to see Courtney on the couch. Her face was hard, and she was ready to resume their argument of the night before. Darren walked to the couch, his shoes and coat still on, and sat next to her. He returned her gaze and it was clear she was waiting to hear what he had to say in his defence. All he could say were the words that had been hanging on his lips since he had been on the nursing station.

"I'm sorry. I didn't know." Tears sprung to his eyes and he buried his head against her shoulder. She returned his embrace but was surprised and unsure of what to make of his appeal.

"What are you sorry for?" Just moments before she was sure that he had many things to be sorry for, but this was unexpected.

"I'm sorry for everything," he answered. "There has been so much suffering around me that I've avoided seeing any of it." He paused. "And that includes yours."

Courtney was still surprised and not sure what to make of his confession. "What happened today?" she asked.

"Mr Sutherland and Mr Doering are dead."

"Oh no." She held him tighter, realizing why he was now so suddenly saddened, but was still not entirely certain of what he was feeling. She tried to catch up with the story. "Was one of them the old soldier we had talked about?"

"Yes. Mr Sutherland." He sniffed loudly, still holding her tight.

"And was the other man the one you said was so mean and unpleasant?"

"I didn't know him. I didn't know anyone."

"I see." She was beginning to. She waited a while and then asked, "Are you going to tell me about it?"

"I'd like to," he answered, remembering now how much he had hurt her feelings. He thought of how he had run from their confrontation the previous night, "if you still want to listen to me."

"Of course I do," she answered. "Let's get you out of your

coat." She helped him put away his shoes and coat and they returned to the couch. Darren blew his nose and they sat quietly for a moment.

Courtney gave Darren time to speak, but when he did not begin, she prompted him.

"You know, whenever we talk with someone about you being a doctor, they always say the same kind of things: 'Oh, it must be tough to be around all that blood,' or 'I could never deal with people dying all the time.' When you talk to actual doctors, all they tell you is about the long hours they work."

"I guess it's easier to say you feel bad about some things than about others. I guess it was easy to tell you about my hours." Darren answered with his eyes closed.

"Why don't you tell me about those other things?"

Darren told Courtney about Mr Doering and Mr Sutherland. He told her about the time he had spent at Mr Sutherland's bedside, and the paradoxical feeling he had afterwards that he had been wasting his time. He told her about "the stroke lady". He told her about how he had tried to emulate other doctors who seemed untouched by the tragedy around them and how he had only today realized the toll that the patients' tragedies had taken on him. Then he told her what he had been realizing as he spoke.

"Courtney, I haven't told you how much I appreciate you. All this time you have been here ready to hear me tell you how I feel, and I guess I took it for granted while I wasn't ready to talk. I just want you to know how important it is to me that you have been here to hear it."

"And how do you feel?" asked Courtney, begging the question that he had not quite answered.

"I guess I feel really bad."

"That's good," she began to answer. "Well, it's not good to feel bad, but it's good to let yourself feel that way if that's what you need. You know, I've got a tough year ahead of me when I start articling, and I'm going to need you there with me then."

"What do you think will be toughest about it?" Darren asked, feeling that he had let a load off his chest and was ready to talk about something different.

"Probably the long hours." She smiled.

Chapter 33

Bill was relieved to receive the order from Sergeant Whalen to lead their new prisoner into the rear area. Although tempted to believe the order suggested that Whalen did not trust him in combat, Bill felt that he had had quite enough combat for the day. Bill walked behind Kurt with his rifle slung over his shoulder. Kurt hardly seemed likely to try and escape; in fact, he had been quite a docile prisoner. Bill was glad for that, given that this German seemed easily strong enough to overpower him.

The two men walked together for some distance and drew looks from other Canadian soldiers they walked past. There were boisterous comments made at the sight of a German prisoner, and many of the Canadians gave Bill a thumbs-up or a 'V' sign. Kurt did not seem to mind and continued to walk quietly and unaffected. Bill had seen many German prisoners being led to the rear, but Kurt was different. Far from hanging his head with a forlorn look of defeat about him, this man seemed quietly proud. Given the sacrifice he had made for his fellow German soldiers, Bill thought he had reason to walk with his head high.

Soon the two men were walking side by side, with Bill hardly making an effort to guard Kurt. Because the Canadian advance in this area had been rapid, the density of men thinned out behind the lines quickly and it was difficult to ascertain where their headquarters were located. They arrived at a cross roads, and Bill puzzled briefly over the road signs. He knew they would be of little help, given that the retreating Germans would have moved many, but he tried his best to look like he had some idea where he was going. There was a hill on their left behind which Bill thought they should go. He elected to walk off the road and to the summit, hoping that if it were not in fact in the right direction, at least it would give him a vantage point from which to look around. He smiled at Kurt and pointed towards the hill. Kurt, continuing to be agreeable, ambled along in the direction Bill had indicated.

Now Bill was really lost. There was no one around to ask for directions, and as they climbed the hill he did not see anything that would be of help. Soon they were at the top of the hill, but Bill was no closer to sorting things out. He decided that it was an appropriate time to stop for a break. He gestured to the ground and sat down beside Kurt, who also quietly took a seat.

Bill began rummaging through his pockets to find a cigarette, but quietly cursed as he realized that he had none.

"Cigarette?" asked Kurt, speaking the word in English.

"Yeah. I've got none." Bill answered with a shrug. Kurt then searched his pockets and produced two cigarettes, handing one to Bill and keeping the other for himself. He paused and mimed the action of lighting the cigarette in a way that suggested he had no matches. Bill, grateful enough for the smoke, produced a match and lit both of their cigarettes. After a moment, Kurt gestured at the patch on Bill's shoulder that indicated he was Canadian.

"You are Canadian?" Again he spoke heavily accented words in English.

"That's right," Bill answered. Kurt looked thoughtful again, but somewhat surprised. Bill thought it likely that not many Germans knew there were so many Canadians fighting in this sector.

Having just searched his pockets, Bill had realized that he was carrying a chocolate bar, so he broke off a piece for himself and offered some to Kurt. Kurt took some gratefully and ate it quickly. Kurt had realized how long it had been since he had had anything to eat, and the fact was obvious to Bill. Bill offered him some more when he finished.

They sat together for a while smoking and occasionally

communicating with a combination of mime and broken fragments of each other's languages. Kurt's English was considerably better than Bill's German. Bill knew only about twenty German words, most of them profane.

Bill looked around the French countryside and admired the many small hamlets dotted by church spires. A small creek flowed lazily by in the valley at the foot of the hill. Bill realized that he could not see any people. The French civilians had likely fled or taken to hiding as the battle approached, but oddly Bill realized that there were no Canadian soldiers evident to the immediate north. He knew that if he turned around he would see the advancing waves of troops that he had just left, but elected to enjoy the pastoral scene for a few moments while things were quiet. It concerned him for only a moment that he now had no idea where he was taking Kurt. Things would work out all right.

While enjoying the countryside Bill suddenly became aware of a sound that he had not heard in a very long time. Silence. It seemed in recent weeks that there was a constant chatter of nearby small arms fire, and even when that was absent, the distant percussion of the artillery was a constant background to everything he did. The battle must have quieted, he realized, if the sounds of combat were gone. In that moment, the war seemed removed across a gulf of time. Now he and his one-time mortal enemy sat here together enjoying chocolate and cigarettes in a pure and wonderful silence, unblemished in any way by the fight that had brought them together. *Funny*, thought Bill, *my ears aren't ringing*. In the last few days whenever the din had quieted, Bill had been aware of a constant ringing, testimony to the damage done to his hearing by the perpetual assault levelled on his cochlea.

Turning, Bill noticed that Kurt was quietly staring at the horizon. As Bill watched, a tear appeared in the German's eye. Bill wanted to reassure him he would be well treated as a prisoner, but somehow he knew that was not what was on Kurt's mind. He realized that despite their brief conversation, he did not know his prisoner's name. For a reason he could not be sure of, he elected not to ask. He was happier not knowing this former enemy's name. He reached out and patted Kurt on the shoulder and Kurt smiled in return. They each resumed their silent enjoyment of a peaceful horizon and noticed that both the sun and moon were in the sky over the picturesque countryside. Bill recalled a time as a child when he was told that if he stared long enough he might be able to see the movement of a clock's minute hand. He had spent a long time trying to master the patience to watch carefully enough but had never succeeded. Now he stared at the sun near the horizon with the same rapt interest. As minutes passed, he was sure that he could see it move. It was still morning, but the sun appeared to be setting.

The End

Acknowledgements

I would like to thank the following individuals for their invaluable help with this novel:

Michael Leahy and Melanie Klingbeil for their enthusiastic editing.

Craig Carney, my Canadian military consultant.

Adam Kelly, for his assistance on points of historical accuracy.

Monica, Nancy, Bob and Aurea Penner and Kurt Wechselberger for their patient reading of early drafts, and their tireless support of the work in progress.

A note on historical accuracy:
The characters represented in this work are entirely fictional, but the historical battles and military formations described, at a scale of battalions and larger, are as historically real as possible in the context of this work of fiction. At times in the book, a small military formation strays from the historical location of its parent unit. This is intentional, and meant to portray the disorganization of a partially surrounded army in retreat.

Also Available from BeWrite Books

Back There by Howard Waldman

Harry Grossman sees his world through the viewfinder of a battered camera. And he photographs it all, from the peeling posters and graffiti on grubby city walls to the most intimate moments of his mysterious French sweetheart. He becomes a permanent guest at her family's ramshackle country cottage, thirty miles and a century away from modern Paris. Harry, the New York outsider, calls it paradise and photographs the Model T Ford on the roof, the archaic well and scythe, the top-secret wild mushroom spots, and the reluctant Lauriers themselves.

They assume that outsider Harry will soon be a member of the family, but the strange photographer with his growing mountain of prints and negatives and imperfect French is not a man for snap decisions. Aren't things already perfect in this paradise? Someone once said, though, that the only paradises are lost paradises.

Back There is a touching and powerfully nostalgic transatlantic love story, sometimes verging on the comic, sometimes on the tragic. France and the French, too often caricatures of their own special reality, are presented with absolute authenticity.

With soft-focus subtlety, Howard Waldman shows that Europe and America are two continents divided by a perceived common culture of art and love - and that light-years separate Paris and Manhattan and the lives and values of the Lauriers and the Grossmans.

Paperback ISBN 1-904492-88-6

Heads Up for Harry by Hugh McCracken

It was a long, long war for Harry Cassidy.

He was a strip of a lad in short pants when Hitler's bombs forced him out of the city to the remote countryside.

He was newly out of high school when he put on his khaki army uniform, picked up a rifle, and drilled to kill for his country.

He was a university student when he was lured into intelligence work where he lost his innocence in the murky depths of espionage, and his treasonous first young love to an assassin with a license to kill.

Names have been changed to protect the innocent -- and the guilty -- and to keep faith with the Official Secrets Act the author signed almost a lifetime ago.

But Heads Up for Harry is the true story of a casualty of war whose childhood and youth were sacrificed to the most evil years of the Twentieth Century ... without ever firing a shot in anger.

Paperback ISBN 1-905202-44-X

BeWrite Books

Also Available from BeWrite Books

A Stranger and Afraid by Arthur Allwright

Tens of thousands of youngsters are evacuated to the English countryside as Hitler's bombers prepare to rain death on their city streets.

But the refugee trains with their cargo of frightened children often take a route from one hell to another.

Arthur, an eight-year-old evacuee from inner London, is thrust upon strict Quaker, anti-war, relatives in a remote village where locals speak such a strong dialect it's like a foreign language and where a vindictive headmaster delights in handing out brutal corporal punishment to the unwelcome little 'vaccies'.

Arthur experiences the depths of despair, the bursts of innocent pleasure, the terrors and the uncertainties of a forgotten war generation too young to fight, too precious to die, too bewildered to understand.

And every single word is true! This is young Arthur Allwright's story.
A moving tale, masterfully portraying the resilience of the human spirit.

Paperback ISBN 1-904224-31-8

Magpies and Sunsets by Neil Alexander Marr

James McPherson has made a huge success of his new life in a new country. He has a thriving business, a wife and three daughters, a beautiful home, a public image, and a private shame.

A voice from his secret past, a voice calling from thousands of miles across the Atlantic Ocean in the thick dialect of the Edinburgh gutters haunts him.

So he returns to his native Scotland to confront his personal demons and exorcise the evil memories that bedevil him. Can he ever recapture the simple, guiltless pleasure of watching Magpies and Sunsets, forgiving the past and laying its ghost once and for all?

In a magnificently crafted and courageous book, Neil Marr makes no concessions to the English language as he throws his reader into the deep end of heavy, rough, tough dialect. A delight for all Scots, a journey of adventure for millions of expatriate Caledonians around the world and a challenge to all Sassenachs!

Paperback ISBN 1-904492-29-0

BeWrite Books

Also Available from BeWrite Books

Whispers of Ghosts by Ron McLachlan

Up here, forget everything you thought you knew about the weather. On this mysterious yet enchanting island strange things can happen: omens, magic, restless spirits ploughing the night on their endless quest for peace, the very land and sea can speak to you of secrets, and of their very own character. When you leave, the dull ache of longing will claw in your heart drawing you back. It's a place like no other. The Isle of Arnasay.

Three generations of the Waters clan lie at the centre of this powerful tale about what happens when families and communities fall apart.

Told through the eyes of Madeline, from twenty years in the future, by which time she has become a successful, Manhattan-dwelling novelist, we are transported on a roller-coaster-like emotional voyage through the Sea Kingdoms of the Hebrides.

Steeped in Celtic, Viking, and Pictish cultural heritage, this gripping novel of close-knit family and community dynamics tells how these forces come into play and wreak havoc with the lives of the Hebrides islanders.

This tale will have meanings, echoing the harsh realities of island life, for all Gaels, at home and abroad. But its appeal goes much wider than that. You can't choose your family; all too often you can't choose your friends either. Sometimes, you can't tell the difference.

Paperback ISBN 1-904492-62-2

Plato's Child by Ron McLachlan

An innocent, seventeen-year-old Hebridean boy, with the gift of second sight, who has recently lost his father in a fishing accident, alone in the comparative sprawl of the City of Edinburgh, struggles to come to terms with his developing sexuality and emerging adulthood. The towers of the University of Edinburgh, as well as sailing the River Forth out of Port Edgar, provide the backdrop for a tale of unparalleled intensity, as this pure-hearted boy fights to come to understand his place in the fast-moving city life so different from the light pace of the islands to which he belongs.

His life, compared to that of his Hebridean home, is accelerated beyond his expectations as he finds himself being forced into the confusing sophistry and ambiguities of the metropolitan life.

Paperback ISBN 1-905202-06-7

BeWrite Books

Printed in the United States
47331LVS00002B/91-105